THE STAR OF CEYLON

CLARE FLYNN

Storm
PUBLISHING

Ebook ISBN: 978-1-83700-066-1
Paperback ISBN: 978-1-83700-068-5

Cover design: Debbie Clement
Cover images: Shutterstock
Map design by JD Smith Design Ltd.

Published by Storm Publishing.
For further information, visit:
www.stormpublishing.co

ALSO BY CLARE FLYNN

MAP OF CEYLON

JAFFNA

● MARICHCHUKKADDI

● ANURADHAPURA

● KANDY

● COLOMBO

● NUWARA ELIYA

HAMBANTOTA

GALLE

● MATARA

Indian Ocean

ONE

February 1906, England to Ceylon

Norton Baxter stood at the stern of the *Dambulla* watching the ship's wake plume like a feather boa below him. He was enjoying the rare luxury of weeks without responsibility, without deadlines, with no looming exams, no need for hours spent poring over complex differential equations or struggling to solve problems and riders for the Cambridge Mathematical Tripos.

From a lower deck, one of the crew hurled a bucket of kitchen waste into the Indian Ocean and out of nowhere a flock of brown seabirds swooped and dived to scavenge the scraps. Norton watched them feast then vanish as quickly as they'd appeared. The tropical sun seared his skin, despite the cooling breeze and the movement of the vessel. How could it be as hot as this while they were still at sea? He supposed after a while he'd acclimatise. He'd better – it would be three or four years before he'd be eligible for a long home leave.

Here he was, steaming down the Indian Ocean between Bombay and Colombo on an ocean liner, Cambridge now a distant memory. His younger sister had presented him with the complete collection of *The History of the Decline and Fall of the Roman Empire* as a farewell gift, suggesting, cheekily, that he might learn from it before he got too big for his boots and began throwing his weight around the British Empire. Norton smiled as he thought of Winnie. He was going to miss her down-to-earth manner and zest for life. How long until he'd see her smiling face again?

With less than a week until the ship reached its destination, the stack of six volumes remained unopened in his cabin. The shipboard days which he'd expected to be conducive to reading had drifted by as he wrote letters home, studied his fellow passengers and stared at the ever-changing panorama of sea and sky. He loved watching the seabirds, flying fish and the occasional pod of dolphins. Never in his life had he been so idle. He told himself it was natural to enjoy a period of total relaxation after the intense years of study at Cambridge. This passage to the East was the first time since early childhood that he had been free of all and any responsibility. Norton was determined to make the most of it.

After graduation, he had aspired to a position in Whitehall – the Treasury ideally – creating policy, making recommendations to cabinet ministers and generally exercising influence. He'd imagined himself the architect of ideas, the planner, the change-maker. This was what his father had done before him. At no time had Norton ever contemplated a role where he'd be required to implement, to do rather than think, much less that it would involve a posting overseas.

When he failed to secure a First-Class degree, he'd been obliged to settle for an administrative placement in the colonial civil service. Expecting, like most of his graduating colleagues, to be sent to India or East Africa, he'd been posted to the Crown colony of Ceylon, the small teardrop at the base of India. Although its capital, Colombo, was a strategic hub for the

British Empire, his father had described the island as a backwater and his posting there as the death knoll for his career ambitions. Norton wanted to prove him wrong.

There were worse fates for a young, single Englishman in 1906. He heard the voice of his mother in his head – 'Positive thinking, Norton! Treat it as a great adventure.' Norton intended to do so – and at least in this distant corner of the empire he would be out of range of his father's scorn.

On board the *Dambulla*, he avoided the games of deck quoits, shuffleboard, and deck tennis, finding them a poor substitute for a proper game of tennis or cricket. After graduation he'd spent the summer walking and climbing in the Swiss Alps, so being on a ship surrounded by the same people was confining. During the day he found a quiet place at the stern of the ship away from the crowd. When the weather was poor, he sat in the rarely used ship's library trying to get to grips with the textbook he had bought on the Sinhala language.

In the first-class dining room, he was placed at a table with Godfrey Wellington, an elderly architect, and Mrs Holloway, a middle-aged woman accompanied by her fifteen-year-old son. She told Norton she was married to the government agent for one of the eastern provinces and had lived in Ceylon for almost twenty years. A frail-looking woman with eyebrows knitted into a permanent frown, Mrs Holloway spoke with a voice that managed to combine nervous tension with condescension. After the initial pleasantries, Norton struggled to find anything to say to her. As for her son, he sat rigid beside his mother, mute, sulky, resentful, replacing greetings with silent nods. Norton felt sorry for the lad but failed to find any common ground with him.

In the absence of anyone interesting on his table he amused himself by making up stories about the people on nearby tables. The man with the monocle, slicked-back black hair and a waxed pencil moustache was a spy selling secrets to the French government; the young couple who couldn't take their eyes off each other had fallen in love when he came to measure her father for a new suit and had eloped – and the rather tubby gentleman at a table in the corner was a private detective sent by the angry father to track her down and return her home. Norton liked to think that the evident devotion between the couple had softened the detective's heart.

On the second evening aboard as the ship made its way along the English Channel, Norton had noticed a tall handsome man sitting alone at the other side of the dining room. He'd spotted him the previous day on a large table with a group of other men, all apparently tea planters. In his imaginary game he decided this man had been ostracised by his fellow planters after making passes at their wives.

Later, as Norton left the dining room he was behind two of the planters as they passed the solitary man's now empty table. Norton couldn't help catching their exchange.

'At least the fellow took the hint and buggered off.'

'I feel bad that he's all on his own now.'

'Don't. We don't want his kind. You've heard the rumours.'

'They may not be true though.'

'No smoke without fire.'

The other man shrugged. 'True. But he doesn't *look* like a pansy to me. And it's a bit miserable for the poor chap being stuck on his own for the next three or four weeks.'

So, far from playing Romeo to their wives, it seemed the man was 'batting for the other team'. That evening while strolling on deck, Norton noticed the lone man leaning against the railings staring up at the sky, smoking. Curious, he joined him and offered a greeting. The man spoke with a slight Yorkshire accent. 'Too cloudy tonight to see the stars.'

Norton declined the man's offer of a cigarette. 'You're interested in astronomy?'

The man laughed. 'No. I haven't a clue about it. I just like looking. Makes everything down here seem small and insignificant.'

Norton glanced at him. 'I suppose you're right. I'm just glad to be able to look at the stars without the anxiety that went with studying them for my examinations.' He told the man he'd studied Newtonian astronomy as part of the Mathematics Tripos. 'Once we get into the tropics, we'll probably have clearer skies and a better view.' Norton stretched out his hand and introduced himself.

The man shook his hand. 'Carberry. Paul Carberry. I'm a tea planter. When we get a clear night will you point out some of the stars for me? I'd love to know what I'm gazing at. In Ceylon I spend a lot of time staring up at them.'

Norton increasingly warmed to the Yorkshireman. Two or three years older than him, Carberry explained that he had been on his first home leave since arriving in Ceylon six years earlier. As well as his undeniably handsome looks, he had an athletic build, a shock of sun-blond hair and skin that, despite weeks spent in England over a rainy spring and early summer, retained its tropical tan.

They chatted for a while and Norton found himself extending an invitation to the planter. 'I say, I couldn't help noticing you're sitting at a table on your own. I don't suppose you'd like to come and join our table?' Seeing Carberry draw back a little, he added, 'You'd be doing me a favour. I don't have a lot in common with the others.'

'You're not making it sound very appealing.' Then seeing Norton's expression, Carberry laughed. 'Thank you. It's most kind of you. I didn't get along too well with some of my fellow planters, so I moved tables. But if you're sure...'

'I'll have a quiet word with the maître d'. There's plenty of room as it's a table for six and we're only four.'

After he'd gone back to his cabin to turn in, Norton asked himself if he'd been rash to make the offer. He didn't know the man. But first impressions had been good. And he couldn't be any worse company than the others on his table. If those men were right and he was what they'd called a pansy, it didn't matter to Norton. There had been several men in his college rumoured to go with other men and they'd never done him any harm.

The following evening, the maître d' showed Paul Carberry to their table. Mrs Holloway, on discovering Carberry was a tea planter, jerked her head back and frowned. Norton pretended not to notice. It was evident from that first evening that Mrs Holloway disapproved of the planter. She refused to address any remarks directly to him, tilting her head and flaring her nostrils whenever Carberry spoke.

Wellington, the architect, accepted Carberry's arrival with equanimity, presumably glad of another person to listen to his lengthy architectural monologues. The skin on his face hung in heavy folds like an old bloodhound and he tended to spray his companions with flecks of spit when he spoke – in a slow, unin-flected manner. After two weeks of Norton and Carberry enduring Wellington describing a lifetime of his past works, none of which appeared to have any lasting significance, the architect left the ship when they docked at Port Said, diagnosed with peritonitis.

Carberry proved to be more congenial and durable company. There was something about the planter that signalled dependability. He was the kind of man, Norton concluded, who avoided fuss and drama and went about whatever he was doing with a calm competence. With growing nervousness about leaving Britain, Norton asked what had led Carberry to move to Ceylon and become a tea planter.

'My older brother will inherit the family farm in Yorkshire, so I needed something else to do. Came out East after leaving school. I've been on the same plantation ever since.'

'What made you want to be so far from home?'

'Same as you I imagine, Baxter. Aren't we all looking to escape?' He tilted his head to one side, studying Norton. 'Being brought up on a farm, I wanted to work on the land and the prospects are much better than in England.' He grinned. 'I've managed to save enough to set up on my own. Worked my way up, learned the business inside out. I'm ready now. I'll be starting small, just growing and picking, then when I've built up more capital, I'll build a tea processing factory.'

Mrs Holloway looked away, her lip curled at the references to his plans, and Norton couldn't help wondering whether it was something about Carberry in particular or the plain fact that he was a planter that she found so uncongenial.

He found the answer one evening after they'd passed through the Suez Canal, when Carberry was late to the table. Mrs Holloway bent forward and spoke to Norton in a conspiratorial whisper. 'I do think it's a poor show that the maître d'hôtel put that man on our table, Mr Baxter.' She inclined her head towards the other end of the dining room. 'He ought to be with the other planters over there instead of being foisted on us. I told the maître d'hôtel but he's adamant that he won't move him again. Says the fellow is happy where he is. Perhaps if you had a word?'

Irritated by Mrs Holloway's snobbery, he said, 'Mr Carberry is a thoroughly decent chap. It was I who invited him to join us.'

She gave a visible shudder. 'Really? *You?* And without consulting me?'

Norton held her gaze. He wasn't going to apologise. 'Mr Carberry was dining alone. I assumed that being a good Christian woman you would welcome him joining us. Are you saying I was wrong?'

Her face reddened and she sucked in a breath. 'It's just

that... I find planters dreadfully uncouth. The man speaks with a North Country accent that sounds extremely common. A very poor example for Frederick.' She patted her son's hand. 'If my boy ever expressed a wish to become a planter his father would disinherit him.'

The young man, who was pale faced and still resolutely mute, looked down. Norton couldn't imagine anyone less likely to do a physically demanding outdoor job. It wasn't Frederick's fault. The poor lad was coddled and cosseted by his overbearing mother. He decided to try drawing the boy out of his silence.

'What would you like to do when you leave school, Frederick?'

It was in vain, as Mrs Holloway gave no quarter to her son, answering on his behalf. 'Frederick intends to become a Church of England minister. He dislikes the tropics, don't you, dear?'

Norton felt a surge of pity for the lad, whose head was now bent, eyes fixed on his place setting. It was hard to imagine him ever managing to stand up in a pulpit and deliver a sermon to his parishioners.

Frederick was spared from further embarrassment by the arrival of Carberry.

'My apologies for being late, Mrs Holloway. I took a late afternoon nap in my cabin and overslept. Must be all the sea air.'

Mrs Holloway didn't deign to reply, affording him only the slightest inflection of her head.

Norton, relieved that he would be released from the strain of manufacturing interest about anything more the woman had to say, greeted the planter with enthusiasm and the two men talked to each other for the remainder of the meal.

'I say, Baxter.' Carberry leaned forward. 'The sky's very clear this evening. How about I take up your offer to give me an astronomy lesson?'

'As long as you understand I'm just an enthusiastic amateur, not an expert.' He turned to Mrs Holloway, and invited her and Frederick to join them, confident of a negative response.

As soon as the pudding had been consumed and after declining coffee and brandy, the two men escaped from the tension at the dinner table.

Out on deck the air was sultry but tempered by the motion of the ship and the dark of the night. Norton and Carberry stood side by side, leaning against the guard rails.

'That's Jupiter there to the right of the Milky Way.' Norton extended his arm to point up into the sky. 'Let your eyes adjust to the dark. Can you see the Milky Way?'

Carberry tilted his head back and gazed up at the dark sky. 'That hazy, cloudy-looking area?'

'That's it,' said Norton. 'Hard to believe, but there are hundreds of billions of stars up there like our sun. They're so far away and so numerous that you can't distinguish them as separate points of lights and they all merge into one cloudy mass.'

'Which star is Jupiter?'

'It's not a star. It's a planet. Look about halfway up and then slightly to the right. It's that bright light on its own.' Norton pointed again.

'Got it.' Carberry tilted his head back and swept his eyes over the sky. 'What about the constellations you mentioned?'

Norton screwed his eyes up and identified the various visible constellations, pointing them out patiently to Carberry.

After a while, they lapsed into a companionable silence, Carberry smoking as they continued to study the night sky.

Eventually the tea planter spoke. 'Where will you be heading when we land?'

'Don't know yet. I have to report to the government office in Colombo and I'll be assigned somewhere. Of course I'm the lowliest of the low. A mere cadet, which makes me sound like a schoolboy.'

'I play golf and tennis with a few civil servants and know

most of them through the Kandy Club.' Carberry turned, leaning against the railings, his back to the sea. 'I think you'll find that even a cadet has quite a bit of responsibility. All very hierarchical in the big provinces, but if you get sent to a quiet backwater where there's just you and an assistant government agent, you could end up with a lot of decisions falling to you. Especially if you get an AGA who's lazy and wants a quiet life. He'll be happy to shift a lot of the workload onto you. On the other hand, if you're in Colombo or Kandy, you'll be shuffling paper for a few years, bored out of your mind.'

'You seem very well informed about the civil service.'

'You mean for a brainless planter?'

'Come off it, Carberry.' He gave his friend a playful punch in the arm. 'Don't put words in my mouth.'

Carberry frowned, then, just as quickly, relaxed. 'As it happens, I was friends with the office assistant in my district. We played a lot of tennis together. Until he got cholera and died.'

'I'm sorry.'

Cholera. That was another thing to worry about as well as the infernal heat. All sorts of tropical diseases. Norton shivered as the ship chugged along through the inky night waters.

'You all right, Baxter?'

Norton hesitated. 'It's just that being sent to Ceylon wouldn't have been my first choice. In fact, I didn't really want to be overseas at all.'

Carberry gave him a sympathetic smile. 'Give it a while. Ceylon will steal your heart. It's a beautiful country with beautiful, gentle people. The life's good. You'll see.'

'Will I?' It was his fate now, so he'd better get on with it – and that meant making a success of it. He had to prove his father wrong.

· · ·

The *Dambulla* took on four new passengers in Cochin. That evening, Norton watched them across the dining room as they took their seats. The party was led by a bespectacled white-haired man in his sixties, wearing a linen suit inappropriate for dinner. His companions were two younger men and a young woman – likely all in their early twenties.

The novelty of new passengers – there had only been disembarkations at Bombay – meant that the group was under scrutiny from the other diners, particularly Mrs Holloway. The matriarch revealed the knowledge she'd gleaned from the purser. 'He's Sir Michael Polegate, a professor from Oxford University.' She uttered his name and title reverentially, but her voice was scornful when she added, 'Studying the natives.' She sniffed and dabbed her brow with a lace handkerchief. 'Why anyone in their right mind would want to waste their time on such nonsense I can't imagine. He clearly isn't aware of the social niceties – or chooses to ignore them – as he hasn't dressed for dinner.'

Norton exchanged glances with Carberry but neither said anything.

Mrs Holloway was undeterred. 'He's travelling with his son and daughter and one of his students. It doesn't seem right for a respectable young woman to be tramping around India and Ceylon. She's unmarried.' She spoke the last word in a hushed voice. 'Most improper. The mother must be dead as I can't imagine her allowing it otherwise.'

Mrs Holloway bent forward to address Norton in a stage whisper. 'In my day, a young woman would never have been allowed to accompany three men on an *expedition*.' The last word was spoken with distaste. 'But these modern girls are so flighty.'

'She doesn't appear flighty.' Carberry always relished the chance to counter Mrs Holloway. 'Looks a bit of a bluestocking. Rather serious.'

Norton, curious, turned his head slightly, sitting back in his chair to afford himself a better view of the party. Carberry was right: the woman did look rather serious – even stern. Her hair was drawn back from her face into a voluminous untidy bun, secured with a tortoiseshell clip. As to her face, her features were handsome rather than pretty, with a nose that was slightly too large. But it was her eyes that caught his interest: they sparked with life and intelligence as she listened intently to her father. He'd seen many young women like her in Cambridge – struggling to prove themselves in a man's world. But there was something about the way she held herself that made him hesitate from pigeonholing her. A quiet intensity. A still point in the midst of the noisy dining room. Conscious that he was staring, he was about to look away when something her brother said made her laugh. Laughter transformed her. There was a lack of inhibition, a giving up of herself to the moment. He heard Mrs Holloway tut loudly. Miss Polegate glanced over in their direction and stopped laughing immediately, looking away.

After the waiter served the soup, Norton switched his inspection to the two young men, both around his own age. The brother was good-looking, but in a bland conventional way, his expression and posture indolent. Now that he was no longer the centre of attention with whatever he had said that had so amused his sister, he slouched in his chair, evidently bored by the topic his father was expounding upon.

The third man at the table was sitting upright, rigid. Of a stocky build, he reminded Norton of his least favourite lecturer at Cambridge, a humourless and rather arrogant man. Like the woman, he listened intently to the professor, but kept glancing sideways at her, as if to read her reactions, tailoring his own to match. This interest did not seem to be reciprocated. Norton was surprised at his own satisfaction in this observation.

When the group eventually rose from the table, the man

held the woman's chair and moved to take her arm in a proprietorial manner that made Norton wonder whether they were engaged. But a slight movement of resistance and the twitch of her lips indicated the attention was not welcomed.

The following evening there was to be a farewell dance before the voyage ended in the port of Colombo. As he dressed for dinner, Norton, who found such occasions something to be endured, realised he was looking forward to it. He would invite Miss Polegate to dance and satisfy his curiosity about what she was doing on an expedition with her father and brother, and perhaps discover what her relationship was to the other man.

But when the men of the Polegate party arrived for dinner, the woman wasn't with them. Norton was surprised to find he was disappointed. He didn't linger for the dancing, after fulfilling what he felt was his obligation to invite Mrs Holloway to dance. Duty done, he went to his cabin to enjoy an early night before his new life began the next day.

When the *Dambulla* docked in Colombo, caught up in bidding goodbye – he hoped for the last time – to the ghastly Mrs Holloway and her son, Norton didn't see the Polegates and their travelling companion again. After disembarking, he checked into his hotel – the Grand Oriental near to the port – then set out to explore Colombo on his last afternoon as a free man.

The heat and humidity were oppressive, and his shirt was soon stuck to his back. He was going to need more cool cotton clothes. He strolled through the streets around the Fort area, wandering through the ground floor of Cargill's, a large red-brick department store with a colonnade of Romanesque arches, where he bought two pairs of lightweight trousers and half a dozen cotton shirts, arranging for them to be dropped off at his hotel.

Now that he was here amidst the bustle of this tropical city, any doubts he'd had about his future faded. It felt like an adventure and Norton was determined to make the most of it.

TWO

Stella was out of sorts. Joining a ship so late in its passage was awkward. She was acutely aware of the interest the arrival of her party had caused among the other passengers. As was the norm on a long voyage, they had formed alliances and friendships, and she felt both an unneeded intruder and a specimen under a microscope. No doubt people were curious about her presence among three men. She was sure they'd realise one was her father but hoped no one assumed she was married to either her brother or Gordon Blackstock.

When her cabin steward told her there was to be an end-of-voyage gala dinner and dancing, she feigned a headache and requested a tray in her cabin. It wasn't just that she didn't want to mingle and be sociable, it was that Gordon Blackstock would undoubtedly assert a proprietorial claim over her and press her into dancing with him. Before leaving India, at a party in Ooty, he'd monopolised her, his clammy hands with their bitten nails damp through the fabric of her gown as he propelled her round the dance floor, always slightly behind the beat. But then, she was the only woman in their little group and Gordon wasn't endowed with much in the way of social graces, so she supposed it was easier for him to claim her, than risk approaching a lady he didn't know.

As she sat down to eat her meal at the small fold-out table in her cabin, Stella told herself not to be so uncharitable about Gordon. Wasn't her brother, Ronald, always accusing her of being too judgemental? She thought his sweeping statement was unfair – the only person she was judgemental about was Gordon Blackstock and she believed she had ample grounds for being so.

As their time in India had gone on, Stella had increasingly found herself thrown together with him. She suspected her brother might be trying to bring them closer. He was wasting his time if that was the case. She had no interest in her father's doctoral student, and she was sure he had none in her – other than as a convenient source to tap for the knowledge he himself lacked in his subject of study.

That was the root cause of her growing dislike of Black-stock. As the expedition had progressed, Stella had started to resent him. She would make a far stronger doctoral candidate than he did. But women, while permitted to study for a degree, couldn't be awarded one, let alone gain a doctorate, no matter how well they performed. In her case, even studying on an undergraduate degree course was denied to her, since her father disapproved of female students. She considered herself fortunate that at least he'd permitted her to travel to Ceylon with them. Back in Oxford he'd allowed her access to his books and said nothing when she sneaked into the back of lecture theatres to listen. Acting as his unpaid secretary had also given her the chance to learn directly from him, the pre-eminent expert in Indo-Aryan and Dravidian ethnography.

The more knowledge she acquired about anthropology, the more she realised how weak Blackstock's grasp of it was. He wasn't a stupid man, just not academically oriented and slow to make connections between ideas. He had a good memory for facts but little facility for complex arguments, and lacked a capacity for original thinking. But her father had accepted him as his PhD student, so it was his problem not hers, and Stella told herself there was no point wasting her energies fretting over their relative situations.

As soon as she'd finished her supper and the steward had taken away the tray, she sat down at the dressing table and pulled the pins from her hair before brushing it out.

This trip to India and Ceylon was a dream come true. It was a wonderful opportunity to participate in her father's fieldwork, to see India and Ceylon, to meet its native people and study their customs and way of life. When her father had agreed to her coming, she'd been overwhelmed with happiness – and with not a little disbelief. It was the first time she had felt truly content since the death of her mother, Delia, two years earlier from a heart defect. Stella's sorrow at the loss of Mama was like an open wound. But it had brought her and her grieving father closer.

Had her mother been alive, by now she'd doubtless have been shepherding her towards a suitable marriage. Thinking of that, Stella shuddered. Now that her eyes had been opened to the possibility of academic study, she hated the idea of being trapped by what she saw as the tedium of domesticity. The notion of joining her father on a lengthy overseas research trip would never have been entertained had her mother been alive. But the expedition had been life-changing, giving her a new sense of purpose and a hunger for anthropological research.

She picked up a well-thumbed photograph of her mother she always kept with her. She'd found it in a trunk after her death, along with a collection of opera programmes. The image was a publicity bill showing her mother as Aida, wearing an elaborate Egyptian bejewelled collar and headdress. It was the first time Stella had seen any evidence of her late mother's former musical career. There was no piano or gramophone in their Oxford house and her mother never sang or went to a concert. She discouraged any mention of her past performances and Stella had the impression that her career had been curtailed by Sir Michael when they'd married. It was still a source of sadness to Stella that her mother – Delia Devine as the handbill attested – had never spoken to her about what must have been a significant part of her life.

Settled in bed, Stella picked up the novel she was reading. In between her intensive studies and the copious note-taking she had to do for her father, she allowed herself the small indulgence of escaping into the world of fiction. The book she was immersed in now was the debut of a young author, E M Forster, and Stella was rationing herself to no more than a chapter at a time – which was proving a challenge as she was so gripped.

Exercising some self-discipline after reading a few pages, she inserted her bookmark, turned out the light and settled down to sleep. The cabin window was ajar to let in some air due to the tropical heat, and Stella could hear the strains of the ship's orchestra. They were playing a waltz, and she was grateful to have been spared the awkward embrace of Gordon Blackstock.

She listened to the music, drifting towards sleep. In her imagination she was being whirled around the dance floor by a partner. She could see him clearly: eyes that were both warm and intense, hair that was slightly too long, a clean-shaven face. A face that seemed both new and interesting and yet simultaneously familiar, as though she'd known him forever. Drowsy, she tried to recall where she'd seen this man before.

Then she remembered. It was a fellow passenger. The previous evening he'd been sitting on the other side of the dining room, at a table with a tall, blond, handsome man, an older woman and an adolescent boy. Stella had wondered what their relationship was and had concluded that other than mother and son, there was probably none. She wouldn't have noticed him at all were it not for the disapproving tutting from the woman, but as soon as she'd turned her head and seen him, she had the impression he'd been watching her.

The semi-conscious waltzing was pleasant so, rather than resist, Stella gave herself up to it. She'd never see the man again so why not enjoy their imaginary dance?

THREE

Norton had arranged to meet Carberry for drinks on the terrace of the Galle Face Hotel. It was a loose arrangement, since Norton had no idea how long he'd be in Colombo and whether his stay would involve any social engagements with his future colleagues. But there had been no invitations left at his hotel – just a brief memo to report to the secretariat at Government House the following morning at seven thirty when he would be briefed about his posting – to Kandy in the Central Province.

Carberry had pressed his address into Norton's hands before leaving the ship. 'If you can't make it to the Galle Face, write and let me know where you are. I'd hate to lose touch.' There was an intensity about Carberry's request that made Norton slightly uncomfortable: a neediness underneath the planter's bonhomie. Norton reflected that the life of an unmarried planter must often be a lonely one.

After buying his new clothes and with a couple of hours to spare before he was due to meet his friend, Norton ambled along Galle Face Green, a long grassy esplanade, parallel to the ocean. The Green had been the site of a gun battery under the Dutch, a parade ground for the British – as well as the place of execution for mutinous soldiers. More recently it had served as a racecourse and a golf links. Now it was a place to walk, picnic, fly kites and watch the waves breaking against the shore.

Norton loosened his tie and wiped a handkerchief over his damp brow. It was such a curse being British and a representative of His Majesty's Government – expected always to be fully suited-and-booted. He envied the local fishermen, dressed in loose shirts and cotton sarongs. He asked himself why his own countrymen placed so much store by formality. It made them look slightly ridiculous rather than bestowing the aura of dignity that was clearly the intent. It was as if they had been plucked from the streets of central London with its cool temperate climate and dropped into the steaming cauldron of Colombo. The one concession to the heat and burning rays of the tropical sun was the ubiquitous pith helmet. Wearing one now, he felt its weight and the dampness of his hairline under it.

As the appointed hour to meet Carberry approached, Norton walked back along the Green to the Galle Face Hotel. An overlarge colonnaded structure, it was topped by terracotta roof tiles, its frontage facing the Green sideways on to the ocean.

He passed the uniformed doorman and porters, all in full regalia, and entered the reception hall, grateful for its cooling ceiling fans. The place could have been a grand hotel in Piccadilly or St James – much wood panelling, marbled floors and a profusion of cut flowers.

The bar was on the right. Norton pushed open the door into a room that looked as though it belonged in a London gentlemen's club. Carberry was at a table, reading a newspaper and drinking a beer. He got to his feet and greeted his friend. 'You made it, Baxter!' He swigged down what was left of his beer. 'Let's go out to the terrace. Best place on the planet to enjoy a sundowner.'

A few minutes later they were installed in rattan chairs and supplied with whiskies and soda.

'So, my friend, do you know where they're posting you yet?' Carberry appeared genuinely interested.

'They're briefing me tomorrow, but apparently I'm being sent to Kandy.'

Carberry grinned widely and clasped his hands together. 'Top hole! I live in the Central Province too. Between Nuwara Eliya and Kandy. I'm in Kandy at least once a month.' His eyes shone and he gave Norton a friendly punch on the arm. 'So glad we'll be able to stay in touch.'

They talked about what Norton could expect of life in Kandy. Once again, he was surprised by how much Carberry, a planter, knew of the workings of the provincial government. 'I have a lot of contact with the provincial office in Kandy and with the district office in Nuwara Eliya. As you can imagine, we planters need to keep on the right side of the government agent and the assistant GA. I have to make the purchase of my land through them.'

Before Norton could question him, they were diverted by the arrival of a group of people at the other end of the terrace.

Norton cocked his head in their direction. 'Aren't they the people who came aboard at Cochin? The professor and his family.'

Carberry was unsurprised. 'Yes. They're staying here at the Galle Face before heading up north.' He took a sip of his whisky. 'I spoke to the son as we were disembarking. Name's Ronald Polegate. They're doing some kind of survey about the Tamils.' He shrugged. 'Comparing the ethnic Tamils up north with the hill country Tamils who came over from India to work in the tea gardens. I told him to look me up when they eventually get down our way and I'll arrange for them to interview some of our workers.'

A few minutes later, Norton glanced again at the four. The

older man and his daughter were drinking tea while the two others had whiskies. 'What's the woman doing with them?'

'She's the old boy's daughter, Ronald's sister. Acts as her father's secretary.' Carberry stuffed the bowl of his pipe with tobacco.

'And the other chap?'

'Not related. A research assistant I believe.'

Norton grinned. 'You're remarkably well informed, Carberry.'

The planter chuckled. 'I was chatting to Polegate while we were sorting out porters. Struck me as louche. Not the sort to last long out here.'

Norton raised an enquiring eyebrow.

'Wanted to know about the horse racing in Nuwara Eliya. A gambler apparently. Gave me the impression he might cut loose from the expedition as he has no interest in the stuff the rest of them are doing.'

'And the woman?'

Carberry shrugged. 'No idea. Looks pretty intense. Not at all like her brother.'

Norton glanced in their direction again just as Miss Polegate looked up and their eyes met. She frowned and looked away immediately. There was definitely something about her he found intriguing. Those eyes that hinted at much more than the serious features and the severe clothes.

He looked out at the ocean, watching the sun sink below the horizon, setting the sky ablaze in orange and pink.

When he next glanced in the Polegates' direction the woman had gone.

Later, over dinner, the realisation registered fully with Norton that he was in Ceylon for at least four years before he'd be eligible for a new posting or a permanent return to the UK. The voyage out had been more like the prelude to a holiday, but as of tomorrow he would be embarking on an experience which, while unknown, would doubtless shape the rest of his life. He felt ill-equipped and inadequate, yet now that he was here, curiously elated. And above all, determined.

'Do you think you'll eventually go back to England?' he asked Carberry. 'I don't mean on leave again, but for good.'

Carberry gave a little snort. 'Never. In fact, I doubt I'll go back at all, even on leave. England holds nothing for me now.'

'What about your family?'

'There's just my father and brother. We've never got on and they're both absorbed in running the farm. My brother has his own family now. Two children with a third on the way.'

'Have you thought of marrying?' As soon as Norton had asked the question, he regretted it. Too personal, even intrusive.

But Carberry was unperturbed. 'That was the reason I went back.' He gave a dry laugh. 'To find a wife.'

'Someone in particular?'

Carberry looked down, toying with his fish curry, shuffling it around the plate. 'Not really. There were a couple of girls I'd known before I came out here, that I thought might do. But they're both married now.'

Taken aback by the choice of words, it sounded to Norton as though Carberry was talking about choosing a birthday gift for a distant relative.

'Besides,' Carberry continued, 'what woman in her right mind would want to marry a planter and leave behind her family and friends to live on the other side of the world?'

'Yet many do. I suppose for love.' Norton put down his knife and fork. He didn't know what to make of Carberry. The usually cheery man seemed morose and introspective.

'Love?' Carberry snorted, his voice sounding cynical. 'Does it even exist?'

Norton frowned. 'I like to think so. Well – I hope so.'

The tea planter looked at him intently. 'Do you? Really? Is there someone in your life?'

Norton leaned back in his chair, uncomfortable at the turn the conversation had taken. 'No. No one. I suppose there were one or two girls while I was up at Cambridge but nothing that lasted. No one I could imagine spending the rest of my life with. But I'm younger than you. I hope that the right girl will come along at the right time. The right time certainly isn't now. Maybe in a few years, once I've proved myself and had a couple of promotions. The only thing that matters to me now is my career. Besides, I couldn't afford a wife on the pittance they'll be paying me as a cadet.'

Carberry nodded and smiled. 'I made my mind up when I was in England. I don't care if people expect me to marry, I want none of it. They can keep all their hearts and flowers. Give me a good set of servants any day.' Carberry reached into his pocket for his pipe and fiddled about with a pouch of tobacco before eventually lighting it. He fixed his gaze on Norton. 'To tell you the truth, Baxter, I'm not that interested in women. More trouble than they're worth.'

At first, he thought the planter was about to confess that he was indeed a homosexual, but immediately dismissed the thought. No one in their right mind would openly admit such a thing with the risk of disgrace and imprisonment. He framed his words as tactfully as possible. 'But what about... you know... sex... children?'

Carberry shrugged. 'One's overrated and the other's a weight around your neck. No, Baxter. As far as I'm concerned, it's better being a bachelor.' Carberry tilted his head slightly, his eyes fixed on Norton as he spoke. 'Women may seem all right at first, but they all end up like that dreadful Mrs Holloway on the ship.'

Norton laughed. 'A bit harsh, Carberry. You can't condemn

all womankind on the strength of an encounter with one insufferably snobbish woman.'

'I can. She epitomises everything I dislike about women. The pettiness, the gossiping, the crass stupidity, and the tendency to fixate on the trivial.'

Norton raised his eyebrows and was about to protest but realised it was pointless. Carberry was evidently in a strange mood this evening. He couldn't help feeling sorry for the man and his cynicism. 'I'm in no rush to be married myself, but I hope in time that I'll find the right woman and I promise you, she'll be nothing like Mrs Holloway.'

Later as Norton prepared for bed in the poky little hotel room with its view over an ugly back street, he reflected on the dinner conversation. What had made Carberry so categorical about marriage? When they'd parted, they'd done so over the customary handshake. Perhaps it was Norton's imagination, but it had seemed as though the planter had been reluctant to release his hand. The look in his eyes had been the same one he'd noticed when they left the ship – a sense of loneliness, of need.

The following morning, all thoughts of Carberry vanished as soon as Norton set off for the secretariat, where he was to meet briefly with Hugh Clifford, the colonial governor.

Clifford had been appointed less than a year earlier after the sudden death of his predecessor from appendicitis. A lifelong servant of the empire – having spent twenty years in the colonial service in Malaya from age seventeen – he told Norton he was delighted to be out East again after four years in Trinidad and Tobago.

'We're at the beating heart of the empire here, Baxter. India may be the jewel in the Crown, but Ceylon is the gateway to the Far East. I'll never love it the way I loved Malaya and especially Singapore, but this is the next best thing. And the port of Colombo has more traffic than Calcutta, Rangoon and Bombay combined.'

He went on to deliver a discourse on the importance of empire, stressing that Norton must always uphold the dignity and privilege of the colonial service. The speech struck Norton as a series of empty platitudes, and he wondered how often Clifford had delivered these words during his quarter century as a civil servant.

Dismissed by the great man, Norton spent the rest of the day first with the principal assistant colonial secretary, then with the second assistant, each adding their own version of the same homily already delivered by Clifford. Eventually, he was left to the mercies of a man called Monty Adamson, the senior office assistant who had until recently been stationed in Kandy.

Adamson was all too happy to provide him with the scuttlebutt about the Kandy office: who could be trusted and who not, who was competent and who was not.

'Are you writing this all down, Baxter?'

Norton was not, preferring to reach his own conclusions when in post himself, but in the interest of preserving goodwill, he dutifully made a few notes.

'The GA, Julian Metcalfe, is a decent enough cove, but woe betide you if you cross him. And steer clear of his daughter, Cynthia, if you want to keep in his good books.'

'His daughter?'

Adamson narrowed his eyes. 'Just steer clear of her, Baxter.'

Norton could tell he wasn't going to offer more information so let the matter drop.

The day dragged on as Adamson showed him the records he would be expected to keep and the numerous forms to be filled in. All his misgivings about whether life as a colonial civil servant would suit him returned in a flood. He had several more days of this to get through before he was due to travel to Kandy.

Using a large map on the wall, Adamson explained how Ceylon was divided into nine provinces, each controlled by a government agent, with the provinces sub-divided into districts under the management of an AGA. All of this was already known to him, thanks to Carberry. But to show the expected level of enthusiasm and conscientiousness he duly made notes in one of a dozen leather-bound notebooks his mother had given him as a goodbye gift.

As well as emphasising that, as a cadet, Norton was on the lowest rung of the ladder, Adamson explained that government offices were referred to by their Sinhala name of *kachcheri*. This was one of many minor concessions to local culture that seemed to be intended to mask the more significant ways that the destiny of both Sinhalese and Tamils had been subsumed by the strong arm of the British Empire.

Adamson, who was tall and skinny with a plummy Home Counties accent, exuded an air of superiority and smugness. There was something about him that reminded Norton of a school prefect, lording it over junior boys. He was glad that their acquaintance would be brief as he wouldn't have relished sharing an office with him longer term and being at the man's beck and call.

Walking back to his not so grand room at the Grand Oriental, Norton waited to cross the street while a small herd of cows blocked the way. Inside the hotel was an open-to-the-sky tropical garden with palm trees, marred only by the tendency of nesting crows to swoop down for pickings off the tables below. As he went up the stairs to his single room at the back of the building, Norton marvelled at the craziness of this city which, no matter how strong the rule and dominance of the British colonial powers, would always be its quirky chaotic self.

FOUR

Stella's right wrist was hurting. She'd sprained it while playing tennis before they left India for Ceylon. The brief respite from writing she'd hoped would be offered by the sea voyage was not to be, as her father, who made no concession to infirmity, continued to work on his findings. Her job was to transcribe these into a series of foolscap notebooks, adding the necessary punctuation and carefully recording the time, date and location. Even for someone as passionately interested in the subject as Stella, it was tedious work. And now, any hope of her wrist recovering quickly was gone, thanks to repetitive use.

Sir Michael dictated rapidly, consulting the little leather notepad in which he made jottings and always kept in his pocket.

Stella winced with pain, struggling to keep up, knowing her father wouldn't notice the wince but would pounce like an eagle on any errors or omissions.

As she worked by the light from an oil lamp, she looked up,

hearing her brother, Ronald, make a whoop of triumph outside the tent, where he was playing cards with Gordon Blackstock.

'Pay attention, Stella,' her father barked. Professor Sir Michael Polegate, an Oxford academic, was here on a six-month expedition to study differences in societal norms between the Tamil population of Southern India and that of the island of Ceylon.

His voice droned on, and her wrist throbbed as her pen formed the words on the page. 'Sorry, Papa.'

Stella was present on the expedition solely as her father's amanuensis, his scribe, denied a voice when Sir Michael and Blackstock discussed their findings. Doubly frustrating, since Blackstock relied on her as his critic and sounding board before presenting his conclusions to her father. *Her* conclusions would be the more accurate way of putting it.

Stella had wondered why her father had agreed to act as Blackstock's supervisor, and concluded it had everything to do with the endowment promised to the college by Blackstock's father, a wealthy industrialist. She was puzzled what had attracted Blackstock to studying anthropology in the first place, when he showed so little enthusiasm or aptitude for it.

She bit her lip as the pen scratched across the paper and she strained to see in the faint light from the guttering lamp. Above the murmurings of the two young men outside the tent, Stella heard the surf breaking on the beach a hundred yards away. She wanted to put her pen down and go there, kick off her shoes and walk barefoot along the shore in the moonlight, feeling the warm water lapping underfoot. Free to think, to form her own conclusions without Blackstock appropriating them.

Anthropology fascinated Stella, but her own interest lay primarily in exploring the roles of women. This was skated over by Sir Michael and his student, who focused their attention on religious customs, work practices, family structures, coming of age rituals, and dispute resolution, only as they pertained to men. For them, women held no interest other than as the wives of men and the mothers of their children. Stella knew there was so much more to explore and ached to do so.

Eventually, her father snapped his notepad shut, slipped it into the oilskin pouch he carried it in, stuffed it into his pocket and rubbed his hands together. 'Time to turn in. Make sure those two don't stay up all night playing cards. They need to be up and ready to leave at first light.'

The plan was to make a diversion along the coast before taking a boat to Ceylon's pearl fishery to witness the return of the pearl divers and the division of the spoils overseen by the British. Pearl diving had been carried out for millennia and, strictly speaking, had little relevance to Sir Michael's research, which was focused on agrarian communities, but it was a spectacle Ronald wanted to see, and their father chose to indulge him – perhaps in the hope of sparking interest in something other than gambling, drinking and – Stella suspected – loose women.

She pecked her father's cheek, bade him goodnight, then went outside. Sitting on a canvas stool she watched the two men finish their game. Somehow since Ronald's earlier triumphalism, Blackstock had managed to turn the tables – as he nearly always did. Ronald slid a ten-shilling note across the folding canvas card table.

'You're playing for money.' Stella sighed, looking up when the lamp sizzled as an insect flew into the flame. 'Honestly, Ronald. You promised Papa never to do it again after losing all that money in Ooty.'

Her brother gave her a sheepish grin and held up his hand to show her a pair of crossed fingers. 'One last time. Blackstock says I deserve a chance to redress the balance.'

Stella looked at Blackstock, who shrugged and looked away. 'Which it appears you've failed to do, so no doubt Mr Blackstock will offer you yet another chance and so it goes on.'

Ronald waved a hand dismissively. 'Don't be a shrew, sis. It doesn't become you.'

She bit back the temptation to respond to that. 'It's time we all turned in. Papa said to remind you we've an early start tomorrow.'

Without waiting for them to answer, knowing they wouldn't comply with her request, she went into her tent. The heat inside was suffocating. Stella undressed and washed quickly, relishing the splash of tepid water against her skin, then slipped under the mosquito net and settled on her camp bed, drawing the cotton sheet over her.

The following morning, Stella rose before the break of dawn. She walked the short distance to the shore and stood watching the sun rise over the gently lapping sea, turning the sky flamingo pink. The shore was interspersed with palm trees and inland there was thorn scrub and strange, fat-trunked baobab trees.

She strolled back to their encampment, where one of the bearers was frying bacon and eggs. Two bullock carts were waiting to transport them after breakfast.

They had travelled by train from Colombo to Anuradhapura but then had to forgo the speed and comfort of the train for bone-rattling bullock carts over rough and uneven tracks through the jungle. Most of the time, Stella chose to walk alongside the cart.

She wondered why the pearl harvest, a centuries-old tradition, should now be under the control of the British Empire. She'd never questioned the status quo before coming on this trip to the East: the empire was simply a fact of life. Britain's dominance of world politics and trade was something one took for granted. But since she and her travelling companions had docked in Cochin three months ago to begin their survey of ethnic Tamils, she had started to ask herself by what right the colonial power from the other side of the world controlled the strange, beautiful, and ancient Indian subcontinent and its people.

Stella had tried airing this with her father, but he'd brushed her doubts aside. 'The British are bringing enlightenment and civilisation to the native peoples. Without us they'd have no railways. We build schools, provide structures for governance.'

'But aren't we forcing our culture upon theirs?'

Her father had laughed and shaken his head. 'Stella, Stella, you can't begrudge the natives the chance to progress. That's what makes my work here so important. Change will come anyway and through the mechanism of empire it will come all the faster. So, understanding the native peoples and their customs and practices has an urgency and importance.' He frowned, suddenly impatient. 'Surely I don't need to justify myself to you?'

She'd bitten back her response, knowing better than to rub him up the wrong way. 'Sorry, Papa. I didn't mean to question your work. Rather the role of the empire in general.'

He shook his head. 'Never mind all that. Politics doesn't interest me. My job is to record, understand and interpret. The rights and wrongs have no bearing on the work.'

Sighing inwardly, Stella concluded her best option was to keep her doubts to herself – at least for the duration of the expedition.

They set off for the town of Mannar, from where they were to complete their journey to the pearl fishery by boat. They were accompanied by the bullock drivers, as well as local bearers responsible for setting and breaking the camp and preparing the food, and one who acted as guide and interpreter.

Ronald and their father rode on the bullock cart, the former sleeping off what Stella guessed was the after-effect of the previous night's drinking – she'd seen the empty bottles discarded behind the back of the tents. Sir Michael sat upright, notebook in hand, keenly watching his surroundings as the carts made their slow bumpy progress on the rough dirt track that followed the coast.

Stella preferred to walk, finding this stretch more interesting than the endless green walls of trees that had lined the track through the jungle from Anuradhapura to Mannar, and was annoyed when Gordon Blackstock chose to do the same. There was something about him that she didn't fully trust. She couldn't put her finger on exactly what it was, but her unease around him increased whenever she caught him looking at her. His eyes gave nothing away, his manners were always impeccable, yet there was something about him that increasingly made her recoil. She was only too aware that he used her as a means of retaining her father's good favour, by rehearsing his presentations with her, soaking up her ideas and conclusions in a manner intended to flatter but which, she knew, was because he was pirating them. She bristled every time she overheard him repeating her theories to her father as though they were his own, and hearing her father respond with, 'Excellent point, Blackstock, well observed and reasoned,' or excitedly, 'Good Lord, man, I think you're onto something there. First rate analysis.'

There was no point in telling the older man what was going on. He simply wouldn't listen, much less believe her. Whenever she'd tried to broach the subject with him, she'd been brushed aside with, 'I'm busy, my dear. Later?' but later never came. She knew she ought to be angry with Papa but settled for taking a quiet pleasure in getting one over on him. As for Blackstock, she'd begun to feel contempt for him, tempered by pity that despite her coaching, he never got any closer to forming his own conclusions. He could amass the facts, collect the data, but when it came to interpretation it might as well have been hieroglyphics. Stella grudgingly accepted she owed him some gratitude for being the channel to give her ideas the means to be tested by her father.

Blackstock's build would have made him a useful rugby prop had he not been disinclined to team sports. His light brown hair was flattened to his head with a strong-smelling dressing and formed a straight line across the top of his forehead from a low-lying parting just above his left ear. The combination of small, wide-set eyes framed by overlarge ears made her think of an elephant. His lips would have been the envy of most women – plump and sensual, and he tended to lick them when concentrating.

As they walked at a stately pace behind the second bullock cart, Stella was grateful for the silence. She avoided looking at Blackstock and let her eyes wander beyond the heavy carts and the road ahead to gaze at the sea on one side and scrub jungle on the other, with the occasional saltwater lagoon. Overhead, an eagle glided on a thermal, following the line of the coast. Stella swatted away a fly and strode on, pretending Blackstock wasn't there.

No matter how frustrating it was to be sidelined by her father, treated as a means of recording his work, and used by Blackstock as his borrowed brain, on mornings like this one she was thrilled to be here. How many women of her age would get the chance to visit a place like Ceylon, to witness the things she was seeing every day? Otherwise, she'd be at home in Oxford during the long vacation, walking by the river, reading, reading, reading, drawing on the thoughts of long-dead men rather than observing for herself and reaching her own conclusions.

Her reverie was interrupted by Blackstock. 'Miss Polegate?'

She turned to face him. He rarely spoke to her outside their academic interludes.

He cleared his throat. 'It can't have escaped your notice how much I respect and admire you.'

Stella caught her breath. She looked away, fixing her eyes on the bullock cart in front. Her chest pounded.

'For a woman, you show a keen intelligence, and I believe we have much in common, a great shared interest in anthropology and once we return to Oxford I propose that we—'

'Mr Blackstock. Please—'

'Allow me to finish.' His eyes narrowed. 'As I was saying, our shared interests offer a solid platform for a life together. Your father has spoken of recommending me for a teaching position in the college; indeed, he has hinted at grooming me to be his successor. I am twenty-seven years old, and it is time I took a wife. I consider you the ideal candidate. You are an attractive young lady, well-mannered, intelligent and I believe you would make a worthy helpmate to support me as I rise the academic ladder, to keep house for me, and in due course provide me with children.'

He stretched his hand out to touch her on the arm. She shrank away, stepping sideways and turning her head to avoid his gaze.

'What say you, Miss Polegate, or if I may, Stella?'

She quickened her pace to draw closer to the cart which had pulled ahead slightly during Blackstock's proposal.

As she was about to respond, he raised a palm to halt her and continued. 'I have discussed this with Ronald, who agrees it's a first rate idea. I haven't yet raised it with Sir Michael as I think it would be best if we were to seek his permission together, offering an already united front. What better for the daughter of one of the world's most preeminent anthropologists than to wed his protégé?'

Stella struggled to speak. She was dumbstruck. First, at the idea of Blackstock proposing when she'd given him not the slightest encouragement; then that his intention was to perpetuate his theft of her thinking and pass it off as his own for the rest of his life. And what form of self-delusion caused him to describe himself as Sir Michael's protégé?

The arrogance was breathtaking. Enough! As soon as this expedition was over and they were back in England, she would have done with it all. No more acting as her father's unpaid secretary. No more feeding her analysis to Blackstock for him to serve up as his own. No more being the overlooked and ignored woman. She was going to emerge from her chrysalis and pursue her studies openly. Her heart was set on Cambridge, away from her father and Blackstock. The awarding of a degree might be an impossible dream – indeed about ten years ago there had been protests in Cambridge when the idea was voted on, with effigies of women scholars burned in the streets while rampaging male students threw fireworks at the windows of women's colleges. But she was tired of studying in secret and having Blackstock as her surrogate. Degree or no degree, she wanted the freedom to learn in her own right.

'Mr Blackstock—'

'Gordon, please.' He smiled and she realised he was utterly confident she would accept him.

'Mr Blackstock, I'm sorry if I've ever inadvertently given you reason to believe in the possibility of a future between us. It has certainly never been my intent.' She swallowed and squeezed her hands into tight fists in an effort to summon up courage. 'I have no plans to marry *anyone*. Ever. The time has come for me to pursue my interest in anthropology seriously and independently. I intend to apply to the University of Cambridge, to one of their women's colleges.'

He gasped audibly. 'Does Sir Michael know?'

'Not yet. I'd be grateful if you'd keep this between us until I find an appropriate time to tell him.'

'It's preposterous. Pointless. Marry me and you'll have all the benefits of study with none of the drawbacks – at least until

I am established as a don, when you can focus your attention on bringing up our children.'

'There will be no children. I have no intention of marrying anyone, much less a man whose only interest in me is as a means of hoodwinking my father into believing that you actually know something.' Now that she'd started, she couldn't hold back. Anger was fuelling her. 'You show no capacity whatsoever for disciplined thinking in the field. Magically, when writing up your findings, your muddled thoughts become lucid well-argued conclusions. *My* lucid well-argued conclusions.'

He gave an embarrassed laugh, a guffaw, as though disbelieving what he was hearing. 'You're pulling my leg! You can't mean it. What a ludicrous accusation. You seem to be implying I steal your ideas!'

'More than implying.'

He frowned, causing the wide-spaced eyes to move closer together and shrink further into his face, like two blackcurrants in a ball of dough. He opened his mouth to speak, gripped her arm like a vice, then abruptly released her and strode away to walk at the rear of the first cart which was carrying all their luggage and equipment.

Stella let out a breath, sucked in her lips and fought the urge to cry. She had meant every word she said, but something told her it had been a mistake to make an enemy of Gordon Blackstock. And there was no doubt that was what she had just done.

FIVE

She could smell the pearl fishery as soon as their boat pulled close to the shore. The stench rose from heaps of oysters piled inside wooden canoes and left to rot away in the sun, leaving the pearls.

Stella put up a hand to cover her mouth and nose. Putrid, rancid, foul. She resented coming to this place, all too aware that their father had been indulging Ronald when the latter said it would be an interesting thing to do. Not for the first time she wished her brother had stayed in England. Sir Michael's tendency to pander to his son's whims was a growing irritant. Yet she supposed Ronald's presence diluted Gordon Blackstock's. Had her brother not been there to distract Blackstock, Stella would have been obliged to spend more time in the doctoral student's company. The dark bruise on her arm where he'd gripped her was a reminder of how undesirable that would be.

The pearl fishery was an enormous temporary encampment accessible only from the sea. It consisted of a collection of hastily assembled wooden huts thatched with coconut palm and arranged in an orderly grid of streets. The site was situated on the northwest coast at Marichchukaddi near Arippu and inhabited only during the pearl fishing season. The most striking feature of the place was that stinking midden of rotting molluscs.

It was odd how something as beautiful and refined as a pearl should be found amidst rottenness and decay. Stella had always treasured the string of pearls that had belonged to her late mother. She thought of how the surface of each pearl was warmed by her skin. She loved to wear the necklace but couldn't help wondering if she'd ever feel the same way about it now.

When the party reached the makeshift encampment, Stella realised what the appeal had been to Ronald. As well as the thousands of pearl divers, the site housed a motley crew of attendant people. There were those associated with the pearl industry – dealers, clerks and oyster counters, jewellers, and drillers, then ancillary workers, boatmen, navigators, cooks, hawkers, shopkeepers, policemen, entertainers, including snake charmers, conjurors, female dancers, musicians and prostitutes. There was a magistrates' court, a prison, a hospital, and a cemetery. Overseeing the whole operation were representatives of the British colonial government, the provincial government agent, the district AGA, and the fishery superintendent, a man who looked careworn, nervous, and exhausted.

They pitched their tents on the periphery of the settlement. Although used to sleeping under canvas, Stella had never done so in such a heavily populated place. In towns and cities they tended to stay in rest houses, and she was not looking forward to spending a night here. She knew better than to complain though, and didn't want to give her father a chance to regret agreeing for her to come.

While Sir Michael and Gordon Blackstock went to meet with the fishery superintendent, Stella persuaded her brother to accompany her on a walk along the shore, away from the chaos and decay. She would have preferred to wander off alone but there was something about Marichchukaddi that made her feel the need for Ronald's protection. And getting him alone would give her a chance to find out why on earth he'd encouraged Blackstock to propose.

'Why did you want to come to this awful place?' she asked him as they strolled along the beach, trying to put a distance between themselves and the putrid smell.

'It'll be a lark. A chap I met in Ooty told me all about it. I'm hoping to do some deals on pearls at a knockdown price.'

'Isn't it all heavily controlled?'

Ronald shrugged. 'Outside the auction someone will be willing to sell at the right price. It'll be interesting.'

'Assuming we survive that smell. Honestly, Ronald, I don't think I've ever experienced anything so foul. Do what you want to do quickly so we can get out of here.'

'Gordon and Father seem to think it will be an excellent spot to gather information for their study.'

Stella groaned inwardly. Her father hadn't mentioned that. He'd described the visit as a minor detour. Their work was focused on the practices and rituals of agrarian communities not the tradition of pearl fishing. She felt sick at the thought of being stuck here, breathing in this stinking air.

'Father says a few days here will furnish him with enough material for his annual lecture to the Royal Asiatic Society.'

Stella bristled. Why had he told Ronald about this rather than her, when her brother didn't give a fig about their work? She bit her lip, determined not to let her brother see that she was put out.

Ronald slowed his pace and glanced at her sideways. 'Did Gordon speak to you?'

Stella looked away towards the sea. 'About what?' – although she knew exactly what was coming.

'About you and him marrying. I think it's a splendid idea, actually.'

She turned to look at him. 'Was it your idea?'

'No, but I don't know why I didn't think of it myself. Solves the problem.'

'What problem?' Stella felt a sinking sensation in the pit of her stomach.

Ronald glanced at her then looked away again. 'Don't be obtuse, Stella. You know perfectly well. You must marry someone.'

She narrowed her eyes. 'Why? Why do I have to marry someone? And why do you imagine I'd want to marry him of all people? Have I ever given the slightest indication of any interest in Mr Blackstock?'

'Well, yes, as it happens. You and he are always talking about the research, going over your notes together. Lord knows why the three of you find all that stuff interesting but it's clear you do.' He bent his arms behind his neck and stretched. 'Gosh, I'm stiff as a board after that abominable bullock cart.' He looked at her. 'So? Answer my question. Did he ask you?'

'Yes, he did. What were you thinking, cooking that idea up between you? Surely you know me well enough to realise there's no way on earth I'd marry Gordon Blackstock.'

'You could do a lot worse. It's not as though you're spoiled for choice. I happen to think he'd be a good match. You can help him with his work, just as you do now for Father.' Ronald kicked absently at some sand. 'Besides, how else would you get the chance to travel like this? Father won't be around forever. In fact, he's told me this will be his last expedition.' He took off his sun helmet and scratched his head. 'You love these trips, Stella. Married to Gordon you'd be able to carry on. At least until you have children.'

Stella shuddered at the thought of what that implied.

Her brother continued, oblivious to her distaste. 'Otherwise, you'll be stuck in England. You can't travel alone as a woman.' The last word was spoken dismissively.

Stella's eyes stung but she was determined he wouldn't see how upset she was. Besides, he was right. Some intrepid women did travel alone – but unlike her they were all wealthy and able to support a large retinue of protective guides and servants.

'Gordon's my friend,' said Ronald, folding his arms. 'Him marrying my sister is a capital idea. Come on, old girl, you have to marry somebody, so why not him? A chap in the same field as Father. A field you're interested in. Seems ideal.'

'You and Mr Blackstock have it all worked out, don't you?' She took a gulp of air. 'I'm going to spoil your little scheme as I'll never marry him.'

Ronald made a snorting noise. 'Be practical, Stella. Once Father's gone, who's going to take care of you? By then I'll doubtless have a family of my own to provide for. It's my responsibility, as the future head of the family, to see you settled.'

The sun was moving lower in the sky, the shadows of the palm trees lengthening, but the heat was still intense. She tried to contain her frustration as she wiped her brow with a hand-kerchief under the brim of her straw hat. 'Mama left me a modest sum of money. Not enough to live grandly but enough to support myself for a few years. I intend to apply for a place at Cambridge.'

Ronald guffawed. 'And what then? Even supposing they'd take you.'

She ignored the barbed comment. Ronald was hardly in a position to judge the academic potential of others. 'Then I will teach. Like Papa. Or become a researcher. Or work in a museum or a library.'

He raised his eyes. 'Don't be daft, Stella. You're a *girl*.'

It was pointless arguing with him. She pushed her hands

deep into the pockets of her skirt and squeezed them into tight fists.

Ahead, on a low promontory above the sandy beach, was a large building, in a state of dilapidation. A big square structure, it had been built in the classical style with a portico of Doric columns. The plasterwork on the pillars had crumbled away, revealing the red bricks beneath. Part of the structure had collapsed into heaps of rubble on the shore. What was left stood alone, roofless, and incongruent, on the empty plain facing out to sea, defiantly inappropriate to its surroundings.

Ronald was already crossing the sand towards the doorless entrance. He called back over his shoulder. 'I've read about this place. It's known as the Doric Bungalow because of the Grecian columns. It was built for Lord North, the first British governor of Ceylon, over a century ago.'

Stella stood on the shore and looked up at the building. She decided it was a bit creepy.

Ronald went on. 'I've been reading a book I picked up in the Charing Cross Road before we left. Written over fifty years ago by some chap called Baker. It's mostly about game hunting but he has a chapter on the fishery.' He stretched out a hand to help his sister up the sandy slope to the ruined bungalow. 'He reckons even back then the place was falling apart. It was folly to build it in the first place in such a desolate spot when it was only going to be used for a couple of months a year when the governor inspected the fishery. Neglect and bad weather saw to it.'

Stella followed her brother inside the ruins, mounting the stone staircase that bisected the building and emerging onto what was left of an open roof terrace. They stood side by side in silence, staring out to the sea and the pale grey sky above it.

'It's so bleak. Imagine living here all the time.'

Ronald grunted. 'I expect that's why the governor didn't

linger once the fishery ended and wasn't tempted to spend more time here.'

Stella turned from the sea and crossed to look over the back wall of the ruined building. Ahead was an ugly sandy wasteland, treeless with just scrub thorn. The ground looked barren, infertile, hostile.

'Even the huts in the settlement don't last apparently. Once the pearl fishers leave, the wind blows them away.' Ronald had moved across to stand beside her.

She hoped he wasn't going to bring up Gordon Blackstock again. She didn't want to think about him. 'It's a horrible place. Gives me the creeps. Come on. It'll be dark soon. Let's get back to the camp.'

As they approached the settlement, the faint sound of a gramophone playing Gilbert and Sullivan floated over to them from a more substantial structure, on a slight rise in the ground and set apart from the mêlée of shacks. Stella recognised the song as 'A Wandering Minstrel, I' from *The Mikado*. She looked quizzically at her brother.

'Must be the government agent's bungalow,' he said.

As he spoke, a manservant emerged from the building and bowed. 'Mrs Moreland would like to meet you. She invites you to join her in taking tea.'

He indicated the building, where a woman sitting at a table beside the open front door waved to them. 'Looks like we've no choice,' she muttered to her brother.

The woman jumped up to greet them, stretching out her hand. 'Violet Moreland,' she said. 'I'm afraid my husband didn't warn me to expect guests.' Mrs Moreland appeared to be in her mid to late forties. She was dressed in an unfashionably loose-fitting white cotton gown and cooled herself energetically with a large painted fan.

Ronald shook her hand. 'Ronald Polegate and this is my sister, Stella. We're travelling with our father and one of his students. Father is an academic, an anthropologist. Your husband wouldn't have known about us, as this is an impromptu visit. I rather wanted to see the pearl fishing in operation.'

'See it? Not a lot to see. The pearl banks are twenty miles out to sea. More like smell it,' said Mrs Moreland, dismissively. 'Still, one does get used to it I suppose. And at least it's not every year. Only when there are enough pearls to declare a fishery. If you're interested, Mr Polegate, my husband or the AGA will be more than happy to give you as much information as you need.'

Stella wondered whether to tell their hostess that Ronald's interest was not scientific, then decided it was up to him to speak for himself. They accepted a cup of tea, which Mrs Moreland poured from a silver pot, before winding the crank, lifting the arm of the gramophone, and setting the needle once more in the groove for another chorus of *The Mikado*.

'I do so love Gilbert and Sullivan. Don't you, Miss Polegate?'

Stella murmured polite assent.

'I keep meaning to set up a little theatrical group in Jaffna and put one of their operas on. Maybe *HMS Pinafore*.' She sighed. 'There's not a lot of us in Jaffna and I suppose not everyone has the voice for it, do they?' Without waiting for either of them to answer, she addressed Stella again. 'Frightfully intrepid of you to come out to the fishery, Miss Polegate. It's not for the fainthearted. In fact, it's plucky of you to come to Ceylon at all. We don't get many visiting ladies. Other than families accompanying their menfolk. There's only one other white woman here at the fishery: Mrs Porter, married to the police superintendent. Frightfully young. And rather horrified by this place, poor dear. Wishes she'd stayed in Mannar. But they're newlyweds so I imagine they didn't want to be parted. The poor girl isn't very sociable. Shuts herself away reading novels all day as far as I can gather.'

Mrs Moreland took a sip of tea, then turned to Stella. 'How long are you going to be at Marichchukaddi, Miss Polegate?'

'Only a day or two. My father is keen to continue his work. We're gathering data on the customs and practices of the Northern Tamils compared with those of India and of the central highlands.'

Mrs Moreland screwed her face up. 'Sounds grim. And you have to tag along with him? What does your mother think of that?'

'Mother is dead.'

'Oh, my dear, I'm frightfully sorry. Out here? The East is hard on us women.'

'No, she died in Oxford. Where we live.'

'I see.' Mrs Moreland took another sip of tea then put down the cup. 'You will stay here with us, of course, Miss Polegate. We can't have you camping in the fishery. Completely unsuitable. It's like the Wild West down there. I'll have the servants make up a bed for you.'

Stella looked at the woman more closely and realised she was probably about ten years younger than she'd first assumed. It was perhaps not surprising as the climate here was hardly kind to a woman, and Mrs Moreland was also the mother of four.

Ronald spoke for the first time since the introductions. 'What a marvellous idea, Mrs Moreland. Stella's been bunking in a tent most of the time. It will be nice for her to enjoy some home comforts.'

'But—' While the thought of a bed was appealing, she had only just met Mrs Moreland and was hesitant to presume on her hospitality.

'No buts, Miss Polegate. It's settled.' Mrs Moreland put her hand on Stella's wrist. 'This is not the most comfortable of bungalows – it's only used for a couple of weeks every year or so. It gets rather wild out here. The back of beyond.' She laughed. 'Half the Venetian slats blew out last year. No point getting them replaced.' She sighed. 'I'm afraid the privy is in an outbuilding.' She smiled. 'Still, a jolly sight better than being among that lot.' She waved a hand vaguely in the direction of the fishery settlement. 'With more than forty thousand people there now, you'd never guess it's completely deserted once the fishery's over.'

'How long does the fishery last?'

'A couple of months. Between the two monsoons. Of course, this year's the last time we will have to be here, thank the Lord.'

'How so?' Ronald raised his eyebrows.

'The government has leased the fishing rights to a private company. A London syndicate. They have the lease for twenty years. The new company has even bought the inspection ship. So, I won't be here, but I'll remain here in spirit since the ship's named after me: the *Violet*.' She grinned. 'I wonder what kind of a job a private firm will make of it. Keeping the peace among tens of thousands of men and women of different nations, speaking different languages and dialects, is no mean feat. I doubt the new company has a clue what they're letting themselves in for.'

Mrs Moreland looked towards the ocean. 'Over there!' She pointed. 'They're coming back.'

Stella and her brother stood up and gazed towards the horizon where the sun was sinking rapidly. Numerous boats of different sizes and styles were heading for the shore.

'They finish diving at noon, before the breezes get up, but it can take a couple of hours or even days to get back, depending on tides and winds.' Mrs Moreland looked wistful. 'Those poor creatures. Do you know they dive from sunrise until noon. Imagine! They tie a heavy stone to their big toes and the weight pulls them down to the pearl banks. They stay down there without breathing for up to ninety seconds, filling up their baskets with oysters, then they pull on another rope and the men in the boat draw them back up as fast as they can. The divers work in pairs so the other one goes down while the first one has a few minutes to recover, and then off he pops again. It's rather like a Swiss cuckoo clock. One in and one out.'

'Sounds dreadful,' said Ronald. 'Have you been to see it, Mrs Moreland?'

'I did a trip on the *Violet* but once was enough. I couldn't stand the tension waiting for the chaps to surface again. One of the poor fellows died last year.'

'Sharks?'

She gave Ronald a disdainful look. 'They're just basking sharks. Harmless. No, it was a heart attack or a collapse of the lungs. The pressure down there is strong and if they come up too rapidly, they get what they call "the bends". As for sharks – for centuries the natives had a nice little number in shark charmers – chaps who peddled amulets and trinkets to keep the sharks at bay. They'd go out with the boats and got paid in pearls – lots of them – for doing nothing other than feeding the natives' superstitions. The British put paid to that. Got rid of them years ago, and not a single shark attack since.' She turned away from the ocean. 'Well, I won't keep you any longer or your father will be sending out a search party. I'll expect you both back here later with the rest of your party to dine with us tonight. I'm just sorry I can't offer accommodation to you all. My husband will be leading the auction at six, so we dine after that. About eight.'

Stella was relieved to be spending the night apart from the others. 'It really is most kind of you, Mrs Moreland.'

The GA's wife gave her a radiant smile. 'Not at all. I'm delighted to have some civilised company. And don't worry – we don't stand on ceremony here at the fishery. No need to dress formally.'

Stella and Ronald walked back towards the settlement, along a shore empty of everything except coconut palms, with the desolate plain beyond. The manservant walked behind them, keeping a discreet distance.

Ronald spoke first. 'Don't believe what she says about the sharks being harmless. In that book I was telling you about there's a story about some British soldiers jumping off a cliff into the sea and there was a lad of just fifteen – the son of one of the sergeants. He dived in, surfaced, then screamed and never came up again. One of the chaps dived down to look for him and came up with just his top half. The shark had bitten right through and eaten him from the waist down.'

Stella felt sick at the thought. 'Here?'

'I think it was at Trincomalee.'

'That's the opposite coast of Ceylon.'

'It's still the Indian Ocean. I for one won't be sea-bathing while we're here.'

Keen to change the subject, Stella asked if her brother knew where they were going. All the shacks looked the same and she was struggling to remember where they'd left the others.

'We're right at the end. As far away from the stinking shell tip as we can be.' He pointed. 'Not sure how Father will feel about dining with the GA and his wife,' said Ronald. 'He was rather hoping to spend the evening talking to the divers.'

'I expect the divers will want an early night since they set off again at three in the morning. Besides, it's frightfully kind of Mrs Moreland to invite us.'

'I suppose so – and we need to get in the GA's good books if Gordon and I are to arrange to go out with the fishing boats tomorrow. I want to see this diving business close up and there'll be plenty of relevant information for Gordon to glean for his thesis.'

Stella didn't want to talk about Gordon. She didn't want to listen to Ronald talking about him either. She was still smarting over their conversation earlier. Inside her, the resentment, which had abated during their brief visit to Mrs Moreland's bungalow, was bubbling away.

The pearl fishery was a hive of activity. Boat after boat of pearl divers returned to shore to unload their catch. The divers were a mixture of Arabs and Moors who travelled from the Persian Gulf each year for the pearl season, as well as Tamils, more of them from India than from Ceylon. Their faces were etched with strain and exhaustion from the repetitive dives they had made – over fifty submersions in a single morning. Stella didn't linger to watch them, conscious of Mrs Moreland's manservant who was waiting to escort her and her bags back to the GA's bungalow.

An aroma of spices and hot oil pervaded the air. Presumably the women were cooking for their returning men. Stella realised she was hungry.

She left her brother watching the scene on the beach and made her way to her tent.

SIX

His induction complete, Norton left Colombo to make his way by train to his posting in Kandy.

A rickshaw deposited him at the Colombo Fort railway station, just a few minutes from his hotel. He was glad to be free of the heavy-handed tuition of Adamson and the depressing room with no view at the Grand Oriental, and was eager to get started in his new role.

The train chugged along, crossing the Kelani River, leaving the city behind. After the rice paddies of the low coastal plain, it began its slow ascent into the hill country. Norton stared out of the carriage window, hungry to see more of the island that was to be his home for the foreseeable future. The train climbed higher, through cuttings and over viaducts and bridges. While acknowledging the railway as a triumph of Victorian enterprise and engineering, he knew it had been built with the sweat and backbreaking labour of local men who had hewn the rock to build the tunnels and embankments for their colonial masters.

You're not supposed to think like that, he told himself. Wasn't it also true that, back in England, great cathedrals and castles had been built by English peasants – often for the invading Normans? Didn't it simply mean that Britain was further along the evolutionary continuum than the natives of Ceylon? This was the kind of argument Adamson would use, but Norton wasn't so sure himself. Britain was the latest in a long line of invaders, following the Portuguese and then the Dutch in capturing Ceylon. The railway had been built under the British to transport tea from the highlands to the port of Colombo, thus bringing prosperity to this small island in the Indian Ocean. Yet how much of that prosperity reached the men who hewed the rocks, cleared the jungles and picked the tea? *You're turning into a Fabian, Norton. That won't wash in Whitehall.* It was even less likely to wash in Kandy.

When the train arrived at the provincial capital, Norton's new boss, the office assistant, a young man called Bertie Frobisher, was waiting at the station to meet him. Inordinately tall – at least six-foot-four Norton guessed – he was prematurely balding and sported an enormous compensatory moustache. He was visibly sweating in a heavy wool suit with a stiff high-collared shirt. The temperature in Kandy, cooler and more pleasant than Colombo, was still above seventy, even now in the late afternoon. Norton was to discover that this attire was the norm for Frobisher, who preferred to roast rather than exhibit even the most minor concession to the tropical climate. For his part, Norton was grateful for the colonial clichéd cream linen suit he was wearing.

'Righty-ho!' Frobisher declared. 'Let's get you installed in your lodgings. You're in the same bungalow as me. Not exactly the Savoy, but comfortable enough and with fine views of the lake and the mountains.'

As they made their way in a pony and trap, Frobisher pointed out places of interest. 'The *kachcheri*'s down there.' He gestured towards a large Palladian-style building that housed the government offices. 'And that's the Queen's Hotel and St Paul's church – and the police courts are over there.' Norton turned to look as they rattled along, thinking how out of place the traditional British architecture was, more suited to Piccadilly than Ceylon.

The Kandy Lake was in the centre, beside the Temple of the Tooth Relic – the most sacred site for the Sinhalese as it housed the supposed tooth of the Buddha himself. He listened while Frobisher recounted the history of Kandy and its role as the capital of the ancient Kandyan kingdom. The lake was encircled by hills, now purplish against the setting sun, and there were flowering trees offering shady walks to the city's inhabitants. Running around about half of the two-mile perimeter was a decorative white scalloped wall, which his colleague told him was called the Cloud Wall. It reminded Norton of his mother's white embroidered table runner.

'The lake's man-made,' said Frobisher, clearly keen to show off his local knowledge. 'It was created by Sri Vikrama Rajasinha, the last of the Kandyan kings, in 1807.' Frobisher gave Norton a potted history of each of the three wars between the invading British and the Kingdom of Kandy. Norton, who had read up on his Sinhalese history before leaving England, let the words drift past him as he gazed at the lake and surrounding mountains.

'The king was a bit of a brute. In order to put down a revolt he impaled forty-seven rebels on sharpened stakes.'

'Gruesome.'

'But the rebel leader, a chap called Ehelapola, evaded capture, so the king seized his wife and children. He decapitated the children, starting with the eldest son, an eleven-year-old, then gave a pestle to the wife and forced her to pound the boy's head in a mortar, repeating this act with each of the remaining children, before binding heavy stones to her and ritually drowning her in the lake.'

Norton couldn't help thinking Frobisher was relishing this bloodthirsty tale. 'What happened then?'

'When Ehelapola found out, he joined forces with the British and they overthrew the king once and for all. The tyrant was exiled to Madras where, thanks to his gargantuan appetite, he died of the dropsy.'

'What happened to Ehelapola?'

'He took umbrage when the British didn't make him king. They exiled him too. Packed him off to Mauritius.'

Frobisher went on to describe the early days of the British administration. Norton wished the office assistant would stop talking. He wanted to drink in his new surroundings without the constant drone of the man's voice. Already, Kandy made him feel uneasy. It was a strange mixture of ancient royal palaces and monasteries with symbols of British colonial power. It seemed to him that neither was comfortable co-existing with the other. The lake and surrounding mist-wreathed mountains were beautiful, but the stories of cruelty told with such relish by Frobisher had already tainted the place for Norton. And he was to share a home with this man. His stomach sank at the prospect.

The bungalow was accessed by stone steps from the lake-side road. The men were deposited at the foot of the stairs where two servants were waiting to carry Norton's bags. He followed Frobisher up through trees towards the building which was invisible from the road. It was a white-painted single-storey dwelling with a green tin roof. In front was a small lawn and the house had a veranda with views to the lake below and the mountains opposite. Norton liked it – a secluded sanctuary distant from the bustle and noise of the town.

The servants lined up to greet him. Frobisher did the introductions then asked whether Norton had met Adamson in Colombo. When he said he had, Frobisher grinned. 'Decent chap. I miss him.' He looked at Norton as if trying to assess whether he might be capable of filling the other man's shoes, and appearing to conclude it was unlikely. 'He started out in your post as cadet and worked up to OA. I learned everything I know from him. First rate fellow.' He turned and spoke to one of the servants in Sinhala before addressing Norton again. 'Supper at seven thirty so I'll leave you to settle in until then. By the way, I forgot to ask, how's your Sinhala?'

Norton had been dreading that question. 'I have some of the basics. Rather hoping it will improve with practice.'

'I'll line up a teacher for you. A Buddhist monk and scholar. Essential you get to grips with the lingo as quickly as possible. Of course, Adamson spoke it fluently. Tamil too. Focus on the Sinhala. You'll need to do an exam before you can hope for advancement. Not that you can expect promotion for several years.' He indicated a door. 'Your room's there. See you at supper. All meals on the veranda, weather permitting.'

With that, Frobisher vanished into his own bedroom and Norton was left to inspect his. It was at the rear of the bungalow with a French window with views of the lawn, and the jungle and mountains beyond. He looked around him. A single brass bed draped with mosquito nets, a dressing table with a basin and jug, a clothes-stand and a small wooden table under the window which would serve as a writing desk. It would do. He was glad he didn't have a lake view, pretty as it was, preferring the quietness and seclusion afforded by being at the back. And he didn't like to think of that poor woman forced to brutalise the remains of her own children, and whose grave lay beneath the tranquil surface of the water.

After laying out his shaving gear and comb on the dressing table, Norton unpacked his suitcases and placed two framed photographs on the desk. One was a formal family portrait, his father standing on one side, ramrod straight, him on the other and his sister and mother sitting in between. The second was a more relaxed image of Winnie taken a couple of years ago. She was grinning, her head tilted to one side, even though her mother had told her to maintain a dignified and serious look.

Dear old Winnie simply didn't do dignified. He missed that broad smile and her infectious laugh. He stacked the six volumes of Gibbons on the window ledge and added the Sinhala language primer. He picked it up, glanced at the curling squiggly letters, then put the book on the nightstand. He would force himself to spend half an hour on it every night before sleeping.

The meal that evening was very British: mulligatawny soup, lamb chops with mint sauce, boiled potatoes, and runner beans, followed by orange jelly. Norton couldn't fault the cooking but would have preferred the local cuisine. He thought wistfully of the fish curry he'd enjoyed with Carberry in Colombo, and the excellent Ceylonese dishes served as an option on the *Dambulla*.

Over dinner, Frobisher had a book open and read while he ate. 'Office hours are long, so I like to catch up with recreational reading in the evenings.'

Norton's face broke into a grin. The best news he'd had since arriving in Kandy. What a blessing not to have to listen to Frobisher's adenoidal voice and grisly anecdotes.

The next day, as they were eating breakfast, Frobisher had evidently decided to travel back even further in time for his discourse on Ceylon's history. Norton wondered whether last night's reading matter had guided this morning's monologue. He let the words float past him, as his colleague told him how Ptolemy had mapped the island and that its ancient name was Taprobane. As Frobisher's voice droned on a like a drowsy bee, Norton focused instead on the view of the mountains, wreathed in mist and clouds, and the play of light on the surface of the lake.

· · ·

The *kachcheri* was a hive of activity when Norton and Frobisher arrived that morning. The many native civil servants were hurrying about, filing reports, compiling statistics, and dealing with queries. It was a large open space with private offices for the government agent and other senior civil servants – all of them white men. But it seemed to Norton that the real work was entirely conducted by locals.

As the cadet, Norton's job was general office dogsbody, lowest in the pecking order of the white civil service. Quickly, he realised that if he were to avoid years of mindless drudgery and earn more responsibility, it was imperative to get to grips with the Sinhala language.

It soon became apparent that once most of his colleagues had spent a couple of years in Ceylon, their main priority was to do as little work as possible. The higher up the hierarchy people rose, the less they appeared to care for the actual job itself, preferring to spend their time on other pursuits. Frobisher, having recently progressed from the rank of cadet, was intent on devoting as much time as possible to Sinhalese history; Adamson had apparently been a naturalist, with a fascination and expertise in the local flora; Jackson, the police superintendent, had a weakness for drink and a fondness, when sober, for game hunting. There was Edison, the chief magistrate, who had a wife and seven children but divided his time between his two native mistresses. It seemed to Norton that for many or indeed most of his British colleagues, once they had passed two or three years in Ceylon, the climate sapped any energy or enthusiasm for what they were there to do. If he were to avoid that being his destiny too, Norton would have to choose to be different. The colonial service's slow and steady advancement up the career ladder discouraged ambition. If one served one's time, kept one's nose clean, and turned up each day in clean pressed clothes and well-polished shoes, eventually one would slot into a higher rank, making room for a new fresh-faced underling.

He could see the future stretching out before him in a progression of paperclips and sharpened pencils. A future of endless days pushing pen across paper, jumping to attention to carry out the requests of the person one rung higher up the ladder. Already on that first morning under the whirring electric fan in the *kachcheri*, Norton decided he would be different. He would make himself an expert in the country, its people, and language. As he looked around the room at the brown-skinned men in suits and ties and their white-skinned overlords, Norton determined that although he had the lowliest rank of cadet, he would carve a job for himself that would keep his interest and fuel his ambition.

After he had been in Kandy for about ten days, he was summoned one afternoon to meet with the government agent, Julian Metcalfe. The GA was a tall, dignified yet affable man with piercing blue eyes and a neatly trimmed moustache.

'Good Lord, they get younger every year.' Metcalfe narrowed his eyes. 'How old are you, Mr Baxter?'

'I'm twenty-three, sir.'

The GA looked him up and down and considered for a moment. 'You play bridge?'

Norton nodded, resisting the temptation to say, only if he must.

'Good, good. Looking for a partner since Adamson shipped off to Colombo. Tennis?'

'Yes, sir. Passably.'

'Passably will do. That chap Frobisher doesn't know one end of a racquet from another. My daughter's been forced to play with planters and their wives since Adamson left. Don't play myself. Golf's more my game. Need to go to Nuwara Eliya for that though. No course here in Kandy.' He looked at Norton as though it was his fault. 'You'll come to the residence tonight for dinner, then? Chance to meet my daughter, then you can arrange a tennis game with her. We'll have a rubber of bridge after dinner.' The eyes narrowed again. 'Twenty-three, eh?'

Norton left the office and returned to his desk. Frobisher looked up. 'Well? What did the great man have to say?'

'Invited me for dinner tonight.'

Frobisher's eyebrows furrowed. 'Really? I've never been invited. Other than formal receptions.'

'Apparently you don't play tennis.'

Frobisher's head jerked back knowingly. 'Ah. The daughter. Cynthia. Watch out. He'll have you halfway up the aisle before you know what's hit you. Getting desperate to marry the girl off. She's rather picky. Adamson put up a good show, but the girl wasn't having it. The GA is at the end of his tether. She's twenty-seven already. Time's running out for her.'

'What about you?'

'Failed at the first hurdle. No tennis. As far as I know, that's all she cares about. It's why everyone was confident Adamson had it in the bag. They won lots of matches together. He had the old man's blessing, but it all went south. He proposed and she turned him down flat. He was cut to bits about it.' Frobisher lowered his voice. 'That's what got him his promotion. Seems the old man wanted him out of the way.'

'What's she like, this Cynthia?'

Frobisher pushed out his bottom lip. 'I'm not really the one to ask. I'm not exactly a connoisseur of female beauty. But she looks all right to me. And she's an only child, apple of the GA's eye, and according to Adamson, has a nice fat inheritance from her maternal grandfather.' He grinned, then quickly added, 'Not that I suspect Adamson of venal motives in courting her, but I'd have had a go myself if it wasn't for the tennis. Rumour has it the girl had a thing with a planter chap, but the old boy would never consent to that. I bet he has his hopes up for you, Baxter.'

It was with a mixture of curiosity and dread that Norton made his way that evening to the government residence.

SEVEN

When Stella entered the tent she found her father alone, bent over his papers. Sir Michael looked up. 'I gather Mr Blackstock wants to marry you.'

Stella gasped.

'He told me while you were walking with Ronald. Says you've turned him down.' His tone was even, and a half smile hovered around his mouth.

She felt a surge of relief. At least he wasn't going to try to put pressure on her like Ronald had. 'Yes, I did. I hope I made it clear that I'm not going to change my mind.'

'He's confident you'll come round in the end. Of course, the man's a fool. An idiot. Don't think I don't know you're feeding him what to say in his presentations and exactly what he needs to write. He must think me a fool too, not to be aware of that.'

Stella was taken aback. 'But you often praise him, Father.'

'Not him. Just the conclusions he presents.' He tamped the tobacco into the bulb of his pipe before lighting it. '*Your* conclusions. I know they aren't his. He's flummoxed whenever I ask him about something he hasn't prepared and learned in advance.'

'So, why—?'

'Why do I keep up the pretence?' Her father looked up as though he was wondering how to answer, his bottom lip protruding.

She waited.

'Because the dean of college has made it clear that a substantial sum of money hangs in the balance.' He looked away, curling the fingers of his left hand in and out, forming and releasing a fist. 'And, yes, before you say it, that does mean I'm compromising my standards and rewarding idiocy. Sometimes I don't know how I live with myself.'

Stella was stunned. She'd never heard her father speak this way before. He'd never taken her into his confidence. Never shown any sign of weakness. She wasn't sure whether to be pleased or anxious.

'But I could just as easily ask you, Stella, why you persist in helping him in his efforts to deceive.'

She looked down, examining the back of her hands before answering him. 'It's the only way I get to test my own conclusions. You never ask me. You've always made it clear that you disapprove of women in academia.'

He ignored her answer and said, 'The greatest disappointment of my life is Ronald.'

Stella's head jerked in surprise at the sudden change of subject.

'I wanted him to follow in my footsteps, to carry on my legacy, but the boy's a wastrel. He shows no interest in academic matters. In any subject.' He stared up at the flickering oil lamp. A moth circled it, settling on the rim. 'If only you'd been a boy.' He shook his head. 'I blame myself for what he's become. I gave him too much leeway. I suppose I hoped he'd settle into academia eventually.' He sighed, a deep sonorous sigh. 'This trip was my last hope. Perhaps an old man's delusion, but I was sure that being in the field would spark a flame inside him; that he'd finally discover the fascination of serious study. I thought the East would open his eyes to a world beyond card games and pretty girls.'

Stella didn't know what to say. She hadn't expected such a serious conversation. But before she could reply, she remembered Mrs Moreland's manservant, still waiting patiently outside the tent. 'Father we've been invited to dinner by the government agent's wife, Mrs Moreland. She's offered me a bed and her servant's waiting to take my bag.'

Sir Michael flapped his hand impatiently to dismiss her and she went to gather her things together. When the servant had departed with her holdall, she went back into the tent only to find Blackstock and Ronald were there. She'd have to wait for another opportunity to continue her talk with her father.

An hour later, the four of them set off together. The men were going to watch the GA conduct the pearl auction. They made their way between the wooden shanties, the cooking smells now even more prevalent. There was a ragbag collection of men in the camp: arguing traders, pearl divers doing deals with them, turbaned snake charmers sitting cross-legged, playing their pipes while the cobras rose in a hypnotic dance in front of them. Stella noticed with dismay the numerous small groups engaged in card games and other forms of gambling, and suspected her brother would be staking his cash against their pearls, doubtless egged on by Blackstock, his co-conspirator and chief encourager.

When they reached the wooden stockade, known as the *koddu*, where the pearls were auctioned, Stella bade them goodbye and made her way to the GA's bungalow nearby, to settle in and unpack before they all assembled for dinner.

The room Mrs Moreland had shown her into contained only a camp bed, a folding table and a wooden chair. There was no mirror, so she settled for smoothing her skirt down, putting on a clean blouse, patting her hair, and hoping for the best, before venturing outside to the enclosed area behind the bungalow where a table was laid for dinner. Her hostess was sitting in a rattan chair, next to her trusty gramophone player, a spaniel curled at her feet. She motioned for Stella to take the other chair, then stood to put on a record – this time 'Take a Pair of Sparkling Eyes' from *The Gondoliers*.

'My husband won't be back for half an hour or so. If the auction isn't over by seven o'clock, he's promised to let the superintendent continue it without him.' Mrs Moreland paused to listen to the refrain, waving a hand in time to the music. 'If there are lots of buyers it can go to several rounds with the price rising. I'll never get the hang of the system. It's not like a normal auction.'

Stella accepted a glass of mango and lime juice from a servant and took a grateful sip.

'Tell me about yourself, Miss Polegate. I'm starved of female company and want to know everything. What exactly do you do for your father? It's most unusual for a young woman to travel this way.'

Stella took another sip. 'I sort through his notes and transcribe them.' She smiled. 'Father's handwriting is atrocious and I'm the only person who can decipher it. I cross-index everything so that when we return to Oxford he will know where everything is when he comes to write up the findings.'

'You must be frightfully clever to understand it all.'

'Anthropology is my passion. I hope to go to Cambridge and study it in my own right.'

'Can women do that? How extraordinary.' Mrs Moreland's eyebrows lifted.

'We can do the studying and sit the exams, but they won't award us the degrees.'

'Jolly unfair.' Mrs Moreland frowned. 'If you put the work in and attain the same standard as the men you should get the degree.' She sighed. 'But then so much in life is unfair for women.' She hesitated then added, 'I wanted to be a nurse. My parents were horrified. Insisted I marry. I had no choice in that either.' She gazed up at the stars, then called to the servant, saying something in what Stella assumed was Tamil. Turning to Stella she said, 'I need a proper drink and it looks to me like you'd welcome one too. I've asked Kavalan to bring us each a gin and lime. Here in the tropics, it's quite normal for women to drink. Otherwise, how would we cope with the boredom?'

The record had stopped, so Mrs Moreland got up and turned it over, cranking up the handle before carefully steering the needle into the groove. There was a slight hissing noise under the singing then the needle got stuck so the same phrase repeated. She jumped up and knocked the arm into the next groove. 'Must have got scratched on the way here.' Her mouth turned downwards.

Kavalan returned almost immediately with a tray of drinks.

'Now where was I?' Mrs Moreland took a gulp of her gin. 'Oh yes, I was telling you something of my own story. My husband was my parents' choice not mine. Percy is almost twenty years older than me. We've nothing in common – apart from the children. He can't abide music. I hate being stuck here in the back of beyond. I thought the world had ended for me the day I married him. I cried myself to sleep on our wedding night.'

Stella wasn't entirely comfortable with this sudden switch to confessional mode.

As if reading her mind, Mrs Moreland added, 'You're wondering why I'm telling you all this. But I like you, Miss Polegate. And I can tell you're not the sort to gossip. Not that I care about gossip anyway. It would be nice to do something worth gossiping about, but stuck here in this godforsaken place there's nothing.'

'But you're only here for a matter of weeks, aren't you?'

'It's not much better in Jaffna. It's just a collection of villages all clumped together. There's no society to speak of. No culture. Nothing to amuse and divert. I long to return to England.' She opened a mother-of-pearl box on the table beside her and took out a cigarette. 'I don't suppose you smoke, do you?'

Stella shook her head. She'd never seen a woman smoke before.

Lighting the cigarette, Mrs Moreland inhaled, leaning back in her chair, staring again at the night sky. 'Yet I fear that returning to England will never happen. Percy loves it here. Not the job. He's too lazy to care much for that. But the way of life. He adores the tropics. The way he's treated as a godlike figure.' Her voice sounded bitter. 'He's a member of the Royal Asiatic Society and is always writing papers on rare plants and birds. He plays cricket and tennis and likes to bathe in the sea. Whereas I am stuck at home dying of boredom, listening to music, and playing the piano. Is it any wonder I enjoy a drink and the occasional cigarette?'

Stella didn't know how to respond to this outpouring, but Mrs Moreland didn't seem to care. She went on. 'If I had my time again, I'd put up more of a fight to follow my dream and become a nurse. I'd live in a city and save up all my money to go to the theatre and the opera.' She downed what was left of her gin and signalled to Kavalan, who was hovering discreetly in the background. Stella had barely touched hers, preferring the more refreshing fruit juice.

'What about you, Miss Polegate? Is there a young man?'

Stella felt herself blushing. 'No. Definitely not.'

'Don't you want to marry? I mean eventually. Once you've completed your studies?'

'They'll never be complete. I'd like to devote my life to them. Just as my father has. There's always more to discover.'

'Very wise. Stay away from men. They ruin your life.' She reached down and stroked the dog. 'I'd always imagined I'd marry for love. Naive I suppose. But I think you're right. Better not to marry at all.'

Stella was relieved of the need to respond by the arrival of Mr Moreland, accompanied by Ronald and Gordon Blackstock.

'Where's Father?' Stella asked her brother.

'Said he was tired and wanted to turn in early.' Ronald stepped forward to greet Mrs Moreland.

Stella was introduced to Mr Moreland then turned again to her brother. 'Is he unwell? Perhaps I should go and check on him.'

'He's fine,' said Ronald brusquely. 'Says he'll have something light to eat then go to bed.'

Stella wasn't reassured. But there was no time for further discussion as their host led them to the table. She was seated between Mr Moreland, who occupied one end of the table, and Blackstock. Mrs Moreland sat at the other end and Ronald was opposite Stella and Blackstock.

The conversation was dominated by the men with both Blackstock and Ronald quizzing their host about the mechanics of the pearl auction, the methods used by the divers, and how the pearls were extracted from the oyster shells.

'While they're out in the sun they attract flies, and the resultant maggots eat the flesh. The dugouts are then filled with water and shaken to wash off the debris so all you're left with is sand, empty shells and the pearls.' Mr Moreland drained his glass, which was immediately filled with more wine by Kavalan, hovering in the background. 'We keep police guards there day and night. We have to watch the divers like hawks to make sure they don't secrete a few pearls for themselves before they bring them in.' He finished eating and wiped his mouth with his napkin. He was a portly man with a large round paunch, a red veined nose and thin, heavily oiled hair. Stella could smell the hair oil – sickly with a spicy overtone. He was clearly much older than his wife and Stella felt a surge of sympathy for the woman and her loveless marriage.

Moreland continued his discourse. 'As soon as the boats come in, the pearls are divided – two-thirds to the Crown and the remaining third to the divers. Then the Crown's share is auctioned.'

'How much is the industry worth?' Blackstock put down his knife and fork.

Stella thought it was typical of Blackstock to hone in on the financial aspects. He seemed more at home talking to the GA than to the Tamil men who were the subjects of their studies.

'It varies. Some years nothing at all if no fishery is declared. Last year was a record. More than two and a half million rupees to the Crown. A valuable contribution to the imperial coffers.' His voice was a drawl and Stella remembered his wife had described him as lazy. But Blackstock appeared to be fascinated.

Stella's thoughts drifted and she suppressed a yawn as the men discussed the reasons for the variations in yield from the pearl banks, which were apparently known as *paars*. She watched Mrs Moreland, observing how she behaved in the company of her husband, noticing that she continued to drink but barely contributed to the conversation. The gramophone was silent.

The following morning Stella joined her hostess for breakfast. She'd barely eaten at dinner and was now hungry and appreciative of the bacon and eggs and fresh tropical fruits. There was no sign of Mr Moreland.

'I hope you slept well, Miss Polegate?'

'Very well indeed.'

'And what plans do you have today?'

'I must check on my father. I'm sure he'll have notes for me to write up. He always keeps me busy.' She smiled.

'That chap – what was his name? Mr Blackstock. You didn't tell me you and he have an understanding.'

Stella put down her knife and fork. 'Because we don't. He's my father's doctoral student. There's nothing between us.'

'According to my husband, Mr Blackstock implied you were betrothed – or about to become so.'

'Well, the implication is wrong. I am not and have no intention of becoming so.'

'Good.' Mrs Moreland brought her palms together in a prayer-like motion. 'I didn't like the man. Arrogant. Unattractive too. I wondered whether perhaps he had hidden depths.'

'He hasn't.' Stella smiled, grateful to have an ally at last.

'All through dinner last night he was watching you. Barely took his eyes off you.' Mrs Moreland pushed her plate aside, her breakfast barely touched. 'If I were you, Miss Polegate, I'd be careful where he's concerned. I hope you don't mind me saying this, but he has a predatory look. I'm an observer of people – I am compelled to do a lot of entertaining because of Percy's position. Since the conversation is usually exceedingly boring, I entertain myself by studying others. Mr Blackstock reminds me of a jackal, stalking his prey. And unless you're careful, my dear, you are likely to be that prey.'

Stella's appetite vanished. She couldn't face the rest of her breakfast. Forcing herself to take a sip of tea she felt a wave of nausea.

'I'm sorry. Perhaps I shouldn't have said anything, but as someone who went through it myself, I recognise the signs. My husband decided he wanted me and set out to stalk then claim me, like a tiger hunting its next meal. I hope I'm wrong, but my advice to you is to keep your distance from Mr Blackstock.'

Before Stella could reply they were disturbed. One of the Polegates' Tamil servants appeared, breathless.

'You must come, Miss Polegate. Your father sick. I call the doctor.'

Mrs Moreland waved her hand to indicate Stella must leave at once and she needed no more encouragement.

EIGHT

The government agent's residence was a long, white, stuccoed building, topped with a clay tiled roof and fronted by an arched veranda. The property was encircled by well-manicured lawns with high hedges to mark the boundary. As Norton walked towards the building, he could hear the strains of a piano. Chopin. Played with fluency but perhaps a lack of feeling.

He walked up the steps and was greeted by a turbaned manservant who took his hat and showed him into a double aspect drawing room, cooled by an enormous ceiling fan. Open French windows gave onto a shaded terrace at the rear of the property.

The music stopped and a middle-aged woman rose from the pianoforte to greet him. Mrs Portia Metcalfe introduced herself and apologised for her husband's absence. 'Julian is in his study signing some papers. He'll only be a moment. Apparently, it's something urgent. I find he claims everything to be urgent, whether it is or not.' She rolled her eyes and extended a hand towards Norton, who was unsure whether she expected him to shake it or kiss it. In the end he took it and dipped his head over it, hoping to cover both.

The GA's wife was short and stout with gunmetal grey hair. She was wearing a high-necked gown in an unflattering shade of lavender. She was as affable as her husband and made Norton feel relaxed at once.

'Cynthia!' she called in the direction of the terrace. 'Do hurry up. Our guest has arrived.'

A black and white Border Collie bounded into the room from outside, followed by a young woman. She was carrying a basket of canna lilies. 'I decided to pick some flowers for the table in honour of our guest,' she said. 'I'm Cynthia. You must be the new boy. Daddy says you're a good tennis player.' She gave Norton a smile that lit up the room.

Norton was momentarily tongue-tied. She was like a beautiful whirlwind. Eventually he recovered his wits. 'Good evening. Norton Baxter. Not sure I'd go so far as to say I'm a good player. Certainly not to the standards of the All England Club. I played for my college but, I'm afraid, without distinction.'

'We'll have to see about that. I'm sure you'll be a jolly sight better than your colleagues. The courts are at the top of the lake. Most of us are there every afternoon.' She gave him another winning smile. 'Please excuse me while I put these flowers in water. I'll only be a few minutes.'

Before her mother could protest, the young woman swept out of the room, leaving Norton looking after her. What he'd expected to be a dull evening of duty was turning out to be much more promising.

'Really. I despair of my daughter sometimes. What on earth does she think the servants are here for?' Mrs Metcalfe raised her hands palm up and shook her head.

Norton was saved from responding by the arrival of the government agent himself.

'Baxter. You're here. Excellent. I had a couple of death warrants to sign. The prison warden wants to get the executions done tomorrow morning. It's *Vesak Poya* the day after and there'd be hell to pay if we were to dispatch anyone on a holy day.'

'*Vesak Poya?*' Norton asked, not wanting to think of the poor souls whose imminent demise was so breezily referred to.

Cynthia returned to the room in time to hear his question. 'It's one of those silly Buddhist feast days. The most important one. Such a bore as no one works. Can't even get a game of tennis.'

Ignoring his daughter, Metcalfe answered. '*Poya* days are the days of the full moon each month and are revered by the Sinhalese, especially here in Kandy. The one in May is called *Vesak* and is said to be the Buddha's birthday.'

'As if anyone knows when the Buddha was born or if he even existed,' said Cynthia.

Norton was tempted to point out that you could say the same thing about Christmas but knew the observation wouldn't be welcomed.

Julian Metcalfe carried on. 'Of course, the Dutch had the right idea when they banned Buddhism and refused to recognise *Poya* days. Lord knows why we bowed to pressure to reinstate them. At least the Buddhists tend to keep fairly quiet – they just trot off to their temples with offerings and then stay at home. Not like the blessed Tamils who make a dashed awful racket on their feast days.'

Mrs Metcalfe interjected. 'Enough talk of religion. It's not a suitable conversation topic before dinner.'

'Talking of which,' said her husband, 'the sun is long past the yard arm.' He rang a handbell and a uniformed servant appeared bearing a tray of pre-dinner drinks.

'I'll have a gin fizz, Sandun.' Cynthia flopped into an armchair.

'You'll have a lemonade,' said her mother.

'Daddy! Tell her I can.'

The GA raised his eyes then nodded to the servant. 'Just one.'

'It's such a bore. I'm not a child.'

Mrs Metcalfe tutted. 'Don't embarrass yourself in front of our guest, Cynthia. It's not seemly for an unmarried woman to drink alcohol.'

'I don't see why.' Cynthia sprawled in her chair, her long legs stretched out in front of her. She extended an arm to ruffle the fur of the dog. 'Sometimes I think Muffin's the only one in this house who cares about me.' She pushed out her bottom lip and fixed her eyes on Norton. He wasn't sure whether she was being flirtatious or sulky. 'Don't you think I should be permitted to have a drink, Mr Baxter? Daddy acts as though we were living in the Dark Ages, not the twentieth century. All those old-fashioned conventions are too silly for words.' She released a long sigh. 'I consider myself a modern emancipated woman. What do you think, Mr Baxter?'

Norton disliked being put on the spot – particularly by a young attractive woman. And whatever else he might think about Cynthia Metcalfe, he had to acknowledge she was easy on the eye. Her skin was like porcelain, crowned by blonde hair arranged in a thick plait coiled at the back of her head. She was wearing a gown of pale blue silk chiffon with a darker blue satin wrap draped over her bare shoulders. Bending forward, she lowered her eyes and blinked rapidly to reveal the longest eyelashes he'd ever seen. It was apparent that Cynthia Metcalfe was all too aware of her own beauty and how to deploy it.

He smiled at her, trying to convey sympathy without actually articulating it and risking the displeasure of his new boss. She looked at him expectantly, so he felt obliged to answer in some way. 'Are you perhaps a follower of Mrs Pankhurst?'

'Oh Lord, no. I can't abide politics. If someone gave me the vote, I wouldn't know what to do with it. That kind of nonsense is best left to men.' She smiled again. 'Rather than votes for women it ought to be drinks for women. Maybe even cigarettes for women. I could sign up for that. Why should men have all the fun?'

'Perhaps because they do all the work,' said her father.

Norton was unsure whether Cynthia was putting on a show for his benefit. He'd met women like her before – privileged, spoiled only-daughters of wealthy parents. But perhaps this was an act. Even a cover for shyness. No, he told himself. There was nothing shy about Cynthia.

When it was time for dinner, they passed through the rather grand dining room with its oversized table and crystal chandeliers, and went out onto the veranda, where a smaller table was laid ready for them.

'When it's just the family, we like to dine quite informally,' explained Mrs Metcalfe.

'Mr Baxter isn't family,' said Cynthia. 'I do hope you'll forgive us for this shabby behaviour.' Her eyes twinkled as she spoke. 'Clearly, my parents are lining you up as a potential future family member.' She glanced at her father. 'Daddy is determined to find me a husband, but I'd like you to know that you can relax, as all I'm seeking is a decent tennis partner.'

Norton felt his skin redden. She was so direct.

Reading his thought she added, 'I like to be frank and remove any uncertainty then we can both enjoy ourselves.'

'Really, Cynthia, I despair.' Mrs Metcalfe swivelled in her chair to look directly at Norton. 'I am sorry for my daughter's outspokenness. I do hope we haven't caused you embarrassment, Mr Baxter?'

'Not at all.'

Norton looked towards his host and saw Julian Metcalfe's mouth was turned down. 'Nonsense, Cynthia,' the GA said. 'You know perfectly well it's my custom to invite all the new members of the *kachcheri* for dinner.'

Norton remembered Frobisher telling him earlier that no

such honour had been afforded him. Across the table he could see Cynthia rolling her eyes.

There was an awkward pause for a few minutes while everyone addressed their attention to the fish that had been placed in front of them. The silence was broken by Mrs Metcalfe. 'I trust you're finding your accommodation satisfactory, Mr Baxter? I understand you're sharing a bungalow above the lake.'

'Indeed. It's delightful. Beautiful views.'

'You're bunking with that dreadful bore, Frobisher, aren't you?' Cynthia locked eyes with him across the table then forked a piece of fish, put it in her mouth and chewed it slowly. Norton was all too aware she was trying to be as provocative as possible in front of her parents. Was she seeking to annoy them or was she testing him?

'Bertie Frobisher has proved a well-informed guide to the delights of Kandy,' he said, diplomatically.

She put her head back and laughed. 'The delights of Kandy? As far as he's concerned the only delights are to be found between the pages of history books. I told Daddy if he ever invited him here, I'd never speak to him again. I've only met him once and that was more than enough. He used to drive Monty Adamson round the bend. Followed him around like a faithful dog.' She tilted her head on one side. 'And if there are delights in Kandy, they've passed me by.'

At the mention of Adamson, the GA's mouth had tightened into a narrow line. Norton wondered whether what Frobisher had said was true and Cynthia had given Adamson the brush-off.

But Cynthia was evidently enjoying herself. She leaned towards Norton and said, 'Daddy wanted me to marry Monty Adamson, but I don't see why I should be expected to marry anyone at all. Unfortunately, when I turned him down, Daddy packed him off to Colombo and I lost a perfectly good tennis partner. I hope you'll prove more durable, Mr Baxter.' She twirled a finger through a stray lock of hair. 'I thought if I made the lie of the land clear from the start, we could avoid any embarrassing misunderstandings.'

Mrs Metcalfe's patience was exhausted. 'Enough, Cynthia!' She waved a hand at the waiting servant, signalling him to clear away the plates, before changing the subject to quiz Norton about the Sinhala lessons he was having at the Temple of the Sacred Tooth each morning, while the sirloin of beef was served.

By the time dinner was over it was too late for the threatened rubber of bridge and Norton was able to make his excuses and leave. He decided Mrs Metcalfe was the consummate governor's wife, gracious, able to make conversation on any topic, and exuding warmth. Her husband, under his veneer of affability, had a steely core. This judgement was underscored by the patronising attitude displayed towards his servants and the frequent contemptuous references to the native population. Norton found this both surprising and disturbing as the civil service and the judiciary would be unable to function in Ceylon without the Sinhalese who formed most of its members. He could see no rationale himself why so many colonial institutions such as the gentlemen's clubs were barred to any aspiring members with brown skin. With such articulate and highly educated people, it struck him as odd that his co-patriates persisted in this petty snobbery. The more he thought about it, the more he found the concept of members of a distant nation ruling the roost over people who had lived here for centuries, absurd. He'd not spent long in Ceylon, but long enough to appreciate the charm and intelligence of its people and the significance of their own cultural heritage. What was it that made men like Metcalfe so convinced of their own racial and societal superiority?

As to Cynthia, he found her undeniably attractive. She was

lively and flirtatious – if occasionally petulant and childish. But was that any wonder? he asked himself. She was an only child, clearly the apple of her father's eye and subject to constant correction from her mother. It was apparent that both parents infantilised her – a woman of twenty-seven. Norton was looking forward to seeing her again the following evening when he had promised to put in an appearance at the tennis courts. Perhaps out of the orbit of her parents he would meet a different Cynthia?

'Well?' Frobisher looked up from the book he was reading. 'How did it go? What did you think of the nubile Cynthia?'

'Charming.' Norton decided discretion was required.

'Come on! I bet she had you wound around her little finger. Poor Adamson was a slave to her every whim. Adored her. Of course she wasn't worthy of him.' He pushed his spectacles up. 'It still makes me seethe to think he got sent to Colombo just because she wouldn't marry him.'

'I'm sure that wasn't the case. He got a promotion.'

'Long overdue and much deserved. But not the real reason. Once Cynthia Metcalfe made it clear she wasn't going to marry him, the old boy had to find another option. That's you.'

Norton laughed and shook his head. 'If Miss Metcalfe refused a man of such evident talents as Adamson, she certainly won't be interested in the *kachcheri* cadet.'

'Fair point.' Frobisher nodded sagely. 'You're not in the same league as Monty Adamson.'

Amused by his housemate's hero worship of Adamson – a man Norton had found pompous and dull – Norton cut short the conversation by announcing he was off to bed.

NINE

When Stella reached her father's tent, she found him lying ashen-faced on his camp bed, his breathing rapid and jagged, his brow burning hot and wet with sweat.

She kneeled beside him. 'Father, it's me, Stella. Tell me what's wrong.'

He opened his eyes and looked at her but said nothing. There was a sour smell in the tent. He must have been vomiting. She took a damp cloth from the servant who had summoned her and wiped her father's face. 'Bring me a bowl of cold water, please, Ravi, and a glass of water for him to drink. Make sure it's been boiled.'

As the servant went to fulfil the request, the flap of the tent parted, and an Indian man entered. 'I am Doctor Patel.'

Stella moved aside, watching while the doctor took her father's temperature and pulse and listened to his chest with his stethoscope.

Eventually, he turned to address her. 'Your father has heat-stroke. He should recover within a couple of hours or so if you keep him cool. Lots of water. Damp cloths. He won't want to eat for a while. As soon as he's well enough to move I suggest you remove him from this place. It's not healthy here in Marichchukaddi. Get him away from the coast and up to the central highlands. The air's fresher and the temperature lower. How old is he?'

'Sixty-three.' Stella took the glass of water from Ravi and helped her father take a sip.

'Not a young man. And unused to this climate I imagine.'

The doctor inquired how long they'd been in Ceylon, and she told him, adding that they'd previously spent four months in India, based near Ooty.

'Exactly. That's up in the hills. Cooler.'

'We plan to be in Jaffna next.'

'Change your plans. This gentleman needs to stay out of the direct sun especially around midday, wear his sun helmet, get plenty of rest and sleep and drink lots of water. Don't forget to boil it first. Somewhere up near Nuwara Eliya will be the best place for him.'

Stella's heart sank. Her father would never accept being exiled to the town known as Little England. As an anthropologist, he would have no interest in surrounding himself with the British.

'Your father has a weak and irregular heartbeat. I can't answer for the consequences if you don't get him to somewhere he can recover and rebuild his strength.'

The doctor turned to Ravi and spoke to him in Tamil before addressing Stella again. 'I've told your man to give your father *aam panna* to drink once he's stabilised. It's made with mangoes and spices and will help keep him cool. Now I must take my leave. Good morning.' He nodded and left the tent.

When he'd gone, Stella sat beside her father's bed, mopping his brow with the damp cloth.

'Where are my brother and Mr Blackstock?' she asked Ravi.

'They went out with the pearl boats before dawn.'

Funny how they managed to rise early when it suited their

own purposes but had to be roused otherwise. It meant they wouldn't return until late afternoon at the earliest. Stella silently cursed them. They should never have gone without checking on Sir Michael. He had clearly been ill all night. She decided to make the necessary arrangements to leave before Ronald could try to derail the plans.

She was giving instructions to Ravi when the tent flap parted again, and Mrs Moreland entered. She glanced at Sir Michael and recoiled slightly, presumably from the smell. 'Heatstroke? I suppose he hasn't been wearing his hat?'

'He hates it. Complains it squashes his ears.'

'Better pinched skin than sunstroke.' Mrs Moreland patted Stella's arm. 'I've no need to tell you that, my dear, of course. But men are a law unto themselves.' She looked about her at the cramped space. 'It's like a furnace in here.'

'The doctor says we need to get away from the coast as soon as possible. Ideally up to the highlands.'

'The supply boat leaves for Mannar the day after tomorrow. I'll ask my husband to arrange for you all to be on that if you think your father will be up to the trip.'

'Dr Patel says the sooner the better.'

'Where will you go?'

'We'd originally planned to go to Kandy *after* Jaffna. Father's old schoolfriend is the government agent there.'

Mrs Moreland nodded. 'Julian Metcalfe.'

'But Father won't be happy bypassing Jaffna, as it's a vital part of the trip.'

'Perhaps Mr Blackstock and your brother could go to Jaffna without you and your father.' Mrs Moreland paused, her head on one side and her mouth in a knowing smile. 'That would keep Mr Blackstock out of your way.'

Stella was dubious. 'Unfortunately, my brother knows nothing about our work. He just came along for the trip. And I doubt Mr Blackstock would know where to begin without Father's guidance.'

'I thought he was meant to be a doctoral student. Surely, he's up to gathering the data you need if your father gives him instructions.'

'I suppose so.' But Stella had her doubts.

'In the meantime, we'll move your father to our bungalow. I'll have a bed set up in the drawing room. There's a generator and a fan to keep him cool. A bit more civilised than a tent.'

Stella thanked her and was glad it meant she too would be able to return to the bungalow and not have to keep vigil here in the hot, oppressive atmosphere of the tent.

Once Sir Michael was installed at the GA's bungalow, his temperature began to drop, and he slept peacefully. Stella sat outside with Mrs Moreland on what passed for a terrace at the hastily constructed bungalow.

'We were talking about Mr Blackstock this morning when we were interrupted.' Mrs Moreland fixed her eyes on Stella, who looked down, uncomfortable at her hostess's directness. The GA's wife continued. 'If you want to avoid being hounded into marrying him you need to be wary.' She reached for the mother-of-pearl box on the centre of the table, took out a ready-rolled cigarette and lit it, slowly blowing the smoke out through her nostrils.

'When I first met my husband, I was a naive young girl, ignorant of the ways of the world. He was in England on leave, in need of a wife. My parents invited him to dinner. My guard was down as it simply never occurred to me that a man nearer their age than mine would have any interest in me. The following morning over breakfast, my father told me Percy had asked permission to marry me, and Papa had given his consent. My own views didn't matter at all.'

Stella gasped. She thought of Mr Moreland, his paunchy stomach and ruddy large-pored complexion, the thinning hair plastered with brilliantine. Hardly an attractive prospect for a young woman.

'I was nineteen and he was thirty-nine. I'd never left England, yet I was expected to abandon home and family and travel to Ceylon with him. A stranger. I knew nothing of men or the physical obligations of marriage.' She drew on her cigarette again. 'He'd been stuck in a remote town on the east coast as acting district judge. There were no other British there, so he was isolated and probably starved of company.' She paused, stubbing out her cigarette. 'Starved of sexual intercourse too as I discovered on our wedding night.'

Stella listened in horror, not knowing what to say.

'Sorry if I'm embarrassing you, Miss Polegate. Only I'd hate for you to have to go through what I did. Mr Blackstock is a much younger man of course, but when he looks at you he's got the same hungry look in his eyes as I saw in my husband.' Mrs Moreland got up and chose a record from the stack. This time, rather than light opera, she chose 'A Bird in a Gilded Cage'.

The song and singer were incongruous in this arid tropical wasteland. But the music clearly held significance for Mrs Moreland.

'All my husband had to say when I wept after he'd had his way with me was "Pull yourself together, girl". Can you imagine how that felt? How utterly alone I was? Honestly, if it wasn't for the children coming along in quick succession I'd probably have walked into the sea and drowned myself.' She fixed her gaze on Stella. 'You think I'm exaggerating, don't you? But you've seen my husband. It may be hard to imagine me as an innocent young girl, but I can assure you I was. Pretty too. Hard to believe now. Too much sun and a miserable marriage put paid to my looks.'

Stella struggled to respond. 'I'm terribly sorry that

happened to you.' She touched Mrs Moreland's arm in a gesture of sympathy. 'At least my father agrees with me that marrying Mr Blackstock is out of the question.'

'Then you're fortunate. It felt like a terrible betrayal when my father handed me over.' She removed a fleck of tobacco from her lip. 'I think he genuinely believed he was doing the right thing. Settling my future. Marrying his only child to a man with excellent prospects.'

'And your mother?'

'She only ever echoed Father. I suppose she was married in a similar manner herself and brought up to believe that one's husband was god and master. One thing's certain. I'll burn in hell before I let Percy put any of my daughters through that. They'll marry for love or not at all.'

'My parents married for love,' said Stella. 'But my mother sacrificed a lot for marriage.'

'How so?'

'She was a talented opera singer and gave up her career to marry Father. She travelled with him when he was undertaking research. To Java and Sarawak. Then when I was born, she had to stay at home while he was away for months on end. After Ronald was born, Father travelled to South America for eighteen months. She must have been very lonely, left at home with a baby and a small girl.'

'Did she still sing?'

'No. Never. We didn't even have a piano. I suppose Father would have bought her one, but it seems she turned her back on music. As though if she couldn't perform professionally, she didn't want to sing at all.' Stella wondered why she was speaking so freely to Mrs Moreland when she barely knew her, but the older woman's disclosures had encouraged her to reciprocate. There was also something about her that inspired trust. 'Mother never complained. But before she died, she urged me not to live my life vicariously through someone else. She stressed the importance of having passions and interests of one's own.'

'Strange then that she gave up her music.'

'At the beginning I think it was her choice. She was in love with Father and giving up her singing career was a symbolic gesture. Then as time passed it was too late and singing for pleasure would have felt worse. But even as a child I was aware of a sadness about her – a sense of loss. She never talked about her musical career. It must have been too painful.'

'What a pity.' Mrs Moreland looked thoughtful. 'Odd, isn't it, that no matter what the circumstances it is always we women who make the compromises and sacrifices? Never the men.' She crushed out her cigarette in an oyster shell that served as an improvised ashtray. 'What's your passion, Miss Polegate? What would you be reluctant to sacrifice?'

Stella told her about her love of her father's subject and how she wanted to study anthropology in depth. She found herself explaining how she coached Gordon Blackstock as her capacity to analyse and interpret the data they gathered was greater than his.

'Let him flounder.' Mrs Moreland folded her arms. 'You've made yourself indispensable to him. If you're to be free of the man, then start now. Stop helping him.'

'But it's the only way I get to contribute to the project.'

'That makes no sense. You said your father is aware that this Blackstock fellow is parroting your conclusions.'

'Yes. But my name can never be cited as a contributor. Gordon's father is a major benefactor to the college and Father's funding is dependent on him.'

Mrs Moreland shook her head. 'My advice to you, dear girl, is to keep as much distance as possible from him.'

Stella's lips stretched into a tight line. 'The other consideration is my brother, Ronald. He and Mr Blackstock are friends. Ronald's told me he supports the idea of me marrying Gordon. I wouldn't put him past pressuring me into it. He's already said that when Father is no longer around, he will be head of the family.'

'Fortunately, your father *is* around and it's all the more important you follow the doctor's advice and get him up into the hills.' She looked up at the sky. 'It must be nearly time for tiffin. Then it won't be long before your brother and his horrible pal are back. After luncheon we can take Coco here for a walk and watch the boats returning.' She reached for the dog curled sleeping at her feet and ruffled his fur.

Stella liked Mrs Moreland. She realised how much she had missed having a confidante – missed the company of women in general. The conversation had made her feel even more determined to keep Gordon Blackstock safely at arm's length.

TEN

The following afternoon, Norton left the *kachcheri* and went straight to the tennis club. He'd brought his whites with him, presuming correctly that there would be a changing room at the courts.

When he arrived, Cynthia Metcalfe was playing a game of singles with another woman. After changing in the clubhouse, Norton went to stand at the side of the court to watch the game and wait for a partner.

Cynthia saw him and called out, 'Mr Baxter! As soon as Val's husband arrives, you can join us in a game of mixed doubles.' She waved her racquet in the direction of the woman she was playing. 'Val, this is Mr Norton Baxter, the new man replacing Monty Adamson. Mr Baxter, this is Mrs Valerie MacDonald.'

'I'm not actually replacing Mr Adamson. That's Frobisher. I'm just the cadet.'

Cynthia, who had been about to serve, lowered her racquet and grinned at him. 'I don't mean in your dreary old office, Mr Baxter. I mean as my tennis partner.' She swung her racquet back and smashed the ball over the net so powerfully that her opponent didn't get near it.

Baxter felt stupid. But neither woman paid him any further attention as they got on with their game. They were both excellent players. Valerie MacDonald was petite, graceful in her movements and fast on her feet. Cynthia Metcalfe was agile, with a powerful athletic service despite her slim build, and a strong forearm. Her play reminded Norton of the ladies' champion Dorothea Douglass, whom he had seen at Wimbledon the previous summer. He stood, watching entranced, under the shade of a rain tree.

When Valerie's husband arrived, the women's game was halted. Snod MacDonald was a Scotsman and a tea planter. Gruff and laconic, he towered over his diminutive wife. He shook hands with Norton but appeared keen to get the game of doubles started.

Norton was surprisingly nervous. He asked himself why – it wasn't as if he was anxious to impress, being here at the behest of Cynthia. Left to his own devices he'd probably have chosen to spend the early evening studying Sinhala, conscious that before long he would be facing an examination in the language. His entry-level salary would not be increased until he passed the exam.

The two pairs were well-matched. The brute strength of Snod MacDonald complemented the lithe speed and movement of his wife. Norton found himself quickly attuning to Cynthia's play and adjusting his own accordingly. After taking a set each, the final set went to the MacDonalds at six–four.

'Not bad for our first time together.' Cynthia dried her racquet handle with a towel and grinned at Norton. 'We'll beat them tomorrow.'

'I'm afraid I can't make tomorrow.'

She smiled at him. 'Of course you can. What else have you got to do? You barely know anyone in Kandy yet.'

'I have to study. I'll eventually have to take an examination in Sinhala.'

Cynthia gave a peal of laughter. 'Did you hear that, Val? He says he has to study. The new boy. Keen as mustard.' She placed a hand on his arm. 'Forget that, Mr Baxter. There's no one to impress. Daddy couldn't care less. Like most senior civil servants he's lazy as sin. You'll pick up the Sinhala as you go. For heaven's sake, even I can manage a few phrases and I have absolutely no call to use it.' She smiled at him, her lips plump and moistened by the tip of her tongue before it disappeared so quickly, he wondered if he'd imagined it. He couldn't help imagining pressing his own mouth against hers and wondering how it would feel. Not for the first time he thought that she seemed to be deliberately taunting him.

They went inside the small clubhouse, and she called out to her friend. 'Can you and Snod drop me off on your way, Val?' Turning to Norton, she said, 'Daddy's expecting you at the Kandy Club for a rubber of bridge later since you didn't get to play last night. Rather you than me. I loathe bridge. See you here tomorrow. Same time.'

'I told you, I can't make it,' he called. But she was gone, leaving Norton feeling as though he'd had his autonomy removed. It was clear that Cynthia Metcalfe was used to getting her own way about everything. He wasn't sure how he felt about that. On the one hand she was disarmingly attractive, and he'd enjoyed the game today. On the other, he wasn't ready to concede to the whims of a young woman he barely knew. There was something about Cynthia that made him uncomfortable. It would be all too easy to give in and let the river of her determination sweep him up and carry him away. Yet something told him that were he to give in once, he'd be in her power forever.

He would drop into the gentlemen-only Kandy Club after dinner. Not to do so risked displeasing the GA and getting

Cynthia into trouble for failing to pass on her father's message. But he wasn't going to turn up for tennis the next day.

The Kandy Club fulfilled Norton's worst expectations. A gloomy place, it was the exclusive domain of white men. The atmosphere reminded him of his days at public school – it was like a series of common rooms. The air was heavy with the smell of pipe smoke and embrocation, underpinned by a slight odour of stale sweat. In a large drawing room, they sat around drinking and smoking while reading the *Ceylon Observer*. Passing another room, he heard the clink of billiard balls.

He found Julian Metcalfe in the bar, doing the newspaper crossword. Cynthia's father looked up and greeted Norton. 'Ah, Baxter! You took your time.'

Norton explained that he had come straight from his supper but had difficulty finding a rickshaw.

Metcalfe waved a hand in the air dismissively. 'How was the tennis? You and the gal get along?'

Feeling his face reddening, Norton said, 'We were narrowly beaten by Mr and Mrs MacDonald.'

'Did she blame you?' The GA made a noise that was half laugh half snort. 'Don't stand for any nonsense, Baxter. My daughter can be headstrong. Stand up to her or she won't respect you. That was the trouble with Adamson. Like a fawning pup when she was around. Damn shame as he was fearless dealing with other men. But he was putty in Cynthia's hands. And when she scents weakness, she goes for the kill.' He folded the newspaper and got to his feet. 'We're playing tonight with one of the local doctors and the district judge.' As he led the way to the library where the game was to take place, he continued to regale Norton with advice about Cynthia. 'If you're to have a chance at wooing my daughter you'll have to play with a straight bat.'

Determined not to be browbeaten, Norton tried to respond diplomatically. 'Miss Metcalfe is charming, sir, but I can assure you I have no designs on her. My focus is entirely on my career.'

Metcalfe placed a hand on his arm. 'Never mind that, young man. If you do right by Cynthia, you'll do right by your career.' By now they had reached the library, but the GA held him back. 'A word to the wise. Do as you're told, keep your nose clean, don't frighten the horses and you'll be fine. Trying too hard at the job isn't cricket. Not gentlemanly. Now let's see how your bridge game is.' After this excessive mixture of clichés, the older man ushered him into the room and introduced him to their fellow players. As the four settled down to play bridge, Norton tried not to feel a sense of foreboding at Metcalfe's words, but there was a queasy feeling in his stomach that was difficult to ignore.

As it happened, Norton did go the tennis courts the following evening. Not to play with Cynthia and her friends, but in the company of Paul Carberry. The tea planter had turned up at the *kachcheri* to inquire about a plot of land he was interested in buying. Once his business was concluded, he sought out Norton and invited him to join him in a tennis game.

'I'm staying in town so I thought we could have a bit of a knockabout at the courts, then you can join me at the Queen's for a few pegs and dinner. Can't do a late one as I'm riding back to Glenross first thing in the morning.'

'Glenross?' Norton was puzzled by the Scottish name.

'The name of the plantation where I work. You'll find there are more Scottish and English names than local ones.'

Cynthia and Val MacDonald were on the courts when the two men arrived. Leaving Carberry to make his way to an adjacent court, Norton went across to explain to the women that he wouldn't be able to join them that evening.

Cynthia stared at him in disbelief. 'But without you we can't play doubles. What about poor Snod?' She knocked the ball she was holding ready to serve out of the court in a gesture of frustration.

Norton bristled. 'I told you yesterday I couldn't make it.'

'No. You told me you'd be studying, and I told you not to bother. It's very bad form to turn up here with another partner when we're relying on you.'

'I apologise for the misunderstanding, Miss Metcalfe. I should have made it clear that I can't commit to playing with the three of you every evening. And I did intend to study this evening until my friend Mr Carberry happened to be in Kandy and invited me to dine with him at the Queen's Hotel tonight.'

At the mention of Carberry's name, Cynthia spun round and looked over to the court where Carberry was waiting. Her face crinkled into a look of disgust. 'You consider that loathsome man your friend? Clearly you don't know him very well.'

'We met on the voyage out. I find him a splendid chap.' Norton's patience was wearing thin. But Cynthia's father was his boss, and he couldn't afford to alienate her so soon in his tenure in the job. He didn't really want to commit to playing again the following evening but decided to placate her.

Cynthia wasn't going to be placated. 'Tomorrow, I have other plans.' She moved away and bent down to retrieve her discarded ball. 'You need to be more particular about the people you choose as friends, Mr Baxter. Paul Carberry is not considered acceptable company.'

Taken aback, he said, 'Why? Because he's a planter?'

She gave him a piercing look with narrowed eyes. 'No. Not because he's a planter. I couldn't give a fig what work people choose to do. Snod's a planter and he and Val are probably my best friends. But Mr Carberry is no gentleman and that's all I have to say on the matter.'

Turning her back on him she tossed the ball upwards and

hit a slammer of a shot, taking Val completely by surprise. As a cry of protest went up, Norton left the court and went to join Carberry.

'What was that all about?' Carberry was frowning.

'Miss Metcalfe appears to have assumed that because I played with her last night, I am now her permanent mixed doubles partner. I was explaining that I'd made no such commitment.'

Carberry raised his eyebrows. 'So, she's cast you as the new Adamson?'

'You know her? And Adamson?'

'Everyone knows everyone.'

'Her father seems to be grooming me as his future son-in-law.'

Carberry made a sound that was part chuckle part snort. 'And how do you feel about that?'

'I barely know the woman.'

'But you must have some feelings on the topic.'

Norton grinned. 'I've no intention of marrying anyone for at least five years. I want to focus on the job. As for Miss Metcalfe, she's undeniably attractive but clearly spoiled and used to getting her own way.'

'An understatement. You know she's known by some as Ayesha?'

Norton shook his head, puzzled.

'She-who-must-be-obeyed. Haven't you read your Rider Haggard?'

Norton grinned. 'Of course. *She*. Does Miss Metcalfe know?'

'Lord, no! She'd be hissy.'

To his credit, other than this, Carberry offered no further opinion on Cynthia Metcalfe and Norton detected no sign that the extreme animosity Cynthia had shown towards the planter was reciprocated.

. . .

Later that evening, after dinner in the Queen's Hotel, Norton and Carberry sat nursing their pegs of whisky on the terrace overlooking the hotel gardens. The croaking of bullfrogs echoed into the ink-dark night. It was cooler now, still warm, but not as sultry as it would have been at the coast.

'What brought you to the land registry today?' Norton leaned back in his chair and looked up at the stars.

'I told you I want my own plantation. I've learned the business and can't wait to be my own boss. It would have been years away in spite of me saving hard, but I was left a slug of money. A piece of unexpected good luck. An uncle I'd never met made a ton of money as a gold prospector in South America. He never married and left a legacy to me. Like me he was a second son so when my father inherited the farm he got nothing. I suppose he was trying to redress the balance. I've signed the papers, and the funds should clear probate within a matter of months. So, I wanted to register my claim to the land and pay a deposit using my savings.'

'That's marvellous news. So, you'll soon be a man of property.'

Carberry chuckled. 'I suppose I will.' He chinked his glass against Norton's. 'You must come and see the plot. I'll have a lot of work to do. Jungle to be cleared. All the planting. I'll need to build a house too, and lines for the coolies.'

'Lines?'

'Living quarters.'

'Sounds like a massive undertaking.' Norton grinned. 'I'm happy for you, my friend.'

Later, after he took his leave of Carberry, he decided to walk back to his bungalow rather than take a rickshaw. He marvelled at his friend's enterprise. He couldn't imagine taking on a project of such proportions himself but envied Carberry's imminent emancipation from the yoke of employment. He thought of the conversation he'd had before the bridge game the previous evening, when Julian Metcalfe had told him that if he did right by his daughter his career would benefit. Had it been a veiled threat that the opposite was also true?

Norton strode along beside the lake, following the fluorescent glow of the white scalloped Cloud Wall. He told himself that he wasn't going to be bamboozled into anything. Whilst he was perfectly happy to cultivate a friendship with Cynthia Metcalfe and to partner her at tennis, he wasn't going to let himself be pushed into becoming her suitor by her father. And as far as the job was concerned, he wasn't willing to seek short-cuts. He wanted to succeed – not just for the job itself, but to prove his father wrong.

ELEVEN

After two days, the Polegates and Blackstock set off by boat from the pearl fishery to begin the journey to the central highlands. Sir Michael was still feeling debilitated. Despite the rough and bumpy track, he slept in the back of the bullock cart as they made the trip to Anuradhapura, from where they would take the train to Kandy.

In light of the doctor's warning, Stella had been firm with her father and insisted on the reorganisation of their research trip. To her surprise, after some initial resistance, he had capitulated. A telegram was dispatched to his friend Julian Metcalfe, the government agent in Kandy, and a response had arrived by return to say Sir Michael and his party would be welcome to stay at the GA's residence as his guests.

The provisional plan was for Sir Michael to enjoy a few days to relax and complete his recovery, before the party moved up into the central highlands, where they would conduct their studies into the Indian Tamil workers on the tea plantations of the area. Assuming the long spell in more temperate climate sufficiently improved Sir Michael's health, they would then travel back north to the Jaffna peninsula to complete a parallel study into the indigenous Tamils there. If he was still considered unfit, the professor would return to Kandy, while Blackstock, Ronald and Stella finished the research. There had been much discussion preceding this agreement, with Stella torn between a wish to remain with her father and a desire to see the project through. She was uncomfortable at the thought of spending weeks in Blackstock's company, with only her brother as chaperon. In the end she decided to wait until the time came before determining what to do.

They were to spend the night at the rest house at Anuradhapura before taking the train soon after dawn the next morning.

Over dinner, Ronald announced that while they were in the highlands he wanted to do a hunting trip. 'I've heard the game there is excellent. That book I've been reading mentions all manner of deer species, not to mention elephants and leopards.' He grinned and rubbed his hands together. 'I'd love to bag a leopard and get it made into a rug.'

'I'm not sharing the house with a dead leopard,' said Stella. 'Why on earth would you want to kill a beautiful creature like that? And for a rug.'

'Leopards kill livestock. As for elephants, not so long ago there was a bounty on their heads. According to Baker's book the government would pay between seven and ten shillings for every elephant shot.'

'Not anymore, thank goodness.' Stella folded her arms and glared at her brother. 'And no leopard skin, thank you, Ronald.'

'I'll store it in the loft until I have a place of my own. Besides, why should you care.' He glanced at Blackstock. 'You'll be married and in your own home before long.'

'That's enough, Ronald,' said their father. 'Stella's right. I won't have a poor dead creature in the house.'

'But it's all the rage.'

Sir Michael fixed his gaze on his son. 'I don't care if it's "all the rage" – whatever that's supposed to mean. You badgered me into bringing you on this expedition and I agreed on condition you helped your sister out with some of the transcription and dealt with the logistics. You've done nothing.' He took off his spectacles and polished them with his napkin. 'I let you come in the hope that you might learn something. That a spark of knowledge might ignite within you. Instead, you've distracted Mr Blackstock from his studies, you've wasted your money gambling and doing Lord knows what other unsavoury activities, and you've been no help to me whatsoever.'

Ronald pulled a face. 'Oh, come on, Father. Don't be a stick-in-the-mud. I'm young, with my whole life ahead of me. If I can't have a bit of fun before settling down, I don't know who can. There'll be plenty of time for being solemn and serious when I'm old like you.'

'It'll be a miracle if you get to be old. You've no plans. You've no idea how to earn a living. I won't always be around to support you.'

'There's plenty of time to find a boring old job when I'm back in England. Better still when I'm ready to settle down. Meanwhile I've my trust fund.'

Sir Michael shook his head but declined to respond.

'So?' Ronald wasn't giving up. 'How about we do a spot of hunting? It'd just be a day. Give you time to rest up a bit more before the next phase of your research. I'm sure your old friend can sort something out for us if he's the governor.'

'Government agent,' said Stella, wishing Ronald would shut up or – better still – grow up.

'Same thing.'

'It isn't. There's only one governor for the whole country. The government agents all report to him. There are nine of them including Papa's friend.'

Sir Michael scraped back his chair and got up. 'Enough. I'm

turning in for the night. I suggest you all do so too as we've an early start tomorrow. Goodnight.' He left the room.

Ronald and Gordon Blackstock exchanged glances, then Ronald produced a bottle of whisky from his canvas knapsack The two of them were clearly making a night of it. Stella, glad to escape, went to bed.

As she undressed, Stella reflected on how disruptive her brother's presence was. His inclusion in the expedition had been at the last minute and had it been up to her he would not have been allowed to come. Yet here he was calling the shots, demanding diversions, and failing to behave as a responsible member of what should be a serious academic study trip.

Not for the first time she cursed the system that pushed women to the back of the queue. Why should she, academically gifted, who would have been a diligent and enthusiastic student, be deprived of the chance for higher education? Her brother, meanwhile, had had every opportunity showered upon him – only for him to fritter his life away on idle pleasures and indulgences.

The germ of the idea of using her own means to fund her attendance at Cambridge was growing stronger every day. As soon as they were back in England, she would make solid plans. Surely, her father wouldn't stand in her way. He might not approve, but he wouldn't actively try to stop her – any more than he tried to prevent Ronald from wasting the opportunities offered him. And their brief conversation before he was taken ill had shown that he knew everything good in Gordon Black-stock's work emanated from her.

She drifted off to sleep, dreaming of sitting in a crowded lecture theatre, and poring over books in the library at Newnham.

· · ·

During the train journey to Kandy, Stella sat alone at the far end of the carriage, claiming she wanted to be quiet and try to sleep. Instead, she stared out of the window watching the countryside. It was raining heavily, water running in sheets down the windowpanes distorting the view of the grasslands and scattered trees. Out of the corner of her eye she could discern her father deep in conversation with Ronald and Gordon Blackstock, their voices a low murmur. Every now and again she sensed one or the other turn to look at her. She closed her eyes and tried to shut them out of her mind. The possibility of travelling to Jaffna in a couple of months with her brother and Blackstock weighed on her, but she wouldn't think about it yet. Soon they would be in Kandy, then in the cooler climate of the uplands, away from the stifling humidity of the coast and the savanna.

After an hour or so, her father rose from his seat and made his way down the swaying compartment to join her. He sat down opposite her, took out his pipe, lit it and leaned back, watching her as he smoked. He looked exhausted. Stella hoped he would take a little time to recover when they reached Kandy.

'We didn't finish our conversation about Mr Blackstock's proposal,' he said eventually.

'I think we did, Papa. There isn't much more to say. I won't marry him. But there is something else I'd like to discuss.' She gulped in a large breath of air. 'I want to go to Cambridge to study. I intend to apply to Newnham College.'

The professor said nothing at first, puffing on his pipe and keeping his eyes fixed on her. Eventually he drew his lips into a taut line and said, 'Not a good idea. For a start there's no point as they can't award you a degree.'

'Not yet, but I'm sure that will change. Already London University is awarding degrees to women. It can only be a matter of time before the others follow. Cambridge has two women's colleges.' She squeezed her hands into fists and urged herself to go on. 'You know I'd be a good student, Papa. You know how passionate I am about the subject. You acknowledged yourself that Mr Blackstock has been presenting my conclusions as his own. Surely you can see that I've earned the right to study the subject for myself.'

'That's as may be, my dear, but I don't make the rules. Society isn't kind to women who try to forge a path of their own. In the world of academia, it's even more so. If you wish to follow your dream and gain the satisfaction of study, the best way to fulfil that dream will be to accept Mr Blackstock's proposal of marriage.'

Stella gasped, disbelieving.

'Look, we both know the man's never going to make a reputation on his own in our field. But the college is determined that make his mark he will. There's a lot at stake. We're not one of the richer colleges and the endowment promised by his father will be transformative. Yes, sometimes I feel ashamed that I support this subterfuge but I'm a pragmatist at heart and if it's for the greater good then I've reconciled myself to turning a blind eye on the man's shortcomings. I won't be here forever, but I want my legacy to endure. You can make it so.'

'Then let me do so by going to Cambridge!'

'How would that benefit the college? The dean and Blackstock's father have determined that my work will be continued by him. Don't you see, Stella, you will have the satisfaction of knowing that it's your work. Of witnessing your conclusions shared across the whole world of anthropological study. That could never happen under your own name, but it can under his.' He re-lit his pipe and sucked on it until it caught. 'You're not in this for fame and reputation; you do it for the sheer love of our subject. It matters not a jot if it's not your name on the cover of a paper if your findings are inside it. Or are you saying you're hungry for glory?'

'Of course not. It's the research that matters.' Stella felt like a cornered animal.

'And the glory could never be yours anyway. Like it or not, Stella, but the men of Harvard, Oxford and Cambridge would never give you credence or credit. This way you'll have the pleasure and satisfaction of getting one over them.'

Stella felt hollowed out. 'You're asking me to marry Gordon Blackstock even though I have nothing but contempt for him in order to cement your legacy.'

He shook his head, a trace of annoyance around his eyes. 'If you're serious about the subject nothing else should matter.'

Stung, she bit her lip. How could he be so callous? It was a terrible betrayal. Stella had believed her father to be her ally. Her lip trembled but she was determined not to let him see how much he'd hurt her.

Feeling utterly alone, she thought of her mother, wishing she were still alive and might prevail upon him to see her point of view. Yet hadn't her mother given up her beloved musical career to marry him? And he had stood by and let that happen. The realisation struck Stella that her father was a selfish man.

Oblivious to her inner turmoil, he smiled sadly at her, a look of disappointment in his eyes, as though she were failing to live up to his expectations. 'Or perhaps you don't care as much about anthropology as I've always believed.'

Emotional blackmail. Stella was outraged and felt the sting of threatened tears. 'Of course I care. How can you doubt it?'

'Because you're not prepared to make this sacrifice in order to pursue a life dedicated to its study.' He bent forward and patted her hand. 'Strong marriages have been built on less than this. The life of the mind and the rewards of study endure long after romantic notions have faded. You'll realise that eventually, Stella.'

She wanted to scream at him, insist that nothing could make marriage to Gordon Blackstock palatable to her. But her father was already on his feet. He smiled at her again. 'Think on it, Stella. But not for too long.'

TWELVE

'Well, well, Mr Baxter, it seems you've made quite an impression on my daughter.' Julian Metcalfe paused beside Norton's desk in the *kachcheri*. 'She's asked me to relay the message that she'll see you at the courts this afternoon. We're expecting house guests from England, and my wife and I would like you to join us all for dinner at the residence this evening.' Without waiting for an answer, the GA swept away into his office.

Frobisher, whose desk was opposite Norton's, raised an eyebrow. 'I say, Baxter, looks like you've hit the jackpot. Already in the chief's good books. Must be doing something right with the daughter.'

Norton gave a false chuckle but was distinctly uncomfortable. 'The only jackpot I'm interested in winning is passing the Sinhala examination so I can start to climb my way up the ladder.'

Frobisher cast a derisive glance. 'You won't pass first time. No one does. You've only been here five minutes. It'll take you at least a year to pass the language test and then you'll still be at the bottom of the heap. Do you realise it took me five years to move up from cadet? The civil service is built on dead men's shoes, Baxter. Your only hope of early advancement is if you play your cards right and become Julian Metcalfe's son-in-law so he'll pull some strings for you. But if I were a betting man, which of course I'm not, I'd put my money on Cynthia Metcalfe turning against you and asking Daddy to arrange for your transfer. If Monty Adamson couldn't win the girl's heart, you're unlikely to do so.'

'That's preposterous, Frobisher. I've no intention of marrying Cynthia Metcalfe – even assuming she'd have me, which I'm sure she wouldn't. Therefore, my preference would be for the transfer – especially if as in Adamson's case it comes with promotion as well.'

'Not a chance. The GA will just shunt you off, still as a cadet, into some beastly backwater.'

Norton decided a response was pointless. Frobisher appeared to be a bitter and angry man. It was as though he blamed Norton for the departure of Adamson. Yet if the bond between the two men was so strong, wouldn't Adamson have tried to find a position for Frobisher in Colombo? Norton had a hunch the man hadn't given another thought to his hero-worshipping former housemate since leaving Kandy.

As soon as he walked onto the tennis court, Cynthia remarked that Norton was late.

'I wasn't sure I'd get here at all. I had a stack of paperwork to finish off.'

Cynthia looked astonished. 'You can't be serious, Mr Baxter. You're actually saying you'd have worked late even if it meant missing tennis?'

Norton swung his racquet in a practice stroke. 'Of course. Work comes first.'

'But everyone is here in the late afternoon. No one expects

you to miss a tennis game. Certainly not Daddy. Not unless the governor himself turns up from Colombo. But even the governor knows we all play tennis in the late afternoon. Daddy would be horrified to think you're stuck behind your desk when you should be here with us.'

Rather than argue, Norton shrugged. 'Well, better late than never, I suppose.'

Snod MacDonald was looking impatient, so they took up their positions on the court and began what proved to be a fast and furious match. This time Cynthia and Norton prevailed, winning in straight sets.

'Daddy says you're joining us at the residence tonight, so I'll give you a lift. Just give me fifteen minutes to shower and change.'

'Don't worry about me. I haven't brought my dinner suit as I wasn't expecting to dine out tonight so I'll head back home to change and will see you at the residence later.'

Cynthia touched his arm and turned her smile on him. 'I told you I'll give you a lift. Daddy's syce is picking me up so we'll go via your bungalow.' As usual, she was determined not to be gainsaid.

But Norton was getting bored with her spoiled girl antics. 'If it's all the same, Miss Metcalfe, I'll head home straight away and see you later.' He wanted her to stop assuming he was at her beck and call. He wanted her to leave him alone – even if it meant losing her as a tennis partner. While he enjoyed partnering her, he hated to be taken for granted, and attractive as she was, he was beginning to find her behaviour tedious. Without waiting for her to respond, he waved cheerily to the MacDonalds, left the court and set off on foot to his nearby bungalow.

When he got there, a letter from his mother was awaiting him. It was a long newsy missive, full of harmless gossip about local people he didn't even know, mixed with humorous diatribes about incompetent politicians and a protracted discourse on the running aground in the Bristol Channel of a naval warship. Norton read it, experiencing an unexpected wave of homesickness. At the end his mother had added a postscript to say she would let his sister tell him her news. There was another letter on a single sheet inside the envelope. Opening it he read:

Dearest Nortie

This will be brief so Mama can catch the post.

Even though now they were both in their twenties, Winnie persisted in using the childhood name she had adopted for him. Were anyone other than her to use it he'd resent it, and she knew not to utter it aloud on pain of death. In school he'd been called Nortie Boy until he'd landed a punch on the chief culprit. It had earned him detention along with six of the best, but it had been worth it to nip the name in the bud.

I have some frightfully exciting news. Now that the season's over and I haven't managed to get engaged to anyone, Mama and Papa have decided I'm a hopeless case. I did have an offer from a chap called Peregrine Fraser-Robertson, but I couldn't possibly have contemplated marrying him as he is a terrible bore and lives in the middle of a grouse moor up in the wilds of Scotland. Imagine! Me as the wife of a laird! I'd turn completely bonkers like Lady Macbeth. So it looks like I'll be back on the market next season. Yawn!! In the meantime, after much pestering from me, Mama and Papa have agreed that I come out to Ceylon for a few months to stay with you. Help you settle in. Organise your social life while you learn the ropes in your job. I think it's a topping idea and I do hope you think so too.

Papa is arranging a passage for me on the Scimitar *leaving in a couple of weeks. Will send the exact details later.*

I can't wait to see you, darling brother, and to meet all your friends and colleagues.

Your loving sister,
Winifred

He started to read it again, imagining he could hear his sister's voice, her delight at making her first trip to the East. He was delighted she was coming out. Winnie was an eternal optimist, fizzing like a glass of champagne but never annoying. Until now, he hadn't realised how much he missed her – indeed his whole family – even his father. He was about to read the two letters through a second time when he was interrupted.

'I've been sitting outside in the carriage for ten minutes waiting for you, so I decided to come and investigate.' Cynthia Metcalfe was a vision in pink chiffon silk. 'Goodness, Mr Baxter, what on earth have you been doing? You haven't even changed. Hurry up and get cleaned up. Daddy can't abide lateness and no doubt I'll get the blame.'

'I'd already told you I'd see you there,' he said, testily. He knew he was being rude, but his patience was stretched to its limits. Cynthia was hounding him. 'I've had a letter from home, so I wanted to read it.'

'Never mind that. Hurry up! Chop chop!' She clapped her hands and flashed him a smile. He had to admit to himself she was uncommonly pretty. Why did she have to be so bossy? Without further argument he went to his room to wash and change.

As they drove through Kandy in the GA's carriage, Cynthia edged close to him. It seemed the cooler he was to her, the more she was interested in him. She was evidently one of those people whose interest heightens as soon as they discover the object of their desire is unattainable.

He could feel the warmth of her leg where it was pressed up against his – quite unnecessarily, given the spacious carriage. Norton was enveloped by her perfume. Gardenia. His mother was fond of the scent.

She turned to look at him, her eyes shining in the glow from the carriage lamps. He caught his breath.

'I like you, Mr Baxter. I like you a lot. Although you don't deserve it at all, you bad boy. You seem to take pleasure in hurting my feelings.' Her lips formed a pout. 'I know you think Daddy spoils me. You're probably trying to teach me a lesson by being so beastly, aren't you?'

Was she serious? If poor Adamson had given her the cold shoulder, he'd likely have been a married man by now. But Norton didn't want to court her. Cynthia Metcalfe was an unwelcome complication to his life.

There was a different atmosphere at the GA's residence that night compared with Norton's previous visit. No informal family dinner on the terrace: this was a grand affair in the formal dining room under the twinkling candles of a crystal chandelier with a full complement of uniformed flunkies. The two men Norton and the GA had played at bridge were present with their wives, as well as the chief of police.

Cynthia had positioned herself beside Norton and casually slipped an arm through his as Mrs Metcalfe prepared to introduce the remaining guests to the late-arriving pair. Cynthia was clearly trying to convey, within the bounds of propriety, that they were a couple.

Norton gave a start as he recognised the other party. It was the woman who had joined the SS *Dambulla* in India. The girl with the beautiful eyes. He barely registered as he shook hands with Sir Michael Polegate, the brother and the third man, who was introduced as Mr Gordon Blackstock.

As soon as the introductions had been made, dinner was announced, and the assembled guests were led by their hosts into the dining room. Norton wished he'd saved the letters from home until later and thus might have had a chance to speak with the woman from the ship, who he had discovered was called Stella.

At dinner, he was placed between his hostess and her daughter. Stella Polegate was at the other end of the table. He consoled himself that since she was on the opposite side he could see her without having to lean forward.

It was just as well, as Norton soon found his eyes were drawn to her. She looked sad, downcast. Not conventionally beautiful, but interesting. And those extraordinary eyes – dark limpid pools. He wanted to gaze into them, to plumb their depths. He was sure there were secrets hidden there. She seemed the very opposite of Cynthia. The GA's daughter was an open book: if she wanted something she demanded it; if she loved something she showered it with affection; if she disliked a person, she made no effort to hide her contempt. Even from a distance where he could observe her freely, Stella Polegate was hard to read. As Cynthia entertained the table with a blow-by-blow account of their earlier vanquishment of the MacDonalds on court, he stole every opportunity to glance down the table to where Stella was deep in conversation with the district judge and his wife. He strained to hear what she was telling them, but Cynthia's cultured tones and musical laugh prevailed.

On Cynthia's other side was the younger Polegate sibling. Norton had already forgotten his name. He seemed to be hanging on her every word and she appeared to be lapping up the attention. He was a good-looking chap, probably no more than twenty, with unkempt hair that gave him a rakish appearance. Norton was grateful for the respite from Cynthia he was affording him.

He realised with a start that the man seated directly opposite him – the Blackstock fellow – was addressing him across the table.

'Sorry, I didn't catch that.'

'I was asking whether you're a hunting man, Mr Baxter. My friend, Mr Polegate, has heard that there's an abundance of game in the highlands and is keen to bag some trophies.'

'I can't help you with that. I know nothing of game hunting. I'm new to Ceylon. In fact, I believe we arrived on the same ship, the *Dambulla*.'

'Really? Then you must join us when we set up our hunting expedition. We can all discover the fascination of stalking wild animals together.'

'No thank you, if it's all the same to you. I don't think killing animals is my thing.' As he said the words, he realised he had probably forgone the only opportunity he might have to get to know Miss Stella Polegate – and get to know her he most certainly wanted to do.

Later, when they had finished eating, the party transferred outside to the terrace and lawn, now lit by flaming torches interspersed with oil burners releasing the scent of citronella and lavender to keep the mosquitoes at bay.

Norton stood slightly apart, surveying the groups of people as the strains of music from a gramophone drifted across the warm evening air. He was trying to spot Miss Polegate but there was no sign of her.

'How do you like Kandy, Mr Baxter?'

He jumped as the voice came from behind him. Turning, he saw it was Stella Polegate. He felt the blood rush to his face and was grateful for the dark half-light. 'Miss Polegate!'

'Sorry. I rather crept up on you there, didn't I?'

'Not at all. To be honest, I haven't yet had much time to

explore Kandy. Mostly the tennis courts and the *kachcheri*, I mean the office where I work.'

'Yes, I gather your fiancée is a keen player.'

'My fiancée?' he spluttered. 'Gosh no. I'm not engaged.'

She frowned. 'My mistake. I thought Mrs Metcalfe implied there was an understanding.'

Norton realised his mouth was gaping open. She must think him an idiot. 'I barely know Miss Metcalfe, delightful as she is. I've only been in Kandy a few weeks.' It was mortifying. Had Portia Metcalfe told her guests that he and Cynthia were to be married?

'We were on the same ship, weren't we? I remember seeing you. With your friend. And again, at the Galle Face Hotel.' She smiled. 'I must have misinterpreted something Mrs Metcalfe said. Please forget I ever said it.'

But Norton couldn't help a feeling of rising panic. Stella Polegate was letting him save face, but he knew she hadn't made a mistake. Now here he was, talking to her at last and all he wanted to do was crawl into a corner and hide. *Pull yourself together, man. Change the subject.* 'You're staying here as guests of the Metcalfes, I hear?'

'Mr Metcalfe is an old schoolfriend of my father. I'm afraid Papa took a bad turn thanks to the heat when we were up in the north and the doctor prescribed a retreat to higher ground. We're here for a few days then we'll be going to the highlands where the climate is more temperate.'

Norton felt a twinge of disappointment. 'Where in the north were you? Jaffna?'

'No. Not yet. We planned to go there next but will do so later. We made a diversion as my brother was keen to witness the pearl fishery operating. With hindsight, not a good idea.'

She told him about the bleakness of the place. 'It's all tree-less scrub, infertile soil, ugly and arid thanks to the burning sun.' Stella wrinkled her nose. 'And the stench! They pile all the oysters up and let them rot away to release the pearls. Just thinking about it and I'm haunted by the smell again.' Her hand covered her mouth and nose for a moment.

'It sounds a terrible place.'

'Make sure you're never posted there, Mr Baxter. I met the local government agent and his wife. She hates the place and must put up with it whenever there's a pearl harvest. Almost every year for about six to eight weeks. Ugh.' She shuddered. 'Enough about me. Tell me about you. What does an important civil servant do in Kandy?'

'I'll let you know if I ever get to be one.' He grinned. 'I'm merely the office dogsbody. The cadet gets all the dull, mechanical drudgery. The stuff no one else wants to do.'

'I'm sure there are interesting things too. You're being modest.'

'If there are I'm yet to discover them. I can't wait to be sent out to deal with problems directly. I know I'm impatient. I suppose I must earn my stripes, but honestly, Miss Polegate, any idiot could do what I'm doing at the moment. Compiling statistics, recording complaints. Petty stuff. Pushing a pen all day.' Keen to keep her in conversation but nervous about giving a bad impression, he asked, 'What brings you and your family to Ceylon?'

'My father is a Professor of Anthropology at Oxford University. Mr Blackstock is his doctoral student. I work as Papa's unofficial assistant, compiling his notes, indexing references. That kind of thing.' She gave him a mischievous look. 'The sort of work you'd find mechanical and tedious.'

Again, he was thankful to the darkness for concealing the red of his face. 'I'm sure what you do is much more interesting,' he said, lamely.

'It sounds rather similar. You see, we study all the small details of daily life and rituals among the Tamil population. Everything from religious practices to marriage customs.'

'Now that *does* sound interesting. My problem isn't with the nature of the subject matter I'm dealing with – just my role in it. I get to listen while my colleague, the chap I share a bungalow with, handles disputes. He makes the decisions. I take the notes.'

'I think we have more in common than you imagine, Mr Baxter. That is exactly the source of my own dissatisfaction. My father and Mr Blackstock get to ask the questions and publish the findings while I write up the notes.' She looked away. 'My dearest wish is to be able to study it all in my own right.' Her voice was sad, a colder, more distant note entering. 'At least in your case if you're diligent and serve your time you'll get to progress. Right to the top of the tree. As a woman I'm denied being anything more than a helper. For the rest of my life.' She took a step backwards, moving herself slightly out of his orbit. 'Now I must go. I'm neglecting my father. I need to make sure he retires to bed before he's exhausted. Goodnight, Mr Baxter. Delightful talking with you.'

He watched her move across the lawn to where her father was sitting talking with the GA. A few moments later she led Sir Michael back inside the residence. Now that she was gone Norton felt as though a light had been turned off. He wanted to leave. There was nothing for him to stay for.

'Darling boy!' Cynthia appeared from nowhere and once again slipped her arm through his. 'Ronald – Mr Polegate, has been telling me he plans to organise a hunting party. He'd like us to come too.'

Norton shivered. *Us?* Here she was again, behaving as though they were a couple. He drew away from her. 'Mr Blackstock mentioned it. I told him I have no interest at all in killing wild animals. Besides, I have work to do.'

'Work, work, work. It's all you ever think about. Don't be such a bore. What's the point of being in Ceylon if you behave as though you're in London?'

'Miss Metcalfe, I've only been in the country five minutes. I'm still learning the ropes. I can't drop everything to go gallivanting about taking potshots at wildlife.'

'Actually, you jolly well can. I've already spoken to Daddy, and he thinks it's important that someone from the government accompanies the Polegates, and he's agreed that should be you. So, you'll be on official business.' She grinned and gave him a playful punch. 'And please stop addressing me so formally. Call me Cynthia. Now come and talk to Ronnie and Gordon.'

Seething at Cynthia's scheming, Norton looked at his watch. It was almost midnight, and he had his daily Sinhala lesson at six o'clock tomorrow morning before work. He hadn't liked the look of Blackstock nor was he keen to discuss plans for a hunting trip. 'I'm sorry, Miss... er... Cynthia, but I must take my leave. I have a very early appointment tomorrow.'

She started to protest but Norton had already turned away and headed across the lawn to thank Portia Metcalfe for her hospitality. When he had done this and climbed into one of the waiting rickshaws outside, he looked back and saw Cynthia, deep in conversation with Blackstock and Polegate.

As the rickshaw rattled along, he pondered what to do regarding Cynthia. He was caught in a cleft stick, as displeasing her would likely bring the wrath of her father upon him and that could destroy his career when it had barely started.

But back at the bungalow, as he lay in bed trying to sleep, it was Miss Stella Polegate who filled his thoughts, not Cynthia Metcalfe.

THIRTEEN

When Norton arrived at the tennis courts, a mixed doubles game was already underway. Instead of himself and Snod MacDonald, Cynthia and Valerie were partnering Ronald Polegate and Gordon Blackstock. Surprised, Norton turned to leave, not wanting to interrupt their game, then noticed Stella Polegate sitting on a folding chair in the shade of the rain trees. Although she was pretending to watch the play, he could tell she was concealing a book from view of the courts with her reticule. She glanced up, saw him and smiled, shielding her eyes from the sun, now low in the sky.

Norton felt a clutch at his insides. Why did she have this effect on him? She wasn't conventionally pretty like Cynthia, but her face was full of character, so he was drawn to her, keen to know more about her. He hesitated to say he was attracted to her – more that he was interested, fascinated indeed, but couldn't work out exactly why. All he knew was he wanted to be near her. To get to know her.

Involuntarily, he moved closer, removing his hat in greeting. 'Miss Polegate, a pleasure to see you. Don't you play?'

'I do, but there's a full complement. Besides, it's quite hot today and rather than run about, I'm happy here in the shade. What about you?'

'I was expecting to play with Miss Metcalfe and Mr and Mrs MacDonald.' He looked about him but there was no sign of Snod.

'I understand the gentleman with the unusual forename has an important meeting. Miss Metcalfe asked Ronald to step in, then since he was already here, Gordon Blackstock was roped in too. I'm sure if you go over, he'll step aside. After all, yours is a regular engagement.'

But Norton had no wish to enter the game. 'As it happens, I'm relieved. You're right about it being hot this afternoon. I think I'll take a turn around the lake.' He hesitated for a moment. 'I don't suppose you'd care to join me?'

Stella pushed her book inside her bag and got to her feet. 'An excellent idea. I'd love to see more of the lake.'

They left the club and began walking along the carriageway that ran around the lake's perimeter. It was cool and well shaded by the proliferation of trees. The carriageway was a popular place for the Europeans to stroll or ride but that afternoon it was deserted. The blue water of the lake shimmered in the sunshine and reflected the greens and pinks of the flowering trees that surrounded the lake as well as the terracotta roofs of the traditional buildings.

Stella spoke first. 'I can't make my mind up about Kandy. It's undoubtedly beautiful.' She swept her arm out to indicate the lake and the mountains beyond. 'But there's something sad about it. It's full of Europeans compared with everywhere else I've been in Ceylon, and yet it feels as though we don't belong, or aren't welcome here.'

'I know what you mean. The Kingdom of Kandy held out for centuries against invaders. The Portuguese and the Dutch never managed to conquer it, and it took multiple attempts by the British. Even now that it's part of British Ceylon there's an undercurrent, a sense that they're going along with us, but they aren't really.' He thought for a moment. 'Perhaps it's all the history. As though we've come along and built on top of it, but we won't endure. As though the Kandyans are waiting for the day when they'll prevail over us and wipe the veneer of British culture away.'

'But they won't, will they? The British Empire rules most of the world. That's not likely to change, is it?'

'Would you like it to?'

She looked at him. 'Until coming to Ceylon I'd never questioned it. Perhaps I should have done.' She frowned. 'Just because something is the norm doesn't mean it's right, does it?'

He smiled. 'To be honest, I never gave it much thought either. But I've started to ask myself why we have the right to lord it over people who have lived here and built their own civilisation for millennia? These aren't views I'd share with the GA – or anyone in the *kachcheri*. I'm an officer of the Crown and hence expected to uphold everything about the great British Empire without question.'

She smiled. 'I detect a note of cynicism. Surprising from someone who's only been in the country a matter of weeks.'

Was she criticising him? Usually, he didn't give a damn what others thought of him, but he realised what Stella Polegate thought mattered a lot to him. 'I'm sorry. I'm being self-indulgent. It's just that I've been having Sinhala lessons from a Buddhist monk each morning before work. As the lessons have progressed, I've learned so much more than the language. We talk about his life and religion, and it's become the highlight of my day. Compared with most of the English chaps at work I find him fascinating. I leave our session each morning feeling stronger and calmer, but increasingly inclined to question things.'

'What else are you questioning?' She looked at him, her gaze intent.

'Sorry, you don't want to hear my ramblings. I probably sound like a raving idiot.'

'Not at all. Do tell me.'

'Just that so much of what we do seems trivial and interfering. What right have we to sit in judgement over whether a couple are entitled to a divorce, or whether one man has stolen another one's cow? They've been resolving those kinds of disputes for centuries without us stepping in and deciding things for them.'

'But there are a lot of native judges and lawyers, aren't there?'

'True. Practising law as laid down by us and using our systems of justice. Are we so sure there was anything wrong with their own methods?'

She smiled. 'Your disillusionment runs deep, Mr Baxter. There are those who say we bring civilisation, education, a durable and consistent bureaucratic structure that will serve all the countries of the empire well for years to come.'

'Is that what *you* think?' He looked sideways at her trying to read her expression.

'I'm the daughter of an anthropologist, not a historian or a politician. I observe and record. But what has always given me enormous satisfaction is trying to understand the ways and means, the rituals and traditions of other peoples. Everything that contributes to a society and culture. Do we really want to replace all these things across the continents with "the British way"? A homogenisation of the world.' She put up her hands. 'I'm merely the scribe but in my time assisting my father I've learned that those who many of our countrymen would call savages have a vast and rich culture. Just look around us. The beauty of the temples and palaces and how long they've endured.' She frowned, remembering something. 'When we were at the horrible pearl fishery place, Ronald and I visited a ruined building. It was the former mansion of the first British governor of the island. It had been built in an exposed position on the coast and was crumbling away, battered by the elements. Apparently, it started falling apart almost as soon as it was built.'

'Sounds like they built it in an unsuitable place.'

'Undoubtedly. But I'm sure the Kandyan kings wouldn't have made that mistake. The governor was only there for a few weeks each year, yet he wanted a symbol of his power and influence – grandiose and complete with Doric columns. Instead, it's now a symbol of transience and hubris.' She paused then said, *'My name is Ozymandias, King of Kings; Look on my Works, ye Mighty, and despair!'*

'Shelley? I remember it from school.'

'Indeed. *Nothing beside remains. Round the decay Of that colossal Wreck, boundless and bare The lone and level sands stretch far away.* It was one of my mother's favourite poems and that desolate place was just like that – boundless and bare.'

He was entranced. He'd never known a woman like her before. He tried unsuccessfully to imagine Cynthia speaking this way. Desperate to keep her talking he said, 'Tell me about the research project that brought you to Ceylon.'

She looked surprised and glanced at him, presumably wondering if his interest was genuine. 'My father is studying ethnographic differences between indigenous Tamils and those who arrived here from India to work on the plantations. Religious practices, concepts of justice, family structures. All manner of things.'

'It sounds fascinating.'

'It is.' She gave a long, heartfelt sigh.

'What's wrong?'

She hesitated, looked at him, then evidently deciding to trust him, said, 'It's what I mentioned last night. I want nothing more than to go to university myself, but my father is set against it. His reasoning is that it would be a waste of time as I couldn't be awarded a degree.'

Norton nodded. 'A terrible injustice to women. I'm sure that must change soon. The right to vote too.'

'Exactly. In the meantime, I want to study anyway because I care passionately about the subject. I want to go to Cambridge.'

He grinned. 'My alma mater. I did the Mathematics Tripos. Failed to distinguish myself. Unlike the legendary Miss Philippa Fawcett a few years back. Her marks were way higher than the highest scoring man, yet he was awarded the Senior Wrangler title, and she didn't even get a degree.'

'I heard about that. I was still a child, but I remember my mother commenting about the unfairness when she read about it in the newspaper.' She pursed her lips. 'The papers were more exercised by how extraordinary it was that a mere woman could perform so well – with barely a squeak about how unjust the system was. Almost as though she were a freak of nature rather than a talented student. The *most* talented. Not only to be denied the rightful honour as the Senior Wrangler but to be refused a degree as well.'

'Will you go to Cambridge anyway? – and will it be Newnham like Miss Fawcett, or Girton?'

'I'd like to go to Newnham. Although my father is trying his utmost to dissuade me. He says not only will I not be awarded a degree for my efforts, but no academic will be interested in my work.' She appeared to hesitate then plunged on. 'Papa wants me to marry his student and support his research. He claims it's the only way my work will ever see the light of day.'

'Not Mr Blackstock?' Norton stopped walking abruptly, a chill running through him. 'Has he asked you to marry him?' Then realising he was stepping into dangerous territory, he quickly apologised. 'Of course, it's none of my business... forgive me... but you seem an ill-matched couple.'

'Like you and Miss Metcalfe?'

'I told you; I'm not engaged to Miss Metcalfe.'

'Not yet, but if she has anything to do with it, I imagine that will change.' Stella smiled. 'Sorry, I'm being presumptuous. And the answer to your question is yes, he has proposed, and I've refused. I have no doubt he will press his suit again with encouragement from my father and Ronald.' She turned to look at him. 'They're determined to wear me down.'

'What about your mother? Can you enlist her help?'

'Mama is dead I'm afraid. No, Mr Baxter, I have no one in my corner.'

He wanted to tell her she had him. Right now, he'd gladly go into battle on her behalf. He felt sick at the thought of her yoked to the Blackstock fellow. While he'd barely spoken to the man, it had been enough for Norton to sense he had nothing in common with Stella. Summoning his courage, he asked, 'Do you get on with Mr Blackstock?'

'I was able to rub along well enough with him as a fellow member of the expedition until he declared his intentions. It's the thought of being his wife – it makes my flesh crawl.' She blushed. 'I'm frightfully sorry. I've no idea why I'm telling you all this. It's just that... I don't know... you're easy to talk to.'

'I feel that about you too,' he said before he could stop himself. 'I felt it at once. Last night. When we spoke on the lawn after dinner. I could have talked to you all night.' He was going too far now. He told himself to shut up before he scared her away.

Stella looked at him for a moment, her gaze intense, and then turned away and continued explaining how Gordon Blackstock used her to shape his own academic work and tried to pass it off as his own. 'He hasn't fooled Papa though.'

'Yet your father still wants you to marry him?'

'That's *why* he does. A significant endowment to the college and the creation of a sizeable bursary in anthropology depends on Blackstock getting his doctorate. My father wants me to do the work that will get him through his doctoral thesis and eventually win him a reputation in the subject. So, you see, Mr Baxter, I am the ventriloquist and Blackstock is my dummy.'

They had almost completed the circumference of the lake but he didn't want their walk to stop. He was dismayed by the injustice of what she had told him. He barely knew the woman, yet he burned with anger on her behalf.

'It will be getting dark soon,' she said. 'I need to get back to the tennis club before they notice I'm gone.'

Norton held her arm. 'Don't marry him. You can't marry him. Not when you feel that way.'

Stella turned her sad eyes upon him. 'I don't want to, but it might be the only way I'll ever have to study my subject. I wish I were as free as a man. Able to do what I want, go where I want, live the life I want. But I'm a woman so I don't get to follow my own path.'

'It doesn't have to be like that.' He was still holding on to her arm.

She looked down at his hand until he moved it away.

'In my case it does, Mr Baxter. I'm afraid it does.' Her mouth formed a tight line.

They walked the last yards in silence and as they entered the gates of the club the foursome was leaving the court.

'There you are!' Cynthia bounded up to meet them. 'Where have you been? We were halfway through the first set when we realised Miss Polegate had vanished. I'm afraid Mr Blackstock jumped into your shoes, Norton. You were late so you've only yourself to blame. Snod will be here in a few minutes and then we're all going for cocktails at the Queen's. You coming?'

Norton was surprised she'd offered him the choice. 'If you don't mind, I'll duck out this evening. I need to do some cribbing before my language lesson tomorrow.'

'Good heavens, Norton, you're such a swot and a spoilsport.

Never mind. The rest of us will just have to manage without you.' With that, she brushed past him, and Norton noted that she didn't seem too disappointed. His only regret was forgoing the chance to spend more time with Stella Polegate.

As he walked back to his bungalow and the prospect of supper with only the company of Frobisher, Norton couldn't stop thinking about the conversation with Stella. He'd felt an immediate connection with her, one that had intensified the longer they'd talked.

After his evening meal, when he sat down to study the Sinhalese text he was to discuss with his tutor the following day, he struggled to concentrate as he tried to rid his head of the image of Stella Polegate, the sound of her voice and the unfairness of her situation. Until now he'd given little thought to the difference in opportunities between men and women. His sister, Winifred, had never shown any interest in academic subjects and appeared perfectly content with her lot. But listening to Stella had changed his views. How could a woman like her be treated so shabbily?

Later, when he settled down to sleep, her face filled his thoughts. How could he let her be pushed into marrying that brute Blackstock?

Since coming to Ceylon, Norton had the strange feeling that everything was being speeded up. His life was moving at a dramatically faster pace than it had back in England. There was Cynthia Metcalfe acting as though they were engaged when their acquaintance was only a matter of days. And now Stella Polegate, who, unless his heart was playing tricks on him, he was already falling in love with. They'd spoken for the first time only last night, yet he already felt he understood her better than anyone. Indeed, if he were honest with himself his fate had been tied up with hers from the moment he had seen those eyes across the dining room of the SS *Dambulla*.

FOURTEEN

After Norton Baxter left the tennis club, Cynthia marshalled them all into rickshaws to head off for pre-dinner drinks at the Queen's Hotel. Stella wasn't used to going out in the evening in this way. At home in Oxford, she had virtually no social life and apart from attending the occasional classical music concert, spent her evenings reading. That evening at the Queen's, the conversation was banal, dominated in turn by Cynthia and Ronald – both excitedly planning the hunting expedition.

To Stella's distress, the assumption was that she would join them. Cynthia insisted. 'Certainly, you must come, Miss Polegate. Otherwise, Daddy will never let me go. Or he'll insist on Mummy accompanying us and then none of us will have any fun.'

Ronald jumped in. 'Of course Stella will join us.' He'd turned to face her, fixing his eyes on her in unspoken challenge. 'She wouldn't dream of spoiling the party for everyone else.'

Stella bristled. Her younger brother had no right. But she didn't want a row in front of these people she barely knew.

Once the topic of the hunting was exhausted, the chatter droned on around her with Stella's attention drifting in and out.

By the time they eventually left the hotel to return to the residence, she was ready to crawl up the walls with boredom. She dearly wished Norton Baxter had come along to the Queen's Hotel too.

Stella was restless and unable to settle. She was sharing Cynthia's bedroom. While the GA's daughter hadn't uttered so much as a word of complaint, Stella sensed she was less than happy about it. As she lay in bed, unable to sleep, Stella conducted a post-mortem of her conversation with Norton. She asked herself why he'd so abruptly refused to come to the Queen's Hotel and had made a rapid escape. Had she made a fool of herself by explaining all the details of her situation to him? It had been one thing to confide in Violet Moreland – Stella had needed the sympathetic ear of another woman. But to unburden herself to the civil servant? A man. A stranger. And one courting their host's daughter. Stella wanted to curl up into a tight ball like a hedgehog and pretend it hadn't happened. What on earth had possessed her? She'd overstepped the boundaries of acceptable behaviour. What must he think of her?

She lay tangled in her sheets, sleep elusive, cringing as she forced herself to replay their conversation. He'd been such a generous listener. And he'd practically begged her not to marry Blackstock. But as soon as they'd returned to the tennis club, he'd fled. Couldn't get away fast enough. She'd painted such a grim picture of her personal circumstances that he'd doubtless felt sorry for her. She'd put him in a difficult position. Stella tossed from side to side, consumed with mortification. But thrashing around in her bed wasn't going to make what had happened unhappen.

Why had she opened her mouth? Stella thumped her pillow. All that complaining about university and Blackstock.

What if he told Cynthia Metcalfe what she'd said? God forgive her, but she couldn't help but dislike the woman. Over-privileged, indulged by her doting father, lording it over everyone and making no attempt to disguise her contempt for Stella. At the tennis club that afternoon, she'd positively relished leaving Stella sitting on the sidelines while she co-opted the two men to join her and Mrs MacDonald. Like a queen bee. Cynthia was everything Stella disliked in a woman – she appeared to despise her own sex, preferring the company of men to other women – apart from one chosen acolyte in Valerie. Off the tennis court, her life appeared to be entirely filled with flirting, teasing, and talking trivia.

Glancing over at the other bed, where Cynthia was sleeping soundly, her breathing audible, Stella asked herself if her dislike was because Cynthia had set her cap at Norton Baxter. As soon as the thought took shape, she tried to dismiss it. Just because Mr Baxter had been friendly and sympathetic didn't mean anything, did it? Surely, she wasn't jealous. Yet why was she unable to banish him from her head?

She had been stung by what her father had said to her on the train: that she was deluding herself if she thought anyone would take her seriously as an academic. It had hurt when he said it would be vanity on her part to want the credit and reputation more than simple satisfaction in the work itself, and if she truly cared about her subject she'd put her personal life second and marry Gordon Blackstock.

The thought of marriage to Gordon was abhorrent. She didn't want to imagine those fat fingers with their bitten nails pawing at her. The overgenerous wet lips kissing her. Those widely spaced dull eyes.

Stella remembered what Violet Moreland had told her about being forced to marry Percy. That had surely been an even worse fate as Percy Moreland was about twenty years older than Violet – and for Violet there had been no compensatory benefit in the way access to academia would be for Stella. Why was she any more deserving than poor Violet? Was it time to accept that this was simply the fate of a woman – destined always to be at the beck and call of a man? Her own mother had married for love but where had it got her? A constant sense that there was a huge part of her life unfulfilled.

Stella missed her mother desperately. She regretted that she had never spoken to her directly about the sacrifice of her career for love and marriage. But then she'd sensed that the topic was not one her mother had wished to explore.

Perhaps if she were to give Blackstock the benefit of the doubt she might begin to discover more positive qualities in him. Was she being over-fussy? In India and indeed in many cultures, men and women had no say in whom they got to marry and yet the custom produced many happy marriages. Perhaps one could get used to anything or anyone, given time. It wasn't as though she harboured romantic notions. Indeed, she'd never imagined marrying anyone at all. Her aspirations had always centred on the life of the mind not of the heart. But as she mooted the thought, she felt a wave of nausea.

Norton Baxter had been sympathetic, agreeing her situation was intolerable. But he was probably only being polite, and was no doubt embarrassed by her outpourings. Stella turned over onto her other side, swept up into a private hell of humiliation.

Eventually she gave up the struggle for sleep, got out of bed, tiptoed across the bedroom and went to sit beside the window, where she gently eased open the shutters to wait for the sun to rise.

The sky began to lighten, then a rosy glow spread from behind the distant mountains above the trees that encircled the residence's well-groomed gardens. There was a lingering scent of citronella mingled with the damp freshness of the early morning dew on the grass. She breathed it in deeply.

Could she and Blackstock reach an accommodation with

each other? After all, his motivation for marrying her was doubtless a practical one. Could they agree that it would be a marriage of convenience? Maybe they could reach an arrangement that would place it on a purely academic footing.

Next time Blackstock brought up the subject of marriage, she would set out her terms. A marriage in name only. A partnership where each would get what they wanted, without need of any of the usual physical implications of matrimonial union. She remembered reading that the French had a term for it – *un mariage blanc*. Until he had proposed to her, Stella had never seen any indication of Gordon Blackstock being attracted to her. His academic goals could be achieved without them having to consummate the union. She would agree to him having other relationships outside the marriage so he would leave her in peace. *Please let him agree!* But even if he did, would he honour the arrangement? It would mean forgoing any possibility of a family. She had never given children a thought before now – and certainly didn't want his. But would he settle for that? Above all else Gordon Blackstock was a vain and ambitious man. She held the academic cards so perhaps he would accept this as the only way he could achieve his goals.

Outside the window the day had begun, bathing the dew-soaked lawn in sunlight. In a tree a few feet from her window, a pair of red-whiskered bulbuls were singing to each other. Stella smiled, watching and listening to the red-cheeked birds as they trilled away. It was an optimistic sound. Perhaps this was a sign that there was a way forward for her after all.

FIFTEEN

When Norton finished his Sinhala lesson, which took place within the complex of the Temple of the Sacred Tooth Relic, it was already nearly seven in the morning. He liked to be at his desk in the *kachcheri* by a quarter to seven, because the working days in Kandy finished early – he suspected a longstanding commitment to the tennis courts was behind this. This morning, though, he had been delayed by a discussion that went on longer than anticipated with the monk who taught him.

The monk, the venerable Vimal, who was clad as was the custom in saffron robes and with a shaven head, was telling Norton about the *Jataka Tales*. He spoke slowly, pausing to let Norton work out the meaning of unfamiliar words from the context, occasionally supplementing this with a demonstration that reminded Norton of one of Winnie's games of charades. Today's tale was of an elderly bald carpenter who was troubled by a mosquito which settled on his head and was stinging him. The man begged his son to rid him of the insect. "'One blow will settle it," said the son to his now impatient father. With a stroke of an axe, he split his father's head in two, killing him and the insect on the spot.'

Norton frowned. 'What's the meaning, Bhante Vimal? Other than that son was an idiot.'

'The Buddha said, "Better to have an enemy with sense than a friend without it."'

Norton was still puzzled.

'An enemy with sense would know the blow would be fatal and would fear the retribution of the man's friends. Our time is now up, my friend.'

Norton hadn't noticed the passage of time. He would be late for work. As he walked away, he pondered the monk's tale and came to the conclusion that in his own case his friends tended to be clever and his enemies – if he had any – stupid.

As soon as he emerged from the temple, he saw Cynthia at once. She was standing under a portico, haloed by early morning sunlight, wearing a loose linen jacket over a muslin dress. Norton paused, momentarily stunned by her beauty, before she looked up and saw him. Her demeanour was hesitant, her smile nervous, with no trace of her usual confident exuberance.

'Miss Metcalfe,' he said. 'I didn't expect to see you here – and so early in the morning. I've just finished my language lesson.'

'I know. I wanted to catch you before you went to the office. Can we walk for a while? And I've told you to call me Cynthia.'

Norton glanced at his watch. If he agreed, he'd be even later, and Frobisher would want to know why. But he could hardly refuse. He'd use the lesson over-running as his excuse.

They walked beside the moat that surrounded the temple complex. The air was thick with incense and the sickly scent from the flowers that worshippers brought as offerings to the Buddha. Yet under the cloying sweetness there was a freshness from the rain that had fallen during the night. The trees beside the lake were bedecked with sleeping fruit bats, hanging from the branches like a collection of fur stoles.

'You haven't come to tennis for three days,' Cynthia said, opening her parasol. 'I wanted to apologise for letting Mr Blackstock take your place and foisting Miss Polegate on you. I can't imagine what you two managed to talk about. She's such a serious intense person. Makes me nervous. Not at all like Ronnie, who's an absolute poppet.'

'You didn't foist Miss Polegate on me. I invited her to join me. And I very much enjoyed talking to her.'

Cynthia raised her eyebrows but offered no further comment on Stella. 'You don't approve of me, do you, Mr Baxter?' Then seeing he was about to protest, she raised a gloved hand and halted him. 'No, do let me finish, please. I'm not cross with you. I simply want to tell you something.'

Norton waited for her to elaborate.

'I know you consider me to be spoiled. Probably shallow too. The only child of over-indulgent parents.'

At least she wasn't lacking self-awareness.

'You doubtless imagine I enjoy being the centre of attention, bossing people about, getting my own way.' She made a little noise – the breath catching in her throat – then put her hand up again to silence him before he could speak. 'But it's all a facade. Covering up the mess I am inside.' Her head turned away from him, as she stared out over the lake, avoiding his eyes. 'You see, Norton – please, please may I call you Norton? It will make what I'm about to tell you much easier.' She paused, biting her lip. 'No one here knows about this, apart from Mummy and Daddy of course.'

Norton wished she'd get to the point. He wasn't in the mood for self-indulgent introspection. He glanced at his watch again.

Evidently sensing his impatience, she blurted, 'I am a twin. I had a brother. His name was Quentin.' She lowered her head. 'We were inseparable. Two sides of a single coin. We could read each other's thoughts and often finished each other's sentences.

I loved him more than anyone on this earth. But he died when we were twelve.'

'I'm sorry,' he said. Her voice had been different from the usual entitled soprano: lower in register, softer, barely a whisper. 'What happened?'

'He drowned. He got out of his depth and a current swept him out to sea.' She choked off a sob. 'Nobody blamed me, but it was my fault.'

Norton listened, unsure what to say or do.

'We were holidaying on the Isle of Wight. We used to rent a house there every summer.' She swallowed, evidently summoning the strength to continue. 'We weren't supposed to be at the beach, but I persuaded Quentin to get up early and slip out while our parents were sleeping so we could swim before it became crowded.' Cynthia closed her eyes for a moment or two before continuing. 'It's painful telling you this but it's important you know. I challenged him to a race. We were both strong swimmers. A couple of fish, Mummy used to say. But that day Quentin wasn't meant to be in the water. He'd been ill with a bad summer cold. He was getting impatient at missing the fun – but was still quite weak. I thought it would give me an advantage. Not consciously, but I've always been too competitive for my own good. I was desperate to win—' She made a sound like a whimper.

Instinctively, Norton reached out and placed his hand against her lower back. It was an intimate gesture but clearly welcomed.

She turned to look at him. 'I knew you'd understand. You're such a kind man, Norton. But please let me finish. Not a day goes by when I don't torture myself over what happened to Quentin. How it could have been different. How he'd still be alive if it weren't for me.

'I was edging in front and sensed he was weakening but he put on a spurt. It would have humiliated him to be beaten by a girl. I should have slowed down. Settled for a tie. Acknowledged to myself that it wasn't fair to race under these circumstances.' She touched her forehead with her hand. 'But I wanted to trounce him. So, I put all my effort into it and raced to the buoy that was the finishing line. I didn't realise he was struggling until it was too late. When I got to the buoy, I looked back but he'd vanished.'

She leaned against the decorative wall that edged the moat, her back to the lake. 'I thought he was clowning at first. That since he couldn't win the race, he was playing a trick on me. Swimming underwater. I expected him to pop up from nowhere and duck me. But he didn't. There was no sign of him on the beach, so he hadn't gone ashore. I looked out to sea and saw an arm raised in the air some distance out. He must have been fighting the current. He was there for a fleeting moment then he disappeared.' She inhaled a deep lungful of air before continuing. 'I should have gone after him but instead I clung onto the buoy rope and stared at the sea, expecting him to emerge again.' She wiped her eyes. 'But he didn't.'

'I'm so sorry, Cynthia.'

'Why didn't I sense he was in trouble? Why didn't I go after him immediately?' She released a long sigh. 'Someone on the shore saw what happened and two men swam out to look for him, but it was too late. He was gone. They sent boats out to search.' She closed her eyes, squeezing them tightly shut and Norton saw that she was shaking. 'The worst bit was telling Mummy and Daddy. The look in their eyes. They didn't get angry with me. They didn't realise it was my fault. That made it worse. They treated me like a little broken creature, lavishing me with affection as though if they didn't, I might vanish too.' Her gloved hands went up and covered her mouth, before she let them fall again. 'I wished they'd blamed me, shouted at me, punished me. It might have helped me feel less weighed down with the burden of guilt. Losing Quentin broke my parents' hearts. That's why Daddy took the job out here. Fifteen years ago. They couldn't bear to be in England anymore.'

'Did you ever find him?'

'His body washed up on the rocks a few miles further round the coast of the island.'

A single tear ran down her cheek. Norton took out a linen handkerchief and blotted her face.

Eventually she spoke, her voice now calm. 'They can't stand to look at me, you know. I'm a constant reminder of Quentin. They don't really see me. Not *me*. They see his absence. It's why Daddy's so desperate to marry me off. So, yes, if I behave like a spoiled child it's because I'm actually broken inside.'

'I don't know what to say, Cynthia. I'm so very sorry.'

'There's no need to say anything. I just wanted you to know. To understand something about me that no one else does.' She gave him a sad smile. 'Now, I've kept you long enough from your work.' With that she leaned forward, dropped the lightest of kisses on his cheek and hurried away.

Norton stood gazing after her, stunned.

As soon as he got to the *kachcheri*, thoughts of Cynthia's tragic story vanished when he was told by Frobisher that he must accompany him to the prison to witness a flogging.

'A flogging?' Norton shuddered at the thought.

'Yes. The good old cat o' nine tails.'

'It sounds barbaric.' Norton had no idea such punishments still took place. He was sure they had long been banned back in England. He pointed this out to his colleague, whose answer was smug.

'Only in the army and navy. It's still used in prisons and as a punishment for petty crimes. Better the birch for the public purse than keeping a man in a cell.'

Frobisher took off his reading glasses, tucked them into his jacket pocket, replacing them with a second pair of spectacles, and rose from his desk. 'Come on then, Baxter. We're already late because of you.'

Bogambara Prison was in the centre of the city. One of the first structures built by the British after the conquest of the Kingdom of Kandy, it was a white crenelated building, its entrance flanked by two solid round towers. Inside, the cell blocks surrounded a central court. It looked a dismal place even under the brightness of the sun that morning.

Frobisher rubbed his hands together. 'Hope you've a strong stomach, Baxter. Floggings are not for the fainthearted.' Despite the disclaimer he seemed to be relishing the prospect himself. 'Adamson always said it's worse witnessing floggings than hangings. If the hangman gets his calculations right it's all over quickly, whereas the beatings involve repeated infliction of pain. But at least you survive a flogging. And after all, the law must take its course, don't you think?'

Frobisher didn't seem to require a response, so Norton didn't offer one.

The office assistant gave a groan when he checked the paperwork. 'Dr Madashanka's on duty. He's over-particular about what he calls prisoner welfare.'

Norton's head jerked in surprise. 'What do you mean? Over-particular? How can you be over-particular where welfare is concerned?'

'If they make a racket or bleed a lot, he insists on stopping the beating while he checks their pulse and temperature and all that palaver. Better to just let the warders get on with it. The rules are to check every ten strokes, but he often intervenes more often. Such a time waste.'

Norton was horrified. For a man who was the epitome of the pen-pushing civil servant, bookish, lacking in social graces, Frobisher exhibited a blood lust that was unnerving.

Seeing Norton's expression, Frobisher said, 'I mean it's

crueller really. Spinning it out. As the bard said, "*If it were done when 'tis done, then 'twere well it were done quickly*". When it's Dr Kingsford or Ranasinghe, they let the warders get on with it. But Madashanka is one of those bleeding hearts who doesn't approve of corporal punishment. Probably doesn't even support the death penalty. Imagine! Although I doubt he'd admit it.'

Norton bit his tongue rather than comment about the quote from *Macbeth* and what the consequences of doing that deed quickly had been for the Scottish king. Frobisher was starting to take on the characteristics of a monster in Norton's eyes.

They went inside one of the prison blocks, diverting briefly for Frobisher to show Norton the gallows chamber. 'We have to be present at hangings too, to certify them.' He pointed towards three large metal hooks set in the ceiling above a wooden gallery accessed by a staircase. 'They can do up to three at a time here. We had a triple the other day, just before *Vesak Poya*. I would have brought you along, but you needed to finish writing up those notes from the appeals court.' He smiled. 'You'll get your chance to witness a hanging soon enough.'

He pushed open a door and led Norton into another room. 'Here we are.' He pointed to an iron frame, about six foot high, fixed to one of the walls. 'The chap will be tied by the arms and legs to the support while the sentence is carried out.' He consulted a file. 'Judge Milton's a bit of an old softie. Only ten strokes. Just bruising and grazing I expect. Unlikely even to break the skin.' He sounded disappointed.

'What did the man do?' Norton felt sick about what lay ahead. He remembered the only time at school he'd been physically punished. The six strokes of the cane had reddened his skin, and the stinging and tenderness had lingered for days. It had been an effective deterrent in his case.

'Stole a hopper from a stallkeeper.'

'A hopper?'

'A kind of pancake thingy the natives like to eat. Apparently rather tasty though I can't say I've ever tried one.'

'So, a minor misdemeanour. Presumably the man was hungry?'

'Boy really. He's fourteen. But you must understand, Baxter, it's to teach him not to steal again. If we nip it in the bud while he's pinching hoppers, we can stop him going on to commit more serious crimes like armed robbery or murder.'

Norton could see no reason for a hungry boy chancing his luck in snatching a hot snack from a food kiosk turning into a hardened criminal. The theft had probably been motivated by hunger or, at worst, a moment's opportunism. If anything was going to turn a man to a life of crime it was probably resentment against authority for such a harsh punishment. But he wasn't prepared to debate the question and risk what would doubtless be a protracted and pompous lecture from Frobisher.

After the introductions to Dr Madashanka and the prison staff had been made, Norton and Frobisher were shown to some chairs in front of the punishment wall. Norton declined to sit. It seemed decadent and prurient to sit like spectators at the theatre while a young man was beaten in front of them.

Frobisher, annoyed, turned to him. 'Don't forget to do a count.' He brandished the file. 'Afterwards we have to record it in here and sign as witnesses, along with the attending doctor.'

'What will happen to the prisoner?'

'Once the doctor's checked him, he'll be free to go. The flogging is instead of a custodial sentence.'

Norton supposed he should be thankful for small mercies. He hoped the lad would be strong and could bear his punishment with fortitude.

When the young man was led in, Norton was aghast. The boy was small and shabbily dressed. He looked so skinny that it would be hard not to assume he'd been driven to steal the hopper by starvation.

Frobisher spoke in a stage whisper. 'A Tamil. Claims to be an orphan. Probably spinning the judge a yarn in the hope of a reprieve.'

Norton clenched his fist at his side. Watching what was about to happen was going to be hard.

The cat o' nine tails was wielded with force by the heavily built prison warders who took turns, one delivering five strokes before handing over the whip to his colleague while the doctor checked the prisoner's vital signs.

Norton had averted his eyes during the first round, but he looked up as the doctor examined the boy. His bare back was striped with ugly weals, and blood was seeping from the wounds. The lad was so thin that his ribcage was visible. During those first five strokes he had never cried out... the only sounds being the crack of the whip as the leather knots hit his back, and the grunt-like expulsion of air from his lungs as he braced himself for the next stroke.

The second warder took over. Norton counted backward in his head as each stroke burst onto the boy's bloodied back. This time, the youth couldn't help screaming as the lash cut into the open wounds. When it was over, his wrists were unfastened from the bars to which they'd been shackled, and he collapsed in a heap on the ground. The doctor stepped forward and helped him to his feet.

Norton grabbed the chair he hadn't used and moved it forward so that the doctor could ease the boy onto it.

'Not in here, Dr Madashanka. Not on the visitors' chairs,' said the prison governor.

'I need to dress the wounds.'

'You can do that next door.'

The boy looked as though he hadn't the strength to walk the short distance so Norton stepped forward and helped the doctor support him into an anteroom where there was a wooden bench on which they helped him to lie on his stomach.

'Thank you,' said the doctor. 'I'll clean him up then he'll be free to go.' Addressing the boy he said, 'You were very brave, Pradeep. It's all over now.' He turned away to fetch his holdall and said to Norton, 'Your first time at a flogging?'

Norton, who thought he'd lost the power of speech, nodded.

'At least it was only ten lashes. Wait till you have to witness fifty or more. This isn't why I became a doctor. But if we medical officers don't attend, who will treat the poor souls afterwards? You're new to Kandy?'

'I'm the new cadet.'

'Well, Mr Baxter, be vigilant counting the strokes. Sometimes, if you don't call a halt, they'll add a stroke or two if they don't like the cut of the prisoner's jib. Some floggings involve prison inmates and resentments can build up between prisoners and their jailers.' His voice was cultured, patrician, betokening an English public-school education. 'Now, you, sir, would do well to go back in there before your colleague gets too upset.' He jerked his head in the direction of the doorway and set about swabbing Pradeep's wounds.

As they headed back to the *kachcheri*, Frobisher made his displeasure clear. 'What the devil did you think you were doing in there, Baxter? You and Madashanka practically carried the chap out of the room. You're there to represent His Majesty's Government not to minister to the unfortunate. The fellow was getting the punishment the law laid down. It's not our job to question that.'

'It was brutal. The most horrible thing I've ever witnessed. He was only a *child*.'

Frobisher shrugged. 'You'd better toughen up quickly as you'll be seeing worse than that. Like it or not, Baxter, it's part of the job.'

Norton didn't like it. No, he didn't like it at all.

. . .

When the rest of the day's business was completed, Norton left the *kachcheri* but couldn't face the tennis club, or spending the evening in their bungalow with Frobisher. He walked aimlessly through the streets of the city, wandering between bullock carts, food stalls, down alleyways, past churches, Hindu temples, and the more prevalent bell-shaped Buddhist stupas.

He decided to console himself with a drink and went into the Queen's Hotel, where he sat at the bar nursing a whisky.

He didn't want conversation but hadn't the energy to remove himself to a corner table, listening in silence as the barman polished glasses and told him how part of the hotel building had been prefabricated in Britain and shipped to Ceylon in kit form by the Victorians. After the man told him the hotel had previously been a governor's residence, Norton slugged down the rest of his whisky, bade him a good evening and left.

The experience at the Bogambara prison had depressed him. Not just the cruelty of the punishment and the youth of the boy, but the way it exemplified everything Norton was starting to see as wrong about the system – that the boy had been punished for staving off hunger, and the severity of the punishment relative to the trivial nature of the crime. But most of all he believed the natives of Ceylon – men like Dr Madashanka – ought to be deemed capable of meting out their own justice – and not be subject to decisions made by British judges and overseen by men like himself and Frobisher.

The latter's behaviour had been particularly disturbing. Superficially, he came across as a quiet, bookish type. Norton's first impressions had been that he reminded him of several chaps he'd known in his schooldays – a swot and a bit of a ninny. But he realised now there was a strong undercurrent of cruelty. Not that he could imagine Frobisher hurting anyone – it was more a pleasure in the sufferings of others. It had even come across on Norton's first evening in Kandy when he'd seemed to relish recounting the terrible story of the wife of Ehelapola and the cruelty of the last King of Kandy.

Norton meandered through the streets, still wanting to delay his return to the bungalow where he would be under the same roof as Bertie Frobisher. He checked his watch. He'd missed supper. But he had little appetite anyway.

He thought of the boy, Pradeep, remembering his stick-thin body. Would he have been tempted to steal food again since his release? Norton wondered what circumstances had caused him to be in a state of hunger. Frobisher had mentioned he was an orphan. What had happened to his family? Hadn't the judge seen fit to inquire? Norton felt guilty that he didn't know and never would – unless the boy was unfortunate enough to be caught again.

He passed the Temple of the Sacred Tooth Relic, now illuminated by lanterns along its perimeter wall. The scent of incense and lotus flowers hung in the air and made him remember his strange encounter with Cynthia that morning. He'd seen another side to her. An unhappy woman ravaged by guilt and sustained grief. How much effort it must take to put on her veneer of jollity when every day she must grieve the loss of her brother. He tried to imagine how he would feel if something like that happened to Winnie. It was unthinkable. And the loss must cut even deeper when it was a twin. Yet he couldn't help wondering why she had told him. Why had she revealed such intimate secrets about her brother's death to him – when they'd known each other such a short time?

Tomorrow, he would turn up at the tennis courts and treat her kindlier. He hoped that having dropped her guard with him, Cynthia wouldn't revert to her usual self-centred behaviour.

But whether she did or not, despite his sympathy for her, he realised he couldn't feel anything more than friendship for Cynthia. She was a beautiful, damaged creature, but Norton knew he would never love her.

SIXTEEN

Stella was going out of her mind with boredom. They'd been stuck in Kandy for five days already while her father recovered, and thanks to Ronald's insistence on the hunting expedition, they were now about to waste another two days. She decided to tackle her father.

He was sitting in a steamer chair on the terrace of the residence, his nose buried in a type-written manuscript.

'What are you reading, Papa?'

'A doctoral thesis sent to me by my opposite number at Cambridge. He thinks I'll find it of interest.'

'And do you?'

'Most certainly. It's about the Andaman Islanders. Absolutely fascinating. First-rate research. If only our friend Mr Blackstock could match this level of scholarship. There's a section here on ceremonial weeping that you'll find fascinating. If I'd read this while we were still in India, I might well have suggested we make a diversion to the Andaman Islands.' He chuckled, knowing full well he would never have dreamed of such a thing.

'Actually, it's about diversions that I wanted to speak to you,

Papa. We've already lost a lot of time since coming to Ceylon. We've completed no fieldwork here at all.'

'My fault, my dear. Entirely my fault. I didn't expect to be taken ill.'

Stella reached out and put her hand on her father's arm. She was still smarting about what he'd said to her on the train but had decided the best course to rebuilding trust was for her to exercise patience and continue to work on him, hoping he'd eventually come around to her point of view. 'It wasn't your fault at all, Papa. It was Ronald's idea to drag us all to the pearl fishery. And now this hunting trip will be more time wasted. I understand him wanting to find some entertainment since he has no interest in the purpose of our expedition, but he can do this without involving Mr Blackstock – and now he's also inveigled Miss Metcalfe into the trip, so her mother insists I go along too.'

Sir Michael pushed his spectacles back onto the bridge of his nose. He glanced down at the manuscript on his lap, clearly eager to return to it. 'Surely, you can sort this out amongst yourselves. After all, it's only a couple of days. By the time you get back from the hunting trip I shall be restored to full health, and we can make up any lost ground. I was thinking we could go straight to the area near Nuwara Eliya as soon as you return. We can use the town as our base while we conduct the field work on one or two plantations. Julian is kindly arranging with the various planters for us to spend time with their workforce. I'll make it clear to Ronald that, after this, no more distractions or side trips.'

Stella was at the point of snapping. Much as she loved her brother this was supposed to be a serious academic study, and he was reframing it as a latter-day Grand Tour. Unlike her father, she'd known exactly what would happen. Her brother's entire *raison d'être* was pleasure. But it seemed that where Sir Michael was concerned, Ronald would get a long leash and a high degree of tolerance. She, on the other hand, would not.

That evening after dinner, when Sir Michael had retired, Ronald dropped his bombshell. He and Cynthia Metcalfe had been chatting animatedly during pre-dinner drinks on the terrace, and now he made their plans clear.

'I say, everyone, Cynthia and I had a good old chinwag with that planter fellow, Snod MacDonald, at tennis this afternoon and he reckons that these days the hunting up in the highlands isn't up to much. The government has put a lot of restrictions on it and so much jungle has been given over to the tea plantations that it isn't at all like that chap Baker wrote about in his book. I suppose it was half a century ago after all. Before they'd even built the railway.' He glanced at Cynthia, who gave him an encouraging smile. 'Snod reckons if we really want a chance of bagging some beauties we need to go to the Southern Province. Near some place called Hambantota. There's a large area the government has reserved for game hunting down there and we can hire a native tracker to take us to all the best spots. Snod reckons it's the cat's whiskers.' He laughed. 'Literally! We're sure to bag a leopard or two there.'

Stella breathed a sigh of relief. If the MacDonalds were going along too, she would be reprieved from the obligation of joining the trip.

Portia Metcalfe seemed to read her mind. 'So Snod and Valerie are going to join you?'

Cynthia pushed out her bottom lip. 'They can't. Such a shame. Snod has the bosses from the tea company coming for a factory visit and Val has to be there to entertain them for dinner.' She smiled and looked at her father. 'But Daddy's going to get Norton Baxter to come with us.' Addressing Stella directly – and unusually – she added, 'Ronald says you'll be happy to come along, Miss Polegate. I do hope you will, as otherwise I know Mummy won't let me go.' The lower lip drooped forward again in an exaggerated pout, designed to ensure that should Stella refuse, she'd be cast as selfish.

Cynthia and Ronald had placed her in an intolerable position. How could she say no without appearing a spoilsport? What was worse, Norton Baxter was to join them on the trip, which would make her humiliation complete.

The day after the young boy's flogging, Norton accompanied Frobisher to an outlying village where the OA was to preside over the gathering of witness statements for a divorce hearing. Norton had already gathered something of the principles of matrimony operating among the Sinhalese, with polyandrous relationships relatively common, even though prohibited by the British for almost half a century. The previous week he had come across an instance of two brothers happily sharing a wife between them. The two men came to register the birth of a child and wanted both their names on the birth certificate.

On the way, Frobisher briefed him on the case they were to hear that day. 'Your job is to take notes not to ask questions. Leave that to me.' His tone was supercilious. 'There are several grounds for divorce under Kandyan law. Quite lax compared with Britain. There are the obvious ones such as desertion or adultery, but they can also ask for one by mutual consent. It gets tricky when one wants it and the other doesn't. Oh, and the criterion is straightforward adultery by the woman, whereas if the man is the adulterer, then for there to be grounds for divorce it has to be in combination with incest or extreme cruelty.'

Norton wondered whether Stella Polegate was aware of this example of the lack of parity between the sexes. Then he remembered her studies were related to Hindu Tamils not Buddhist Sinhalese. In any event, he was sure she'd find it interesting and filed it away in his head to discuss with her the next time they met.

'How do we decide whether to grant the divorce?' Norton wasn't sure the bookish bachelor was the best arbiter of matrimonial discord.

'Not *we*. I told you, Baxter. You're there to take notes.' He steepled his fingers under his nose. 'I will hear from each party. Then from the witnesses.'

'The witnesses?'

'Yes. That's the way it works here. A long procession of villagers and relatives offering their observations on the marriage.'

'How extraordinary.'

'Extraordinarily dull. As you can imagine, we have to listen to a lot of tedious trivia.'

'I don't suppose it's either tedious or trivial to them.'

'True. Unfortunately, they see it as a matter of life or death. Sometimes I'm tempted to just toss a coin. But as the colonial power, it's our responsibility so I tell myself to get on with it.'

He opened his attaché case and took out a file. 'There are two forms of Kandyan marriage. Marriage in *binna* where the husband lives in the wife's family house, and marriage in *diga* where the wife lives in the husband's home, and her dowry is incorporated into his estate, and she cannot inherit. A *binna* wife remains part of her own family and can inherit from her parents. Husbands in *binna* have no right to inherit their wives' estates. It's made clear at the marriage registration which one it is.'

'So which do we have today?' asked Norton.

'A marriage in *binna* where the wife now wishes to divorce and the husband is objecting.'

'Does it mean that if the divorce is granted, he's thrown out of the matrimonial home?'

'Probably. That's what we have to determine. Of course,

normally this would be dealt with by one of the judicial staff. But the district magistrate is on home leave.' Frobisher looked thoughtful. 'Look, Baxter, I might as well do you a favour and tell you. If you want to get ahead, stay in the administrative branch of the service and don't let them push you into a judicial post. The highflyers get the administrative positions. What's more, some of the men on the judicial side are perhaps... how should I put this?... less of gentlemen. Don't need to spell it out for you. You know what I mean. The chap who's on leave, Clitheroe, is a case in point. He speaks with a North Country accent. Not *one of us.*'

Norton's aversion to Frobisher was getting deeper every day. He wondered if this was also the root cause of Cynthia Metcalfe's dislike of Paul Carberry, who also had a North Country accent.

'Where was I?' Frobisher consulted the case file again. 'As I expected. It's a cross-cousin marriage. They're the most frequent. It's between cousins where they're the children of a brother and sister.'

Norton gasped. 'Incest?'

'Good Lord, no. The offspring of a brother and his wife and his sister and her husband. First cousins. Oddly, they regard this as the most desirable type of marriage, yet the children from the respective marriages of two brothers or two sisters is regarded as incestuous. It's bizarre. But not for me to question the twisted logic of the natives.'

At this point, Frobisher went off into a lengthy discourse about the historical origins of cross-cousin marriages, based on the example of the Buddha himself. Had anyone other than Frobisher been conveying this, Norton would have been riveted. As it was, he couldn't wait to reach their destination. He made a mental note to find out more about matrimonial customs from Bhante Vimal at his next Sinhala lesson.

The deposition of witnesses took most of the day. It taxed

Norton's knowledge of Sinhala to the limit – but he was able to follow the gist of what was said. The husband of the marriage was accused by his wife of adultery and failure to provide for the family, preferring to spend his days lying about doing nothing but drink *arack*. This was strenuously denied by the husband. A succession of witnesses attested to the fact that the man was lazy and often drunk, countered by two of the man's brothers, his father and a friend who all maintained he was a good and dutiful husband. Most of the neighbours and members of the wife's family cited numerous negative examples of the young man's behaviour.

When all the witnesses had been heard, Frobisher adjourned the proceedings to consider his decision. 'Well, it's straightforward. No incest and no extreme cruelty. The marriage will stand.'

Norton, who had found the wife's testimony far more convincing than her husband's, thought his colleague wasn't taking full account of the evidence. 'Surely the fact that the husband is drunk all the time and fails to provide for the family is additional grounds.'

Frobisher's eyes narrowed. 'Are you questioning my judgement, Baxter? I told you, you're here to take notes not cast an opinion. Idleness and drunkenness do not constitute extreme cruelty. That will be my ruling. These are their laws. My job is to apply them. Tell the two parties they can come back in for the verdict.'

Norton was about to protest but thought better of it.

The husband was jubilant but the woman looked devastated when told the divorce petition had failed. She was swept away on a tide of wailing relatives. Norton couldn't help but think that justice had not been served by Frobisher's literal interpretation.

They returned to Kandy in silence. Frobisher, as usual, was reading and Norton was frustrated at how the day had gone.

The following morning, he was due to join the hunting party. While he was eager to see more of the island, he had no desire to join the hunt. He imagined Stella Polegate was similarly vexed.

It had been bad enough when Ronald Polegate's hunting party had been in the locality. It would have meant missing a day's work, two at the most – but now Julian Metcalfe had informed him the trip would be to the southern part of the island, to a completely different province.

'I hoped the GA down there could spare his OA to accompany them, but they've got a bad outbreak of rinderpest so he's out going from village to village trying to get them to isolate and enclose their cattle.'

Unable to curb his curiosity despite his fury at being asked to nursemaid Cynthia and the Polegate party, Norton asked what rinderpest was.

'A nasty cattle disease. Leads to a dashed awful death. The poor cows get their faces eaten away by maggots.'

Norton wished he hadn't asked. 'But, sir, I've barely had time to make any inroads into the backlog of land registrations you asked me to sort out.'

'That can wait.'

He couldn't help but wonder what possible justification there was for a pleasure trip for the GA's daughter and her friends taking precedence over the normal duties of the provincial office. But he knew better than to object.

'How many will be on the trip, sir?'

Julian Metcalfe thought for a moment. 'Five including yourself. Cynthia, the Polegate siblings and that fellow who's with them. What's his name? – Blackstow.'

'Blackstock, I believe, sir.'

'Whatever.'

'How long will I be away?'

Julian Metcalfe waved a hand dismissively. 'No idea. Talk to Frobisher. And probably my daughter.'

When Norton emerged from the GA's office it was apparent that Frobisher had already been briefed.

'So, you get to skive off work to go hunting. You really have wormed your way into the boss's good books, Baxter. Ten out of ten.'

'If you'd like to go instead, you're welcome. I'd rather get on with my work.'

Frobisher eyed him over the rim of his spectacles and gave an awkward laugh. 'Me? Hunting? You've got to be joking. Besides, the charming Cynthia has requested your presence. Otherwise, the GA would never countenance you being out of the office on a jolly.'

'Believe me, as far as I'm concerned it will not be a jolly. Any more than witnessing that flogging was.'

Frobisher sniffed but said nothing. Norton couldn't help thinking that for the OA it had probably been an excellent morning's entertainment.

Picking up a slip of paper, Frobisher signed his name then stamped it with a rubber stamp and handed it to Norton. 'Here you are. Six days' leave plus the two days of the weekend which are on your own time.' He smiled. 'Sorry.'

Norton was sure he was not. 'Why so long? It was to be just one or two days.'

'You're going to the Southern Province.'

Norton's jaw dropped.

At least the silver lining to this cloud was that Stella Polegate would be on the trip. Norton wondered whether she was a keen hunter, then immediately dismissed that possibility. He barely knew her, yet he was sure that she welcomed the prospect of this hunt as little as he did.

SEVENTEEN

On the way south, they travelled the first leg by train before descending the steep escarpment to the coastal plain by road. The journey would take two full days. The return trip was to follow a different route – skirting the coastline by train from Matara via Galle and Colombo and thence on to Kandy.

Norton sat alone on the train, across the aisle from the rest of the party. Cynthia had called out to him to join her and the two men, which would have left Stella Polegate to sit on her own. Naturally he had taken the seat beside Stella, only for Cynthia to insist that Stella move across to join them. Stella had protested that she was perfectly happy, but Cynthia, narrowing her eyes at Norton and taking Stella by the hand, drew her across the aisle to join the others. 'You don't want to sit with Norton. He plans to do his boring old paperwork. Come and join us in a game of cards.'

To Norton's dismay, Stella Polegate complied. Had he over-stepped the mark when they'd walked round the lake? He'd practically begged her not to marry the Blackstock chap. It had probably scared the living daylights out of her – since it was none of his business. He cursed his own intemperate behaviour. Anxious not to upset her further, he avoided looking at her for the entire journey and buried his nose in his paperwork.

Surreptitiously, he listened to the conversation across the aisle. It was mostly related to the card game, with Stella contributing next to nothing. Norton was convinced she welcomed this hunting excursion as little as he did.

Cynthia held court, her laughter filling the first-class carriage as she flirted with both Blackstock and Ronald Polegate. This was clearly intended as a dig at Norton for refusing the invitation to join them. Today there was no trace of the tearful girl who had witnessed her twin brother drowning. For a moment, Norton wondered whether the story had been fabricated, then felt ashamed – her grief had been tangible and could not have been faked. But why had she shared the story with him – even rising early and seeking him out to tell him? One thing was clear, women were a complete mystery.

It was hot and airless as they bumped down the mountainside in the bullock carts. Norton found himself riding with Gordon Blackstock, while Cynthia travelled with the Polegates.

Norton took the opportunity to study the anthropology student. The man was stocky with big ears and hair that was plastered to his head by an over-enthusiastic application of brilliantine, now reinforced by sweat. He was smoking a noxious-smelling pipe, which at least was keeping the insects at bay.

He leaned forward and fixed his gaze on Norton. 'You're not a hunting man, Mr Baxter? Not even to hounds?'

'Strictly a city dweller. You?'

'I've ridden out with the Quorn,' Blackstock said, puffing out his chest. 'Didn't take to it. Horses aren't my thing.'

'So only Mr Polegate is a keen hunter?' Norton was feeling

increasingly disgruntled about being dragged more than one-hundred-and-fifty miles to appease a whim of Ronald Polegate's.

Blackstock smiled. 'Actually, no. Since horses aren't involved, I too am relishing the prospect of game hunting and bagging a leopard. A true predator. No comparison with foxes. They're not even game, they're vermin.' He sucked on his pipe. 'How do you feel about sleeping under canvas in the jungle, Mr Baxter?'

'It wouldn't be my choice of a way to spend the night.'

'Come on, old boy, don't tell me you're windy. Scared a leopard might get you?' He guffawed, then glanced behind at the other carriage. 'You don't want the little ladies to know you're chicken.'

Norton stiffened. Not just because his courage was being called into question. He could imagine Stella's reaction to being described as a little lady. Reflexively his fingers curled into two tight fists. 'Firstly, Miss Polegate and Miss Metcalfe deserve to be addressed more respectfully than that, and secondly, the fact that I wouldn't *choose* to sleep in a tent doesn't mean I'm afraid of it.'

Blackstock put his hands up in the classic gesture of surrender. 'All right, all right! Steady on. No offence intended to you and certainly not to Miss Polegate or Miss Metcalfe.' He turned to look back at the carriage behind. 'Miss Polegate knows the deep admiration I have for her.'

Norton shivered. So Blackstock continued to nurture expectations where Stella was concerned. Determined to cut him off before he went further, Norton said, 'Perhaps I'm being presumptuous, but I have the sense that the prospect of hunting wild animals is as unappealing to Miss Polegate as it is to me.'

Blackstock's eyes narrowed. 'I'm afraid you *are* being rather presumptuous, Mr Baxter. Although you couldn't be expected to know.' He smirked at Norton and drew on his pipe. 'Just between you and me, Miss Polegate and I will be joined in matrimony once we return to England. Our engagement is still unofficial, but I expect that we will announce it before we leave Kandy next week.'

The words were a punch in the stomach. Norton twisted round in his seat and looked back to where Stella was sitting beside Cynthia, opposite her brother. Their eyes met and she looked away immediately. He turned back. Swallowed. Took a deep breath. 'I didn't know. Miss Polegate gave no indication of your plans.' Was Blackstock expecting him to proffer congratulations? 'I had understood that she intended to apply to Cambridge.'

'That won't happen. What nonsense,' Blackstock scoffed. 'Women at university? What's the point? Where will it all end? Votes for women? Degrees for women? Anyone would think they deserve to be treated like men.'

'Well, don't they?'

The doctoral student took his pipe out of his mouth and banged it against the outside of the open cart to empty the bowl. 'For a start, it's clear the fairer sex is not cut out for the rigours of academic study. It affects their health. They're simply not constitutionally adapted for it. There's scientific evidence.' Seeing Norton was about to disagree, he added, 'Good grief, don't tell me you're one of those Fabian socialist wallahs? A supporter of Votes for Women?'

Norton wanted nothing more than to be outside this vehicle and away from this obnoxious man. He had no wish to reveal his political leanings and it was none of Blackstock's business. 'As a servant of the Crown, I claim no political views. And I'm not comfortable discussing Miss Polegate in her absence.'

Blackstock visibly bristled. 'Quite.'

They passed the rest of the journey in silence. Norton

fumed. It was unbearable to think of Stella Polegate marrying this Neanderthal.

The local men who drove the bullock carts set up the tents for the overnight stop in a clearing close to the road. It was agreed that the party would make an early start in the morning to reach Tissamaharama by nightfall. There they would establish their base for the two or three days of hunting.

Everyone agreed to retire early but Norton struggled to sleep. The silence of the scrub jungle was punctuated by heavy snoring from the adjacent tent which Blackstock shared with Ronald Polegate. Norton needed to stretch his legs after hours in the cramped bullock cart. Outside the tent, two of the native servants were talking in low whispers as they sat in front of a campfire, kept burning to keep animals at bay. The men didn't notice him, and he walked over to the edge of the clearing. It would be wise to remain within sight of the fire as he had no wish to get lost in the unfamiliar terrain.

The night sky was clouded, and it took a few moments for his sight to adjust to the dark. He didn't see Stella until she spoke to him.

'Have you been avoiding me, Mr Baxter? I want to apologise.'

Norton's heart skipped a beat – partly as she'd made him jump, but also at being near to her at last. 'Apologise? For what?'

'I was indiscreet when we walked by the lake. I put you in an awkward position. It was wrong of me to presume on our brief acquaintance. Forgive me.'

A wave of relief and gratitude swept over him. 'On the contrary, Miss Polegate. It is I who should apologise for rushing off rather than joining you all for drinks. I hope you didn't think it was anything to do with you. I thoroughly enjoyed our walk and would have happily prolonged it. But I needed to study and knew if I diverted to the Queen's it wouldn't happen.'

'I enjoyed it too.' As she spoke, the clouds shifted, and her face was lit by moonlight.

'That's better,' he said. 'I can see you now. I presume, like me, you couldn't sleep?'

'Not a wink.' She smiled at him, and he relaxed. 'I have the feeling you're not looking forward to hunting?'

'Is it that obvious?'

'No. You're the soul of discretion, but I confess I'm dreading the whole enterprise too and I'm mortified that my brother is the architect of our misery.'

'With not a little encouragement from Miss Metcalfe.'

Stella smiled. 'We must find some other diversion while our friends are indulging their blood lust. Any ideas what?'

Norton tilted his head on one side and thought. 'We could chase butterflies, listen to birdsong, or collect wood for the campfire.'

Just as he hoped, she chuckled. 'As long as no one puts a gun in my hands and tells me to shoot. The very idea of putting animals to death for sport is anathema. But Ronald has been reading a book by that chap Samuel Baker – you know – the explorer who claimed he'd traced the source of the Nile to Lake Albert. For some reason the book has brought out a blood lust in my brother and he wants to follow in Baker's footsteps.' She sighed. 'It's totally derailed the progress of our research, but my father seems incapable of saying no to him. Especially with Gordon egging Ronald on.'

Norton hadn't intended to raise the subject of Blackstock's boast about their forthcoming nuptials, but he had to satisfy his conviction that the man was fabricating the story. 'Mr Blackstock told me this afternoon that you and he will be announcing your engagement soon after we return to Kandy.'

He had expected her to deny it, but instead she frowned.

'We're not engaged,' she snapped, then gave a sigh. 'But it may be the only option if I want to pursue my studies, albeit vicariously.'

'I see.' The blood was pounding inside his head.

'Do you? Do you really see?' Her voice sounded bitter.

'But... I thought you were set on going to university. Isn't there some way for you to do so?'

'I had hoped to use my small trust fund, but Papa says it's pointless since no one will take my research seriously if it's published under my own name. And anyway, Ronald has to sign off on my use of the funds until I'm married, when oversight will fall to my husband. Ronald has made it clear that he'll block my using the money to pursue my studies. He's very keen on me marrying Gordon.'

Norton seethed at the thought of Ronald – who struck him as a layabout – controlling the life of his older sister. 'There has to be a way.' For a moment he was tempted to offer to marry her himself so he could ensure she had access to her money. But that would not resolve the problem, as it would be unlikely she'd be permitted to study at Newnham or Girton as a married woman. He looked at her, at the sadness in those beautiful intelligent eyes. 'I'd like to help you. Perhaps I could talk to your brother. Plead your case.'

She shook her head. 'Why would Ronald listen to you? I can tell you now, he wouldn't.'

'How can he let you be handed over to that dreadful man?' He clenched his fist inside his pocket. Turning back to look at her, he said, 'After spending this afternoon in Blackstock's company it was enough to convince me that you can't possibly marry him. Talking to him I was reminded of Shakespeare's Coriolanus – "*More of your conversation would infect my brain.*"'

Stella roared with laughter, then just as quickly frowned. 'You've summed him up perfectly. But it changes nothing.'

Norton was about to respond but was cut short by the sudden arrival of the man they were talking about.

Blackstock's scowl made him appear even uglier than usual. 'What's going on? I say, Baxter, are you trying to compromise Miss Polegate? What kind of cad are you?'

Norton would have liked to punch him, but instead said, 'It seems neither Miss Polegate nor I could sleep. Thanks to someone's snoring so loudly that it could have been heard in Kandy.'

'I'm going back to bed before we wake everyone up.' Stella moved away before Blackstock could stop her.

When she'd gone, Blackstock moved closer to Norton, thrusting his chin out. 'Look, Baxter, I don't know what your game is, but I thought I'd made it clear today that Miss Polegate and I are getting married.'

'Yes, Mr Blackstock. You made it very clear. That doesn't make it true.' Without waiting for Blackstock to respond, Norton went back to his tent.

Inside, he lay in the darkness staring unseeing at the canvas roof. If he'd had any doubts before, he had none now. He was head over heels in love with Stella Polegate and he wasn't going to let her marry Gordon Blackstock.

It was his first experience in the jungle. As Norton followed the Sinhalese tracker, he told himself it would be his last as well. The trees were too sparse to shield them from the harshest rays of the sun; the heat and humidity were suffocating; sweat blinded his eyes; his shirt was plastered to his body and chafed against his damp clammy skin. A few feet away, he could see Ronald Polegate and Cynthia, Ronald with his rifle across one shoulder, while Cynthia's was carried by one of the bearers. Somewhere behind were Blackstock and Stella, the former evident by the noise he was making as he crashed through the undergrowth. Norton thought it likely that any wild animal within a mile of them would have fled.

Geethan, the native tracker, lithe as a cat, moved rapidly, his footsteps making no sound, so Blackstock seemed like a lumbering bear in comparison. Without the tracker to guide the way, they would be lost amidst the thick thorny scrub. It appeared impenetrable but somehow the tracker always knew exactly where there was a passable pathway. The man had grown up surrounded by this forest so it must be as familiar to him as the gravel walks of his local park were to Norton.

Geethan turned and put up his hand to signal a halt. Around them, the jungle was silent. It wasn't dense as a rain-forest but consisted mainly of thick thorny scrub with a mixture of saplings and small trees and the occasional tall one rising above them. Norton listened, straining to discern what had caused the man to stop, but heard nothing.

After a few moments, Geethan signalled to them all to follow and they moved forward slowly until they arrived in a clearing surrounded by tall trees, where a solid rock face rose up above them between the trees and thorn bushes. There was a terrible stench about the place and Norton looked around for its source. Eventually he realised it came from the dark purple flowers hanging from a tree. The flowers, dangling in panicles, were as beautiful as their smell was foetid. He covered his mouth and moved away towards the unperfumed shelter of a banyan tree. As the others realised the source of the odour, they followed suit. Geethan however appeared insensible to the stink.

The tracker put a finger to his lips and pointed at the top of the rock face. At first Norton could see nothing. He strained his eyes trying to make out what was the source of the tracker's attention in the gloom of the forest canopy.

And then he saw the beast. The leopard was lying stretched out on the rock surface in front of what appeared to be a cave.

The creature was about nine feet long from nose to tail, its breast and legs speckled with black spots and the bulk of its taut muscular body covered in black rings with brown centres. Its eyes were the colour of amber. Norton watched intently as Geethan kept one hand raised to indicate they should all wait. Beside him he sensed Stella, her gaze fixed on the beautiful animal.

A shot rang out, wide of the target, exploding against the surface of the rock sending birds skywards, and previously invisible monkeys scrambling higher into the leaf canopy, screeching a chorus of terror.

Of the leopard there was no sign.

'Sir,' said Geethan. 'I tell you not to fire until I give signal.'

Ronald shrugged. 'Had to seize the moment.'

'But you didn't. Did you?' Stella's voice was icy. 'You missed and it got away. I'm jolly glad it did too.' She looked at her brother with an expression that bordered on contempt.

'It's gone inside the cave,' said Cynthia. 'If we're patient it will eventually come out and you can have another crack at it.'

Geethan shook his head. 'It won't come out. Not till we are gone.'

'Maybe we can smoke it out,' said Blackstock. 'We could light a fire on that ledge and drive it out of the cave.'

Norton had never heard anything so stupid. He exchanged glances with Stella, who clearly thought so too.

Cynthia was the one who responded. 'Are you volunteering to climb up there and do it?'

'Perhaps not.' Blackstock pointed at Geethan. 'But this chap could.'

There was a snort of disgust from Stella. 'I have a better idea,' she said. 'We do exactly as Geethan says, keep quiet and let him do his job.'

Norton smiled and nodded. 'Well said, Miss Polegate.'

Blackstock was visibly seething. He scowled at the tracker then at Norton.

Geethan paid him no attention but looked at Stella with gratitude. 'River is nearby. We go there. Elephants, deer, maybe crocodiles. Please, no shooting until I give signal.'

Based on Ronald's performance so far, it was looking unlikely he'd manage to hit anything, but Norton remembered Carberry saying that lots of the trackers positioned themselves close to prospective hunters and shot at the same time to guarantee the result, declaring that the European was the one who had hit the target. He imagined this dishonesty earned them a nice tip at the end of the hunt.

It started raining as soon as they moved on through the jungle. The trees were denser than they'd been until now so that often there didn't appear to be a track to follow, but Geethan found the way through for them. They moved through wet undergrowth, grateful for the leech gaiters they had been kitted out with.

Norton had slipped back behind the others. Ronald and Blackstock were now immediately behind the tracker, with Stella and Cynthia following. Four native bearers brought up the rear behind Norton.

Noticing him, Stella slowed slightly and as the track widened, Norton was able to walk alongside her. They talked, their voices low and muffled by the rain.

'This is my first experience of a hunt, and I hope it will be my last,' she said.

'Me too. Animals are far more beautiful alive than stuffed and hung on walls as trophies.' He gave her a wry smile. 'How did we get dragged into this?'

She shook her head, returning his smile. Norton loved the way her whole face changed when she smiled, grateful that she appeared to do it rarely and mostly at him. Might she feel something for him too? She had given him little cause for hope. Yet he sensed she sought his company too.

He reflected how extraordinary the effect she had on him was. He wanted to be near to her whenever possible. Never before had a woman exerted such a pull over him – and the irony was that she seemed completely unaware of it.

As they trudged through the undergrowth, they talked. She asked him about his years at Cambridge, eager to hear how he'd spent his time outside lectures and tutorials. She listened intently, constantly prompting him with more questions.

He told her about his sister, Winnie, and how much he missed her. 'Winnie's a very practical girl. She'd never entertain the idea of academic study. She loves to read, go for long walks and is partial to pranks and parlour games.' He shook his head. 'She was at boarding school for a while but managed to get herself expelled after an episode involving itching powder and the deputy headmistress.'

'Not like you at all then?' Stella laughed and raised her eyebrows. 'You seem far too serious for that kind of thing.'

'Maybe I was just better at not getting caught!' He gave a shrug. 'We are very different, but we still have much in common. I love reading and enjoy nothing more than a long hike – and no matter my own inclinations, my dear sister won't let me get away with trying to sit out a game of charades.'

Stella rested her hand on his arm for a moment. He felt a shiver of electricity run through him. 'You must miss her dreadfully,' she said, softly. 'She sounds great fun.'

'You may get to meet her as she's coming to Ceylon soon.'

'I'd like that very much.'

Eventually he was able to switch the subject to her. But Stella was reluctant to say much about herself. 'You don't want to hear about my dull life. I may live in the heart of Oxford, surrounded by students, but I'm an outsider, an interloper, there solely by dint of my father's position.'

'Did he foster your interest in anthropology?'

'Not really. He's never encouraged it, tending to treat me simply as his willing scribe. On the other hand, he's always tried to foster an interest in the subject in Ronald – sadly a futile effort.' She brushed away an insect from her cheek. 'But since we've been here in the East, he's treated me more as he might one of his students – actually taking time to explain his thinking, sometimes even seeking my views.'

'Yet he doesn't want you to study the subject in your own right?'

'Papa is rather old fashioned.' Her mouth formed a smile, but her eyes were sad. 'My mother had to give up her career when they married, and he expects the same of me.'

'That's hardly an unusual view. Very few women continue their chosen path after marriage.'

'True. But Mama was a professional opera singer. Many singers go on performing after they marry. But Papa wouldn't countenance it.'

'Was she aware that would be the case before they married?'

Stella looked thoughtful. 'I don't know for sure, but I imagine he made his wishes clear. All she told me was that she had sacrificed everything for love.'

Norton looked at her. 'Then I hope she felt the sacrifice was worthwhile.'

Stella said nothing but her lips moved into a tight downward line.

At that moment Cynthia turned and called to them, 'Hurry up, you two slowcoaches.'

Blackstock, hearing her, looked round and, next thing, he moved back to join them, blocking Norton's path so Stella was forced to walk beside him. Norton, fuming, followed behind.

After tramping along getting damp from dripping overhead branches, the party was looking increasingly dishevelled. Eventually they emerged on the bank of a dirty slow-moving river. It was lined by a ribbon of tall trees with scrub jungle everywhere else. Within the brown waters of the river, Norton could see the silvery flash of scales and watched transfixed as a kingfisher swooped down and caught a fish.

Even though most of the animals drank at dawn or in the evening, the hunting party was rewarded by the sight of a group of sambar deer about two hundred yards away. This time, Ronald was given a signal by Geethan. His shot rang out and one of the deer stumbled and half fell into the water, scrambling back onto its feet again. Blood ran down its rear flank. Norton and Stella exchanged glances.

'Not dead. Must finish or die in pain,' said Geethan.

Ronald was exultant. 'But I got it, didn't I?' Geethan threw him a look of disgust then moved off along the bank. A moment later another shot rang out and the beautiful creature crumpled to its knees then rolled over dead.

'You ready, Cynthia?' Ronald had evidently moved on to a less formal footing with Miss Metcalfe.

'All set!' she replied. She nodded to one of the bearers, who opened the haversack he was carrying and produced a camera and tripod for her and helped to set it up.

Norton watched, dumbfounded, as Ronald, gun over his shoulder, posed proudly with one foot on the flank of the dead animal.

Stella's voice was quiet but angry as she materialised beside Norton. 'Sometimes I am deeply ashamed of my brother.'

By the time they returned to their campsite near Tissama-harama, they were all footsore and very damp. The day's haul consisted of that first sambar deer and a couple of boars, the latter both shot, unassisted, by Cynthia.

Lying in his tent that night, Norton was in turmoil. The more time he spent in Stella's company the more he was convinced he wanted to marry her. Not just to rescue her from an unthink-able fate with Gordon Blackstock, but because he loved her and wanted to spend his life with her. He told himself it shouldn't be possible to fall in love in such a brief time, but he had never been more certain of anything.

Yet how could he marry her? He had no money to support a wife. He was on the lowest rung of the ladder and stuck here in Ceylon when she wanted to be in England – at best studying in her own right at Cambridge or at worst vicariously in Oxford. Even if he had the means to marry her, how would it enable her to follow her dream? It was out of the question for a married woman. He went round and round in circles desperately trying to think of a way but could find none.

From their conversation the previous night, it seemed to Norton that Stella was starting to accept defeat. Marrying Blackstock, however unpalatable, would allow some proximity to the academic world she wanted to remain part of. If Norton truly loved her, he ought not to begrudge her that. But as he tried to reconcile himself to the prospect, the contemptuous words of Blackstock in the bullock cart came back to him. How could he let her throw herself on that man's mercy?

Trudging through the damp jungle, he decided he had to find an opportunity to speak to Stella in private, rather than the snatched conversations as they walked. But Blackstock was always there to thwart him. If he had time to talk with her prop-erly, he'd suggest she try to persuade her father to allow the status quo to endure. Why did it take marriage to Stella for Blackstock to earn his doctorate? Surely, they could continue as now until the man got his degree and Sir Michael secured the bursary. There was no reason for the marriage to make either of those things possible. Norton had barely exchanged more than a few sentences with the professor, but he had seemed a sensible, down-to-earth man. He had to encourage Stella to talk to him again.

Assuming she succeeded in this, it still wouldn't give Norton what he wanted himself – to marry Stella and spend the rest of his life with her. But it would buy him time and save her from Blackstock. If she returned to Oxford and remained single, one day when he was able to offer her a future he could find her again. In the meantime, he'd know she was able to continue to work in her chosen field – albeit unacknowledged and unrecognised. It wasn't entirely satisfactory, but it was better than the alternative.

EIGHTEEN

Stella struggled to think of a single day in her life that had been as miserable as the three they'd spent in the southern jungle. If she never again went anywhere near a hunting expedition it would be too soon. Day after day of wading through scratchy undergrowth, having to watch as her brother bungled his shots while Geethan unobtrusively hit the target and allowed Ronald to claim the kill. The subterfuge was so obvious, yet her brother was triumphalist – an overgrown child.

Ronald claimed to have killed a buffalo. He removed the horns as trophies, while the carcass was abandoned for the jackals to pick over. He had wanted to have it skinned but despite the natural plenitude of salt in Ceylon, there was none available for the curing process, salt being strictly controlled by the British government. They operated a scarcity policy to keep prices of this essential commodity artificially high.

Norton didn't shoot at all. Blackstock, like Ronald, failed to hit anything himself, while Cynthia proved to be the best shot, killing several deer and a pair of wild boars.

For Stella, the only redeeming feature was glimpsing the animals that got away, including another leopard. They came upon a small herd of elephants but on Geethan's advice chose not to take a pot at them, as they included a couple of babies, and the tracker warned them that the mothers would charge if they sensed danger. The highlight for Stella was entering a clearing and coming upon a dozen screaming peacocks, tails open as they grazed in the long grass.

Hunting over, they travelled from Tissamaharama via the district capital, Hambantota, towards Matara where they were to spend their last night in a guest house before taking the train. Outside Hambantota they passed close to the salt pans along the coast near the town – the only source of naturally formed salt in the country. Whilst the rest of the party went to look at them, Stella told Blackstock she wanted to speak to him privately. She couldn't put it off any longer, even though she felt sick to the pit of her stomach at the prospect.

They walked along the beach. Such a picture-perfect setting was too beautiful for a conversation that filled Stella with dread. The ocean was turquoise, topped with white crested waves which crashed thunderously onto a sandy beach fringed by coconut palms. A boy and his father were casting nets into the sea, and a colony of white egrets clustered in the branches of a fig tree. As they walked along the shore, Stella couldn't help wishing she was experiencing this idyllic scenery with anyone other than Gordon Blackstock.

'Have you given further consideration to my proposal, Stella?'

She hated him calling her by her first name. It was an intimacy taken rather than offered. But it was important to handle the conversation with tact. She took a few slow breaths then turned to face him.

'If I am to accept your offer there will be conditions attached.' She saw his eyebrows draw closer and his eyes narrowed. Stella told herself not to lose her nerve now and not to be bullied into anything. 'It's fair to say that any marriage between us would have to be a mutually beneficial one. Wouldn't you agree?'

He looked uncomfortable but gave a cautious nod.

'I think we would be best advised to view it as a business arrangement. May I be frank?'

He nodded again.

'Marriage between us could offer me the opportunity to continue my studies. It would offer you...' She hesitated – how could she say it would give him access to her brain? 'Offer you... offer us both a way to carry on my father's legacy in anthropological research.' She looked down at the sand. 'As such, I am prepared to accept your offer if we agree that it will be a marriage of minds rather than a conventional marriage. The French even have a term for it – they call it *un mariage blanc*.' She struggled to get the words out. Why was this so much harder than when she had rehearsed it in her head? 'I have no wish for children and—'

'Stop!' Blackstock grabbed her by the arm. 'What nonsense is this? Are you suggesting that the marriage isn't consummated?'

She felt the blood rush to her cheeks. 'I suppose I am. Yes, I am. That way, we will each—'

'Enough! This is intolerable.' He dropped his hold of her. 'Do you seriously think I will settle for that? That I will accept a childless marriage without marital congress? I intend to have children. The Blackstock name must endure. No, no. What kind of foolish nonsense is this? What sort of man would agree to his wife denying him his conjugal rights? Ours will be a normal marriage in every sense, and you will be a dutiful wife and will bear me children. Preferably lots of them.'

Stella blanched. She'd been naive and foolish to try. 'Then I am afraid I must repeat what I said when you first proposed. I cannot marry you, Mr Blackstock, on any terms but those I have just set out. If you wish for children, then you must look elsewhere for a wife whose aspirations match yours. I intend to dedicate my life to study.' She paused, desperately searching for some conciliatory words to add. 'I am sure a man such as you will have no trouble finding a suitable spouse.'

His lip curled and he thrust his chin out, then grasping both her wrists he pushed his face up close to hers, his breath laced with pipe smoke. A fine spray of spittle spattered her cheek as he spoke. 'You must think me a fool, Stella. But you're the fool – a silly foolish girl. You've been indulged by Sir Michael for long enough. Marriage will be good for you. Once my tenure is secured, and you accept your natural role as a wife and a mother, I will consent to you supporting my research in the manner you do now for your father.' He was still holding her wrists and his grip tightened.

'Let me go. Please. You're hurting me.'

He dropped his hold and softened his voice. 'You need to lose this silly schoolgirl fantasy and grow up. It's time to settle down and become a dutiful wife.'

'Never!' She almost spat the word out. Then unable to bear another moment alone with him, she hurried back to the road where she saw the other members of their party approaching. Relieved, she went to meet them, with Blackstock following close behind.

Norton Baxter saw at once that something was wrong. He fell into step beside her and several paces behind Cynthia and Ronald as they approached the bullock carts waiting to transport them to the nearby rest house. 'Is everything all right?' he asked, his eyes full of concern.

Stella wanted to tell him what had happened but knew it would enrage Blackstock, so she smiled and said it was. There was something comforting and reassuring about Norton Baxter's presence that made her feel safe from the aggression of Blackstock. Stella ran her fingers over her wrists where they smarted still from his iron grip. She glanced sideways at Norton, whose eyes reflected kindness, but the firmness of his jaw gave her the impression of a quiet strength. She would have liked to carry on walking beside him, free to talk and apart from the rest of the party, but a hundred yards ahead of them the others were climbing into the bullock cart.

Norton paused and looked back over the sandy palm-fringed beach to the vast ocean. 'Apparently, if you set sail due south from here, you'll travel all the way to Antarctica without once meeting any land.'

Stella imagined being on a boat drifting across those empty oceans. It ought to feel a frightening prospect but at this moment it sounded alluring.

She let Norton help her up into the cart, relieved when he clambered in behind her. Gordon Blackstock got in too, sitting on her other side. To her relief the trip was occupied by Norton answering her questions about the salt pans, while she feigned interest and Blackstock silently fumed.

They stopped for a short break and Stella avoided looking at Blackstock during the rest of the journey. He made his anger evident by walking alone ahead of the carts and deigning to speak only to Ronald, who seemed to be oblivious to the tension between his sister and his friend.

She was relieved to have made her position clear to Black-stock. Sir Michael and the dean would have to find another way to secure a grant of money for the college. Now the priority must be to complete the research that was the purpose of their expedition to Ceylon.

Blackstock would have to accept her refusal. She knew he had no romantic feelings for her so her rejection could hardly be the source of heartache for him. It would take only the passage of time to restore his injured pride.

It was late evening, two days after leaving Hambantota when, exhausted, they arrived at Matara. As they were the only occupants in the rest house, Stella was grateful she wouldn't have to share a room with Cynthia.

After eating, Stella elected to retire early when Blackstock and her brother produced a bottle of whisky and gave the impression they wanted to spend the last night of the trip carousing. Cynthia Metcalfe tried to persuade Stella to stay up a while longer, but Stella was obdurate. She would have liked to talk with Norton Baxter but knew it would only antagonise Blackstock and she was weary of conflict.

As soon as her head hit the pillow, she fell asleep.

Stella was trapped, unable to free herself from a heavy weight that bore down upon her. A tree? No – some kind of creature. An animal. Crushing her under its weight, hurting her. Around her was darkness. The jungle?

Her dream was disturbing. A nightmare.

Normally, at this point she would wake up and gasp in relief. But this nightmare wasn't stopping. The weight was real. Substantial. Her eyes wide open, trying to adjust to the pitch dark of the shuttered bedroom. *What is the smell?* Grainy, grassy, woody – but sharp, biting. Whisky. The sensation of warm breath on her face.

Panic surged. *No. No. No. This must not happen.*

His weight prevented her moving. Pinning her down. Squashing the breath out of her. Smell of whisky mixed with stale sweat. Hands. Touching her. Fingers. Grasping. Probing. Under her nightdress. Fumbling. Rough. Invasive.

She tried to cry out. To scream. No sound. That always happens in dreams. Legs don't move when you try to run.

She tried again. But this was no dream. A hand hot against her mouth, blocking her screams. *Can't breathe. Stop. Stop. Stop.*

Fingers down there touching her, forcing her legs apart.

Rasp of fingernails against tender skin. Then pain ripped through her, tearing her apart. She must surely die. Horrible. Thrusting. Pounding. Grunting. Like an animal. Hurting, hurting, hurting. *Let it end. Let me die. Dear God, make it stop.*

Just when she thought she could bear no more, there was a groan. The weight eased. A warm stickiness spread between her legs.

Stella wanted to cry but the tears wouldn't come. She lay motionless, unable to comprehend what had just happened.

Gordon Blackstock shifted his bulk sideways. He sighed a long, contented sigh, then propped himself up on one elbow to better look at her. She wanted to turn away but wouldn't let herself. She had to make him see what he had done to her. He must witness her pain. Her shame. Her horror. Her disgust and loathing.

He smiled. 'You're mine now. You'll have to marry me.' He stroked a strand of hair away from her forehead. 'It didn't need to be like that, you know. But you gave me no choice. If you'd just said yes when I proposed, I'd have waited until we were married.' Stella shivered in revulsion at that creepy, ugly smile again. 'But don't worry. I'll make it up to you. We'll have a honeymoon wherever you'd like to go. No expense spared. Champagne and chocolates in the bedroom. Paris or even Rome.'

Before he could say anything else, taking him by surprise, she thrust her fists hard against his shoulder, unbalancing him and toppling him out of the narrow bed onto the wooden floor.

'Damn you!' he snapped. 'That hurt.'

'Get out. Now. When my father hears what you've done, he'll have you sent down.'

He looked up at her from where he was sprawled on the floor. He snorted in derision. 'Don't be a silly girl, Stella. If your father finds out what we've just done, he'll have the banns called as soon as we get back to Kandy. His only daughter indulging in pre-marital intercourse?'

'You raped me.' The word was alien, ugly, but she knew it was the only one that described what he'd just done to her. 'You raped me while I was sleeping peacefully in my bed. You are a monster.'

Blackstock snorted again. 'You invited me into your bed. We all overindulged on Ronald's whisky tonight. It must have gone straight to your head. Brought out the slut in you. Quite took me by surprise. But strong liquor helps us all to shed our inhibitions.' He got to his feet and adjusted his clothing. 'But don't worry, dear girl. No need for it to come to that. We'll tell your father that I asked you to do me the honour of becoming my wife and you've accepted. No one will be any the wiser.' He bent over her and she felt herself cringing and drawing in upon herself.

'You may not think much of me now, but love will grow. What better basis for marriage than a meeting of minds and shared endeavours. When we return to Oxford you will assist me in writing my thesis, partnering me as we pursue our studies together.'

'I will never marry you. I loathe you. Everything you've done to me tonight makes me even more determined. I will shout what you've done from the rooftops. I will tell the world.'

He gave her a look of pity. 'No, my darling, you'll tell no one. The only women who do so are women of low birth and breeding. That kind of thing never happens to respectable women. Everyone would blame you. They'd say you led me on, that you are a whore, harbouring unhealthy desires. You'd be publicly shamed and shunned. You'd bring disgrace on your father and brother and your good name would be tarnished forever. Sleep on it, dear Stella, then when we get back to Kandy we'll talk, and you'll see that what I say makes sense. You may think it unfair. Perhaps it is. But that's life. I swear if you are a good wife I will be a good husband to you. You'll want for nothing. And once you give this more thought you'll see the merits in the marriage. Goodnight and God bless.'

After he left, she was in shock, reliving the horror of what had just happened. Terrified, she propped a chair under the handle of the door, although she knew he wouldn't come back.

The blood on the sheets and the crusty residue between her thighs bore testimony to her violation. Revolted, she went to the chest of drawers, where the jug of water and washing bowl stood, and washed herself. If only she could wash away what had happened and the memory of it. If only she could turn back time and have already placed that chair where it now secured the door. But how could she have known Gordon Blackstock would do what he'd done? It was unthinkable. Yet it had happened.

After she'd washed, she couldn't bear to get back into the bed where he'd violated her, so she dressed, then sat on the floor in front of the window, her body shaking. She opened the shutters onto the black velvet night to wait for the dawn to come.

She asked herself what she'd done for this to happen. Why hadn't she waited until they were back in Kandy before telling Blackstock of her conditions for marrying him? Why hadn't she seen that he was capable of such violence? What had she done for him to hate her so much?

But she knew the answer to the last question. Her rejection had caused him to do this to her. She'd been stupid. How could she have expected a man like Blackstock to agree to a marriage in name only? He would have seen it as an affront to his manhood. Blackstock was the kind of man used to getting his own way. His father was buying his position in Oxford. Everything was laid out on a silver plate for him. Stella was like any other possession. He wanted her, so he took her.

Tears started to flow. Tears of anger and grief. She had lost something of herself that she would never recover. No, not lost. It had been stolen from her. Gordon Blackstock had ruined her. Savaged her innermost core. Destroyed her trust. Made her feel unsafe. Utterly alone.

She remembered what he'd said about her having to marry him now. As the daughter of an anthropologist, Stella was all too aware of how in many countries and cultures – the Bible too – it was an accepted solution for a rapist to marry his victim.

She'd die rather than marry Gordon Blackstock. Nothing her father or Ronald could say or do would change her mind on that.

NINETEEN

Norton couldn't wait to get back to Kandy. The entire trip had been a trial. He'd hated the hunting and had played no part in it, disgusted by Ronald Polegate's behaviour. Whenever possible, he'd talked to Geethan, finding the tracker's intimate knowledge of the jungle and its flora and fauna fascinating.

He'd trudged along at the rear of the group, wishing himself anywhere but here, or —more accurately – wishing himself anywhere if it was alone with Stella. He told himself his attraction to her was a passing fancy. He'd known her such a short time. But the ache inside him belied the idea that this was a transient emotion. He didn't want to contemplate his future if she wasn't in it. The thought of her soon leaving Kandy and within a matter of months leaving Ceylon altogether was too painful to dwell on.

Shuddering at the thought of her married to Blackstock, Norton wondered again whether to ask her to marry him herself. But how could he? He had nothing to offer. Stella wanted a career in academia, not to be stuck in provincial Ceylon, married to a civil servant on the bottom rung of the ladder, earning barely enough to support himself, let alone a wife.

Besides, she had given him no indication of having any romantic feelings for him.

Yet now that he knew her, how could he possibly think of marrying anyone else? He loved her. Her quiet serenity, her determination, her cleverness, her intensity. And those eyes – he could lose himself in them forever. But on this trip, fate, the jungle, and Gordon Blackstock had conspired to ensure their eyes rarely met.

On the last night, which they spent at the rest house in Matara, Norton went to bed early. Stella had already retired and the other three were clearly determined to mark the end of the trip by polishing off a bottle of whisky. Cynthia tried to persuade him to stay and join them.

'Please stay! It'll be fun. The night is young!'

Norton shook his head.

'Don't be such a fuddy-duddy, Norton. You're being an absolute killjoy.'

Both Ronald and Blackstock sniggered at this.

'You three are welcome to stay up all night as far as I'm concerned, but please remember, Miss Metcalfe, I'm here as your father's representative and I'm on government time.' He avoided addressing her by her first name whenever they were in company. Then realising he probably sounded pompous, added, 'Besides, since we have the luxury of proper beds tonight, I'm looking forward to a good night's sleep.'

Cynthia looked disappointed but didn't argue further. As he made his way to bed Norton felt a twinge of guilt. After all, Cynthia only wanted everyone to have a good time. He thought again of the tragedy of her childhood. Maybe her desire for activity, for entertainment and partying was to counter her loneliness and what must be a terrible hole in her life.

He fell asleep at once and slept deeply until dawn, in contrast with his insomnia when under canvas. To his surprise, when he went down for breakfast the following morning, the only other person present was Gordon Blackstock. The doctoral student grunted a greeting, then turned his attention to his plateful of scrambled eggs.

Norton ate his own breakfast in grateful silence, as the clock on the mantelpiece ticked loudly, accompanied by the chomping of Blackstock's jaws as he demolished a slice of toast.

Eventually they were joined by a bleary-eyed Cynthia and, a few moments later, by Ronald, who looked dishevelled, his hair sticking up like straw on a scarecrow.

'Never again!' said Cynthia, her hand theatrically touching her forehead. 'Whisky is the filthiest of drinks. I can't imagine why anyone chooses to drink it. My head hurts as if a herd of water buffalo have stamped all over it.' She glanced at the table where Norton and Blackstock had just finished their meals, dropping her hand to her bosom as her face contorted. 'Eggs? I think I'd die if I tried to eat one. I feel sick to my stomach.'

'It's what's known as a hangover,' said Blackstock, who appeared to be unaffected himself.

Norton sensed something had changed amongst his fellow travellers. Cynthia and Ronald, despite their overindulgence and claimed reluctance to eat, sat together and each managed to tuck into a hearty breakfast. Norton couldn't help noticing a familiarity between them that spoke of an ease and friendship he'd not been aware of before.

He wondered where Stella was. It was almost time for them to leave for the train. If she didn't appear soon, she'd miss her breakfast. 'Any sign of Miss Polegate? She's cutting it rather fine.'

Cynthia sighed. 'I'll go and check.' She got up and left the room, returning in a few moments. 'She doesn't want breakfast and she'll be down in a few minutes.'

When she appeared, Norton thought Stella looked as though she'd not slept at all. He knew she hadn't been carousing with the others the previous night, yet she looked drawn and distracted. Her face was slightly red and her eyes puffy as though from crying. His chest constricted and it was all he could do not to rush over and gather her in his arms.

Stella avoided his gaze. More than that, she seemed to be avoiding them all, holding herself apart. Something had upset her.

'Righty-ho, we need to get a move on if we're to make the train,' said Ronald, oblivious to his sister's misery.

Cynthia elbowed him playfully. 'Don't be silly, Ronnie, the station's just across the road. It's the end of the line and the train hasn't arrived yet. Stop fussing.' She slipped her arm through his affectionately, no sign of her hangover.

Immediately, Stella followed them, linking with her brother's other arm.

Norton frowned. What was wrong? Uncharacteristically, Stella appeared to be seeking her brother's protection. Norton turned to look towards Blackstock to see if he'd noticed. The man tilted his chin forward, the trace of a smile on his face. Not a smile. A smirk.

Something had happened and Norton felt as though he was the only one who didn't know what.

Once they were on the local train that would take them to Galle where they'd change for the Colombo train, Norton's unease increased. Stella had taken a seat between the window and her brother. When Blackstock sat down opposite her she jumped up, mumbled something about her handkerchief, and went to the end of the carriage. When she returned, she took the seat next to Norton.

His delight at her proximity was diminished by concern for her. He could sense the tension in her.

Blackstock narrowed his eyes. 'Stella,' he said in an accusatory tone. 'Come and sit here, please.'

'No,' she snapped. 'I'm comfortable where I am.'

Norton was shocked. Stella was usually formal but courteous towards her father's student, but today her tone was ice cold to the point of hostility. What was happening? She was still avoiding his eyes. As soon as the train started, she closed her own and kept them shut all the way to Galle.

Cynthia and Ronald both appeared to be sleeping. Norton noticed Cynthia's head slipping onto the young man's shoulders. Had they started a flirtation? Was that what was upsetting Stella? As for Blackstock, he was reading a book.

There was a twenty-minute wait for their connecting train at Galle. Norton was supervising the transfer of their luggage when he heard Stella's voice further along the platform.

'Get away! Don't come near me!'

He turned, alarmed by the strident tone. Stella was pinned with her back against the wall as Blackstock appeared to be grasping her by the shoulders.

Leaving the porters to finish unloading the bags, Norton dashed over and grabbed Blackstock's arm, pulling him away from Stella. 'You heard what Miss Polegate said. Let her go.'

Blackstock squared up to him, hands on hips. 'Stay out of this, Baxter.'

'No, I won't. Miss Polegate has made it clear she doesn't wish to talk to you. Leave her alone.'

There was no sign of Cynthia or Ronald.

Blackstock scowled but appeared to decide that a public confrontation would be ill advised. 'I'll speak to you later, Stella.' As he went to walk away, he turned back and snapped at Norton, 'You need to mind your own business, Mr Baxter.'

Norton said nothing, puzzled by what was going on, but relieved to see Blackstock move to the other end of the platform.

'Can we sit in another part of the train, please?' Stella addressed him, while still avoiding meeting his eyes.

'Of course. Look, Miss Polegate, are you unwell? Has something happened?'

'Wait until we're on the train.'

The platform was crowded when the train drew in. Norton helped Stella into a carriage and settled her in her seat. She turned her head away to look out of the window.

'I'm going to check on the others.'

'You'll come back?' There was a note of fear or desperation in her voice.

'Of course.' He worked his way through the carriage and into the next one. Blackstock was sitting alone, facing the other way. Cynthia and Ronald were further along the compartment and were deep in conversation. Norton was glad he didn't have to contend with Cynthia, although he was surprised at the new dynamic between her and Ronald. But perhaps he shouldn't be. Both had relished the hunting, sharing a love of sport and a sense of excitement. Surely it couldn't be a romantic attachment though – Cynthia must be eight or nine years Ronald's senior.

The train had filled up and Norton made his way back to Stella. The two seats opposite theirs were now occupied by a middle-aged Sinhalese couple dressed expensively in British-style attire. They introduced themselves and told Norton they'd been in Galle for the wedding of their only son, and that the man was a district judge from Kalutara, a town about halfway to Colombo. Their presence deterred any intimate conversation between Norton and Stella, so both looked out at the passing countryside.

It was hot and humid, barely relieved by the breeze from the open windows. The train thrummed along past dense green tropical vegetation, large-leafed banana plants, heavily fronded palm trees, straw thatched huts, lazy rivers and murky palm-fringed lagoons. Norton let the scenery wash over him as he wondered what had passed between Blackstock and Stella. As far as he could recall, nothing untoward had happened over the evening meal and she had been the first of them all to retire. Had she been up early? Had they argued before Norton had found Blackstock breakfasting alone?

After the Sinhalese couple departed the train at Kalutara, Norton turned to face her. He was conscious that Stella was tense, as though she had drawn in upon herself, like a coiled spring. Keeping his voice low, he asked, 'What happened, Stella?'

She looked at him directly. 'I'll have to leave Ceylon. I can't go back to the Metcalfes. I can't bear to be under the same roof as that man. Please, help me.'

Norton felt a swell of rage inside him. What had Blackstock done? 'Of course I'll help you. What do you need me to do? Shall I fetch your brother?'

'No,' she snapped. 'Ronald wouldn't understand. Or wouldn't care.' She sucked in a breath. 'You're the only person I trust in Ceylon. Well, you and a lady called Mrs Moreland, whom I met at the pearl fishery. But she's in Jaffna. I can trust you, can't I, Norton?' At last, she fixed her dark eyes upon him as though trying to see right inside him, searching for reassurance.

Norton's breathing quickened. He opened his mouth, but the words wouldn't come – instead he nodded, waiting for her to elaborate.

Stella closed her eyes and bit her lip, summoning up the strength to go on.

Norton reached for her hand and to his surprise she didn't pull it away. 'Has Mr Blackstock hurt you? Did he hit you?' He was fearful of what he'd do to Blackstock if she said he had.

Stella's mouth stretched into a hard line. 'It's hard for me to talk about. Yes, he hurt me. He didn't strike me. It was worse than that. He has destroyed me, ruined me.'

Every muscle of Norton's body stiffened, and he jerked upright, releasing his hold on her hand. 'You mean? He...?'

She spoke, still with her eyes shut, and he sensed she was willing herself to get the words out. 'I was asleep. I thought I was having a nightmare. He covered my mouth so I couldn't scream.' She drew another deep breath, summoning strength from it. 'He forced himself upon me.' She lowered her eyes. 'And it's my fault.'

Norton bridled. He grasped both her hands in his, squeezing them tightly. 'Don't say that. Nothing you could do or say could possibly make it your fault.'

Her eyes were desolate. 'But it is. Over the past few days, I'd been weighing up my options. There didn't seem to be many. In the end I thought – stupidly, I see now – that perhaps he would agree to a marriage in name only. I assumed his only reason for wanting to marry me was so he could continue to use me to shape his work. A marriage of convenience where I'd have access to everything I need to pursue my research and he would be able to continue passing my work off as his own.' Her eyes teared up. 'I was stupid. I thought that would be enough for him. So, I put the idea to him while you and the others were looking at the salt pans.'

Norton listened, horrified. He could imagine exactly how a man like Blackstock would have felt about that.

Stella looked down. 'He took it badly. Told me he would never accept those terms. That he expected me to bear him children and once he had secured tenure as a don, my life would be centred on keeping his house and raising his children.'

Norton realised his mouth was open. He felt sick to the stomach.

Stella continued, her fingers kneading the fabric of her skirt.

'I told him I wouldn't marry him. So that's why he... forced himself on me.' She said the last words in a voice hard with bitterness. 'He chose to shame me into marrying him. He stole from me the one thing that can never be regained. He did it so I would be ruined, my reputation destroyed, and I'd have no choice but to accept his offer. There's a long tradition of men expecting women to marry the men who attack them.' She choked back a sob.

Norton locked his eyes onto hers. 'Gordon Blackstock is a blackguard. A vile contemptible... sorry, I have no words strong enough.' His fists were so tightly curled the circulation had almost stopped. 'Stella, no matter what he did to you, he can't take away what makes you, *you*.' Her eyes were welling with tears, and he longed to take her in his arms and comfort her but settled for holding her hands in his. He wanted to tell her he loved her and nothing that Gordon Blackstock had done could ever stop him loving her. But if he were to say that it would probably make matters worse.

Instinctively, he knew patience and love must guide him. Stella was broken and his role was to be there for her, while she made herself whole again. She had to heal herself. And that would take time. Norton knew now with absolute certainty he would love and protect Stella Polegate until the day he died. Seeing her at her most vulnerable had made him love her all the more. Even if it proved to be a one-sided love, he knew it would be lifelong.

She wiped a hand across her cheek, defiantly brushing away the single tear that had appeared. 'I won't do as he asks. I'll die rather than marry him.'

'I'll kill him myself if he ever lays a finger on you again, Stella. That's a promise.' Norton's mind was racing as he tried to work out what to do. 'We must find somewhere safe for you. What about the lady in Jaffna? Who is she?'

'The GA's wife. Mrs Moreland.'

'Do you think she'd take you in for a few days, while I work something out?'

Stella nodded.

'Would Blackstock guess you were there? Or your father?'

'I don't think Blackstock is aware of how close she and I became in just a few days. He was too wrapped up in the pearl fishery and only met the Morelands once when they entertained us all to dinner. And Papa was too ill.'

'Good. Then we must get you there.'

She thought for a moment then shook her head. 'It's too difficult. The train only goes as far as Anuradhapura. Besides, it's too risky. We're due to go to Jaffna anyway as part of the research project. Blackstock would find me there. And I need to be in Colombo to get a ship back to Britain.'

His chest tightened. He couldn't bear to think of her leaving Ceylon and him never seeing her again.

'I thought you were all going to the tea growing region next?'

'That's the plan. But part of the research must be done in the Jaffna peninsula. We were due to go there after we finish the work on the plantations. Now we've lost so much time, thanks to the side trips to the pearl fishery and the jungle.'

'Then that's it. You must convince your father that since so much time has been lost it would be better to conduct both legs simultaneously. You and he go to the plantations and let Blackstock and your brother cover Jaffna.'

'Blackstock is incapable of doing a good enough job. And Ronald will make matters worse by talking him into more madcap side trips.'

'But that's good. The more your father realises just how incapable he is, the less likely he is to push you to marry him.'

'But the college bursary?'

'There will be other donors.'

'But without Papa or me the research will likely be compromised.'

'Frankly, Stella, right now I'm thinking it already has.'

'Blackstock will never agree to go to Jaffna without me or Papa. He knows he's not up to it.'

'Is he going to admit that? If your father asks him to do it – trusts him to do it – surely he won't be able to say no without losing face. Besides, I sense that Blackstock's the kind of man who's susceptible to flattery. If your father tells him he trusts him, he'll believe it.'

'But Papa would never say that, because he doesn't trust him.'

Norton thought for a moment. 'Could you tell your father what happened?'

She looked horrified. 'No. He'd insist on me marrying him. He'd see it as the only way to protect my good name.'

Norton frowned. It was unthinkable that a man could treat his only daughter that way. 'How important is this research to him?'

'Vital. His last big overseas trip. He intends to present a series of papers to the Royal Asiatic Society in London. Not to mention a book.'

'Then he needs the data. Surely if you suggest that you divide and conquer, with you accompanying your father, who you've said needs to remain in the highlands because of his health, while Blackstock, supported by your brother, deals with Jaffna, Blackstock can't refuse without losing face and your father can hardly admit publicly that his student is incapable of doing fieldwork.'

Stella thought. 'It might work. Unless Papa suggests Ronald stays with him and I go with Blackstock to Jaffna.'

'Allow his unmarried daughter to travel alone with a man? I can imagine what Mrs Metcalfe would have to say about that.'

Stella pondered the idea for a moment. 'It might work. But what good will it do? It's just delaying the inevitable. It changes nothing.'

'It buys us some time.' Then he remembered Winnie was coming. His sister's arrival would complicate matters.

TWENTY

When the group returned to the GA's residence, they found Sir Michael prowling the terrace like a caged bear. His health now restored, he appeared full of energy and frustrated that they had wasted so much time in Ceylon without doing any fieldwork.

'I had no idea you'd be gone for so long. What kind of madness was it to trudge all the way to the south of the island to shoot animals? I thought the plan was to spend a couple of days hunting locally. You've been gone for eight.' He glared at Ronald. 'I suppose this was your hare-brained idea?'

'Someone at the tennis club told us the supply of game was much better down south where there are designated hunting areas. We thought—'

'I don't care what you thought, Ronald. You've been nothing but a drain on this expedition. I rue the day I agreed to let you come. Wasn't all that time-wasting nonsense at the pearl fishery enough for you?'

Cynthia stepped forward. 'I'm sorry, Sir Michael, it's entirely my fault. I persuaded everybody to change the plans. Please don't blame Ronnie.'

Mrs Metcalfe shook her head at her daughter's confession. 'I might have known.'

'Ronnie? His name is Ronald.' But the steam had gone out of the professor. He gave a heartfelt sigh then turned to Stella. 'I've decided on a change of plan. Mr Blackstock and I will go to Jaffna while you, Stella, can cover the plantation coolies.'

Blackstock folded his arms. 'You can't seriously expect her to do the work on her own. She's an unqualified amateur. A woman. Besides, I thought the doctor said you were to avoid exposure to the sun. Surely, you'll be better off in the cool of the highlands. No, Sir Michael, we must all stick together.' He paused, looking thoughtful. 'Or even better, Stella can accompany me to Jaffna.'

Stella could barely breathe. The thought of being alone with Gordon Blackstock was intolerable. She felt nauseous at the prospect and couldn't even look at the man.

At this point Portia Metcalfe came to her rescue. 'Michael, you can't possibly allow your unmarried daughter to travel unchaperoned to Jaffna.' She fixed her gaze on her daughter. 'Perhaps Cynthia could go too.'

'Certainly not!' Cynthia folded her arms, her expression defiant. 'I'm not trailing up to Jaffna on some dreary research trip. What would I do while they're going round talking to the natives? Besides there's a tennis tournament next week I can't possibly miss.'

Stella dug her fingernails into her palms. The tension was unbearable.

Sir Michael thought for a moment then said, 'I am the leader of this expedition. I make the decisions. My daughter and I will concentrate on the highlands. She is more than capable of collecting the data and she and I can work together in compiling it. Stella may be an unqualified woman, but she has always proved herself to be an invaluable assistant to me. She's lost precious time being dragged round the Southern Province after you and Ronald, Mr Blackstock.'

'But—'

'Unless you're saying you're incapable of doing the work in Jaffna without Stella or myself? Really? It's only simple interviews, observations and data gathering. Stella has already prepared the guidelines for the interviews.'

'But there's so much to do if I have to manage the interviews as well as write up the notes.'

'Are you saying you can't cope, Mr Blackstock?' Sir Michael narrowed his eyes and fixed Blackstock with a penetrating stare. He turned to address his son. 'Since you're the cause of all our tribulations, Ronald, you will go with Mr Blackstock and assist him by sitting in on his fieldwork and writing down everything you hear.'

Now it was Ronald who was poised to object. He exchanged glances with a furious-looking Cynthia.

'But what about the tournament? Ronnie's going to partner me in the mixed doubles,' she wailed.

Sir Michael wasn't prepared to listen to any objections. 'Enough! We are here in Ceylon to work, not for my son to amuse himself playing sport.'

Portia Metcalfe spoke again. 'Inside, now, Cynthia. Leave our guests to make their plans.' She took her daughter by the elbow and led her back into the house.

When they'd gone, Sir Michael fixed his son with a gimlet stare. 'You've caused enough damage. It's time you earned your keep. This expedition has already been derailed by you, and it will be a miracle if Stella and I can retrieve anything from it. I've had enough, Ronald. More than enough. I've let you get away with murder, but these past few days I've come to my senses. I don't want to hear any more.' Sir Michael turned back to address Blackstock again. 'As for you, do you understand what I expect of you? I am entrusting you to collect the necessary information. Surely, you're capable of doing that.'

'Of course I am, Sir Michael.'

'Now get out of my sight. Not you, Stella.'

After the others had left the terrace, Sir Michael turned to his daughter. 'Do you think Blackstock's up to it?'

Barely able to shape her words, she said, 'If he follows the questions, writes everything down and doesn't let Ronald lead him astray.' A burden had lifted from her shoulders now that her father had arranged everything without her having to intervene. 'He doesn't need to analyse the findings. You and I can do that later.'

'Very well. I'll make it clear to him that if he doesn't do this job properly, I'll no longer supervise his doctorate.' Sir Michael rubbed his palms together. 'We will leave in the morning. Julian has lined up a few plantations where we can talk to the Tamil workers.' He studied his daughter's face. 'Are you unwell, Stella? You look pale.'

Stella stretched her lips into a fake smile. 'I'm quite well, Papa. Glad to be done with the hunting and back to doing the work.'

Stella remained on the terrace after her father went to change for dinner. The sun was close to the horizon, and it would be dark in a few minutes, but she was in no hurry to return to the room she was sharing with Cynthia. Better to leave her some privacy, and quickly change for dinner herself later.

A soothing hiss of running water crept over the lawns, as one of the gardeners began hosing the flowerbeds. Stella needed some quiet time alone to reflect on the trauma of the trip to the south and Blackstock's savagery. She had a sudden and unexpected longing for her late mother. It was seven years since her death, and she tried not to think of her often as it was too painful. But it was impossible not to now. She longed to fold herself into her arms just as she'd done as a small child, seeking her solace and comfort.

Yet Stella knew what her mother would tell her. How many times had she warned her of the dangers of letting her heart rule her head? How often had she stressed that love required great sacrifices? She herself had given up everything when she'd married Stella's father. A price that had perhaps been too high to pay. Better to be rational, to look for a course that would bring lasting benefits, since love was such a transient emotion. She'd counselled her daughter not to make her mistake and place her trust in love, but to pursue her own interests. If she were here, she'd doubtless urge Stella to accept the security offered by the odious Blackstock in order to stay close to the academic world.

Then she thought of Violet Moreland. Violet wouldn't have agreed. Stella remembered the fierce passion with which she had denounced her own parents for forcing her into an unhappy marriage. And now Stella had also gone through what Violet had suffered on her terrible brutal wedding night – and had done so without even a ring upon her finger. Would her mother really have advised her to swallow her hatred, her pride and her sense of self, and marry Gordon Blackstock for the sake of appearances? Would she have counselled her that it was better to marry a rich man and retain the possibility of at least being close to the world of academia she loved? Stella asked these questions but was sure she already knew the answers.

Mama would have reminded her that she'd sacrificed her own singing career for the love of Stella's father and instead would have been better served by remaining single – or marrying someone who could have supported her life as a musician – even though it would have meant forgoing love.

She remembered a conversation she'd had with her mother when she was about sixteen. Sir Michael had been away on a research trip and her mother had been unusually talkative. Stella had never forgotten her mother's words that day. She'd taken Stella's hand and said, 'Men do their utmost to hold us back, keep us in what they see as our rightful place. You must find a way to work around them.' She remembered that afternoon vividly. She'd often puzzled about why her mother had been so vehement – Sir Michael had never seemed to be the domineering type, but she had accepted that a daughter can't possibly know the inner workings of her parents' marriage.

Stella thought of the leather-bound scrapbook full of press cuttings that she had found in the attic after her mother's death. Programmes from La Scala in Milan, the Royal Opera House at Covent Garden, and the Paris Opera. A glittering career cut short by Papa's insistence that she live the life of an academic's wife and bring up their children in the quiet backwaters of Oxford. She had relinquished everything she'd cared about to marry Sir Michael and, in the end, had concluded that love hadn't been enough.

Stella thought about Norton Baxter, the kindness he had shown to her, and the way she had felt able to trust in him completely. When she'd looked into his eyes something had stirred deep inside her and for a moment, she'd imagined what it would be like to be married to a man like him. To be loved and cherished and to love in return. But just as quickly she pushed the thought aside. Marriage to a man like Norton was out of the question. It would be to repeat her mother's mistake. Yet marriage to Gordon Blackstock would be to repeat Violet Moreland's.

The only way forward was to return to England as soon as she and her father had completed the plantation surveys – and before Blackstock's return. Somehow, she'd find a means of going to Cambridge. With no money, no home, no support, it would be a challenge, but she had to find a way to make it happen.

The sound of a piano drifted through the open French doors. The pianist was Mrs Metcalfe. Stella recognised a German *lied*. Schubert. Then it occurred to her that it was strange that she had never heard her mother sing. Not so much as a lullaby when Ronald was a baby. It had been as if she'd been struck silent. Perhaps she'd been deliberately making a point to her husband. Or perhaps the thought of singing for simple pleasure after what had clearly been a glittering career had been too painful. Stella wondered why she'd never thought to ask her. And now it was too late.

She got up and wandered into the room where Portia Metcalfe was playing. The GA's wife looked up, saw her guest and stopped at once. 'I didn't realise you were out there, my dear.'

'Please don't stop. It was delightful.'

'I wouldn't presume to play for the daughter of Delia Devine.'

Stella was taken aback by the use of Mama's stage name, surprised that Mrs Metcalfe was aware who her mother had been. 'Have no fear on that score. I haven't a musical bone in my body.'

'Didn't Delia teach you to play?'

Stella gave a hollow laugh. 'There was no music in our house. I only developed a taste for it myself after Mama died and I started going to concerts with Papa. Mama disliked going. I suppose she found it too painful after Papa had insisted on her giving up her singing career when they married.'

Mrs Metcalfe frowned, her mouth open. 'Forced her to give up? What do you mean?'

'She had to abandon singing in order to marry Papa.'

'Whatever makes you say that, my dear? Your father would never have asked that of her. Quite the contrary. It was love for her singing that drew him to her in the first place.'

'You knew my mother?' Stella had believed the connection

to have been solely between her father and Julian Metcalfe from their schooldays.

'Delia and I met at music school. We were close friends. We lost touch after Julian and I married and moved out here to Ceylon. It was clear early on that I was never going to have a career in music – other than teaching it. Julian and I were engaged to be married, and your father was keen to hear the great Delia Devine singing so we went to a recital together and afterwards the four of us went out for dinner. Your father was smitten at once.'

'And Mama?'

'Not interested at first. Your father followed her around the circuit, neglecting his studies in order to hear her sing. He brought her flowers after every performance. Wrote her letters. Begged her to go out with him. But she refused.'

'Why?'

'I don't think it's my place to say. I thought perhaps you'd know all this.'

'No, I didn't. Mama told me she gave up her career because of Papa. She said she had paid a high price for love.'

Portia Metcalfe paled. 'I've probably misremembered. Goodness me! Is that the time? We'd better hurry and dress for dinner or we'll be late.' With that, she hurried out of the room, leaving Stella utterly perplexed.

Why was Mrs Metcalfe so reluctant to discuss the late Delia Polegate? If what she had said was true, then it cast a completely different light on her parents' marriage – and on her father's character. Stella remembered what Norton had said when they were on that southern beach about there being nothing but ocean between that point and the icy polar region. Standing now in the elegant drawing room of the residence, she felt like a castaway in an open boat with nothing but empty waters all around her.

Her thoughts returned to Norton Baxter, remembering his kindness, his empathy, the feel of his hands wrapped around hers, the warmth of his skin against her own. His eyes had seemed to look right inside her, to know her, to understand her. She felt a little flip in her stomach then told herself to stop it immediately. There was no point in forming an attachment to a man with whom she could have no future. Norton's life was here in Ceylon where he was embarking on his career. He was unofficially linked to Cynthia Metcalfe – no matter that he had denied the connection. Stella was too worldly wise not to realise that marriage to the government agent's only daughter had to be an excellent career-enhancing move.

Outside the open French doors to the rear lawns, the sound of the garden hose had stopped, and the sky had darkened the way it did so suddenly and completely here in the tropics. It was time to change for dinner.

As Stella walked along the corridor to the room she was sharing with Cynthia, she told herself to forget about Norton and focus on completing the job she and her father had come to Ceylon to do. She would never be able to risk telling Papa what Blackstock had done to her, but she would have time alone with him, away from his student. Time to make her case again for at best studying in her own right, or at least for maintaining the status quo and continuing to work as Sir Michael's assistant. And time too to find out more about his relationship with her late mother and the reason she had abandoned her singing career to marry him.

TWENTY-ONE

Norton had heard from his sister, Winifred, again. She'd sent a telegram from Bombay to advise him of the date of her arrival in Colombo and to say there was no need for him to travel to the capital to meet her ship when it docked. On board, she had met and befriended two missionary sisters who were travelling via Kandy to take up positions in Trincomalee on the east coast, so she would undertake the train journey with them, and Norton could meet her at the railway station in Kandy. This was a relief to him as he was keen to return to his Sinhala lessons. He needed to make up lost ground in the *kachcheri* after the trip to the Southern Province and get to grips with the sizeable workload Frobisher had assigned him.

Although he threw himself into his work, Norton's mind was often occupied with thoughts of Stella Polegate. Now he worried whether she'd succeeded in arranging for Blackstock to be deployed somewhere where she would be safe from him. It must have taken a great deal of courage for her to tell him what Blackstock had done. He promised himself that the man wouldn't get near her again. He'd never felt such anger and malevolence towards another human being. He would have given anything for Blackstock to be reported, arrested, and punished for what he'd done – but that couldn't happen without compromising Stella and risking the inevitable tarnishing of her good name.

A day after the return from the Southern Province, Norton received a message from Paul Carberry to say the planter would be staying in Kandy that evening and requesting he and Norton meet. He was pleased at the prospect of seeing Carberry again and that he would therefore have a reason for avoiding both a miserable supper at the bungalow with Frobisher and the regular visit to the tennis club. Cynthia had not been in touch with him since their return and Norton wondered how much of that was down to her new friendship with Ronald Polegate.

That afternoon, he asked Frobisher to make his excuses to their housekeeper for his absence from the evening meal.

'Dining at the GA's residence again?'

'No. I'm meeting a pal for dinner at the Queen's.' Not that it was any of Frobisher's business.

'Anyone I know?'

'A planter friend I met on the voyage out.' Seeing his boss's quizzical expression he added, 'Chap called Paul Carberry.'

Frobisher jerked back in his seat. 'Carberry? Good Lord, man. You should take more care about the company you keep.'

'He's a decent fellow. We get along well.' Norton suspected Frobisher's reaction was another example of the snobbery shown by the civil service towards planters as exemplified on the *Dambulla* by Mrs Holloway.

'Steer clear of him if you've any sense. He's a rum one. Not many people would give Paul Carberry so much as the time of day.'

'Why ever not?' Norton was uneasy, remembering Cynthia's similar hostility towards Carberry.

Frobisher lowered his voice. 'Rumour has it he's a sodomite.

It was all hushed up by the plantation manager at Glenross and by the GA, but everyone knew what the score was.'

Norton felt his stomach sink. 'I'm not interested in gossip.'

'It's more than just gossip. There was an office assistant in the district office at Nuwara Eliya, a fellow named Huxtable – George Huxtable, who was pally with Carberry. Played a lot of golf together. Huxtable was regarded as something of a high-flyer in his district with a bright future. They were caught in a compromising situation in the changing room at the golf club. Turns out they were a pair of pansies. The GA dismissed Huxtable and ordered him to return to England in disgrace. The chap couldn't stomach the shame of it all. Drank a bottle of Scotch and flung himself to his death from the top of a water-fall.' Frobisher, still with his voice in a half whisper, folded his arms. 'So, as you can see, Carberry is no gentleman. Not that anyone would expect him to be, being a planter.' He covered his mouth and gave a discreet cough. 'As for Huxtable, until then everyone thought he was a good chap. Clubbable. The fellow couldn't stand the shame of being unmasked as a sodomite and the prospect of being sent back to England with his good name ruined. Mind you the pair of them were lucky the GA took it no further and didn't pursue a prosecution. It was nearly a year ago, but people still blame Carberry. Reckon he led the poor chap astray.' He shook his head. 'Huxtable was highly regarded until then. But I suppose he took the honourable way out; I'll give him that. More than Carberry had the decency to do.'

Norton didn't know how to respond, so chose to say noth-ing. He wondered whether George Huxtable was the chap Carberry had referred to in Colombo: the source of Carberry's inside knowledge about the roles and responsibilities of civil servants. Carberry had said he'd died of cholera – but he could hardly have admitted the truth.

By rights, Norton ought to be shocked by what Frobisher had told him, but instead he felt sorry for Paul Carberry and his friend. Such a waste of a young life. And undoubtedly the source of the sadness and loneliness he had detected in Carberry.

Frobisher was waiting for him to respond to the revelations. 'So, now you can understand why most people shun Carberry. Leonard Kerslake, who's the owner of the Glenross plantation where Carberry works, sent him on leave to England to find a wife to straighten him out. Told him otherwise he'd be out of a job – even though he reckons Carberry is the best manager he's ever had. No excuse for that kind of leniency though. But the man's come back still a bachelor. I understand he's now buying his own place. Just as well after he's betrayed Kerslake's trust.' Frobisher paused, frowning. 'I say, Baxter, you're not queer too, are you?'

Norton didn't deem that question worthy of a response. He'd heard enough salacious gossip and made his excuses. 'I have to collect some documents from the registry.'

'So, you'll be back for supper tonight after all?'

'No. I told you. I'm meeting Paul Carberry for dinner at the Queen's.' He turned on his heels and left the main room of the *kachcheri* to head for the records registry next door. He didn't look back but could hear the indignant tutting from Frobisher.

That evening, he met Carberry in the bar of the Queen's. Once the barman had served them both with beers, since it was a warm evening, they settled at a table on the veranda. Norton decided he was going to tell his friend he'd heard about Huxtable.

'When we were on the *Dambulla* you mentioned a friend in the civil service who died of cholera.'

Carberry froze with his glass between the table and his mouth. He put it back down. 'Yes,' he said, a shadow crossing his features.

'Was that George Huxtable?'

Carberry lifted his glass and took a gulp. 'Who told you?'

'My boss.'

'I'm surprised you didn't cancel tonight.' While Carberry's voice was guarded, Norton saw what he thought was a glimmer of hope in his eye.

'You and I are friends, Carberry. Besides, it's none of my business.'

'Very broadminded of you.' There was a note of bitterness in his voice.

'As long as you know my own inclinations aren't in that direction, I don't see what's changed. I enjoy your company. Your private life is none of my concern.'

Carberry downed the rest of his beer and signalled to the waiter to replenish their drinks. 'I did rather hope you might be the same way as me, but I realised back in Colombo I was hoping in vain.' He released a long sigh. 'I suppose he told you how George died. That it wasn't cholera.'

Norton nodded. 'Yes, I'm sorry.'

'I went back to England to find a woman to marry in the hope that the rumours would die. Mr Kerslake said he'd no longer employ me unless I stopped all that "nasty business", as he put it. Another reason for me deciding to buy my own land. I don't want to be beholden to anyone.'

He waited while the man placed the beers in front of them. 'You remind me of George, you know, Baxter.' He gave another long heartfelt sigh. 'Not a day goes by when I don't think of him. God, I miss him so much.'

Norton took a mouthful of beer. 'Have you always known you were... er...'

'Queer? Yes. And believe me I've tried not to be. I told myself I'd find a nice girl and marry her and maybe it would all be all right. I'd soon forget about George and my perversions as my father calls them. But it was hopeless. I couldn't find one willing to take a chance on living over here.'

'Your family know, then?'

Carberry shrugged. 'The subject's never been mentioned directly. My father makes unpleasant jokes about pansies though. Another reason why I'll never go back to Britain. My life's here now. Even though it's a lonely one.' He lit a cigarette. 'I have to be discreet.'

Norton was shocked at his friend's candour but chose to say nothing.

Carberry inhaled deeply on his cigarette. 'Things will be better when I set up in my own place. To change the subject, how was your hunting trip?'

'How did you know about that?'

'The bush telegraph. Nothing's secret in Kandy.'

'I hated it, if you must know. Pointless butchery. Couldn't wait to get back here.'

Carberry chuckled. 'Now why doesn't that surprise me? What else is new with you, Baxter?'

'My sister's coming out. She'll be here in five days.'

Carberry raised an eyebrow. 'You have a sister? Older or younger?'

'A few years younger. She's just gone through her first London season. Poor thing absolutely hated it. One marriage proposal and turned him down. Some Scottish laird with a grouse moor. Her dislike of hunting appears to be as deep rooted as mine. Must be genetic.'

'What's she like?' Carberry ground out his cigarette in the ashtray.

'Winnie's a good egg. A bit bossy but with a heart of gold.'

Carberry smiled. 'I'll look forward to meeting her – assuming you deem me suitable company for a young unmarried lady.'

Norton grinned. 'Well, it sounds like she'll be safe in your company.'

Carberry shrugged but took it in good spirit. 'No brothers then?'

'Just Winnie and me.'

He turned his mouth down in a mock frown. 'And how's your courtship of the GA's daughter going?'

'Is there nothing you don't know about?' Norton shook his head. 'I told you. No secrets here.'

Norton took another mouthful of beer. 'There is no courtship. Other than in the GA's head. Cynthia Metcalfe is a beautiful girl but there's nothing between us.'

'Nothing?'

'Nothing.'

A waiter appeared and led them into the dining room.

After the young man had taken their dinner order, Carberry continued. 'Why isn't the lovely Cynthia interested in the new boy in the *kachcheri* then?'

Norton shrugged. 'I'm concentrating single-mindedly on my career.'

'Surely the two go hand-in-hand. The fastest way to progress in the colonial service is to marry a GA's daughter.'

Norton laughed. 'I want to get there on merit. No short-cuts.' He speared a piece of melon with his fork. 'To be frank though, I'm having growing doubts about the civil service. About the whole empire thing.' He told Carberry about his recent experience at Bogambara prison. 'The poor boy had his back flayed to pieces for stealing a bite to eat. That's no way to treat a child – an impoverished orphan at that.'

He ate another piece of melon then carried on. 'I'm working for an insufferable fellow. Maybe you've come across him. Name's Frobisher.'

Carberry rolled his eyes. 'The twit in the tweed suits?'

'That's the man. Can you blame me for feeling somewhat disenchanted?'

'Leave.'

'Leave?' Norton echoed his friend.

'Come and work with me. Come and be a planter. I'll train you in everything about growing, picking, and processing tea. Spend your time in the outdoors. Never mind all that pen pushing and form filling. I'm going to need a number two. It would be topping to have you. You'd have no one to be accountable to – apart from me. And a chance to eventually buy into the business.'

Norton was about to protest when Carberry put his hand on his arm. 'Don't answer yet. There's no rush. But think about it. I'll give you a tour of Glenross and tell you about my plans for my own place – it will be called Oaklands.'

'Oaklands? Seems an odd name for a tea plantation.'

'Means something to me,' Carberry said enigmatically. 'That's all I ask. Just let the idea brew for a bit. When your sister arrives, we can show her round too.' He turned a wide grin on Norton. 'It'd be an interesting day out for her. I'll show you both round the Glenross tea factory.'

Norton had to admit there were attractions in the proposal to work for Carberry. It would be appealing to escape from the endless, pointless administrative tasks that underpinned the British Empire. To break away from what he was increasingly regarding as the unjustified rule over the native Sinhalese and Tamils. To help to build something new, to be in at the start of Carberry's enterprise. To move out from the petty rules and regulations of the *kachcheri* and the daily contact with Bertie Frobisher and his ilk. Working for Carberry would mean a life in the open air overseeing Tamil workers, earning a living with the sweat of his brow rather than the exercise of his brain.

But he had come out to Ceylon to prove to himself and his father that he could build a successful future as a servant of empire. Once he'd scaled the ladder here the world would be his oyster – increasingly significant postings across the British Empire – or a chance to return, cloaked in glory, to a home-based post in Whitehall.

Giving up the civil service would render all his struggles with the Mathematical Tripos pointless. He couldn't possibly throw all those years of study away.

As though reading his mind, Carberry said, 'Imagine. You would be applying all your clever mathematical training to help build a business. To work for ourselves rather than a deadly hierarchy of civil servants. If you join me, Baxter, we can create it together.' The planter pinned him with his eyes. 'All I ask is that you think about it. Don't answer me now. Come out to Glenross. Then I can show you the plot of land that will become Oaklands. Just say you'll do that, and I promise I won't put any more pressure on you now.'

Norton wanted to change the subject, to escape the intensity of Carberry's gaze. 'Very well. No promises, but I'll come and have a look some time and I won't rule it out until I've given it more thought.'

Carberry grinned. 'That's all I ask, my friend.'

TWENTY-TWO

With a nostalgic longing, Stella thought about the Oxford she'd known when her mother was alive. A quiet house without music; silent – other than the soft ticking of the long case clock in the hall and the crackle of logs on the fire blazing in the sunny drawing room; big blowsy tea roses in abundance in the walled garden, as well as in pottery jugs throughout the house, their sweet heady scent everywhere, mingled with that of newly mown grass and fresh lavender.

There were no jugs of roses anymore. After her mother's death, it would have felt unseemly to bedeck the house with flowers. A pall of sadness had landed on Stella's shoulders like a heavy cape. Where once the silence had wrapped around her and enveloped her, since Mama's death it had become oppressive. Delia Polegate's passing had left a larger hole than her quiet presence would have indicated. Not a day went by when Stella didn't think of her mother.

But now, after the violence of Gordon Blackstock's assault, the ache of loss inside Stella was a chasm that had grown bigger. Stella felt she had lost something of herself too. Blackstock had damaged her in a way she was convinced she'd never recover from.

The only thing keeping her functioning now was the work. Stella realised she must throw herself into it body and soul. It was the only way to keep going. It was also her only hope of persuading her father that she be allowed to continue her studies and remain unmarried. By proving herself indispensable she had a last chance to win him around – and now she was free to do so without Ronald and Blackstock seeking to influence him to the contrary.

So, it was with an icy determination and a refusal to dwell on the events that had taken place in the guest house at Matara that Stella set forth to the highlands with her father. They travelled in the relative comfort of a horse-drawn carriage and the roads were better than those she had taken on the oxen carts to the Southern Province. As they made their way south, passing tea gardens, intersected by the occasional stream and rocky outcrop, she felt her anxiety lessen. It was as though a weight lifted off her the further they got from Blackstock.

Julian Metcalfe had arranged for them to base themselves at a large tea plantation where they would have open access to the tea workers. Given the significant role women workers played in the plucking of tea, Stella convinced her father that the women's testimony should be part of the project. His priorities were religious rituals, marriage customs, and superstitions – but all seen through the lens of Tamil men. Stella wanted to include a female perspective too.

The plantation where they based themselves was owned by a childless Scottish couple, the McNairs, who had also agreed to put the professor and his daughter up. It comprised around two hundred and fifty acres all planted to tea, on steep slopes with views of distant higher peaks. Stella thought it beautiful and tranquil. The estate was intersected with two streams and waterfalls, leading to a larger river at the foot of the hillside and the whole place had a magical quality like a forgotten Eden. Mr McNair was known as the PD, or *periya dorai* – meaning big boss. The couple lived in a tin-roofed bungalow surrounded by gardens tended by Mrs McNair and planted with poinsettias and hollyhocks with manicured lawns and a small waterlily-covered pond. It would not have been out of place in the Surrey Hills.

The days passed quickly – even though they were long ones. Stella and her father worked alongside an interpreter – although the professor had a rudimentary knowledge of the Tamil language. Stella found the women shy and reluctant to speak to them during the formal interview sessions which took place on the meshed-in veranda of the plantation manager's bungalow. Quickly, she realised that the tea workers were inhibited by being interviewed on the threshold of the boss's home and in the presence of her father. They appeared furtive, nervous, reluctant to answer questions, constantly looking around them to see if they were being overheard saying something that might not meet with approval.

After one of the sessions, Stella wandered down to 'the lines' where they lived in rudimentary wooden shacks, to observe the women in their own spaces as they cooked, washed their clothes, and cared for their children. She went without her father into the tea gardens and via the translator talked to the women while they worked, finding them more open and prepared to talk, away from the possible disapproval of their menfolk and British paymasters.

As the days went by, she became increasingly convinced that the tea industry was built on the backs and shoulders of Tamil women. Without the women to pluck the leaves there would be no tea. Only women had fingers small enough to pick those delicate leaves – the top two plus the bud – as well as backs strong enough to carry the heavy woven baskets from dawn to dusk. It was arduous work – and in addition they birthed the children, raised them, and managed their simple homes. Their wages at fourpence a day were less than those of the men even though their effort was arguably greater.

It became clear to Stella that these indentured workers were little more than slaves. Yes, they were fed, housed, and paid – but only a small amount relative to the hardness of the work and the enormous profits earned in the tea industry. She learned that the plantation labour was recruited in southern India under what was known as the *kangani* system that had operated since the early nineteenth century. The *kangani* – or recruiter-supervisor – came from the word meaning the man who observes – *kan* being the Tamil for eye. The *kangani* exercised significant control over those he hired, often illegally deducting wages in a form of debt bondage in exchange for bringing them across to Ceylon and into secure employment. The consequent rise in income and status among the *kangani* made it a position for workers to aspire to. Stella found it abhorrent.

Yet, as she spent time in the tea gardens with the women themselves, she observed that they were smiling and happy, enjoying each other's company. This made her question her own misery. Compared with these women, her existence had been blessed. Yet her life of ease and access to knowledge had made her no happier than them – arguably less so.

Stella tried to use her growing knowledge of the tea workers' way of life to put her own crisis into perspective but was forced to conclude that there was no point in the comparison. She had grown up in a different world with certain hopes and aspirations and no matter how hard she tried, she couldn't eradicate these in order to reach any form of acceptance about marriage to Gordon Blackstock. It was pointless trying to compare her future with the one facing the Tamil women.

. . .

As time went on, Stella assumed a more influential role in her father's research, suggesting supplemental questions, compiling summaries of the daily findings, and discussing the conclusions directly with her father, while constantly looking for ways to broaden the scope of the project. Before now, her role had been more reactive: that of a secretary rather than an assistant, but as each day passed, she became more of a collaborator. Yet she bided her time and chose not to broach the subject of continuing her studies on their return to England. Better to wait until she was certain of a more positive response.

Other than her father occasionally wondering aloud how Blackstock was progressing without them, they didn't discuss her assailant at all. The professor made no reference to the previous marriage discussion and asked her nothing about the trip to the Southern Province. Stella for her part had no desire to revisit the trauma of that trip, so they proceeded almost as though Blackstock didn't exist.

It was therefore a shock when, after they had been away for several weeks, a telegram arrived from Blackstock, borne to them by none other than Julian Metcalfe himself. Stella and her father were dining with the McNairs, when the GA burst into the room.

He thrust the brown envelope into Sir Michael's hands without so much as a greeting. Stella moved around the table to read over her father's shoulder.

RONALD IN COLOMBO DUE TO SAIL TO ENGLAND. I WILL RETURN TO KANDY FORTHWITH.

YOURS G. BLACKSTOCK.

'What in heaven's name does he mean?' said Sir Michael, waving the flimsy paper in his hand and addressing Stella, who was as mystified as he was. But as well as surprise, a chill of fear ran down her spine.

The GA looked ashen-faced. 'That's not all. My daughter is missing. Portia says she's taken half the clothes in her wardrobe and must have left in the middle of the night. The bloody dog won't stop howling and whining. Portia is distraught.' He scowled at his old friend as though finding him personally responsible. 'I've every reason to suspect Cynthia has run off with your boy.'

Stella gasped. She'd noticed a growing intimacy between Cynthia and Ronald but had assumed it was no more than a passing flirtation. Not least because of the age difference between the pair.

Sir Michael looked bewildered. He scratched his head. 'I don't understand. Why would your daughter run off with my son?'

The GA's voice was clipped, as though he was trying to rein back his anger. 'Why does anyone behave in such a manner? Because they believe themselves to be in love I suppose. At least that's what Portia thinks. I can't accept it myself. What would possess Cynthia to run away with a young idiot like your boy? She's nearly ten years older than him. Her life's here, not back in England. She's too old for schoolgirl infatuations.' He took out a handkerchief and wiped his brow. 'All due respect, Michael, but as soon as I met that boy, I thought to myself that he was a bit of a bounder.'

Sir Michael opened his mouth to protest but Stella stayed him with her hand on his arm.

'When did Cynthia leave?' she asked. 'Are you sure it isn't connected with her plans for the tennis tournament she mentioned? Can you be certain she's gone to join Ronald?'

'Portia says when you sent him off to Jaffna with that other fellow, Cynthia was in a funk. Then there was a flurry of letters, all with a Jaffna postmark. And she refused to play in that tennis match she was so excited about.'

Their hosts discreetly excused themselves, Mr McNair returning a few moments later to deposit a tray with a bottle of whisky and some glasses on the table.

Stella poured out two measures and handed them to the GA and her father.

Sir Michael gulped his down then shook his head. 'I should never have let Ronald come on this trip. It was unprofessional of me and foolish to hope it would be the making of him. I'm sorry, Julian. The boy's a liability. But I never dreamed for a moment he'd seduce your daughter.'

Metcalfe's mouth stretched into a tight line. 'Knowing Cynthia, I expect she played an active part in any seduction that was going on. She's always been a handful. Portia says I treated her with kid gloves after her brother died. Highly strung. I suppose I gave her too much rope.' He shook his head and took a gulp of his drink. 'Lord, I needed that. Yes, Cynthia won't be told. She knows how to twist me round her little finger. I'd rather hoped she'd marry that chap Baxter. She seemed keen enough. Not sure *he* was though. I thought marriage to a young civil servant with a bright future would sort her out. A few children to keep her busy. That's all flown out of the window now. Even if we track them down and bring her back, I doubt Baxter will want to have anything to do with her. Not now that she's damaged goods.'

Stella listened to all this in disbelief. There was too much to take in. When Norton's name was mentioned, she'd felt the colour rising in her face. Then the words 'damaged goods' made her feel sick – a term that could also be applied to herself even though she'd played no part in her own disgrace. And what was the reference to Cynthia's dead brother about? She hadn't been aware of Cynthia having a brother.

Stella looked across at her father, who looked defeated. She had to take control of the situation as he seemed incapable of doing so. She sucked in a breath. 'Do you have any idea if they are already in Colombo, Mr Metcalfe? And whereabouts?'

'The telegram says they are, but just in case I've got someone watching the trains arriving at Kandy from the north and Colombo from Kandy. Although I doubt the two of them would be foolish enough to travel that way as they'd realise they'd be intercepted.' He sighed. 'That girl will be the death of me.' Then with a shake of his head from side to side, like a dog after getting wet, he added, 'Obviously I've put out an alert to monitor passengers boarding outgoing ships. But what do I do? If I drag Cynthia back home she'll be disgraced forever. Perhaps it's better they marry.'

'You realise my brother's only twenty?'

The GA closed his eyes and shook his head slowly. 'Dear Lord. What a filthy mess this is.' He poured himself another whisky. 'Portia will blame me of course.' He looked up at his old friend. 'Maybe if I can get Cynthia back before they try to sail, I can persuade that fellow Baxter to marry her.'

Stella couldn't bear to hear this. She was sick to the pit of her stomach with all the scheming by older men interfering in the lives of grown women. 'Can you hear yourself? You can't just force your daughter to marry one of your employees. Cynthia's twenty-seven. She's a mature woman with a mind of her own. And is Mr Baxter allowed no say in the matter?'

'She's a child. At least she's behaving like one.' The GA slumped with his head in his hands.

Sir Michael spoke at last. 'If my son has damaged the reputation of your daughter then he must face the consequences and marry her. Lord knows what they'll live on. As much as it pains me to admit it, Ronald is an irresponsible fool who never thinks of the consequences before acting. He lives entirely in the present moment and to solely fulfil his desire for pleasure. But your daughter has made her bed, Julian, and she'd better get used to lying in it. Perhaps she'll be able to knock some sense into him eventually. Believe me, I've never managed it.'

He turned to address Stella. 'We'd better pack up and return to Kandy with Julian. This project has been doomed since the day I let Ronald join us. We'll have to patch together what we can from it and hope for the best that Blackstock has done a decent job in Jaffna.' He ran a hand through his shock of grey hair. 'When we're all back in Kandy, I want you to work with him to see what you can rescue. If his work's useless we'll have to modify the scope of the project to limit it to a comparison between the mainland Indian Tamils and the immigrant tea workers and cut out the section on the North Ceylon Tamils.' He shook his head again, this time a slow movement of resignation. 'This expedition was meant to be the pinnacle of my career, my last contribution before retirement, but I'll have to lower my sights.'

Panic flooded Stella at the prospect of spending time one-on-one with Blackstock. She felt the bile rise in her throat and told herself to get a grip. 'Never mind that, Papa. We can worry about the results later. Why not send Mr Blackstock to Colombo to look for Ronald? I'm sure Mr Metcalfe would welcome all the help he can get to try to track them down.'

'I've already sent Baxter. Chap wasn't exactly thrilled. His sister has just arrived from England, and he's had to leave her in Kandy. Naturally Portia and I have had to take her in as she can hardly be left alone in a bungalow with that idiot Frobisher. What a bally mess.'

Stella couldn't help but agree.

TWENTY-THREE

Norton was feeling drained after a morning spent back at the Bogambara jail, witnessing his first hanging. His attendance was unofficial, the responsibility for overseeing the execution lying with the deputy fiscal, who happened to be Bertie Frobisher, the OA. Frobisher had asked Norton to attend as an observer as part of his induction programme.

It was before dawn when they left their bungalow and travelled in a rickshaw to the prison. Norton's stomach was rumbling from missing his breakfast, but it was the custom for all death sentences to be performed in the early hours before the city was up and about.

'Keep your mouth shut the whole time we're there, Baxter. Listen, watch, and learn. That shouldn't be too hard for you, eh?'

Norton swallowed his irritation at Frobisher's patronising attitude and smug tendency to lord it over him. He followed him, along with the medical officer – not Dr Madashanka but a British doctor this time – and the prison superintendent, as they went to the condemned man's cell. They stood awkwardly in the doorway while Frobisher read out the warrant for execution and asked the condemned man if he had anything to say. The man, in his early thirties, convicted for murdering his neighbour in a row over the ownership of a goat, declined. He stood shivering against the wall at the rear of the bleak brick-walled cell as though trying to anchor himself there. Dressed in white with a strange, voluminous cloth hat, he was to be accompanied to the gallows by a saffron-robed Buddhist priest.

The priest spoke to him quietly and led him out of the cell. As the party walked along the corridor to the gallows the condemned man muttered prayers quietly to himself and appeared to be shaking with fear, though he made no protest or attempt to resist his fate.

The previous day, Norton had read the summary of the man's trial and sentencing. It had been a crime of the moment – an outburst of anger between two men who had hitherto coexisted without conflict. The theft of a goat seemed to be a strange cause for a crime of such magnitude – until Norton had discovered this theft had been an act of cynical opportunism that had occurred while the condemned man was at the funeral of his father. The tension and grief had led him to snap, and he'd struck his neighbour with a piece of wood that fractured his skull, causing death. He had been immediately contrite, reporting his own crime to the police. Now, not one but two families would be without a father and two wives without a husband. Norton questioned how capital punishment could be viewed as a deterrent for this kind of crime, performed in a moment of madness.

If he had already been opposed to the death penalty in principle, the reality of watching it performed confirmed that the practice was barbaric. Before the noose was placed over the condemned man's head, the cloth of his white cap was pulled downwards to form a kind of hood to cover his face. Frobisher had already warned Norton that things sometimes went wrong in a hanging – around twenty per cent of times according to the records. He described – with ill-disguised fascination – how at a recent one the executioner had miscalculated the drop, so when the poor man fell through the trap the force almost ripped his head off his neck, covering the priest who had been standing beside him in blood.

That morning Norton watched, horrified, as after the drop, the body continued to twitch on the end of the rope. The executioner, unfazed, grabbed hold of the man's legs and with a quick jerk ensured he was safely dispatched to meet his maker.

Norton couldn't wait to be outside the oppressive walls of the jail. He watched, his fingers balled into tight fists, as Frobisher signed the paperwork to certify completion of the sentence and the medical officer signed the death certificate.

When they emerged from the jail, he turned to the OA. 'That was gruesome. What have we achieved by hanging that man, apart from leaving another grieving widow and a set of orphans with no one to provide for them?'

'He should have thought of that before he battered that fellow's head in.'

'Did you even read the case? It was a single blow with a plank that happened to be lying there. He probably didn't intend to kill the fellow.'

Frobisher was unmoved. 'We have to set an example, or every Tom, Dick and Harry will be running round Kandy bashing their neighbours' heads in over petty theft.'

There was no getting through to the man. Frobisher's world view was immutable. They climbed into a waiting rickshaw and headed back to the *kachcheri*.

As they rattled through the streets, Norton remembered an old lithograph on the wall of the bungalow he shared with the OA. It portrayed a horrible scene – a wretched man kneeling before a block of stone on which his head was laid while an elephant crushed it with one raised foot. Execution by elephant had once been common practice amongst some of the rulers of the Indian subcontinent. Outlawed by the British, Norton couldn't help wondering whether execution by hanging was any more merciful.

When he'd been in England, at university, and before that, at school, he'd never questioned any of this. The topic of capital punishment had been far removed from his daily concerns. Now, forced to confront it as part of his job, he couldn't help but question it. He didn't want to be complicit, but as a colonial civil servant he had no choice in the matter. When he'd accepted the posting to Ceylon, he'd never anticipated what would be involved. He'd seen it as a chance to experience another country and culture, to build a reputation and career and rehabilitate himself in the eyes of his over-critical father. This morning, as the sun rose over the distant misty hills, the offer from Carberry seemed more tempting. Then, as he climbed down from the rickshaw, he told himself to get a grip. Witnessing the workings of the law was only one tiny part of his overall duties for the Crown. It would be foolhardy to let that govern him. Norton told himself to file it away and get on with the job. He was the tiniest cog in the wheel of the empire, and it was not his place to question or seek to change that vast machine.

Inside the *kachcheri*, the atmosphere was tense. As soon as Norton and Frobisher walked into the room, one of the Sinhalese clerks approached. 'Mr Metcalfe wants to see you immediately, Mr Baxter.'

Norton sensed Frobisher stiffen beside him. As he walked towards the GA's office, Frobisher followed, then overtook him. 'It's completely inappropriate for the GA to conduct meetings with the office junior,' he said in a waspish tone of voice.

After their knocking produced a grunt in response, the two men went inside.

'Not you, Frobisher,' Julian Metcalfe snapped and waved an arm in dismissal.

A furious, red-faced Frobisher retreated, closing the door behind him.

Norton turned to face an equally stern-faced Metcalfe.

'Are you aware of my daughter's whereabouts, Baxter?'

'Isn't she at home?'

'Her bed wasn't slept in. She hasn't been seen since dinner last night, and my wife says she's taken a suitcase of clothes with her. What the devil is going on, man?'

Norton was affronted by the GA's accusatory tone. 'I haven't a clue where your daughter has gone and frankly, I take exception to your implying otherwise.' After a short pause, 'Sir.' Metcalfe may well be the big cheese, but Norton had done nothing wrong and was determined to stand up to him.

The GA growled, 'Are you aware of anything untoward going on between Cynthia and that fool Polegate?'

'Ronald?'

'Yes, Ronald, of course. Not Sir Michael.' The GA thumped his fist on the desk.

Norton refused to be cowed. 'I had noticed they'd become quite friendly. But I never witnessed anything improper. I gather they've been playing a lot of tennis together.'

'That was meant to be your job, Baxter.' Julian Metcalfe leaned his chair back, balancing on its back legs, then jerked it forward again. 'Dash it all, man, she was supposed to marry you.'

'*Marry* me? I'm in no position to marry anyone, sir. I've only been in Ceylon five minutes and I'm on the lowest rung of the ladder. I'm here to prove myself. Marriage simply isn't on the cards. As for Miss Metcalfe, we've played a fair bit of tennis together but nothing more than that.'

'Don't play the fool with me, Baxter. You know bloody well I wanted you and her to marry. If she were married, eventually with a few babies, it would sort her out. I'd have done right by you in terms of salary and promotion. Your future would have been secure. But you've stood back like a ninny and let her run off with that halfwit. You realise you've thrown your career away into the bargain?'

Norton bristled and pressed his palms hard against his thighs as he fought to rein back his anger. Metcalfe's words were not only patronising, but they were also threatening. Norton fixed his eyes on his boss, refusing to be cowed. 'I wasn't aware my career was dependent on my matrimonial choices. I joined the service in the belief that advancement was by merit alone.'

The GA waved a hand in the air dismissively. 'Don't be naive, man. It's always been *who* you know, not *what* you know. I'd have thought you of all people, as Hector Baxter's son, would have understood that. Everyone knows Sir Hector's meteoric rise within Whitehall had more to do with him marrying the cabinet secretary's daughter than any God-given talent or hard graft.'

Norton stared at him open-mouthed. His maternal grandfather, Lord Heatherden, had been a distant and rather scary figure to him until his death about five years earlier. Norton was unaware that his father owed his career to Lord Heatherden by marrying his daughter. Certainly, to listen to Sir Hector Baxter when he railed at his only son, one would be forgiven for assuming he was a man of exceptional gifts, cursed with a son full of shortcomings. Norton had been led to believe that for his father, winning the accolade of Senior Wrangler of his year in the Mathematical Tripos had opened the doors of opportunity to him, whereas Norton's failure to secure the top marks had led to his placing in Ceylon rather than a more significant posting. Norton's mother's role in facilitating her husband's rise to power had never even occurred to him.

Metcalfe's eyes drilled into his. 'Lost your tongue? What in the Lord's name is wrong with you, man? How have you let that milksop Polegate woo Cynthia right under your nose? He's even younger than you are. And he hasn't a brain cell in his skull.' The GA slumped back in his chair, like a wounded animal, all the energy and anger drained from him.

The onslaught from the usually affable GA knocked Norton for six. It was not unlike the many tongue lashings he'd received from his father. He pulled his shoulders back, stood tall and stared back at Metcalfe. 'With all due respect, sir, neither Miss Metcalfe nor I have shown any inclination towards marrying. I've always intended to establish my career before considering the question of marriage. As for Miss Metcalfe, she has never shown a sign of viewing our relationship as anything more than tennis partners and good pals.'

'Good pals?' Metcalfe spluttered. 'The gal's twenty-seven. Long past a respectable time for settling down. And your career would be better served by marrying her. Surely you can see that. No, Baxter, I've had enough of your time-wasting. Get yourself down to Colombo and watch every passenger ship in harbour in case they're intending to flee on one of them. I've already put out an alert via Adamson in the Colombo *kachcheri*, but I need you there on the ground.'

Norton, who was still standing in front of Metcalfe's desk, glanced at the chair but knew better than to sit down without invitation. 'What would you like me to do there, sir?'

'Stop the pair of them sailing off. Bring my daughter back here. Then if you know what's good for you, you can darn well marry her.' Reading the expression on Norton's face he added, 'Anyone would think I was asking you to walk to the North Pole instead of marry a beautiful and talented woman.'

Norton kept his voice steady. 'No offence to Miss Metcalfe – but I must be clear to you that I'm not going to be coerced into marrying anyone. It's not part of my terms of employment. I'm here to do a job but not one that includes choosing a life partner. I'd be grateful if you wouldn't raise the matter again or I'll be forced to consider my future and request that the governor moves me to another province.'

'Are you threatening me, Baxter?'

'No, sir, I was rather under the impression that it was the other way round.'

Metcalfe narrowed his eyes. 'Very well. The most pressing thing is to find her. Now get a move on. I want you on the next train to Colombo.'

'The snag is that I must be here in Kandy tonight to meet my sister. Her ship docked this morning and she's travelling up by train today.'

'Frobisher can meet her.'

'Frobisher?'

'Yes. The chap in the tweed suit you supposedly report to.'

'But she's a young unmarried woman and can't possibly stay in our bungalow alone with Frobisher. My parents would be horrified.'

'Damn and blast it! When I see Cynthia, she's going to find out just how much of a headache she's caused me.' Metcalfe took out a handkerchief and wiped his brow. 'Very well. I'll tell Frobisher to bring her to the residence. There's only Portia and me there, so she can stay with us until you get back. But I don't want to see you again, Baxter, unless my daughter is with you. As for that shameless idiot Ronald Polegate, you can stick him in a trunk and ship him off to China.'

'But, sir, if they've... if they've already married?'

'No time for that to have happened yet.'

'But if they're... as good as...?' Norton remembered that last night in Matara when they'd been drinking whisky. Had they spent the night together? Had the alcohol emboldened them the way it had fired up Blackstock?

'If he's had his way with her, you have my permission to horsewhip him before you throw him out of the country and then you can get yourself back here and we can talk again about you putting a ring on my daughter's finger. It's regrettable if it turns out you're getting secondhand goods, but you've only yourself to blame. If you'd been quicker off the mark none of this nonsense would have happened.' Julian Metcalfe stroked his moustache. 'Now get out of here and get yourself on the next train to Colombo.'

As Norton dashed back to his bungalow and crammed a few items into a holdall, he seethed with anger at Julian Metcalfe's arrogance and presumption. How could he think he had the right to order him to marry his daughter? And was it true that his own father had married his mother to advance his career? He had never for a moment thought of his parents' marriage as a love match but that was hardly unusual among their milieu. But there had been an implication in Metcalfe's words that his father's marriage had been a cynical choice based entirely on career advancement. If that was true Norton was damned if he was going to do the same thing.

As he boarded the train, he thought again of Carberry's employment offer. His disillusionment with his role as a colonial administrator had deepened the more he knew about the inner workings of the empire and its dominion over the native peoples of its territories. But joining Carberry as a planter would mean committing himself to a lifetime in Ceylon and Norton wasn't ready to do that.

He told himself it was because despite his misgivings, he still nursed an ambition to succeed. What he wasn't ready to admit to himself was that taking up Carberry's offer would almost certainly mean there was no possibility of a future with Stella Polegate. Not when her own ambitions lay back in England.

TWENTY-FOUR

Stella spent a sleepless night churning with anxiety at the prospect of being back in close proximity to Gordon Blackstock. She silently cursed her absent brother's selfishness and his capacity to derail everything in his path. He had single-handedly managed to ruin his father's last significant piece of fieldwork. Yet again, she wondered why her father had agreed to let him join the expedition. Sir Michael had claimed it was in the hope of sparking an interest in their subject – but it had always been clear to Stella that it was a hopeless cause. Ronald had never shown an iota of interest in anything unconnected with the pursuit of pleasure.

If it had been up to her, she'd have sent him home after the first weeks in India. They had been working at a hill station near Ooty when he had disappeared without word. It transpired he had been locked up in the military garrison at Coonoor overnight after being found drunk and disorderly in public. He had lost all his money gambling and had to be subsidised by their father, and then to cap it all, Stella had overheard Papa in a rage hauling Ronald over the coals after he'd been caught in a compromising situation with the wife of one of the officers. Yet for some reason he had been forgiven and allowed to remain.

Stella told herself there was no point railing against the injustice of it all. A far more imminent problem was their return to Kandy and the reunion with Blackstock. She'd thought about telling her father what Blackstock had done but quickly dismissed the idea. The risk of being compelled to marry her attacker was too great.

That afternoon on the train when she'd told Norton Baxter what happened, he had promised to help her. But how could he help? According to Julian Metcalfe, by now he'd be in Colombo, hunting for her brother and Cynthia. Even if they were found that day it wouldn't change anything for Stella. She wished she'd taken the risk and broached the subject of university again with her father while they'd had these weeks alone here in the tea country. Too late now. They would be returning to Kandy with Mr Metcalfe so there would be no opportunity to talk privately.

But it wasn't just the prospect of being back in Blackstock's orbit that was eating away at her. A far worse fear was churning inside her. Ever since that terrible night in Matara, Stella had been convinced that Blackstock's savage attack had resulted in an unwanted pregnancy. From the moment of her violation, she had feared this. There was no logic in this assumption but that didn't stop her believing it. When, in the days and weeks that followed, she felt her energy sap, her breasts were tender and an almost constant tiredness washed over her, this certainty intensified. She had always been regular in her monthly bleeding, even during this expedition, so when her period didn't arrive at the appointed time her worst fears were compounded. At first, she'd refused to think about it, telling herself it was the change in climate or the stress from the attack. Now, six weeks after that terrible night, she was still overdue and there were none of the usual signs that her period was imminent – the occasional spot on her face, a bloated stomach, and the customary headaches.

Stella knew there was little room for doubt. Her despair mounted. There was no one to advise her. She'd heard stories of women in this predicament dosing themselves with gin and taking red-hot baths, but she had no means of obtaining sufficient gin and asking a servant to draw a steaming hot bath in a tropical climate would raise questions. Even had she the courage to try it, throwing herself down a flight of stairs was not an option as so many buildings were single-storey.

She felt as though a foreign body with no right to be there was growing inside her – a squat evil presence. Parasitical. Malignant. There was no point telling herself that this was the formation of what would become an innocent child, as all she could think of was that Gordon Blackstock had put it there.

It was becoming hard to explain her frequent need to vomit as merely a bad reaction to food. If it weren't for the fact that the professor was so absorbed in his work and now in his anger about Ronald, her condition would have been impossible to keep hidden. As it was, every time Stella was sick, she wished she could as easily eject what was growing within her. She thought of it as an incubus, a tiny version of Gordon Blackstock, planted inside her and clinging on despite her prayers for it to disappear. She wanted no part in it, refusing to think of it as human. She tried to starve herself in the hope that the pregnancy would go away, but morning sickness meant she was barely able to keep food down anyway and nothing made any difference.

She was desolate. How long would she be able to hide her condition? With Gordon Blackstock heading back to Kandy it seemed her fate was sealed. Marriage was an inevitability.

· · ·

When Stella went in to breakfast, she found her father alone at the table, drinking tea and smoking his pipe.

'Where's Mr Metcalfe? I thought we were returning to Kandy together,' she said.

Sir Michael knocked his pipe into an ashtray and looked at her over the top of his spectacles. 'The tea's fresh. More toast is on the way.' He took a sip from his cup. 'Julian's gone. I gave him a reply to telegraph to Blackstock at the rest house at Anuradhapura so it will be waiting for him when he gets there.'

Stella could barely breathe. 'What did you say?'

'I told him to turn around and get himself back to Jaffna. He has no business changing the plans without consulting me. He can damn well get on with the work without Ronald. I can't imagine Ronald was much use to him anyway.'

Relief surged through her. She sank into a chair. 'We're carrying on here?'

'Yes.'

'What about Ronald?'

'What about him?'

'Well... if Mr Metcalfe finds him before he can leave Ceylon, won't you need to do something?' She lifted the lid of the serving dish but the smell of bacon that greeted her made her feel nauseous. She replaced the lid.

'What exactly? Ronald is a grown man. He may be shy of his majority by a couple of months but it's a bit late for me to play the angry father. I'll leave that to Julian. If he decides to horsewhip him and throw him out of Ceylon, he has my blessing. Ronald must learn that actions have consequences.'

Stella stared at her father. Where was all this coming from? It felt out of character. 'And Cynthia?'

'What of her?'

'Well, do you think they'll have to marry?'

Sir Michael tilted his head back. 'If I know Julian, he'll make sure of it. Can't have his unmarried daughter running all over the country with a young man. He's still set on her marrying that other fellow, but I can't see the chap agreeing to that if Ronald's already had his way with her.' He shook his head, exuding an air of resignation. 'I'm sure before long they'll both rue the day they met each other, but they should have thought of that before they embarked on such licentious behaviour.' He put down his teacup and polished his spectacles with his pocket handkerchief. 'Now what do we have for today?'

'For today?' she echoed.

He frowned at her under his bushy eyebrows. 'Yes. Today. What's wrong with you, Stella? Where are we up to?'

'Oh... I see. We were about to investigate the rituals around betrothal and marriage, and how these have adapted since the workers have been here in Ceylon.'

'Well hurry up then.' The professor rose from the table. 'I'll be on the veranda when you're ready.'

The beating of a drum was the signal for the tea workers and the McNairs to rise each day at five in the morning, ready for Mr McNair to be present at the rostering of the workers at six. While her husband was occupied around the tea estate, Mrs McNair, a keen gardener, spent her mornings either tending to her flowers and vegetables or riding on horseback to visit friends – other planters' wives – to play cards and share garden produce. As a result, Stella and her father were usually free to conduct their work without fear of interruption.

Sir Michael had now almost entirely delegated the questioning of the workers to Stella, only occasionally interjecting to clarify a detail. The women's responses were proving to be more interesting than the men's. Stella wasn't sure why that was the case. Perhaps they had more time to observe and think during their long days picking in the fields, whereas the men's work was more varied – sometimes operating equipment inside the factory, sometimes weeding, pruning tea bushes, or collecting and weighing the baskets of leaves. And that day's topic of marriage and the rituals around it was highly pertinent to women. So, it was a surprise when no one had turned up that morning. Usually the workers were gathered ready – around half a dozen at a time for the half hour each group was spared from their duties by Mr McNair. It was a welcome break from work so until now there had always been a steady flow.

Stella looked at her father, who was staring out over the tea gardens, where the brightly coloured saris of the women pickers dotted the slopes. Smoke was rising from the factory chimney, so it was apparent work was underway there too.

'Perhaps there's been some confusion over the roster,' said Stella. 'Shall I go and find Mr McNair and ask him what's happened?'

Before her father could answer, the birdlike figure of Mrs McNair appeared on the steps of the veranda, her gardening gloves in one hand and a wooden trug over her arm. 'Frightfully sorry, but there isn't anyone for you to interview today. We've just found out one of our coolies died during the night.' She stretched her lips into an apologetic smile. 'They're cremating the poor chap later today and beforehand they want to pay respects and go through whatever rituals their religion requires. Alastair has given the family permission to take time off today and everyone else will get some time to lay garlands. It's dreadfully inconvenient as there's a big order to be fulfilled and one of the belts is broken, so you see he really can't spare the workers any more time off to accommodate your work.' She took off her straw hat and smoothed a hand over her hair. 'Would you mind awfully taking the day off today? I'm sure you'll be glad of a rest and things should be back to normal tomorrow.'

'Actually, we'd like to pay our respects too,' said Sir Michael, glancing at Stella, one eyebrow raised. 'One of the topics we are covering is death rituals and funerary rites. Perhaps if we can observe today, it will enrich our questioning when we cover the topic.'

Mrs McNair raised her eyebrows. 'Goodness me. I've no idea what they'll think about that. Alastair isn't around to ask as he left a few minutes ago to collect some machine parts for the broken belt from the railway station.'

Stella intervened. 'Perhaps we can ask the *kangani*. Obviously, we don't want to upset anyone at such a sad time, and we'll assure him of that.'

The planter's wife raised her palms and shrugged. 'Up to you. But tread carefully and don't blame me if they say no.'

Stella and her father, accompanied by their interpreter, set off to find the *kangani*. After assuring him of their good intentions and that they would keep a respectful distance and observe any protocols, the man agreed to take them to the lines to the home of the deceased. 'You only watch. Say nothing.' The *kangani* looked towards Stella. '*Memsaab* cannot watch cremation. No women allowed.' He turned to the interpreter and spoke rapidly in Tamil.

'He asks me to explain you that no ladies follow procession to funeral pyre. Not good for spirit of dead person. Spirit tries to hide inside body of a woman – can't go to afterlife for reincarnation. Bad for woman too. Haunted by spirit.' He looked away for a moment then spoke to Sir Michael in a whisper so that Stella couldn't hear. The professor nodded, glanced at Stella, but did nothing to enlighten his daughter.

The four of them set off for the lines. The blue painted single-storey buildings stretched in rows. Stella wondered what it must be like to live one's life within the confines of these very basic dwellings. She had visited here before to sit outside and talk with those women who were too old to work, too heavily pregnant or nursing babies. But today the usual bustling atmosphere was replaced by a sombre quiet, the distant murmur of voices and the occasional muffled ring of a bell or gong.

Along the guttering above the doors to the dwellings, white funeral flags hung like bunting. The same flags adorned the fences that separated the lines from the tea gardens. The interpreter explained that the flags were there to guide the spirit of the dead man to the afterlife.

'How did he die?' asked Stella.

The *kangani* replied, 'Doctor says infection from cut in arm.'

'Did he have a family?'

The *kangani* nodded. 'Wife and two children. Wife expecting third child soon.'

'How terribly sad.'

By now they had reached the home of the deceased and a steady procession of people bearing flower garlands or carrying rice balls entered the building. Keeping their distance, Stella and her father looked inside the dwelling which was illuminated by burning oil lamps. The interpreter explained that the lamps were also there to guide the spirit of the dead and remove the pollution of his body. He told them that the preparation of the dead man's body – washing and purification – was performed by the women relatives but otherwise the ceremony was the province of the men. 'Usually, the deceased's son leads the prayers and lights the funeral pyre but this was a young man, so it has fallen to his brother to do it.'

Stella edged closer to the doorway, trying to avoid appearing intrusive. Inside, she could see the body was laid out under a white sheet which was gradually becoming covered with flowers as people laid their offerings on top. She wished she had thought to bring some herself. There was chanting of prayers and in the corner a young very pregnant woman was wailing. Suddenly it was too much for Stella: the condition of the woman, her all too evident grief and the claustrophobic atmosphere of the tiny dwelling place crowded with people. She turned to her father. 'I'm going back to the house. You stay and witness the cremation. I didn't sleep well so I'm going to lie down for a while.'

Without waiting for an answer, Stella walked back towards the McNairs' bungalow. As she approached, she noticed a figure standing on the veranda.

He turned around and she saw it was Norton Baxter.

TWENTY-FIVE

When Norton saw Stella walking towards him, he felt an unexpected surge of joy. She was wearing a pale green blouse over a black skirt and her face was shaded by a straw hat. His mind had been focused on how he would impart the news about Ronald to her and her father that he hadn't allowed for his feelings on seeing her for the first time since their return from the hunting trip. She approached, her hair escaping from the loosely tied plait that hung over one shoulder, with one hand shielding her eyes from the sun. He tried to swallow but his throat was dry.

Instinctively, he rushed to meet her, his hands outstretched to grasp hers. It was only when he was holding them that he saw the surprise in her eyes.

'Mr Baxter... Norton. I didn't expect to see you. Mr Metcalfe told us you'd gone to Colombo,' she said, avoiding any mention of Ronald.

He released her hands, conscious of the proprieties. 'Your father?' He looked around. 'Is he here?'

'He's at the funeral of one of the estate workers. We're studying death rituals.' She twisted round to look back over her shoulder towards the lines. 'But Ronald? You have news of him?'

Embarrassed and suddenly awkward, Norton was caught between his feelings for Stella and his duty as the representative of the provincial GA. 'Perhaps we ought to wait for Sir Michael.'

Impatient, she said, 'He'll be ages.' Then evidently remembering her manners, she added, 'You've come straight from Colombo? You must be tired and in need of refreshments. I shall go and find Mrs McNair.'

'No need. I've already seen her. She's rustling up some tea and sandwiches.'

Stella indicated a pair of rattan chairs, and they sat. 'Tell me please. Where is Ronald?'

Norton twirled his hat between his fingers. 'I'm sorry. The news isn't good. It seems he and Cynthia have already left the country. They were never in Colombo. They crossed the Palk Strait from Jaffna to India and from there have taken a ship for England.'

Stella's hand enfolded the locket that hung around her neck. 'So, Gordon Blackstock lied.'

'I can't say. They may have told him they were going to Colombo.'

Stella looked sceptical. 'Are they married?'

'Not yet.' Seeing her crestfallen face, he quickly added, 'But I believe they intend to be. The GA in Jaffna – I understand you've met him – Mr Percy Moreland... well, he tried to talk them into returning to face the music in Kandy, but they'd have none of it. As you can imagine, Julian Metcalfe isn't best pleased. He instructed me to come here to inform your father before returning to Kandy. Look, I'm sorry—'

'Don't you dare apologise. You've done nothing wrong. You're not responsible.'

Norton smiled and raised his eyebrows. 'Tell that to Julian

Metcalfe. I'm the convenient punch bag. Not least because he believes I was remiss in failing to propose to Cynthia myself.'

Stella's mouth twitched as he said this, and Norton wished he hadn't. She removed her hat and laid it on the low table between them. Norton watched as she fiddled with a lock of hair. The sunlight was behind her creating a kind of halo-like glow around her head. His chest tightened.

He was about to speak again when Mrs McNair appeared, followed by a servant with a tray of tea and sandwiches. 'Ah, you've found each other,' she said. 'Frightfully sorry but I can't stay and join you. I have to ride into Nuwara Eliya. Today's my bridge afternoon. And Alastair is off collecting some machinery. Awfully inhospitable of us, Mr Baxter, but I'm sure Miss Polegate will make sure you have everything you need. Are you staying overnight? It would be so nice if you were able to stay and join us for dinner. It's always a novelty having company here. I can't tell you how delightful it is having Miss Polegate and Sir Michael as our guests.'

'I ought to return to Kandy straight away...' He hesitated.

'Nonsense. You must stay. I have a nice piece of mutton and I've asked Cook to make one of his delicious apple pies.' She grinned. 'That's settled then. See you later.'

When she was gone, Norton looked at Stella. 'I hope I won't be intruding. You and your father will want to talk privately.'

She poured tea for them both. 'I'm relieved you're staying. Papa is going to be angry and if you're here it will dilute the effect a little.' Then she looked up and met his eyes. 'And from a selfish point of view, I'm pleased. I'm always glad of your company.'

He brushed a hand through his hair, a rush of pleasure running through him at her words. 'I'm always glad of yours too,' he said.

She handed him a cup of tea and offered the plate of sandwiches.

'How have you been, Stella? No word from Blackstock?'

Her mouth tightened and she sucked her lips inwards. 'When Ronald left, Mr Blackstock sent a telegram to say he was returning to Kandy, but Papa put a stop to that, thank goodness, and told him to turn back to Jaffna.' She took a sip from her cup and Norton noticed her hand was shaking. She looked up at him. 'I don't think I could have coped if we'd all returned to Kandy. Just the thought of being in the same room as that man fills me with terror.'

Norton couldn't help himself. He reached out a hand and took one of hers in his. She drew it away immediately.

'I think I'm expecting a child.' The words tumbled out, but her voice was barely a whisper.

He stared at her, unable to believe what he was hearing. 'A child?' he echoed. 'Are you sure?'

She nodded. 'I haven't seen a doctor but I'm as certain as I can be. I don't know what to do.'

'Does your father know?' He tried to meet her eyes, but she was looking down.

'Lord, no. And he mustn't find out or he'll have me married to Blackstock in an instant.' Her voice cracked and she bit her lip. 'You're the only one who knows.'

He tried to absorb what she'd told him. All he could think was that he wanted to protect her, love her, make everything all right.

'I think I've run out of choices. I thought of trying to get to Colombo and taking a ship back to England and just disappearing.' She pushed a stray lock of hair behind her ear. 'I imagined having the child and giving it to an orphanage then getting a job and earning the money to support myself. But it's all a fantasy. I don't even have the money to cover the passage home. I have a small trust fund from my mother, but I can't access that.' She looked at him at last, her eyes full of despair. 'I feel as though I'm carrying a monster. All I want is to be rid of it.' She made a sobbing sound. 'I know it's sinful of me, but I pray every day to miscarry. Or better still to find out that I'm not pregnant at all.'

Norton, shocked by the vehemence behind her words, put down his teacup, got up from his chair and kneeled beside her. He grasped her hands again, and this time was determined not to let them go. 'Marry me, Stella. I'll take care of you. And the baby.' He was reacting without his usual analytical, mathematical approach to problems, and it felt liberating.

Her head jerked back, and her eyes widened. He felt her straining to escape his hands, but he held on to them. 'I've never been more serious about anything, Stella. I want to marry you.'

He heard her gasp, but he carried on. 'I have little to offer. I'm at the bottom of the pecking order and don't earn much, but I do have prospects, and I promise you I will give my all to caring for you and providing for you.'

Stella gave a little cry and jerked her hands free of his. She stood up. 'You can't be serious. You barely know me. Did you even hear me? I'm carrying another man's child. I've been disgraced by him. Why on earth would you want to marry me? Please, don't trifle with me, Mr Baxter. Can't you see I'm at my lowest ebb?'

Norton was distraught. This wasn't going the way he'd envisaged. But then he hadn't envisaged proposing to her at all today. Yes, he'd known he wanted to marry her but had intended to find a way that would let her fulfil her academic dreams first and allow himself to increase his earning power. But all that was as nothing in the face of her situation. 'I've known for some time that I love you, Stella. I realise you don't feel the same about me, but I hope that eventually you might come to care for me too. In the meantime, I believe you do at least like me, and marriage to me would be preferable to being bullied into marrying Blackstock.'

She stared at him, eyes wide, trying to make sense of what he was saying. Norton pressed on. 'I think I fell in love with you the moment I first caught sight of you on the *Dambulla*. Then as I came to know you, my feelings have intensified.'

Stella slumped back into her chair. 'Norton, I don't think you fully understand. I'm touched by your spontaneous kindness, but I know you'll regret this once you've had time to think about it. Again, why would you want to marry a woman who has been used by another man and is carrying his child? – No, let me finish!' She put up a hand. 'You may think this is a noble thing to do but once the reality of my situation sinks in it will be a different matter. I don't want this baby so why in heaven's name would you? The thought of it makes me shudder. Every time I look at it once it's born it will remind me of him and that horrible night. Believe me I wish I could be rid of it now – the thought of carrying it for months and giving birth to it makes me sick to my core.' She started to cry.

Norton pulled out a clean handkerchief from his breast pocket and handed it to her. He kept his gaze fixed on her as she wiped away her tears and blew her nose. He knew that whatever happened next would shape the rest of both their lives and he didn't want to mess it up. 'I love you, Stella. I can't help myself. Even if you weren't in this condition, I'd still want to marry you. This has just hastened things. But I'm glad. I'd imagined waiting a long time to make an offer – likely after you had returned to England. I was dreading you leaving. As for the child, we'll face the problem together. I'm not going to put you under more pressure. If you decide to give it up for adoption, I'll support you. If you decide to keep it, I'll love it because it's yours. You're carrying it. Blackstock doesn't matter.'

She fixed her eyes on him. He felt as though she was trying to check his sincerity. 'You realise that you're risking a stain on your own reputation. People will assume it's your baby and you seduced me. That could ruin your career.'

He took a deep breath. 'I'm not going to tell you it will be easy. It won't. But we'll work it all out together. Just say yes. I promise you, Stella, if you'll have me, I will do everything in my power to make a good life for us.'

She squeezed the handkerchief into a ball in her fist and sat with her hands in her lap, studying his face. She lowered her eyes, then raised them again to meet his. 'It's not true, you know. What you said just now.' Her voice was soft. 'About me not caring for you. I do care. Surely you know that?'

Norton gasped. 'You do?'

'Yes. When I thought at first you were engaged to marry Cynthia Metcalfe I was consumed with jealousy. I just wouldn't admit it to myself.'

Her hands were curled tightly, her knuckles white. He reached for them again and this time she didn't resist. They sat together hand in hand, their eyes locked.

He could feel his heart hammering against the inside of his chest. 'So, you'll marry me?'

'If you're absolutely sure you aren't going to change your mind?'

'I've never been surer of anything.'

'Then the answer is yes.'

He could bear it no longer. He jumped up and pulled her to him, breathing in the lemony scent of her hair. Her nose was red and her eyes still brimming with tears, but he thought she had never looked more beautiful. He bent his head and kissed her, tentatively.

She returned his kiss with a fervour he hadn't expected – until a voice boomed out at them.

'What the devil do you think you're doing?'

They sprang apart and turned to see Sir Michael mounting the steps to the veranda. 'Mr Baxter. I thought you were an honourable man, but it seems you're just a chancer.'

'Papa, please.'

'Be quiet, Stella. I'm disappointed in you. Ashamed even. What are you thinking?' His face was red with anger.

'Stella has just agreed to be my wife.' Norton squared up to the older man, keeping his voice steady. 'I hope we will have your blessing. I love her and promise you I will take care of her.'

The professor's eyes narrowed, and his voice was clipped. 'My daughter is to marry my student, Mr Blackstock.'

Stella made a sound like a wounded animal. 'I'll never marry him. I loathe him, Papa. My mind is made up. I intend to marry Mr Baxter.' She stretched out her hand and grasped Norton's. She pulled herself up to her full height and fixed her eyes on her father. 'We love each other.'

Sir Michael's expression changed to one of bewilderment. He closed his eyes and seemed to sway on his feet. Norton stepped forward and took his arm, helping him into a chair while Stella poured him a glass of water. He took a couple of sips then said, 'What are you doing here anyway? I thought you were in Colombo looking for my son.'

'That's why I'm here, sir. I'm afraid I have bad news on that front. Ronald and Cynthia Metcalfe sailed to India from Jaffna and by now will probably be on a ship bound for England.'

Stella's father bent forward, head in hands. 'Does Julian know?'

'Yes, and he's not pleased. It seems they're travelling as man and wife, but as far as we know they have not yet married.'

Sir Michael gave a low groan, then shaking his head, said, 'I wash my hands of the wretch. He's been nothing but trouble since we left England. I fear the worst. I can't see the pair of them staying together once the novelty wears off. And now you, Stella. I thought you were the sensible one. I thought you at least would do as I wished and carry on with my work. The only way to do that is by marrying Blackstock. Not this... this... junior civil servant in a far-flung backwater.'

Stella visibly bristled. 'I told you, Papa. I want to marry Norton. I'd rather do that with your blessing, but I intend to do it anyway.'

Sir Michael shook his head then took off his glasses and rubbed his eyes. 'You're throwing your life away, Stella. You have a chance to carry on the research we've been doing, to assist and support Gordon Blackstock and help shape his career. You have a chance to make a real mark on our subject, to make a lasting contribution, but instead you're happy to throw all that away for the sake of a passing fancy for this man. Oh, Stella, I'm disappointed in you.'

'I'm not going to argue with you, Papa. You know that I want nothing more than to study in my own right. I don't want to settle for being the uncredited skivvy to a man with no talent, no flair, no imagination and what's worse, a bully who has shown me nothing but contempt and disrespect.'

Norton wondered whether to add his words in support, but Stella was in full flow.

'I've told you that I despise Gordon Blackstock. I'd rather die than be married to him. If you have any fatherly feelings, you'll respect my wishes.' She was still holding Norton's hand.

He squeezed hers in encouragement and addressed the professor. 'I acknowledge that in marrying me, Stella will be sacrificing her proximity to the world of academia. She and I have not yet had a chance to talk about our future, but I hope that we can find a way for her to continue the work she has been doing here after we're married.' He turned to look at her and was met with a radiant smile.

'Yes, Papa. I can continue to gather information and write up my findings and send them to you. Once you return to England, I'm sure there will be further areas where you'll need more information or wish to dig more deeply, and I can do that for you.' She let go of Norton's hand and placed hers on her father's arm in a conciliatory gesture.

'Don't be ridiculous, Stella. A married woman can't be galli-vanting about Ceylon without her husband, talking to the natives.'

Before Stella could answer, Norton intervened. 'Look, Sir Michael, it's been a shock for you. I think we all need time to assimilate this. Stella had only just accepted my proposal when you came upon us, so this is all very fresh. I would hope to have your blessing and yet again I want to assure you that I will make it my life's mission to make your daughter happy.'

The older man shook his head then took a drink from his water glass. 'What a mess. What a bally awful mess. I wish to God we'd never left England.'

TWENTY-SIX

Stella's anger was close to rage. Her father's bloody-minded attachment to her marrying Gordon Blackstock, despite his contempt for the man, was beyond logic. She exchanged a glance with Norton, drawing strength from the sympathy in his eyes. It was strange how in the space of such a short time – less than an hour – everything had changed. It was hard to believe he wanted to stand by her and assume responsibility for another man's child, yet she knew she could trust him and that whatever happened he would be there in her corner.

She pulled a chair close to her father's, sat down, and took his hand. 'I need you to listen to me, Papa. Please don't interrupt. This is going to be very hard for me to tell you.' She was aware of Norton moving to stand behind her chair and felt his hand on her shoulder. His touch gave her added strength – as well as a warm feeling of security.

'When we were on the hunting trip, something bad happened to me, Papa. Gordon Blackstock renewed his request that I marry him, and I refused. I gave it a lot of thought, but I just couldn't accept him. You need to understand that. I would rather die than agree to be his wife.'

Stella shivered as she spoke, despite the warmth of the afternoon. She took a deep breath then went on. 'He came into my bedroom later that night when I was sleeping and forced himself on me. I thought I was having a nightmare, but it was all too real. All too painful.' She drew breath. 'I've never been so terrified.' She struggled to form the words until she felt the pressure of Norton's hand increase. 'I tried my utmost to fight him off but he was too strong for me and covered my mouth so I couldn't even scream for help.'

Sir Michael made an anguished cry like a wounded animal and pulled his hand free from her hold.

'It was the worst thing that's ever happened to me. I was filled with shame and anger and grief at what he had done to me. He told me it was so I would have no choice but to marry him. He threatened to tell you and said he was confident you would insist on us marrying rather than risk my reputation being destroyed.'

Stella had to fight to retain control of her own emotions. 'Now for the hardest part. As a result, I have good reason to believe I am with child. Until today, I've been at my wits' end, afraid to tell you, frightened about what the future might hold. I've been living with the fear that Blackstock would get his own way and I'd be forced to marry him. Forced to marry a man I despise and now also fear. I've had no one to confide in until I told Norton.'

Sir Michael spoke. He sounded suddenly old and fragile. 'You could have told me. Why didn't you tell me, Stella?'

'Because I knew exactly what you would have said and done. You would have told me you were sorry about what had happened but that it was better to marry Blackstock than to face the inevitable disgrace of bearing a child out of wedlock.'

'But—'

'There's no buts about it, Papa. Be honest! You would have

said that. After all, you wanted me to marry him anyway. You'd made that clear.'

Her father groaned and buried his face in his hands.

'The only person who knows about this is Norton. When I told him about the rape, he wanted me to tell you. He promised to find a way to help me. But once Blackstock went to Jaffna we thought the threat was contained for a while. And then I realised I am pregnant. When I told him just now, he immediately asked me to marry him. I still can't believe he has done so, but he's assured me of his sincerity, and I trust him. I don't know what I've done to deserve him and I'm grateful from the bottom of my heart.' She turned to look at Norton, feeling a rush of emotion that brought tears to her eyes.

Sir Michael's eyes narrowed as he looked at Norton. 'You're willing to take on another man's child? To provide for them both?'

Norton met his gaze. 'It's Stella's child and that's what matters. If she wants to keep it, I will bring it up as mine. If she wants to give it for adoption, I'll stand by that.'

'But that would ruin you. Adoption is out of the question. People would realise it wasn't your child.' Sir Michael's voice was tremulous.

Stella interjected. 'We can say it's a premature birth and the baby died. No one would know the truth.' She glanced at Norton. 'But we'll worry about that later.'

Norton cut in. 'I love your daughter. In other circumstances we might have had a more conventional courtship, and I must be honest that from a financial viewpoint it won't be easy at first. But as soon as I pass my Sinhala exam, I'll get a modest pay rise and then regular increments each year with more substantial increases as I progress into higher grades.'

Sir Michael looked from one to another. 'And you love this man, Stella?'

'I do.' She reached her hand up and placed it over Norton's

where his still rested on her shoulder. 'With all my heart.' As she said the words, she felt a rush of happiness that reinforced the realisation that yes, she did indeed love him. How had it taken her until now to admit it to herself?

'Stella, will you leave us for a while? I would like to speak to Mr Baxter alone.'

She looked at Norton, who nodded. Reluctantly, she left the veranda and went inside the house to her bedroom.

When Stella had gone, Sir Michael took out his pipe and lit it. The woody scent of briar pervaded the veranda. Norton waited as the older man puffed at it, coaxing the tobacco into life. When it was drawing to his satisfaction, he addressed Norton. 'What I'm about to tell you is for your ears only. You must never tell Stella.'

Norton was about to protest that he wanted no secrets between them, but the professor waved a hand in dismissal. 'It's vital you agree. If Stella were to know what I'm going to tell you, it would destroy her. Promise me.'

Norton had no choice – yet it seemed to him unfair to extract such a promise before he knew the implications.

Stella's father continued. 'It may surprise you to hear this, but I can empathise with your situation. When I fell in love with Delia, my wife, she was an opera singer and a friend of Portia Metcalfe. I used my friendship with Julian to meet her. I haunted the concert halls and opera houses where she was performing, following her from city to city, trying to convince her to marry me. But she would have nothing to do with me.'

He took out his wallet and removed a well-worn photograph which he showed to Norton. 'So beautiful. With the voice of an angel.'

Norton was puzzled. Why was this to be kept from Stella? But Sir Michael gave him no chance to ask.

'Eventually I discovered that Delia was in love with another man, a conductor and impresario. He was older than her, an

Italian. Unfortunately for Delia he was married with five children and no intention of leaving them.'

Norton listened intently, still uncertain why, when Delia Polegate was dead, Sir Michael was insisting on keeping this from Stella.

'I won't mention his name. It no longer matters. The man's long dead. But he was a scoundrel. He made promises to Delia, lavished gifts upon her, swore he was going to leave his wife. But he had no intention of marrying her. He seduced her, kept her as his mistress, until she found out she was expecting a child; then he cast her off like a threadbare coat. He dropped her as the soloist while another singer – his new mistress – took her place.'

Norton saw that Sir Michael's anger at this man was unabated even after so many years. He sensed where this was leading and was increasingly uncomfortable.

'Poor Delia was distraught. She loved the man passionately and had believed every word from his lying silver tongue. Now she was abandoned, pregnant, without a job. I had been in love with her since the first time I heard her sing. My feelings for her were as deep and lasting as that devil's had been shallow and fleeting. I followed her from the concert hall the night he abandoned her. You may think me pathetic that I was so besotted, but I could tell she was distressed. I wanted to find out why and try to help. She went to Waterloo Bridge.' As though the memory of that night was still fresh, he took out a handkerchief and wiped it across his eyes.

'She had started to try to climb up the parapet, so I ran forward and grabbed her, holding on to her as she struggled. Eventually she gave up and then we talked for hours. She told me everything. I offered to marry her. No – I *begged* her to marry me. I knew she didn't love me – she was brutally honest about that – but she said her mother had once told her that if you couldn't marry someone you love, then you should try to marry someone who loves you.' He fumbled in his pocket for matches and relit his pipe, evidently taking comfort from it.

'So, Mr Baxter, I married Delia, knowing I would never be more than second best. But in spite of all the pain, I would do it all over again. I sense it is different for you as my daughter appears to love you.'

Norton hoped he was right. 'I am still pinching myself. I am the luckiest man alive.'

Sir Michael went on. 'All of this is a long and circuitous way of getting to the point of this conversation, which is to tell you that the child Delia was carrying was Stella. She is the product of an illegitimate liaison. So, Mr Baxter, I have walked in your shoes before you and I therefore believe I have some right to offer an opinion on the challenge you are about to take on. Firstly, despite my initial doubts because of my loathing for her natural father, I have loved Stella as though she were my own. I say this while admitting to you that it may not always have appeared so. I am filled with shame and remorse when I admit that I favoured Ronald over her. I suppose it was to counterbalance Delia's evident preference for Stella. I overindulged him, gave him too much rope. Privileged him over his sister. Alas, that has come back to bite me.' He squeezed his eyes tightly shut then shook his head. 'Yet despite all that, Stella is the one good thing in my miserable existence. I see her mother in her every day. And I also see myself. Forgive an old man's vanity, but she has become everything I wanted my own child, Ronald, to be. Nurture over nature perhaps. I couldn't be prouder of her and the knowledge and expertise she has built up in the subject that has been my life's work.'

He made a little snorting noise. 'According to Portia Metcalfe, Stella believes I forced her mother to give up her music career when we married. Nothing could be further from the truth. Delia burned all her musical scores and refused to sing another note after that devil abandoned her.' He tilted his head back and closed his eyes again. 'And yet despite what he did she still loved him.'

Norton was dumbstruck. He felt compassion towards Stella's father at being forced to live a lie all those years, at loving his wife without his feelings being returned.

'Why? Why did you let Stella believe you'd forced her mother to abandon her career?'

'What choice did I have? I heard Delia telling Stella she had given up music for love. When Stella assumed that must be love for me, how could I disabuse her? It was the sorrow of my life that I fell in love with her voice first, only for her to refuse to sing again because of *him*.'

'Even though it meant Stella thought badly of you for forcing her mother to give up her passion?'

'Because I loved Delia. And because I love Stella too.' He grabbed at Norton's arm. 'If she loves you, Mr Baxter, you are a lucky man indeed. And if, please God, you are as fortunate as I was, you will be able to love her child too. But your case is different. Unlike Delia, who – even if misguidedly – loved that adulterous bastard until the day she died, Stella hates Blackstock with a passion. That may mean she will find loving the child to be a challenge.'

Norton exhaled. His brain was in turmoil. In sharing this confidence and swearing to keep it from Stella, Sir Michael had given him a burden that he wasn't sure he was up to carrying. How could he hold this knowledge and not share it with Stella? How could he start married life keeping such a secret from her?

But Stella loved both her mother and father, and if Sir Michael was right, it could devastate her to find out that she was the child of another man – someone she had never met and who had treated her mother with contempt and abandoned her. And most of all had rejected Stella herself. How hurtful would that be?

Sir Michael bent forward, elbows on knees, hands clasped.

'Remember your promise, Mr Baxter. Not a word to Stella. She's suffered enough. I couldn't bear for her to suffer any more. But I hope you see why I've told you this. If I could bring up another man's child and love her as though she were my own, then I'm sure you can too.'

Norton's gaze was steady. 'I love Stella and it goes without saying I will love her child too. I promise you, Sir Michael, if Stella wants to keep the child it will be treated as mine. No question.'

The older man leaned forward and proffered a hand to Norton. 'Then welcome to the family, Norton Baxter.'

In the distance, beyond a thicket of trees, a plume of smoke rose.

Norton dropped the handshake. 'What's that? Over there beyond the trees. Is there a fire?'

'Ah! They've lit the funeral pyre,' said the older man. He drew on his pipe again then said, 'I'll walk over there now and leave you to my daughter.' With that, he knocked out what was left in his pipe, put it in his jacket pocket and hurried towards the trees.

TWENTY-SEVEN

Early next morning, Norton returned to Kandy. He went first to the GA's residence to find his sister, figuring that Julian Metcalfe would be safely out of the way in the *kachcheri*. Since he'd had to abandon Winnie to the care of strangers, surely the GA would allow him to spend a few precious minutes with her before returning to duties – but he wasn't going to risk asking permission first.

Portia Metcalfe greeted him warmly, but he could tell she was upset about Cynthia. 'I should have seen it coming,' she said. 'All the signs were there. Letters from Jaffna daily. Cancelling tennis games. Moping in her bedroom. I just hope she'll be happy with this young man.' Her lips were stretched tight, and Norton could tell she was putting on a brave face. 'He *will* marry her, won't he? You don't think he'll leave her stranded when he's tired of her? They say it happens all the time when women give their favours too easily.'

Norton had his doubts, but it wouldn't be helpful to express them. 'Having won Miss Metcalfe's heart, Ronald Polegate would be crazy to let her go.'

She gave him a narrow-eyed look, perhaps thinking that he

himself had done just that. 'I hope you're right, Mr Baxter. At least Ronald comes from a good family. His mother and I were dear friends in our youth.' She swept an arm out in the direction of the rear of the house. 'But enough of my troubles; I expect you are eager to see your sister.'

'Thank you for putting Winnie up at such short notice, Mrs Metcalfe.'

'The least I could do when it's thanks to my daughter that the poor girl was left alone in a strange place. And it has been an absolute pleasure. Winifred is a darling. I suppose you're planning to whisk her away, aren't you? I'll miss her dreadfully and I suspect she'll be bored stuck in your bachelor quarters while you're at work, so why not let the dear girl stay here at the residence. It would be company for me now Cynthia's gone. I can introduce her to other ladies. What do you think?' She paused. 'I took the liberty of mentioning it to Winifred and she likes the idea.'

'Then who am I to argue? Thank you.' Norton was relieved. He'd been anxious about his sister. The hunting trip and the wild goose chase to Colombo had left him with too much catching up to do to request time off.

When he stepped onto the large terrace at the rear of the property, Winnie was at the far end of the extensive lawns playing fetch with the dog. Tall and solidly built she had an infectious smile that lit up her pleasant, freckled face. She turned and saw him, breaking into wreaths of smiles. She rushed to greet him, holding her skirts up as she ran, the dog barking excitedly behind her. She stopped in front of him, flinging her arms around his neck. After planting a kiss on his cheek, she drew back and gave him an exaggerated scowl. 'You absolute swine, rushing off before you'd even welcomed me to Ceylon.' Although she'd every right to feel aggrieved, her eyes were shining with merriment and pleasure at seeing him.

'I'm sorry, Win. If I'd known, I'd have telegraphed to tell you to wait in Colombo, but you tore off with those ladies.'

She grinned. 'I know. I'm not really cross. It's my own fault I didn't stick to the original plan and have you meet me there. But Mrs Metcalfe – Portia – has been terribly kind to me and the most wonderful hostess.' She took a step back. 'Let me look at you.' She adjusted his tie. 'Not too bad. You'll do.' She gave him another hug. Norton noticed that her skin already had a healthy glow from the Ceylonese sunshine. It suited her.

Portia Metcalfe stuck her head round the open doorway. 'Coffee is on its way, and I've sent a message to the *kachcheri* to tell my husband I'm stealing you, Mr Baxter, until after tiffin. You and Winifred have a lot of catching up to do, so I'll leave you alone until it's served.' She raised her voice to call the dog. 'Muffin, come here!' The dog dutifully pattered across the grass and followed her inside.

They sat on the cool shaded terrace and talked over their coffee, first about Winnie's voyage out, then about Norton's life here in Kandy.

'Poor Portia and her husband are frightfully upset about the daughter doing a bunk with that chap. I gather you know them both – she mentioned that you all play tennis and gad about together.' She looked at him with an arch expression. 'I got the impression they'd rather Cynthia had chosen you. Obviously, they didn't say as much – but if it's the case you probably missed out there, Nortie. There's a portrait of her in the drawing room and she's a beauty. Not to mention she's the boss's daughter. Slow on the uptake, were you?'

'Please don't call me Nortie, dear girl. It's not so much that I mind it from you, but I don't want anyone else assuming it's appropriate to call me that. I'd never shake it off.'

'Spoilsport!' She pulled a face, then reached for his hand and squeezed it. 'It's wonderful to see you at last. I've missed you terribly. I was rather hoping you'd find it beastly out here and come straight home to England again.'

He sipped his coffee but said nothing.

'I say – that Frobisher chap's a bit of a rum one, isn't he? Grumpy and frightfully rude.'

'I have to live with him – and report to him.'

'I don't know how you stick it. Pity – as I was rather hoping he might be an SMC.' She grinned and gave him a wink.

'SMC? What the devil is that?'

'A Suitable Marriage Candidate. It's why I'm here. I'm on the hunt for a husband. My London season was an absolute stinker. Only one proposal, from that ghastly Scottish fellow. Mummy is in despair.' Winnie rolled her eyes and laid a hand across her brow in a theatrical gesture. 'She seems to think I don't make enough effort, but the truth is I fall for handsome chaps – the type of men who'd never give me a second glance or who turn out to be confirmed bachelors.' She gave him a sad smile. 'That Frobisher fellow would be even worse than the Scottish laird. Quite apart from his rudeness, he dresses like an elderly parson and certainly doesn't have the sort of face one would be happy looking at every morning over a plate of kippers.'

Norton wasn't going to disagree with that. Amused, he asked, 'What constitutes suitable marriage material then?'

Winnie opened her handbag and drew out a folded piece of paper. 'I've made a list. I have given up on handsomeness as a requirement and will settle for a pleasant face but since I get to define what pleasant is, it's tending to be perilously close to handsome, so I'm trying to give more weight to the other factors.'

'Which are?'

'Good prospects – that one's to keep Mummy and Daddy happy although I don't really give a fig about it myself. There was a chap I was rather keen on whom I met at a promenade concert, but they put the damper on that as he was only a bank clerk.' She counted off on her fingers as she went through the rest of her list. 'A sense of humour – that's essential – I can't abide men like your Mr Frobisher who don't know how to laugh. Intelligence – *obviously* – after all we'll have to find interesting things to talk about for years and years. Sporty—'

'Sporty! Why on earth is that a requirement?'

'I don't want someone who's only ever got his nose in a book. I definitely prefer outdoorsy types.' She paused. 'Unless they're like the Scottish laird and just spend their life in a deerstalker hat shooting at things. I want someone who likes normal kinds of sport like golf or tennis or swimming.' She raised her eyebrows and gave him a cheeky smile. 'Actually, sporty is really just my code for not being fat. I wouldn't care to marry a chubby chap.'

He laughed. 'What other requirements, coded or otherwise?'

'That's it. I want to keep it as broad as possible and not rule someone out until I've given him the benefit of the doubt. Now I'm going to need your help to line up some candidates. Portia says until the situation is clearer with Cynthia she won't be doing any formal entertaining – otherwise that would have been a perfect way to get to know some SMCs. So, I'm dependent on you, dear brother.' She took a fan out of her handbag and began to flap it vigorously. 'Thank heavens you're in Kandy. So much cooler than Colombo. And the place is full of Europeans. You could have been posted to some awful backwater with no one within miles. Portia says there's a wonderful social whirl here.'

'Does she indeed?' Norton dreaded the prospect of finding out where the centre of this whirling scene was and steering his sister into it. It wasn't something he knew himself and was certainly not something Frobisher could advise him about. Then he thought of Carberry. He'd know.

'But you've told me nothing about yourself. Surely your

failure to win the beautiful Cynthia wasn't just because you're being a swot and obsessed with the job. There has to be another lady on the scene – come on – spill the beans!'

Norton decided Winnie would have to know sometime – imminently if Stella was indeed expecting a child. That would be established today as she was going to see a doctor in Nuwara Eliya.

'Actually, Win, I got engaged to be married yesterday.'

Winnie had just poured herself a second cup of coffee and managed to snort it out of her nose. She produced a handkerchief and mopped up the damage. 'Good grief, you know how to deliver a surprise. When did this happen? What will Mummy and Daddy say? Have you told them? When's the wedding? I can't believe it! You crafty devil. Who is she? When do I meet her?' She clasped her hands in front of her.

'You'll meet soon, I hope. But you must tell no one yet. Certainly not the Metcalfes. They're friends of her family and it would be inappropriate for me to be the one to tell them.'

'What's her name? How did you meet?'

'First, promise to say nothing to anyone until it's official. That includes the parents.'

'Deb's honour.' She ran her index finger along her lips.

'Her name is Stella – Stella Polegate.'

'Polegate?' Winnie frowned. 'Where have I heard that name? – Good Lord! It's the name of the fellow who's run off with Cynthia Metcalfe!'

'Stella is his sister.'

'Good gracious, Norton. You dark horse. Is she fast like he is? She certainly seems to have wasted no time with you.'

Norton's light-hearted mood receded. He didn't want to make light of his relationship with Stella. 'She's completely different from her brother. And it's not like that at all. Stella isn't frivolous. Certainly not fast. She's serious. Sometimes too serious – which I hope will change when everything's sorted.'

'Sorted? What do you mean?'

'Just that she's had a raw deal since leaving England. Her father's an Oxford anthropologist and she works as his assistant – his right hand even. They've been on an expedition for months – firstly in India and then over here – studying the Tamil culture. Her brother has done everything possible to wreck things and Stella has been trying to hold it all together. Her father was taken ill in the north and there have been a lot of problems.' He hesitated for a moment, then plunged on. 'One of the reasons for me moving so quickly in asking her to marry me was that she was coming under intense pressure from her brother and father to agree to a marriage proposal from the other member of their expedition, her father's doctoral student. He was extremely persistent and a thoroughly unpleasant man. I knew from almost the first moment I saw Stella – when they joined our ship – that I had feelings for her.'

'Feelings?' She cocked her head on one side, her eyes narrowing as she studied him.

He sighed and pulled at his collar. 'Love – I love her.'

'Gosh. I never expected you to go soppy on a girl. You've clearly got it bad.'

'Look, Winnie, it's all happened quickly. We've had no time to plan anything. The only other person who knows is Stella's father.'

'Where is she? Will I meet her tonight?'

'They're not in Kandy. They're up in the hills on a tea estate doing their research. They have a few things to wind up, then they'll be coming here. I hope to have more news tomorrow.'

Winnie studied his face again then leaned over and kissed his cheek. 'If you love this girl then I'm happy for you and I'm determined that she and I will be firm friends.' She smiled at him, her eyes bright. 'And I promise until you tell me otherwise, my lips are sealed.' Then she grinned. 'But you'd better get cracking on Project SMC as I don't want to be playing the gooseberry while I'm here in Ceylon. And if you've managed to find someone prepared to put up with you, I jolly well ought to be able to find someone too.'

He smiled and squeezed her hand. 'I'll do my best. As it happens, my only real pal will be in town tonight. He knows everyone for miles around so I'll see if he can suggest any eligible bachelors.'

'Good grief, Norton, don't tell him I'm on a man hunt. Show a bit of subtlety.'

'I'll be the soul of discretion. I'll simply suggest that as I'm an antisocial devil myself – something he knows all too well – I need his help in introducing you to the Kandy social whirl.'

'Perfect!' She paused then leaned forward. 'What about him? How would he measure up to my list?'

Norton laughed. 'Carberry? Definitely not suitable marriage material.'

'I think I'll be the judge of that, dear boy.' She patted him on the arm. The gong sounded to signal that luncheon was about to be served. Winnie looped her arm through her brother's. As they went inside to join Portia Metcalfe, she said, 'As for your beloved, she does have a nice name. Stella is Latin for star and it seems she's already shining brightly in your life.'

Norton was touched by her words, if somewhat embarrassed. They went into the dining room and the conversation moved on to safer ground.

Norton returned to the *kachcheri* after the meal. He didn't need to worry about the GA as the latter was closeted away inside his office.

'The old man's like a bear with a sore head,' said Frobisher. 'I gather you messed up and failed to return his runaway daughter.'

Norton ignored him and picked up the first item from a large pile of papers on his desk.

'You thought you were in with her, didn't you? Seems she was oblivious to your charms.' Frobisher made a guffawing sound. 'That fellow snatched her from right under your nose.'

Tempting though it was to put Frobisher right, Norton decided not to take the bait. He crossed the room to one of the filing cabinets that lined the walls and rifled inside, searching for a folder. He returned to his desk with it and buried himself in analysing numbers of live births by ethnic group.

Ever since his experiences at the prison, and the conversation he'd had with Carberry about leaving the service, Norton had felt unsettled. It was paradoxical that he often felt ill-prepared for the weighty responsibilities of colonial government, yet the nature of the work was fascinating and absorbing. Even though Frobisher lumbered him with all the menial jobs he didn't want to tackle himself, the work was often of significance to the lives of others. Norton was only twenty-three and yet before long he would be expected to make decisions on land disputes, marital discord, and law and order in general. It was a huge responsibility, yet he had to acknowledge, deeply interesting. He tried to counter his unease about being a young white man lording it over natives, by telling himself that if he wasn't doing it, someone else would and perhaps less conscientiously. Most of all, someone as junior and insignificant as he was powerless to overturn the status quo.

He looked around the office at all the clerks – young men of both Sinhalese and Tamil ethnicity – and reflected that one day they would be well-equipped to run the whole shebang themselves, thanks to what they were learning now. But would self-government happen in his lifetime? Already much of the judiciary, the medical profession, and the teaching profession were local people. Surely that could eventually apply to all branches of government. He hoped it would but knew the empire was too entrenched, too valuable for Britain to ever let it go without a struggle.

Norton thought again of Carberry's offer. But he couldn't picture himself a planter. Besides, would that be any easier on his conscience? The pay and conditions of the Tamil tea workers left much to be desired. Although estate workers were prepared to accept what were little more than subsistence wages in exchange for the provision of accommodation and security of employment, it didn't justify that they earned less than they deserved for what was often backbreaking work.

Norton sighed and turned his focus back to the preparation of the monthly statistics required for the Blue Book – the annual compendium of information on Ceylon, recording everything from population statistics to rates of production, taxation and public spending, itemising expenditure by category, and revenue earned for the Crown on everything from agriculture and archaeology to warehousing, weights and measures and weather statistics. The data was compiled by the clerks but, as the cadet, Norton was responsible for overseeing their work and checking for anomalies and errors. The mathematician in him enjoyed it and found it satisfying.

He glanced up at the clock. He'd promised Winnie he'd take her to the tennis club for a game before they met Carberry at the Queen's. He returned the files to the cabinets, wiped his pen nib, and packed away his notes to follow up on tomorrow. He still hadn't had to face Julian Metcalfe – something he was intensely relieved about.

After playing a game of doubles with Val and Snod MacDonald, Norton and his sister set off for the Queen's Hotel in a rickshaw. Winnie asked him how the rest of his day had gone.

Norton chose not to tell his sister about his huge backlog of work. 'I was going through statistics all afternoon.'

'Sounds a bit grim.'

He explained about the Blue Book. 'It's not as bad as it sounds. But until I get it finished it means I won't be able to take much time off to entertain you and show you around.'

'Don't worry about me. After all, I invited myself here and I'm perfectly happy spending time with Portia.' She gave him a nudge with her elbow. 'And don't think you have to turn up to play tennis with me every afternoon. Val MacDonald has promised to introduce me to the other ladies and says I won't be short of partners.'

They rattled along the lakeside, past the Temple of the Sacred Tooth, now lit up by lanterns.

'Kandy's such a beautiful place. I could certainly be happy living here.' Winnie smoothed her hand over the skirt of her dress. 'But knowing my luck, I won't find an SMC and you'll have to send me home again. Then I'll have to marry whoever meets with parental approval and is prepared to make me an offer.' She pushed out her bottom lip.

Norton snorted. 'Approval is something I've never managed myself where Father's concerned.'

She patted his arm. 'You worry too much about what Daddy thinks. I know he carries on at you but he himself had it easy. His year at Cambridge wasn't the best so he didn't have a lot of competition to become Senior Wrangler. I had that from a very good authority who shall remain nameless. And he's always had a comfortable ride in Whitehall. Marrying Mummy certainly didn't do him any harm. You, on the other hand, have come out here and are making your own way. I'm frightfully proud of you, Norton.'

'Thank you.' He squeezed her hand gratefully, while wondering how his younger sister appeared to be apprised of his parents' marital circumstances when he hadn't been.

'As for Daddy, I know he's awfully proud of you too even though he doesn't always show it. He's always impatient to read your letters – even over Mummy's shoulder.'

Norton sniffed. 'Looking for things to find fault with.'

She slapped him playfully on the back of his hand. 'Stop it! Don't play the victim, Norton. And don't argue with me. I promise you he only criticises you when he thinks you're capable of doing more. He's often said that you'll go far.'

Norton was surprised, but his sister was always unafraid to speak the truth, so he had to accept his own doubts were possibly unfounded.

'Daddy only wants the best for you, Norton. He may seem to be hard on you but it's only because he loves you.'

Norton felt a rush of guilt. Had he been too quick to assume the worst about his father?

They had arrived outside the hotel and went inside. They were a little early and there was no sign of Carberry yet. Norton ordered drinks and thought of his sister's list of requirements for a spouse, reflecting that, were it not for his claimed sexual orientation, Carberry himself would have fitted her requirements perfectly.

TWENTY-EIGHT

Her father was pacing anxiously outside when Stella emerged from the doctor's surgery. 'Well?' he asked.

Her mouth set in a hard line, she gritted her teeth, determined not to cry. 'Yes.' It was all she could manage.

He winced. 'I'm sorry, Stella.'

'I couldn't help nursing the hope that I was wrong.'

'Will you keep the baby, or have it adopted?' His eyes were full of concern, and it seemed to Stella that the worry lines on his face had deepened. She wished she could do something to reassure him.

'I don't know. I don't want to keep it. It doesn't seem right to foist another man's child on Norton.' She closed her eyes for a moment. 'It doesn't even feel right that he's having to marry me at all.'

Sir Michael looked alarmed. 'You're not having second thoughts? You said you loved him yesterday.'

With a rush of feeling she said, 'I do. I'm sure of that. But that's why I feel bad that he's offering to go through this for me. To marry and bring up another man's child before he's had a chance to make his way in the world. How can I ask that of him?'

Her father looked away. Stella saw he was shaking.

'What's wrong, Papa? Are you unwell? I said you didn't need to accompany me today.'

Sir Michael's expression was anguished. He was silent for a few moments while he appeared to be battling with indecision. Eventually, he suggested they adjourn to the Grand Hotel for some refreshment before returning to the tea estate.

They sat in the extensive gardens in front of the gable-fronted hotel, where they were served coffee and biscuits under the shade of a neem tree. Stella couldn't face eating, and sipped slowly on her coffee, hoping to draw strength from the bitter taste. Her father's countenance was pale, and he seemed preoccupied: probably worrying about her. The doctor at the pearl fishery had said his heart was fragile and she feared her condition was causing him stress.

They sat for a while in silence, as Stella listened to the rich, warbling birdsong from the tree beside them. She looked up into the foliage at a brown bird with a white breast speckled with dark spots. Some kind of thrush. She pictured herself at home in Oxford in their garden listening to the song thrush that nested in the ivy that covered the garden wall.

Her reveries were interrupted when her father put down his cup, cleared his throat and said, 'I must tell you something. I've wrestled with my conscience and have come to the conclusion that you have a right to know this, even though hearing it may be painful for you.'

Stella waited, puzzled and uneasy, her eyes on her father, aware that he was avoiding her gaze. She listened, dumbstruck, as he told her he wasn't her natural father.

It was as though the ground under her feet had been cut away and everything she had ever believed was a lie. 'Who is my father?'

'He's dead.' The professor explained about the man who had abandoned her mother and refused to acknowledge Stella's existence.

'Is that what you were telling Norton yesterday? Is that why he was so quiet over dinner last night?'

The colour suffused Sir Michael's cheeks. 'I put him in an impossible position. I made him swear not to tell you when he was adamant he wanted no secrets between you. Having slept on it, I now realise he was right. I've been protecting myself whilst pretending to protect you.' He choked off an anguished sob. 'The truth is, Stella, I was afraid if you knew the truth you'd want nothing to do with me. I'm still afraid of that now. Afraid because I couldn't bear to lose you and to lose your respect.'

She steadied her breathing. 'Ronald? Does he know?' Then her expression changed. 'Is he also this man's child?'

'No. Ronald's mine.' He looked down, twisting his hands in his lap. 'Stella, you may not be of my blood, but I couldn't love you more if you were.' He paused. 'As you can imagine, I feel some empathy for Norton's situation.' He wrung his hands again. 'The difference is that your mother loved the man who is your natural father. It was hard for me to understand why, since he treated her so badly, yet I believe she loved him until the day she died.'

Stella struggled to hold back her emotion.

'I'm sorry. Believe me, I wish it were different.' Sir Michael's face reflected his misery.

She scrunched a handful of the fabric of her skirt in her fist, trying to process the information he'd imparted. 'I'm going to walk for a few minutes, P—' She couldn't bring herself to say the word 'papa'. 'I need to be alone. It's a shock.'

'Of course, my dear.' He looked distraught.

She walked away, across the well-tended lawn, past formal flowerbeds and a fountain, wanting to get her father out of her sight. She perched on a low stone wall, screened by foliage from where he was sitting and shaded by trees. It was quiet, distant from the terrace where their refreshments had been served: with only the soft tinkling of the fountain and the sound of the birds.

Stella was angry at her father for telling Norton about her parenthood and coercing him into sustaining the lie. A wave of nausea rushed up on her and she had to turn aside as she threw up the coffee she had just drunk onto the grass. She took big gulps of air, hoping it would calm her, as her nerves jangled and her chest pounded. After a while, her breathing settled, and she told herself that she could hardly blame Papa for not being her father. What he had done was exactly what Norton was offering to do for her. The difference was that he had done it in the knowledge that her mother didn't love him in return. Yet he had stood by her; had stood by Stella too. It must have been a lifelong source of pain for him. How it would have hurt him deeply when Ronald, his own son, failed to share his passion for anthropology while his adopted daughter did. A bitter pill. She started to feel some compassion for him, directing her anger instead at her mother for deceiving her and taking her shabby secret to her death bed.

After several minutes, she was ready to face her father. What he had done was above criticism – apart from telling Norton before he told her. And it had been her mother's secret, not his. In continuing the silence he'd merely been respecting Delia's wishes.

She returned and sat down beside him. He looked up, his eyes damp with unshed tears. Stella reached for his hand. 'Let's go back to the estate, Papa,' she said. 'We have work to do.'

Stella and her father skirted the Nuwara Eliya golf course, heading for the post office in order to send a telegram to Norton with the news from her visit to the doctor. As they were emerging from the building, a man almost knocked Stella over as he hurried past. He stopped and took off his hat.

'I beg your pardon, miss, I wasn't looking where I was going.'

As he spoke, Stella took in the man's appearance – there was something vaguely familiar – tall, with a shock of fair hair and classically handsome features.

'You're Miss Polegate, aren't you? Arrived on the *Dambulla* from Cochin?'

Stella stared at him in astonishment. 'Yes, but... we...'

'Haven't met. I know, but I met your brother when we were disembarking in Colombo.' The man looked around. 'Is he with you?'

Stella turned to include her father in the conversation. 'No, Ronald's left Ceylon. I'm afraid you have the advantage of me, Mr...?'

'Carberry. Paul Carberry.' He turned to introduce himself to Sir Michael. 'I'm a tea planter. Your son mentioned that you were conducting a study among the Tamil tea workers. I told him you're welcome to talk the workers at Glenross. I'm the number two there.'

The professor said, 'Most kind of you but we are staying with the McNairs at Hillbrow then we will likely return to Kandy.'

'I'm off to Kandy myself tonight. I'm purchasing a plot of land for my own tea estate. My dinner companion on the *Dambulla* works in the provincial *kachcheri* so I'm hoping he can help grease the wheels for me over a hitch that's come up with the title of the land.'

Then Stella remembered. He was the man who had been with Norton on the ship and the next day in the Galle Face Hotel. Stella blurted, 'Norton Baxter?' She felt the blood rush to her face.

'You know him?' Carberry's eyebrows shot up.

'The government agent in Kandy introduced us all.' Stella felt her face burn and fiddled with the brim of her hat to ease it lower over her face and hide her blushing. Anxious to escape, she slipped her arm through her father's, told Carberry it had been a pleasure to meet him and asked him to convey their greetings to Mr Baxter. Then she steered her father away, leaving Carberry standing on the pavement, his hat still in his hand.

'I'll tell him I met you when I see him tonight!' he called towards the backs of the Polegates as they hurried away.

They returned to the Hillbrow tea plantation in the McNairs' carriage, the sun shining on flaming, blood-red rhododendrons, where they burst in vibrant swathes between the green sweeps of the tea gardens that lined the route. As they swayed along, Stella tried to put her father's revelations into perspective. So much about her past made sense now: her mother's rejection of music, her benign neglect of Ronald, her father's indulgence of her brother, and most of all the sadness that was never far from her mother's eyes. What kind of man would use and abuse a woman like Delia, refuse to acknowledge the child he had fathered and cast them both into the wilderness, denying all responsibility? In contrast, Papa had done nothing to reproach himself about. Stella felt a rush of gratitude on behalf of her mother as well as herself. She hoped Delia, even if she had been incapable of loving him, had at least shown him affection. There had always been a warmth between them – perhaps merely gratitude on Delia's part but genuine devotion on Sir Michael's. No wonder he had thrown himself so wholeheartedly into his work. She glanced sideways at him. His solid jaw and usually closed countenance today showed a raw vulnerability. Stella's heart ached for him. No matter what, he would always be her father.

Her thoughts turned to Norton. How strange that just as they had sent the telegram, they had run into Paul Carberry and discovered the mutual acquaintance with Norton. How she envied Carberry that he would be spending the evening with him.

Stella was certain her marriage to Norton would be different from that of her parents. She and Norton loved each other. A shiver of pleasure ran through her. But Stella was realistic enough to understand that the timing of their union was far from ideal. In marrying Norton, she would forgo the life she loved in exchange for that of a provincial civil servant's wife. A world of tea parties with other European wives, games at the tennis club, bridge afternoons – just like Mrs McNair. Eventually as Norton's career advanced, she would progress to entertaining guests the way Portia Metcalfe and Violet Moreland were expected to do. It all sounded terribly dreary.

And yet, she would have Norton. The thought of him made her stomach flutter. She pictured his hands with their long fingers and prominent bones resting on his thighs – strong hands with skin warm and smooth to the touch. Then Blackstock's stubby fat fingers and bitten nails entered her head and the memory of those ugly hands prodding and probing her body and clamping over her mouth. It was all she could do not to be sick again. Her father seemed to sense her malaise and took her hand, enveloping it in his.

She glanced at him, her gaze taking in his familiar features. Papa may not be her natural father, but he was her true one. He had always been exacting and demanding of her, often seeming to take her for granted but always there for her. She told herself that his wish for her to marry Blackstock had been born of a desire to secure her future. Yes, there was also vanity involved – the desire to protect his own legacy in the field of anthropology – yet even that was because he trusted her. And he had been penitent since discovering what Blackstock had done.

Stella didn't know what the future would hold, but Norton had assured her they would face it together. She took a world of comfort from that thought.

TWENTY-NINE

As soon as Carberry entered the room, Norton saw his sister staring wide-eyed at the planter in what was unmistakably an instant attraction. He knew at once he should have warned her that Carberry wasn't interested in women. But how was one to raise such a delicate subject with one's sister – especially a girl like Winnie who had led a rather sheltered life?

For his part, Carberry was the very model of charm. The bluff northerner was acting the part of a suave matinee idol: he bent his head to kiss Winnie's hand and professed to be delighted to make her acquaintance, barely giving Norton a second glance. Over drinks before dinner, he asked about her impressions of Kandy, her voyage out, laughed at her humorous take on the London season, and altogether behaved as though she were the most fascinating person he'd ever met. To Norton's dismay, Winnie was lapping it up.

Only as they went into dinner did Carberry address Norton. 'This morning, I bumped into that Polegate girl in Nuwara Eliya. Remember? The one from the ship. She was with her father. Apparently, the brother's gone back to England. She asked me to convey her greetings and mentioned that she'd been introduced to you by the GA. You kept that quiet, didn't you?'

Norton glanced at his sister hoping his frown would remind her to make no mention of his engagement to Stella. 'I got to know the family when the GA asked me to accompany them on a hunting trip down south. Neither Miss Polegate nor I enjoyed the game hunting.'

'What happened to the brother? And that other chap?'

'Gordon Blackstock is up north in Jaffna, working on the research project they're doing. I'm afraid Ronald, the brother, has blotted his copybook. He's run off with the GA's daughter.'

'Good Lord!'

'They've left the country, presumably to return to England.'

Carberry shook his head. 'Well, I never. So old Cynthia finally found her man. Although as I recall he's not much more than a boy.'

'As you can imagine, Julian Metcalfe's not exactly thrilled.'

'How do you feel about that, Baxter? I thought you and she had a bit of an understanding.'

Norton gave a shrug, trying to make light of it. 'I think that was what the GA was hoping, but no, there was never anything between us.'

'Naturally, the Metcalfes are very upset but I'm staying as their guest in the residence and Mrs Metcalfe has been awfully kind to me,' Winnie said pointedly, while looking straight at Norton. 'I don't think we should be discussing this.'

'Quite so.' Norton was glad his sister cut the conversation short, hoping it would also rule out further talk of Stella and her father.

The rest of the evening passed quickly with Paul Carberry continuing to charm Winnie, offering to give her a tour of Glenross and show her the plot of land where he hoped to create his own tea estate. He turned to Norton. 'I'm rather hoping you'll be able to fix a problem with the land purchase,

Baxter. There's a finger of land that butts up against a waterfall and a stream. It's only a couple of acres but it cuts into the rest of the plot. I'm pretty sure Lockwood Tea, who claim ownership, are trying it on and I'm hoping you can sort it out for me. If I come to the office tomorrow, we could have a look at the deeds together. I want to get the purchase ratified as soon as possible.'

Norton agreed. Carberry then directed his attention back to Winifred, telling her about his hopes and plans for what would be Oaklands – building a bungalow, clearing and planting the land and eventually building a factory to process the tea. Norton listened with growing discomfort. He didn't need to ask Winnie what she thought of the handsome planter as it was written all over her face.

They said goodnight to Carberry but as soon as they left the hotel, a jubilant Winnie clasped her brother's hand. 'Do you think he likes me? Oh, my goodness, why on earth didn't you tell me all about him?' She clutched the front of the shawl draped around her shoulders, her voice full of excitement. 'He's ticking all the boxes on my SMC list. He's handsome, sporty, charming, and with excellent prospects.' She pulled the shawl tighter. 'And he seems to like me too. Please tell me he does!'

Norton's mouth was dry. He'd never seen Winnie as excited about anyone or anything before. She was giddy with it. An overwhelming sense of foreboding descended upon him. He didn't want to shatter his sister's illusions, but he was certain no good could come from this.

'Carberry's a likeable chap but please don't get your hopes up, Win. I doubt he has any thoughts of settling down and taking a wife for a long time yet. He's taking on a gargantuan task in creating his own plantation. It will take years and until it's done, he'll be in no position to marry and start a family.

You'll be long back in England and married to someone else by then.'

She spun round, eyes narrowing and tears threatening. 'What a cruel thing to say, Norton. I didn't get that impression at all.' With that she swept through the gateway and into the residence.

Norton stood staring after his sister. He knew his words had been harsh and he hated dashing her hopes, but he couldn't in conscience encourage the possibility of a match. He remembered the story of George Huxtable's suicide. For Carberry's illicit lover to take his own life it must have been an intense and serious relationship – and the scandal of its potential exposure more than poor Huxtable could face.

Norton had intended to walk straight back to his bungalow on the other side of the lake, but instead he went back to the Queen's Hotel where he found Carberry nursing a peg of whisky in the near empty bar. He sat down beside him, deciding to waste no time on preambles. 'What the devil are you playing at?'

Carberry frowned, his head tilted on one side in an unspoken question.

'You're leading my sister up the garden path and it's not fair to get her hopes up in that way.'

The planter leaned back in his chair and fixed his eyes on Norton. 'Your sister is delightful and I'm certainly not leading her up the garden path. If I'm not mistaken, she seems rather taken with me too.'

'Because she has no idea about you.'

Carberry's head jerked back. 'On the contrary, I think I gave her a pretty good resumé of my circumstances.'

'You know damn well what I mean, Paul.'

'I'm afraid I don't. I told you that I'd been in England hoping to find a wife but there was no one suitable who wanted to uproot to live here. So, I gave up. Then lo and behold your charming sister appears. She claims to love Ceylon, so I intend to do my utmost to convince her that she's not wrong about that – and eventually to persuade her to marry me.'

Norton's jaw dropped.

The barman was hovering, and Norton, in need of a strong drink, ordered a Scotch. When the man had gone, he continued. 'What about the thing you told me? About your true nature.' Then when Carberry remained silent, he added, 'Damn it, man. About liking men not women.'

Carberry snorted. 'That doesn't stop me appreciating women. I found Winnie extremely congenial company. She reminds me of you. My tragedy is that I can't have you, so who better than your sister?'

A surge of anger rushed through Norton, but his rage was curtailed by the return of the bartender bearing the whisky. He calmed himself with a deep breath. 'Look, you may have forgotten but I remember all too well what you told me in Colombo – that you didn't like women – that they all ended up like that awful Mrs Holloway.'

Carberry shrugged. 'I hadn't met your sister then.'

'Come off it, you even said women are more trouble than they're worth.'

'You have a good memory. Did you take notes?'

Exasperated, Norton snapped. 'I can't let you mislead Winnie like this. She wants a normal conventional marriage. And a family for goodness' sake. She wants to be loved.'

'And why do you suppose she can't have those things with me?'

'Because you've made it clear to me, you're—'

'Queer? Yes, I am. I can't help that. But it doesn't mean I can't still be a good husband.'

Norton took a gulp of his whisky.

'I told you I'm very discreet.'

Norton snorted in disbelief, remembering what Frobisher

had told him about George Huxtable. 'Then why do you want to marry my sister?'

'You make the mistake of assuming that we so-called sodomites are only interested in sex.'

Norton was taken aback at Carberry's bluntness.

'I will make your sister a good husband. I'll do my duty as far as children are concerned if that's what she wants—'

'What do you mean – *if that's what she wants?*'

'Do you know? Have you asked her?'

Again, Norton was taken aback. 'Of course I haven't asked her. Why would I? It's obvious.'

'The classic masculine assumption. I find that arrogant.' Carberry paused. 'Look, my friend, I don't want to fall out with you over this, but I fully intend to court your sister. I like and admire her. Many successful marriages are built on less. As for children I'd like them myself. I'm building a future on that plot of land, and I'd like to have someone to inherit when I die. I'd rather marry Winnie with your blessing, but if that's not forthcoming I'll do so without. Assuming she'll have me.' He drained his glass. 'Now it's late, so I'm turning in. Time you did too. Goodnight.'

After Carberry left the bar, Norton slugged down what was left of his Scotch and left too. He realised Carberry's words about wanting his blessing echoed his own the previous day to Sir Michael.

But as he walked by the lakeside heading back to his bungalow, his unease remained. He knew all too well that many, if not most marriages were built on considerations other than love. Carberry was right that marriage was about more than sex, but it seemed wrong that his sister should be misled into sharing the rest of her life with a man who liked other men. Maybe it was since he'd fallen in love with Stella whom he loved and desired, that he didn't want his sister to have to settle for anything less.

. . .

Before going to bed, Norton opened his heart to Stella in a letter.

My dearest Stella,

I wish I could have been with you today when you received the news you didn't want. I can only say again that whatever you decide when the baby arrives, I will support your decision. I long to be with you now, beside you, supporting you, loving you. I am counting the hours until we can be together.

As you know, my sister has arrived in Kandy and that complicates matters. I have told her about you and our engagement – not about the pregnancy of course. I am desperate to see you again and would like to introduce you to her. When we do meet, she will likely be with me. Meanwhile Portia Metcalfe has invited her to stay on at the residence and that is a huge weight off my mind.

Oh, Stella, why is life so complicated? I don't mean you and me – as far as I'm concerned there is complete clarity and conviction that, come what may, we are meant to be together. But I am now in loco parentis *for Winifred and already I am facing a dilemma. I understand you met my friend Paul Carberry in NE this morning. Tonight, he and Winnie met, and she appears to have experienced the* coup de foudre. *Later Carberry told me he is set on courting Winnie and hopes eventually to offer to marry her if she is prepared to remain here in Ceylon. (Incidentally our future home is something you and I must talk about for ourselves.)*

What I am about to tell you is in confidence of course, but I am much in need of good counsel. Mr Carberry is – to put this delicately – of the Oscar Wilde persuasion. He maintains that it should not be a barrier to his marrying my sister, but I am not convinced. At the very least I don't think I should let any courtship take place until Winnie is fully apprised of his situation. But how do I tell her? She is in so many ways an innocent at large.

It's hard saying all this in a letter. It's late at night and I would much rather be there with you, holding you in my arms and making plans for our own future. (Which we must do without delay.) But I would dearly welcome a feminine perspective on this.

Sorry to burden you with my worries. It's late, I must sleep but I want this to catch the first post tomorrow.

With all my love,
Norton

The following morning, after his Sinhala lesson, Norton went into the *kachcheri* where he found Carberry already waiting for him. Neither man referred to their argument the previous evening and avoided eye contact as they stood side by side, poring over the hastily drawn maps of the territory the planter was intending to buy.

After Norton had established from a perusal of the records that the contested strip of land did indeed form part of the larger plot Carberry wished to purchase, his friend thanked him and extended a hand to shake. Norton hesitated momentarily, then accepted it, before making his excuses to return to the growing backlog of work on his desk. Was he overdramatising the problem? After all it was possible that many outwardly respectable married men were of the same persuasion as Carberry. The only difference was that they kept their orientation a closely guarded secret, whereas he was a party to Carberry's. Yet it hadn't been Carberry who had told him. It was Frobisher, who right now was looking curiously at him across the office. Norton ran a hand through his hair. Frobisher probably suspected him of following the same inclinations. Cynthia too must have been aware. It explained her shunning of Carberry at the tennis club. How could he stand by and let his sister be drawn into potential scandal? Indeed, was it to avoid this that Carberry was so keen to marry her? A wife would lay to rest any rumours.

As he went through columns of figures making the occasional adjustment, Norton felt the weight of the world bearing down on him. He ought to work late to catch up with the arrears. His Sinhala examination was looming, and he needed to spend his evenings studying for it. He desperately wanted time to return to the McNairs' estate to make plans with Stella. Yet he had a responsibility to entertain his sister. He was consumed with guilt that he was keeping Sir Michael's secret from the woman he loved and Carberry's from his sister. Life had become overwhelming.

Stella replied to Norton by return of post. Her letter was exactly like her: calm and reassuring. She told him her father had told her the truth about her parentage.

My first instinct was anger at him for deceiving me. But once I got over the shock, everything made sense. Papa must have loved Mama very deeply to do what he did. I also realised, not only how incredibly generous you are in your willingness to accept me and my unborn child, but that Papa has already proved that it is indeed possible to love and care for a child who is not one's own flesh and blood. I am and will always be grateful to you for this, Norton, and not a day will go by when I won't thank God for you coming into my life.

I have spent today thinking about our future and believe I have come up with the best solution – although it is a painful one. We should marry here in Ceylon as soon as possible but I must then return to England as planned. I will tell the truth – that I am a married woman whose husband is in Ceylon, but we decided I would be safer giving birth in England rather than in a tropical climate with risk of disease and infection. Oh, my dear Norton, it will be the greatest of sorrows to be separated from you for many months – likely a full year when my recovery and travel time are considered. But I will bear it in the knowledge that at the end I will have the rest of my life to be with you, my beloved.

You are doubtless wondering how we will explain my departure so soon after our marriage. I will use the writing up and publication of the Tamil research as well as concerns about my father's health as the reason. In the case of the latter, I would anyway feel duty bound to see him safely returned to England and have no wish to leave him to the care of Blackstock on the voyage home. As to Blackstock, I am determined he shall come nowhere near me again. I have been talking with Papa and he is going to ask him to remain here in Ceylon to follow up some aspects of the research that we have not yet completed to satisfaction. He won't like it, but he knows if he doesn't do as requested, his PhD is at risk. I suppose I ought to feel bad at such deception, but I don't. Gordon Blackstock is not worthy of receiving a doctorate anyway, so forcing him to do more towards earning it is only fair.

I hope you will agree that although painful, this is the best plan. Think it over, dear Norton, and if you have a better solution, please tell me. This is the only way I've been able to think of that protects our reputations and keeps me safe from Gordon Blackstock.

Forgive me for saving your dilemma over your sister until last. I have given this much thought. My encounter with Mr Carberry was so brief that I have no opinion to offer as to his suitability as a husband. I can however see why Winnie would be drawn towards him. He is a very handsome chap!

You mentioned Oscar Wilde – Mr Wilde was himself married for many years in what appears to have been a happy union, producing two children. Mrs Wilde, despite the public opprobrium, remained loyal and never sought divorce. Had it not been for his vanity and recklessness in bringing the libel suit he would have been spared the punishment and disgrace he brought upon himself. If Mr Carberry is prepared to reform his ways surely there's no reason why he too cannot have a happy and fruitful marriage with your sister. If they genuinely like each other's company that is a firm foundation on which to build.

However, I agree with you that Winnie should be made aware of your friend's past behaviour before committing to any marriage proposal, but it is he who should tell her not you. My advice is that you ask him to do so, then leave it up to him. Your sister is an adult – possibly not of age but certainly entrusted by your parents to travel alone to Ceylon. It is not your responsibility to make decisions that will affect her future happiness. I haven't met her but if she is in any way like her brother, she will have a mind of her own and a determination to follow her heart. I don't think you should stand in her way.

How much easier it would be if we were able to talk about this face to face and I were able to read your reactions in your eyes.

I love you and miss you,
Stella

Norton read the letter three times before folding it back into the envelope. Stella's pragmatism regarding Winnie and

Carberry hadn't eradicated his own doubts and worries but it had gone some way to lessening them. But her proposal of a protracted separation was a source of anguish. He knew she was suggesting this to protect him and his future. Her assumption was that they would eventually make their home here where he had embarked on his career. It would mean her sacrificing her proximity to academia, separation from her father and a long exile to have her baby alone. How could he let her do that?

A better solution would be for him to resign from his post and return to England with her and her father and seek another post there. If this sudden departure and breaking of his contract ruled out another civil service position, then he would try his hand at something else. He could become a school mathematics teacher, work in a bank – or even the City of London. He could eat humble pie and seek his father's advice. None of these would offer the interest and fascination he found in his work here in Ceylon – but they would serve to release him from his nagging doubts about the role of empire. Most of all it would avoid any separation from Stella.

He picked up his pen and started to write.

THIRTY

Stella and her father were sitting on the McNairs' terrace surrounded by their papers, drinking a mid-morning coffee. The sunlight filtered through the trees, dappling the lawn in an ever-changing kaleidoscope while a small troop of toque macaque monkeys were grooming each other a few yards away.

Putting down the letter she'd been reading, Stella made up her mind. She couldn't let Norton do it. Throw away all he'd achieved so far. From their conversations in the jungle, she was only too aware how fascinated he was by the variety and nature of his work. He was vested in it – his Sinhala exams were looming; he loved the country and its people – and from her own work here she could understand why. She, on the other hand, had no paid employment, would be constrained from studying as a married woman and even as a single one couldn't receive a degree. Once her child was born – even if she kept it – if she returned here to join him, she would be able to continue to research the indigenous people and the Indian Tamils and contribute to her father's body of work. If she and Norton were to return to England they would both lose out. A lengthy separation was a heavy price to pay, but in the long run, surely the better decision. It was vital to talk this over in person with Norton. An exchange of letters was too cumbersome.

It was clear Norton couldn't spare the time to come to her, so she must go to him. After talking it over with her father, he agreed she should return to Kandy for a few days. He said he would accompany her.

'No! I won't hear of it. There's been enough disruption to your work and you're tired, Papa. It's not far for me to travel – just a couple of hours on the train and Mrs McNair has offered to drive me to the station in the pony and trap.' She patted his arm. 'Don't fret. I'll be perfectly safe, and Mrs Metcalfe has kindly offered to put me up. It's also an opportunity for me to meet Norton's sister and spend a little time with her. I'll only be gone two nights.'

Her father sighed then nodded. 'Very well, my dear. I will get on with the study of funeral rites. I have a lot of supplemental questions arising from the cremation ceremony the other day. It means talking to the menfolk and they wouldn't want you present anyway. When you return, we can start to pull it all together.'

Stella swallowed, hating what she was about to ask. 'Have you had any word from Gordon Blackstock? Has he made any progress on his part of the study?'

Sir Michael snorted in disgust. 'Not a word. He's probably angry about me making him turn back to Jaffna and get on with it on his own. He'll use that as an excuse – too overwhelmed with work to spare the time to write me a progress report.'

She nodded, not wanting to pursue the matter further. Every time she thought of Gordon Blackstock the memory of that fatal night rushed at her. Would looking at her baby when it arrived provoke the same reaction? Might the child resemble him? She covered her mouth with her hands, fearing she would be sick, but mercifully she wasn't.

'Stella? Are you unwell?'

'Sorry, Papa, it was just a twinge. It's passed now. I'll go and pack a case.'

When Stella arrived in Kandy that evening, the station was a buzz of activity – people rushing to catch the train, a crush of rickshaws touting for fares, sellers of street food calling out their offerings, the cloying aroma of hot oil and spices, the scent of flowers from the vendors selling floral offerings to take to the temples. Stella had intended to take a rickshaw to the GA's residence and hoped that Norton would meet her there later.

To her great joy, she saw him pushing his way through the throng, hurrying towards her, eyes shining. She wanted to fling her arms around him, but the proprieties must be observed – especially in such a public place, so she had to content herself with grasping both his hands outstretched towards her in greeting. He pulled her closer then pulled back to look at her. 'I've missed you so much,' he said, his voice tender.

Stella told him how much she'd missed him too. She marvelled at how their relationship had changed so radically since he'd arrived unannounced at the tea estate, and she had told him about the baby. Looking into his clear blue eyes she felt her resolve weaken. How easy it would be to succumb to his suggestion and agree to him accompanying her to England. But that would be selfish. She loved him too much to let him sacrifice his future.

When they arrived at the residence and met Winifred, Stella warmed to her immediately. Norton's sister held out her hands in greeting in a mirroring of her brother's action earlier at the railway station.

She spoke in a torrent of non sequiturs. 'Norton has told me about you but not nearly enough. May I call you Stella? It's such a beautiful name. You know it means star? Winifred means bringer of peace and joy. It's from Welsh. But please call me Winnie. Miss Baxter sounds so stuffy. I love finding the meaning of names. Poor Norton's is really a surname and means northern town which is terribly dull and not true in his case as he was born in Richmond-upon-Thames. How was the train journey? Was it crowded? Did you find other ladies to sit with?'

Stella smiled warmly. 'It was fine. I was in first class and there was a group of half a dozen ladies who were returning to Kandy after performing with their choir. They were a jolly bunch, and the time passed quickly as I eavesdropped on their conversations.' She raised an eyebrow and unpinned her hat. 'And of course the scenery is so beautiful – mountains, tea plantations, waterfalls.'

Portia Metcalfe appeared in the drawing room and greeted Stella. 'How lovely to see you again, Stella. How is your dear father?'

After reassuring her hostess that the professor was in good health, Stella was whisked away by Winnie. 'You and I are to share a room. I've already dressed for dinner so if you don't mind, we can chat while you change. I want to hear everything about you and your work. But I must warn you I'm terrified that you're so frightfully clever I won't understand a word you say.'

Behind Winnie, her brother rolled his eyes then grinned at Stella. 'I'll see you later, ladies.'

Once they were in their bedroom, Winnie flung herself on one of the beds and arranged the skirt of her dress neatly around her. 'Norton says you and he are to be married. He seems to think it's going to be soon. That's all happened very fast.'

Stella didn't want to pre-empt her discussion with Norton about their plans so she decided to sidestep the subject. 'He and

I still have much to discuss about the details. It's why I'm here. It's so hard making arrangements by letter.'

'Absolutely.'

'How about you, Winnie? What do you think of Ceylon?'

'Pure heaven. I adore it. Everything about it. The colourful Hindu temples, those strange bell-shaped stupas where the Buddhists worship, the lake, the mountains, the creepy-faced flying foxes that hang upside down from the trees, the gorgeous saris the women wear. It's so alive, so vibrant.'

Stella smiled. 'It is indeed a special place.'

'I could definitely live here.' Winnie paused, watching as Stella unpacked a gown from her suitcase and smoothed a hand over it. 'In fact... can you keep a secret?'

Hesitant, Stella said she could, guessing what was coming.

'Do you know Norton's friend Paul? Mr Carberry? He's a tea planter and quite shockingly handsome.'

'I met him very briefly but couldn't claim to know him. But yes, his looks are striking.' She tilted her head in conspiratorial acknowledgement.

'I'm afraid back in England I rather botched my London season. Couldn't get anyone suitable to bite – sorry, that sounds rather vulgar, doesn't it? But you know what I mean. So, imagine when I met Paul Carberry and oh my goodness, Stella, he seems to like me too. Maybe I'm getting carried away, but I got the impression that he's as keen on me as I am on him.' She laid a hand over her bosom in a dramatic gesture. 'But Norton is being beastly about the whole thing. He says Mr Carberry can't possibly be interested in marriage until he has established his tea plantation. That he'll have no time for a wife and a family for years and years. But I didn't get that impression at all.'

Stella was uncertain how to handle this. 'I'm sure Norton only has your best interests at heart. He's probably being cautious. And I suppose as a good friend of this chap, he must know something of his mind.'

Winnie frowned. 'Surely having a wife to support him as he works on what sounds like a very ambitious project would be beneficial. I'm not one of those prissy girls who expects to be entertained all the time. I'm quite prepared to pull my weight.'

Stella didn't doubt it.

'Actually, I think it's very mean of Norton. It feels as though he's being a dog in the manger. He's marrying you and he wants to keep his best friend to himself too.'

Stella spun round to face her. 'No, no. Absolutely not, Winnie. I don't imagine for a moment you really believe that yourself. Norton would never be so selfish. He's probably just aware of his responsibilities since your father and mother aren't here. Looking out for your best interests.'

'You think so?'

'I'm certain. I may not have known Norton for long, but I have a very clear idea of his character. I also know how much he cares about you.'

Winnie looked down, entwining her fingers. 'I suppose so.'

'I'm sure he'll come round in the end if you're right about Mr Carberry. Now it's time we joined the others. Would you mind fastening this please?' She turned her back to Winnie, who closed the clasp of the necklace Stella held out to her.

'What a beautiful locket.'

'It was my mother's. She gave it to me before she died. It contains a lock of her hair.'

'So sad that your mother has died.'

'I miss her every day.' Stella gave her future sister-in-law a smile. 'And I know my poor father must miss her even more.' She threaded her arm through Winnie's. 'I don't know about you, but I'm ready for one of those fresh lime and sodas that Portia serves before dinner.'

. . .

The two women had just entered the drawing room and been served by the Metcalfes' butler with the refreshing lime drinks, when a stern-faced Julian Metcalfe arrived. He greeted Stella, welcoming her back, then turned to address them all. 'Apologies for arriving late but I've just received some dreadful news.'

'Not Cynthia?' Portia Metcalfe clasped a hand over her mouth and sank into an armchair.

'No, it's not Cynthia. I'm afraid she's still sent no word. I expect they want to get a large amount of ocean between us before they get in touch.' He looked at Stella. 'I'm very sorry to have to be the bearer of such terrible news but—'

'Papa!'

'No, no. Please allow me to finish. Michael is perfectly well – I imagine he's as you left him earlier today. It's his student. Mr Blackstock. I'm afraid he's... dead.'

Stella gave a little cry and the glass she was holding slipped from her hand and smashed on the floor. One of the servants rushed forward to clear up the mess and Norton shepherded her into a chair. Her face was as pale as her ivory gown and Norton could see her chest heaving as she struggled to breathe.

'Please can we have a glass of water here,' he cried to the butler, who swiftly supplied one.

'How did he die? What happened?' she said, her eyes fixed on the GA.

'I'm sorry and offer my sincere condolences. I've sent a telegram to inform your father. I imagine you both knew Mr Blackstock well because of your extensive travels together.'

Stella nodded. 'Please tell me what happened.'

Metcalfe hesitated then pressed on. 'Nasty business. I heard this from Percy Moreland, the GA up in Jaffna. We spoke over the telephone, and he's promised to send a full report tomorrow. Apparently, Mr Blackstock met a Polish count in Jaffna, and they decided to go on a hunting trip.'

Stella, impatient, interrupted. 'No. Surely not. Mr Blackstock can't have been hunting. He was working. There must be some mistake. They have the wrong person.'

Glancing at Norton, Metcalfe said there was no mistake. 'Mr Blackstock was staying in the rest house in Anuradhapura and was about to come to Kandy when your father telegraphed to send him back to Jaffna. I understand he met Count Krasinsky and his party while still in Anuradhapura and decided to join them on a game hunting trip instead.'

Stella exchanged glances with Norton.

'Apparently the native tracker and several of the count's party tried to save Mr Blackstock's life but there was nothing they could do. He had somehow become separated from them, and they could hear his screams. By the time they found him it was too late.'

Losing patience, Stella slapped the arms of the chair. 'What happened? Please stop skirting round the issue, Mr Metcalfe. Tell me how he died.'

With an apologetic look at his wife and a lowered voice, he said, 'He was savaged by a leopard. He'd fired several shots and continued to follow the animal, who pounced on him from the top of a rocky outcrop. The details will be in Moreland's report, but it seems the poor chap didn't stand a chance. I wanted to tell you the news and I've suggested your father telephones me tomorrow morning. I'll have to liaise with him and Moreland to sort out the funeral and I imagine Sir Michael will want to contact the man's family personally.'

Stella listened in horror mingled with an overwhelming sense of relief.

The GA shook his head. 'Bad business.'

Uncaring whether the Metcalfes noticed, Norton kneeled beside Stella's chair and took her hand in his. 'It's all over now, my darling,' he whispered.

Stella held his hand as though if she let go, he might drift away. She closed her eyes and breathed, feeling the fear that had been choking her like a ring of barbed wire around her neck finally erode. For the first time since Gordon Blackstock made his offer of marriage on the road to the pearl fishery, she felt able to breathe freely and live without fear.

The atmosphere in the room was tense. Winnie broke the silence in the end. 'I'm so dreadfully sorry for you and your father, Stella. Please accept my sincere condolences.'

Stella stared at her blankly.

'Yes, my dear,' said Portia Metcalfe. 'A truly terrible shock. I'm so sorry for your loss.'

Stella looked aghast.

Norton spoke up. 'It's a shock to us all. Not least the manner of the man's death.' He squeezed Stella's hand.

Julian Metcalfe turned to Norton and barked, 'You'd better take care of all this, Baxter. Get on to the Jaffna *kachcheri* first thing in the morning. No question of shipping the body home. Probably needs to be buried up there and fast given the heat. Not that I imagine there's much left of him to bury. Get on to Sir Michael and get the details of the chap's family and send official condolences on behalf of the government. Right. I need a stiff drink.'

Portia Metcalfe called to the uniformed servant. 'And another lime juice for Miss Polegate.'

Stella sat upright. 'If you don't mind, Mrs Metcalfe, in the circumstances I'd rather have a sherry.' She exchanged glances with Norton and let out a long breath.

THIRTY-ONE

During dinner that evening the atmosphere in the residence was subdued. Yet for Stella the bonds holding her had at last been removed, freeing her from fear. She still had the pregnancy to worry about – and the need to hide it – but now she was safe from any attempts by Blackstock to shame her or to claim parenthood of the child and attempt to force a marriage. For the first time since the rape her appetite for food was restored.

Blackstock's must have been a terrible death but while Stella was horrified at what he must have suffered, there was some justice in the way his life ended. She had heard that leopards rarely attacked humans unless provoked. They tended to go for their victim's neck and throat, causing extreme blood loss so it would have been unlikely to have been a protracted death, but there would have been terror and shock. Was she wrong to take some satisfaction from that thought?

After dinner, Julian Metcalfe closeted himself inside his study. Sensing Stella wanted to talk with Norton, Winnie asked Portia to join her in a hand of cards, leaving the couple to walk around the moonlit garden.

It was a huge relief to be alone with Norton at last. They stood out of view of the house under a tamarind tree, their feet crunching on the fallen pods, and he took her in his arms. It was only then that Stella let the tears flow. 'I can't believe he's gone and I'm safe.'

Norton kissed her, then pulled her close and held her against him. She circled her arms around him drawing strength from him.

'I'm glad he had a horrible death,' she said at last. 'I know it's un-Christian of me, but I don't care. Gordon Blackstock was an evil man and it's right that he came to a violent end. Trying to be a hero no doubt – the idiot. If he'd done as Papa asked and returned to Jaffna and the work he was here to do, it wouldn't have happened. No. I don't have one jot of sympathy.' She threw her head back and stared up at the stars through the foliage of the tree.

Norton watched her have her moment of satisfaction, then gathered her close again. 'He's out of our lives forever now. We need to make plans for our wedding and our return to England. Once I've sorted this business out for the GA, I'll tell him I'm resigning and—'

'No! That's why I've come here to Kandy. I don't want you to resign. I don't want to live in England, and I won't let you give up your job for me. There's nothing for us in England. I want to be with you more than anything. More even than my plan to go to Cambridge – and anyway that's out of the question now that I'm expecting this child. We can make a life here. I love my work and as you suggested there's no reason why I shouldn't continue my research after the child is born.'

'But—'

'Please let me finish, Norton. My plan is best. We need to marry as soon as possible. We can have a short honeymoon here in Ceylon – assuming Mr Metcalfe agrees to let you take some time off. Then I will accompany Papa back to England where

I'll tell everyone the truth – that I married overseas and am expecting a baby. I won't even have to hide myself away anymore now that Blackstock's gone. After the child is born I will either give it up or return here with it. My absence and the voyage will cover any discrepancies in the dates, and we can say it was a honeymoon baby. If I give it up for adoption, I'll come back here to you. No one here need ever know I was pregnant. We can explain my trip to England as caring for Papa and completing the publication of our work. As for the English end – it's quite normal for colonial wives to return to birth a child. We will have a watertight story for both places. Your reputation and employment will be safe. No one will doubt the child is ours. That is, assuming you are prepared to accept it.'

'Of course I'll accept it, but I can't accept a whole year apart from you, my darling. A whole year apart. How could I stand it?'

'You'll bear it because you're strong. Because you'll throw yourself into your work. You'll make yourself indispensable to Julian Metcalfe and will be promoted faster than any civil servant ever. Because you're brilliant and clever and I have total faith in you. You'll bear it because you'll know that I will be coming back to you and then we will have a lifetime together.' She ran her hand over his chest then reached up to kiss him again.

'Besides, I have no choice. Papa can't travel back alone. His heart is weak. He has this study to write and publish. It will have to omit the part on the indigenous northern Tamils thanks to Blackstock, but it will still be an important work, and I need to help him complete it – I *want* to help him complete it. He has to have a reckoning with Ronald too and I must support him in that. Please, Norton, painful as this is, it's our best choice and lays the groundwork for a long and happy future.'

'Are you done?' He smiled at her.

'Yes, I'll shut up now.'

'You're a formidably persuasive woman.'

'And you are an eminently logical and reasonable man.' She gave a little laugh. 'So, are we agreed?'

'Reluctantly, painfully, we are. We'll need to tell the Metcalfes, and I'll have to grovel for some leave so we can have that honeymoon you talked about. I'm imagining a long, curving, sandy beach fringed with palm trees and not a single European to disturb us. We can live in a wooden hut and eat fruit all day and bathe in the ocean.'

She laughed again. 'That sounds like paradise.'

'Anywhere will be paradise if I can be alone with you, Stella.'

They kissed again. A long lingering kiss full of tenderness and longing.

When they eventually pulled apart, Stella said, 'I have a request to make.'

'Anything.'

'Let Winnie follow her heart. Don't put up barriers of your own making.'

She felt him stiffen.

'If you're right and your friend Mr Carberry is trifling with her it will become apparent quickly enough. If, on the other hand, she's right and she genuinely loves this man and he has affection for her too, then let them be. Perhaps he does like men but that's no reason why he can't be a good husband to her. He seems a kind man, a hard worker. Better that she's with someone like him whom she genuinely loves than with a man like Gordon Blackstock – or Percy Moreland, the man the GA was talking about last night. His wife told me about the horror of being forced to marry him – much older than her, unattractive, selfish, uncaring.' She looked up into his eyes. 'And who knows, perhaps the love of a good woman like Winnie might cause Mr Carberry to change his ways.' She laid a hand upon his cheek and kept her eyes fixed on him.

Norton released a long breath. When she looked at him like that he felt his resolve weaken. But he had to stand in Winnie's corner. He was terrified she was making a terrible mistake. 'He told me he wants *me* and Winnie's the next best thing. He accused me of thinking it was all about sex. I heard there was a serious relationship with a civil servant – before my time and in another district within the province. There was some scandal – I don't know the circumstances – but the poor chap took his own life. Carberry was devastated. And a fuss with his employer who threatened to sack him unless he found a wife. That's why he went back to England, to look for one.'

Stella nodded but continued to look into his eyes. 'That's awful. Very sad. I can't claim to understand why some men choose other men over women – although Mama once mentioned to me that in the opera and theatre world there were many men like that. We can't predict the future but if what Winnie told me is right, he seems to genuinely like her – and she is besotted with him. Isn't that a basis for marriage?'

He drew her closer so that she laid her head on his chest. 'I suppose it's because I am so blessed in finding you. I don't want a compromise for Winnie. I want her to have someone who'll love her, body and soul.'

But Stella was resolute. She drew away from his close hold and looked up at him again. 'It's not what *you* want. It's what *she* wants, surely.'

'And you think she's serious about him? It's not just a passing fancy?'

'She spoke of nothing else while we were dressing for dinner. She's upset about falling out with you. But clearly not enough to hold her back if Mr Carberry pursues matters.'

Norton knew when he was beaten. He gave a long sigh. 'Then I suppose I'd better stand aside and let her have what she wants.' He stroked her cheek. 'I already know he means to ask her to marry him. He made that clear to me. Said he'd rather have my blessing, but he'll go ahead anyway.'

'Then give your blessing.' She smiled up at him and he bent to kiss her.

The following weeks passed in a whirlwind of activity. Stella returned to the Hillbrow plantation to complete the data collection there with her father, while Norton flung himself into his work. No one from Kandy attended Blackstock's funeral which took place in Jaffna, attended by Mr and Mrs Moreland and other staff from the *kachcheri* there. Count Krasinsky and his party did not attend. Sir Michael wrote to Blackstock's parents, imagining that it would also mark the end of the dean of college's hope for a significant endowment. To his surprise and gratification, a telegram arrived from the dean to say that Blackstock senior was granting a substantial sum for the building of a new college library and a bursary in anthropology in his son's name. Percy Moreland forwarded the papers found amongst Blackstock's belongings. Stella went through them but as she had feared there was little of use to incorporate into the thesis. Half of them were notes taken by her brother before he vanished with Cynthia – incoherent and incomplete. The remainder were in Blackstock's unintelligible handwriting and were superficial, lacking any interrogation of the more salient points. She showed them to her father, who consigned them to the fire.

Stella and Norton were married in a small ceremony in the parish church in Kandy. Stella's father, the Metcalfes, Mrs McNair, as well as Winnie and Paul Carberry were present at the nuptials. Norton had felt obliged to invite Frobisher, but his presence was ruled out by the GA, who claimed he needed to provide cover in the *kachcheri*, it being a weekday.

On the day of the wedding a letter arrived for the GA from

Cynthia to say that she and Ronald had decided to spend some time in Cairo and wouldn't be arriving in England until the following spring or summer. There was no mention of marriage.

Norton and Stella didn't manage the palm-fringed beach beside the ocean. Keen to make the most of their limited time they stayed in a cottage in the hills outside Kandy. Used as a retreat by the Metcalfes, Portia had persuaded her husband to offer it to the couple before Stella and her father left for England from Colombo.

Norton's concerns that consummating their marriage might bring back the traumas of the night in Matara proved unfounded. When they made love he took his time, mindful and caring of Stella. The love and sensitivity he showed her could not have been more different than the violent brute force of Blackstock's attack.

'You've made me so happy,' she said as they lay entwined in the simple bedroom, sunlight pouring through the open shutters. 'You've restored me to myself. Given me back a sense of joy.' She rolled over and lay on her back, shivering with pleasure as he ran his fingers lightly over her stomach. Smiling up at him as he bent over her, she said, 'I never dreamed it would be like this. Mama wasn't one of those mothers who spoke of lying back, gritting one's teeth, and thinking of England, but even so, I'd no idea, Norton. I never imagined feeling so... so... blissful.'

He bent over and covered her mouth with a kiss.

The five days alone in the hills were the happiest of her life – long lazy days walking hand-in-hand beside the stream that ran behind their cottage, sitting on the tiny veranda sipping freshly prepared fruit juices as they looked out over the rolling countryside around them, covered with a rich green tapestry of tea gardens and rising up to tall, craggy mountain peaks. The air was clear and fresh, the sun warm, the sound of birds all around them. An earthly paradise.

'If only we could stay here forever,' she whispered to Norton as they strolled beside the stream.

'You'd soon be bored,' he said. 'Nothing to exercise your mind.'

'All this beauty and you. That's enough for me.'

'No, it's not.' He smiled and drew her into a kiss. 'Once you're back in Oxford you'll forget all this.'

'Not for a moment. I will feed off the memory. It will sustain me. And I'll write to you every single day.'

Parting from Norton was the hardest thing Stella had ever had to do. She clung to him as they stood on the quayside, breathing in the smell of him, feeling the smooth weave of his linen jacket under her cheek. She wanted to imprint the memory of him in her mind to draw on during the lonely nights that stretched ahead of her.

Now, while her father instructed the ship's porters about the disposition of their baggage, Stella felt hollowed out inside. Leaving Norton was like cutting off one of her limbs. The past week had confirmed how deeply she loved him and made leaving him behind heartbreaking. Winnie, standing beside her, took her hand and squeezed it. 'The time will pass quickly, I'm sure. Once you've settled your father back in Oxford you can return to us.'

Not for the first time Stella felt a twinge of guilt about keeping her new sister-in-law in the dark about the child she was expecting and how it would delay her return. 'I want to make sure Papa sees a heart specialist before I come back. And I've promised to help him write up our findings from this expedition – especially now that Mr Blackstock isn't here to assist.'

'Poor Mr Blackstock,' said Winnie, her mouth drawing into a downturned line.

That was another secret Stella would not be sharing with

her sister-in-law. She gave Winnie a weak smile to reflect an appropriate level of sadness and changed the subject. 'How are things between you and Paul Carberry? You spent a lot of time talking to him at the wedding.'

Winnie's face broke into a wide smile. 'He has asked Norton and me to look at the land he's buying, at the end of this week. I'm praying he'll give me some firm indication as to his intentions then.' She slipped her arm through Stella's. 'Assuming he does, I want you to know I have no intention of marrying until you're safely back here with us.'

Stella was touched. How quickly she and Winnie had become close. 'Look after Norton for me.'

'Of course I will. He has his Sinhala examination in three weeks' time so I will make sure he keeps his nose to the grindstone.'

'Thank you, dear Winnie.' She pulled her into a hug. Then, turning to Norton she said, 'Please don't come on board with us, my darling. Go now. Take Winnie to enjoy a sundowner on the terrace of the Galle Face and watch the sun set over the ocean as I sail away.' Seeing he was about to resist, she added, 'Please. Don't make it harder for me, my love.'

'I can never say no to you, Stella, no matter how much I want to.' He bent down and kissed her tenderly, uncaring of the impropriety of such a public display. 'If only I could speed the world up and make the time pass so that instead of saying good-bye, I was already welcoming you back.'

She pulled herself away, feeling she was tearing her heart out as she did so. 'Now I'm going. I don't want Papa standing out here any longer in the blazing heat.'

Stella turned, slipped her arm through her father's and they walked together up the gangway and onto the ship, the tears she'd been holding back now flowing freely down her cheeks.

A LETTER FROM THE AUTHOR

Huge thanks for reading *The Star of Ceylon*; I hope you enjoyed the ups and downs of Stella and Norton's journey. If you want to join other readers in hearing all about my new releases and bonus content, you can sign up for my Storm newsletter:

www.stormpublishing.co/clare-flynn

And if you want to keep up to date with all my other publications, you can sign up to my mailing list:

www.subscribepage.com/r4w1u5

If you enjoyed this book and could spare a few moments to leave a review that would be hugely appreciated. Even a short review can make all the difference in encouraging a reader to discover my books for the first time. Thank you so much!

I absolutely loved writing *The Star of Ceylon*. It all started with a research trip I made to the island of last year. I was captivated by the beauty of the country, especially the tea-growing highlands. I'd made a more extensive tour of Sri Lanka back in the late '90s so I already had a reasonable idea of the place, but I wanted to do a deeper dive into some specific areas such as tea growing and processing.

I loved discovering my characters, Norton and Stella, and felt close to both of them. My first main job after university was a three-year stint in the British civil service so I understood some of the frustrations Norton went through – as well as the desperate desire to make a difference. I wasn't in the foreign service – my role involved managing the financial affairs of psychiatric patients under the jurisdiction of the Court of Protection – so I had to do research to understand what was involved. My expert guide in this was Leonard Woolf, whose excellent memoir, *Growing*, is a fascinating account of his seven years as a civil servant in Ceylon. Like Norton, Woolf's attitude to the job was ambivalent, combining a passionate interest for the country, its people and the challenges of the job with a growing disenchantment with empire. As for Stella, I completely identified with her frustrations with the patriarchy. I was fortunate enough to have had the vote, the right to education and the ability to take a degree and find it abhorrent to think how this was once denied to so many simply on the basis of gender. With so many attempts at the moment to roll back women's rights – particularly in the United States – I was fired up on Stella's behalf.

Thanks again for being part of this amazing journey with me and I hope you'll stay in touch – I have so many more stories and ideas to entertain you with!

Clare Flynn

www.clareflynn.co.uk

 facebook.com/authorclareflynn

 x.com/clarefly

 instagram.com/clarefly

 bsky.app/profile/clarefly.bsky.social

ACKNOWLEDGEMENTS

My thanks as always to the team at Storm, especially my fabulous editor, Vicky Blunden. It is an absolute joy working with Storm – it's so collaborative, collegiate and author-centric.

A big thank you to author Margaret Kaine, who read this book as it took shape and gave me much encouragement along the way. To my fellow authors and friends in The Sanctuary who help to keep me sane and are always so supportive.

Thanks to Lydia Fiondella at Audley Travel for organising my trip to Sri Lanka. To the charming Gayashan Madushanka, who was such a charming and helpful guide to his wonderful country. And to Singh and the staff at the Castlereagh Bungalow, who made me so welcome.

And last but not least, to Gemma Court, who looks after many aspects of my admin and marketing. Everyone needs a Gemma!

Made in the USA
Las Vegas, NV
14 June 2025